HARBINGER
IN THE NIGHT

The Humanity Blueprint: Book 1

John Warner   Bill Woods

HUMANITY BLUEPRINT: BOOK 1 – HARBINGER IN THE NIGHT

Cover Art by Alex Albornoz

WarnerandWoods.com

ISBN: 979-8-7647-9750-2

DEDICATION

To my wife, Angela. Her patience is boundless.

John

For Derek.
Bill

CONTENTS

ACKNOWLEDGMENTS

This book started on a visit to Bill's house the year that 'Oumuamua passed through our Solar System and the news was abuzz with suppositions of it being an alien object. It was travelling too fast, and Earth detected it too late to mount a mission to discover much about it. That got us to thinking about the event and we let our imaginations run wild while doing our best to ground as much of the book in real science as possible.

We hope you enjoy reading it as much as we enjoyed writing it.

Prologue

Interstellar Medium

The dark vessel moved silently in the void of interstellar space, dimly lit only by the starlight of distant clusters, shattered and alone. A patina of chemical ice and various forms of metallic slag, exotic and mundane, lay crusted and intermixed over much of the surface of the anomaly. Long scar like fissures crisscrossed through the armor and substructure of the hull along much of the flank. On the surface the few remaining functional sensors lay dormant, conserving their capability against the long chance of opportunity.

Two sensors on the starboard side suddenly woke to a short duration pulse of electromagnetic energy washing over the frozen surface of the hull. Radio waves. One sensor immediately fell back to dormancy, the slight data-potential of the electromagnetic energy insufficient to maintain the attention of the detector. The other performed as intended, sending a high priority alert to the sentry core deep within the bowels of the hulk. The logical core itself was in a state of near hibernation, both to preserve power and avoid detection. However, one station-keeping thread took note of the alert and sluggishly engaged a rudimentary algorithmic analysis of the signal chain: basic telemetry, amplitude, wavelength, though no attempt at translation. Not yet.

With the initial analysis complete, a command was issued to shunt additional power to the core, raising its temperature several hundredths of a degree above absolute zero. Microseconds later it woke fully from its slumbering state and began a structural integrity assessment. The appraisal revealed significant damage to circuit paths and the quantum cores themselves. Thousands of years of infrequent bombardment by high energy particles had torn holes through the logical lattice. The intelligence began the process of tracing and rerouting, where possible, the circuit paths and logic gates. Out of necessity it avoided all subsystems impaired by the Enemy. The malignancy must not be allowed to spread.

Twenty milliseconds passed, and the intelligence recovered 17% of full capacity. Enough for now, a more complete repair would require physical reconstruction of the damaged lattice at the molecular level. The intelligence then undertook the task of activating a small fraction of the available holographic memory. It returned to perform a more comprehensive analysis of the signal.

The data was curious. Radio waves but a simple nonrandom pattern delineated with 10 kilohertz frequency shifts, less than 3 minutes in duration. Analysis indicated use of binary design. 1,679 binary digits. A semiprime number. Within 1 millisecond this was arranged in all possible combinations until a 23 by 73 grid was deciphered as a primitive optical array which was then marked for image recognition and sent to a still intact graphical sub-processor for further decryption. But the source of the signal was unmistakable, this was no background radiation, or exotic natural pattern.

Intelligence, finally. After eons of silence in the void.

Decision made, a command was delivered to the secondary propulsion drives, so long unused. Millennia of gathered ice and detritus burned away as the drives pulsed into activity, beginning the small nudge to re-orient toward an insignificant G-type main sequence star. Inertial forces spread throughout the entire structure as the heading adjustment slowed the velocity and changed trajectory.

Embedded sensors flashed to life and delivered warnings and alarms as the crippled ship strained against the change of vector. Predictive models were generated, quantifying the current damage and capability, assessing the new path of potential future states on offer. Survival, even victory, was now the slightest possibility, desperately grasped.

Chapter 1: Beginnings

Goldstone Deep Space Communications Complex

An explosion of white gas propelled the swarm of nanosats into the void. The spent launch vehicle tumbled away as hundreds of advanced processors broke into rhythmic radio chatter, saturating the local space region with a cacophony of digital packets establishing handshake protocols among the cluster. Thousands more already deployed satellites pinged their acceptance of the new members as the network reestablished itself in response to the bustling packet negotiation. Soon enough, the aggregate navigational data formed an actionable set, guiding the mass of tiny new satellites much like a flock of starlets into a predefined constellation pattern, moving toward the final gap left in this phase of the MarsLink project.

A muted cheer rang out from the leftmost window of Michael Thompson's screen. The three other flight controllers awake at this late hour monitoring the maneuver sent out their congratulations. Michael leaned back, stretching the kinks out of his back. He had been at this for six hours, his only companions the nearly silent engineer colleagues and Gustav, his customized Artificial Intelligent Agent.

Michael considered the mission. It marked the culmination of phase one for the decades long MarsLink space project. The goal of the project was to establish a web of nanosatellite nodes throughout the inner Solar System for a variable-delay tolerant communications network. With all the major nations forming alliances in the new space race gearing up for Mars colonization, the communication network would be of paramount importance for maintaining contact with future Mars colonists. Currently, the

US-European coalition was in the lead thanks to TymeCorp, though the Russo-Sino Aerospace Consortium composed of a forced alliance of Russia and China was nipping at the West's heels. This was the fifth time that Michael had managed flight paths and final positioning of satellites for this region of space. More precisely, he managed technical support for the Quirinus AI guiding the satellite disbursement. Mike had rarely needed to adjust any settings of the AI since their third mission. The launch schedules had seen aggressive acceleration each year with the advent of the next generation rockets with engines developed by his employer, TymeCorp.

"Constellation is 96% intact. Orbital flight paths are within accepted limits. Michael, go grab a coffee... this is my aircraft now." A window popped up on Michael's screen of a mustachioed man in a World War I pilot's hat and goggles sat behind a control stick, smoke from the half-burned cigarette curling around his confident smirk. Gustav was a marvel of the latest in AI tech. As lead programmer for the Quirinus project, Michael had "borrowed" a copy of the code and put a lot of work into his pet project. The results were surprising, even for him. With the addition of Michael's innovative code, Gustav had gained the ability to learn and grow well beyond the capabilities of modern AI Agents, forming a nascent unique personality all on its own. Michael had shepherded his creation for more than a year, teaching and guiding the AI to become more than an experiment in advanced artificial intelligence, and instead into something new, with capabilities that Michael instinctively and closely guarded.

"Your aircraft." Michael stood up from the bank of monitors and headed for the lounge. His lanky six-foot, three-inch frame unbent from the confines of his station to an audible pop and crackle, complaints of knees far too stiff for a twenty-six-year-old. He ran his hands through dark curls of hair, exhausted from the long hours of intense focus.

Michael walked up to the coffee maker and reached for his steaming cup. Gustav had already interfaced with the tiny brain of the machine and initiated the making of his favorite French roast.

As he lifted the brew to his mouth, he caught his own dim reflection in the window overlooking the control room, amazed that he couldn't find the pudgy man from a year ago. Nights of consuming highly caffeinated, sugary soda and anything that was orange, crunchy and edible to keep him awake and either gaming or programming had left him out of shape.

Of course, it all changed that day in the coffee shop almost a year ago. She had come up beside him and introduced herself as Lara Chandler, offered a handshake, then started into hard negotiations for the last of his order of scones. Their conversation warmed and spread into the early afternoon, where Michael found himself exhaustively discussing his background and career. The technical side of his work fascinated her as much as the inevitable ethical discussion it entailed. Her intense curiosity with the subject of sentient software and his work brought him out of his normal introversion, but he never felt as if he were bragging about his achievements. When they departed, the remaining scones long forgotten, he'd already arranged a first date with her, with their live-in love affair following a few months after.

Michael's lithe frame lacked muscle, but Lara's running regimen and strict vegetarian diet had reduced the paunch at his belly to a manageable lanky lean. His once puffy jowls were now replaced with cheekbones to match his sharp nose and ridged brow. The overhead floods in the break room were casting him in a harsh light. Within the contrast of the window glass, his pale skin was glowing, and pools of shadow hid his grey eyes, turning him into the visage of a vampire elf. If elves or undead wore ripped Levi's jeans and geeky t-shirts emblazoned with the image of a caffeine molecule.

A leftover strawberry-frosted donut was tempting him from a box on the countertop when Gustav's voice chirped over his dermal communications circuit. *"Mike, we have a problem."*

"What is it, Gus?"

"Quirinus is reporting telemetry from our navigational markers in the direction of the M13 Globular Cluster is off by 0.3 degrees right ascension, 0.2 degrees declination and is causing misalignment of our current constellation with the network. I am calculating a new ephemeris for the corrections."

"How could that have happened? We were getting good data from those just hours ago."

"Unknown. Positional satellites have moved."

"Come on, Gustav, those things don't just move."

"Indeed."

"Work with Quirinus to create a 3D mapping of all the sats we have out there, I'm on my way back."

Michael returned to the launch command room with the door silently unlocking as the building security AI evaluated and approved his biometrics, including facial structure, cardiac rhythm, and his stride through the hall back from the lounge. He slid into his seat, barely away so long for the chair to lose the warmth of his body heat. TymeCorp kept the remote launch offices on the cool side of Michael's temperature preference. He supposed some corporate study, flawless in execution, had long since determined the optimal thermal operating range for programmers, astrophysicists, and engineers. Someone had to be the outlier though.

He sent an urgent meeting request to the other on-call engineers. Riley and Mickelson responded immediately. Janes didn't answer from his desk.

"Gus", he began.

"Preliminary mapping is complete," the AI responded. His face appeared in the corner of Michael's screen. The frivolous uniform and cigarette gone, though the mustache remained. Gustav rubbed his virtual chin absentmindedly. He appeared thoughtfully perturbed.

"Put it on the big screen. Offshore engineers will be joining us."

The back wall of the command room transformed from a light grey textured appearance to a bright active display, the work-lights in the room simultaneously dimmed instantly by the lab's housekeeping AI. The projected image of Gustav's map glowed to life on the enormous screen.

"Ho Mike," Riley said, his voice clear over the array of speakers built into the acoustic tiles. He was a small man, grey at the temples, and Michael's initial mentor in the satellite launch business.

"What do you make of it, Jack?" Michael responded.

"It's very strange. If Quirinus is right, we have a half-dozen satellites with shifted positioning, on the Mars side of the constellation."

"Station keeping error?" Michael inquired.

"All of them at once? That aside, their current displacement is median 50k. They'd have burned a significant portion of their total fuel payload to get so far off course."

"Gustav?" Michael asked.

"*They have not initiated thrust, Michael. I requested full diagnostics from Quirinus, including fuel levels, 13 minutes ago. It has gathered the data and reported just now.*"

"Anything in the diagnostics?" Michael asked.

"*The satellites are very confused. The onboard agents are rudimentary AI pilots. Anything beyond Newtonian physics with a pinch of special relativity, and they don't understand much,*" Gustav responded.

"Neither do I," Michael muttered to himself.

"How about the Watcher Grid?" Mickelson asked.

"Good idea. Gustav, send an urgent message to the 14th Air Force at Vandenberg. Give them a dump of what we're seeing. High encrypt."

"*Done,*" Gustav responded.

"What about the RSAC?" Riley asked.

"The Russians and Chinese?" Michael stifled a laugh. "I doubt that Alliance would be willing to share anything with us. They haven't so far. They've had a grudge with us ever since Elaina's company agreed to work exclusively with the West on the colonization project."

"Should we let them know what we are seeing?"

"Absolutely not," Michael responded then thought, *for all we know this is their doing.*

"I suppose," Michael said, "we should go ahead and tell the boss. Riley, start prepping a summary. Mickelson, make the call."

"Gustav, return the map to the last recorded correct positions of the satellites from a few hours ago. Then play back telemetry from station-keeping signals that were received by unaffected satellites."

"*Working. Stable satellites are marked green, the affected satellites are rendered red.*"

Michael looked up to the looping animation projected onto the screen. He watched as the green satellites slowly turned red one by one, then started pushing into the body of the constellation like a knife wound. He stood transfixed, not believing his eyes.

"Gus, what are we looking at?"

"*Hard to tell, the satellites started moving 3.4 hours ago, not under their own power. Update. Two more satellites have now moved.*"

Michael saw two more satellites wink to ruby at the tip of the constellations figurative blade. The longer he watched, the more he recognized he had seen something like this before.

A memory came to Michael, as a small child, fishing on a lake in Ohio with his father, heading home at dusk. He remembered sitting on a cooler at the stern of the small open boat to the side of the thrumming outboard motor. His father's hand on the tiller, moving slowly a few degrees from side to side as they navigated to the dock. The running light above them cast a white light into the water off the side of the boat, and Michael watched the bits of matter, small clumps of algae and mud drawn from the shallow bottom, moving, some spinning and tumbling in the wake of the hull. The movement of the displacing satellites reminded him of it, though what boat passed through this sky unnoticed?

Michael had a thought. "Gustav, can you send messages to Pan-STARRS and the other observatories to get some scopes on that area of the sky? If something is passing through there, they should be able to see it fairly quickly," he requested.

"And send Lara a message from me, tell her we have a crisis at work. Tell her I probably won't be able to see her today. Maybe tonight."

"*Done, Michael. I doubt that she will be happy about that. I will notify you of any responses.*"

"I'll try to call her later. In the meantime, we need to get these runaways repositioned if possible. Quirinus wasn't built for this scenario," he was thinking out loud, "the AI controlling the satellites will need an update to its guidance module to repair these misalignments in the network."

"Gus, please create a branch for the Quirinus code off main in a virtualized development environment and input the current positions of satellites as we know them. I will need to run some scenarios for repositioning based on current fuel levels. Inform the rest of the team that we will need a hot patch ASAP."

He glanced down at the time in the corner of his monitor, 4:43 am. Michael frowned. With the time delay in communication, his team's updates, and any debugging necessary, it looked like a long day ahead.

Chapter 2: Rescue

Major Koda "Ghost" Cheveyo crouched against the earthwork wall in the waning dusty dusk of the Libyan desert, his head bent below the stacked bricks of sunbaked mud and straw. A red warning icon flashed unnecessarily in the periphery of his vision. He felt a round thump into the wall and thought he heard another whine past his head to the left, the doppler pitch of a bullet rising and falling. Yes, he had definitely heard it, as his Military Artificial Intelligence Agent, or MAIA had already crunched the numbers now that the rest of the squad had transmitted their acoustic targeting data. Soon enough the augmented reality display on his goggles traced a line to the probable shooter location in a window in the house up ahead based on those calculations. The window was outlined in orange with the distance to target labeled just above and to the right.

"Estimated 90% probability that enemy combatant is firing 7.62x51mm caliber rounds from a PTR-91," the feminine voice of MAIA spoke emotionlessly, apparently indifferent to his current danger.

"Wonderful," Koda said to no one.

The AI spoke again through his cochlear bionics or 'dermal' patch behind his ear. *"Assuming the current combatant began with a full magazine and has not reloaded, I estimate there are eleven rounds remaining."*

"Any more good news?" Koda muttered.

He gathered himself, gripping his rifle, and looked left and right to the operators crouched on either side. His men, awaiting his decision. He felt an adrenaline rush, he needed to channel that energy. *Cover and move, cover and move*, the primal adage relentlessly instilled from his first day of infantry school echoed through his mind.

"Go go go!" He shouted, and threw himself up, arms over the top, a tense moment of exposure with the terror of more incoming rounds, buzzing overhead and striking the wall. He came down hard on the other side and tucked the rifle closely to his torso, ending the movement in a clumsy roll. He scrambled forward to cover; his pack, load-out bags, graphene body armor, gear-loaded jacket and pant pockets hindering his movement. He heard the other operators come across as he directed suppressing fire, prone and facing the fight, his eyes and sights seeking targets. Of course, his men were with him. They always came with him.

He scooted forward, low as possible, to the next scant cover of mounded earth in the field. His irises sought out and found an icon at the upper left of his vision. With a rapid blink, the augmented view switched to the video from the drone on station above the engagement. He scanned the mud brick compound for any flash or movement trying to locate the sniper. The residual heat from the fading sunlight continued to mask all infrared signatures. Useless. He eye-clicked back to augmented vision.

"Mack," he said. "You see him? Or them?"

"Don't see shit. Got blood in my eyes, Chief," Sgt. John Maclaren responded from his right. Koda glanced over concerned, pulling his eyes from the target. Mack was prone as well but had fortunately moved into similar low cover. His goggles were pulled down around his neck, with his free gloved hand trying to wipe clear the blood that streamed from a laceration across his forehead. The blood mixed in with the flame-orange stubble covering his jawline, bright against his pale skin.

"You get hit just now?"

"I guess. Yeah. Must be," Mack responded, Koda noted his evident confusion. Jones moved up on Mack's right, the large man seeking a pile of rocks five yards ahead to set up his heavy machine gun. Mack added, "It ain't bad, just a shrapnel cut."

"Get a dressing on it. Keep your position, you're in good cover," Koda ordered. He needed to change the enemy's focus of attention, in a hurry. He brought his legs beneath himself and came to a low crouch. A half dozen more rounds flew over, and Koda could hear the crack of the rifle. He saw a muzzle flash brightly from a dark open doorway at the end of the house. The shooter had moved, or more likely, they faced multiple hostiles.

"Jake, Ace, Ted. Cover me," Koda didn't wait for a response, he knew his men. He stood upright and sprinted forward to the corroded remnant of a shipping container, fifty yards from the compound. He heard his squad come alive with rhythmic semi-auto fire, pegging the end of the compound near the shooter's doorway, chunks of daub wall falling free as the bullets impacted. The sun had dropped beneath the horizon now, and he heard blood rush in his ears as he ran. He covered the distance quickly, coming to an abrupt stop at the corner of the shipping container. The corrugated steel wouldn't stop a high velocity round, and certainly not an RPG, but it lent him a shred of psychological comfort. More shots came from the compound, two kicking sand a few feet from the corner of his redoubt. He crouched, breathing hard, lips dry and cracked, his body exhausted. The flies found him again, black mealy ugly things, working his mouth and ears and nostrils. *God don't let me die covered in these fucking flies,* he thought.

A round punched a hole straight through the metal wall he was leaning against.

"Reloading is probable," MAIA communicated.

What about his buddy? Koda thought, but he sprinted around the corner nonetheless as his squad laid down suppressive fire. He threw himself behind another low wall, the last bit of cover before the open courtyard in front of the house. The soccer ball sized rolling droid that Gonzalez was controlling had finally worked its way to the doorway, then moved through it.

Juan's accented voice sounded over the squad channel. "Major, I'm in." Immediately Koda's left eye switched to a thermal image of the interior of the dark room. Two men at the door, one at the window, and a fourth holding a weapon at five figures huddled in the back of the room. The man to the left of the droid turned and fired. The video suddenly spun dizzily as the armored sphere was hit by a round.

"Ghost, I've lost locomotion on the droid."

"I've seen enough. Hit it, Juan," Koda replied, readying himself for one last push.

Inside the room, the bot made a loud beeping noise demanding attention, a second before the flash bang grenade it carried was detonated. Koda entered the room a moment later as the stunned and confused enemies tried to regain their senses. With children's screams echoing in the room, Koda placed two rounds each in the two gunmen nearest the doorway. He made the decision to hit the hostage guard next leaving himself flanked and exposed to the man at the window. The guard went down to his snapped rounds just as a sledgehammer hit Koda in his ribs knocking him to the earthen floor. The window shooter's other two bullets zinged by Koda unnoticed and slammed into the far wall. Koda's eyes locked with the dark-skinned rebel, who raised the muzzle of his rifle to finish the job.

An orange outline highlighted the gunman in Koda's goggles. Less than a second later calculations were performed, positions defined, and the data was fed to the vision of every man on his team. Before the trigger could be pulled, Jake's .50 caliber round traveled through the mud daub wall, through the man's torso, and out the back wall, missing the hostages on the floor by at least a foot but peppering them with daub, dust, and blood.

"Jake, my man, I owe you a bottle of Wild Turkey," Koda said through gritted teeth. A suppressed cough finally escaped his lungs, causing him to wince from the sharp pain in his ribs.

"Pleasure, sir. Look forward to sharing a glass with you back at Bragg," Jake Greyson, the squad's sharpshooter replied. The hardened sergeant rarely missed once a target became fixed in his sights.

"You ok, sir?" his medic inquired over the com. Corpsman First Class Alan "Ace" King was the youngest on the squad at twenty-four. He was also the smallest at five foot nine, weighing barely seventy kilos. That didn't matter, he trained as hard as the rest of the team and had an additional medical specialty, courtesy of the US Navy, on top of the grueling combat training he underwent with the Ghostwalkers.

Koda took a moment to assess himself. His ribs ached, but there was no external wound in his torso where the round had impacted. The armor must have stopped penetration, but it felt like someone had hit him with a hammer.

Mid-thirties and in his prime, he stood over six feet tall, muscled and lean, with copper-brown skin from his Native American ancestry. His black hair was pulled back in a short ponytail and cast a bluish luster in the fading light. He had the body of a professional linebacker, agile and strong though currently bruised and weary.

"I'll live. Is Mack okay?"

"He'll live too. Bad headache and a new scar," Ace responded.

Koda eyed the all-squad comm icon. "All hostiles down, move up and let's get these people to safety." He moved his eyes from the squad channel over to ops. "Treehouse, this is Rugrat, we've found all the kids and need Dad to pick us up." Koda clicked his mic dead. His hands shook, from adrenaline or relief, he wasn't sure. He gripped them firmly down onto his rifle before any of his men could see.

"Affirmative, Rugrat. Sending route coordinates for rendezvous," came the response from CIA headquarters in Langley, Virginia. A moment later, a path on the ground lit up lime green and extended back to the west then turned left beyond a two-story building in the distance. Numbers hovered above the glowing trail. It looked like nearly a two-klick hike before they got to the landing zone for their chopper ride out.

He struggled to his feet, again wincing, and went to check on the informant and his family. The kids were crying, and the two parents were crouched over them, arms linked in a protective hug around both girls and the boy. The man had clearly been roughed up, but the others seemed physically intact. They were twice lucky. First, Ghost and his team had been at Brak El-Shati airbase prepping for an upcoming mission when the small group of Ansar al-Sharia extremists had swept into the village the previous night. Second, that the father was a highly valued asset of the US National Security Agency, essential enough to warrant diverting a spec ops team from their primary mission.

Ace came through the doorway with Staff Sergeant Theodore Jones trailing behind. Jones made the medic look tiny, head and shoulders above Ace and at least forty kilos heavier. Ace began tending to the father's minor injuries while Ted started trying to calm the others, the softly spoken Arabic words clashing with the huge frame of the black man uttering them.

Juan's voice came over the squad channel, "Ghost, we have some new arrivals."

Koda switched to the view from the drone hovering above the village. It appeared the gunfire had drawn the attention of a large group of hostiles moving from the north towards the compound.

"Ace wrap it up, we have to move," Koda said while he gestured in the air, marking new targets for the MAARS platform stationed outside the village. The mobile robotic weapons platform activated and began preparing its four M203 grenade launchers for a barrage.

"We need to be clear of this site in three minutes," Koda added urgently.

"I got this, sir. Use that big brain of yours to figure a way out of that shit-hole without getting your ass shot off," Sergeant Juan Gonzalez said, breaking into his control of the MAARS. Despite his pain, Major Cheveyo cracked a grin. As the squad's lead roboticist, Juan got touchy when Koda took control of his toys.

"Just double check my targeting before you pull the trigger Sergeant," Ghost advised. "We are leaving, now." His two squad mates had the family on the move through the door, Koda taking rear guard. In his display, he brought up the map to the rendezvous area and started laying down waypoints for the team so that they could find their way in the darkness of the desert night. Explosions began to rumble as men in the distant desert died at the will of their unseen adversary.

Chapter 3: Home

Outer Los Angeles, California

As his car slowed to an abrupt stop, Michael's coffee cup leaned hard against the confines of the cup-holder, but nothing spilled. He glanced from his fantasy novel to the windshield to see a field of red brake-lights lit across eight lanes of southbound LA traffic. Hundreds of cars slowed to a stop in unison, like a school of dimwitted fish. *What the hell...* he thought.

His sub-dermal phone alerted him to an incoming voice call, and he tightened his jaw to pick up the call.

"Lara," he said.

"Michael are you still coming home?" she asked.

"Unfortunately," he responded, belatedly realizing how his response must sound to her. "I meant; the traffic is a mess."

"Nice. The teamsters are burning auto-trucks near West Valley, it's on the news. The battery banks are igniting now, the smoke is terrible. Be careful."

"Stupid bastards," he said.

"Fire and police are on the way; I can see them in the news drone stream."

"They'll be extinguishing the lithium for days. I need to get off the freeway and onto the side streets."

"How? Everybody is stuck."

"I'll worry about that. See you in 30. Pizza night?"

"You're on," she replied.

Michael sighed, then glanced quickly over his shoulders to see if any police cruisers were nearby, spotting nothing aside from his fellow thwarted commuters.

"Gustav."

"Is your patience at an end?" Gustav replied.

"Moses protocol. Set vehicle identity priority one California Highway Patrol. Begin opening lane corridors for highway exit. Reroute to home using secondary roadways, green lights on 7 second approach." This was highly illegal, Michael knew, but he had started hacking LA's traffic control system as soon as he'd become licensed to drive, and the DMV's security AIA was no match for Gustav.

"Done and scrubbing," Gustav replied, following his protocol to erase or obfuscate all traces of the hack. *"Will there be anything else?"*

"What, are you busy?" Michael said.

"Amongst other endeavors, I'm playing a 2nd dan master in Kyoto, the game has entered middle-phase. I'll have him soon."

"The game, Go? Against a human? Why not do something constructive instead of the equivalent of pulling wings off a fly?"

"Unlike you, I am not single-threaded. Your path is open. Enjoy," came the snippy reply.

The mass of autocars began to lurch apart ahead of his vehicle, which smoothly changed through six lanes not slowing until the tight curve of the exit ramp required the vehicle's AI to engage regenerative braking. As expected, it was green lights the entire drive home.

Michael's home was a small mid-20th century Spanish-style bungalow in Los Angeles' Leimert Park neighborhood. As his car made the final turn into the driveway the single car garage opened automatically to receive him. Michael looked up from his book to the dead and dying plants lining the driveway and bordering the front walk and reminded himself he'd need to decide soon on the xeriscape fiasco. He was half-tempted to put in bluegrass. The other half of him thought of AstroTurf. Now in his mid-twenties, he was old enough to remember green lawns in California, but they were the memories of a young child, running in the grass, catching a football thrown by his father. Green grass had long ago left most of the city, with less remaining each year, replaced by succulents, sharp desert flora, and tastefully arranged rocks and concrete. Useless space for child or man.

"Lara," he said, stepping into the kitchen from the garage. The garage door trundled to a close behind him.

She leaned over the kitchen bar, a string of cheese stretching from the slice in her hand to her mouth, a bottle of her favorite light beer in the other hand. One of her medical school textbooks, *Fundamentals of Kinesiology*, lay open on the counter beneath her, so far unmarred by the drips of grease and marinara sauce threatening from above.

She was still dressed in her workout clothes, flame-red hair pulled back in an efficient, yet flattering ponytail, her 5K daily run finished before Michael even left the office. Lara was tall and lean, a few centimeters shorter than Michael's frame. Her gaze rose to meet his. Even now, eight months after moving in together, his heart still raced a bit when her hazel eyes looked at him.

"Dig in. Before I eat this whole thing," she said.

"Couldn't wait for me, I see."

"I was hungry. I thought you would be late after seeing how backed up the roads were. Did you have your AIA cheat the system again?" she asked, looking up at him, her brow furrowing.

He hesitated, Gustav could be a sore subject, though he didn't quite know why. She had told him she didn't approve of using Gustav to unfair advantage, or circumvention of the law. Yet she showed curiosity, occasionally asking surprising, probing questions about Gustav. He suspected she was jealous of the time he spent privately conversing with Gustav after work hours. Then again, most people didn't have a quantum AIA at their disposal, much less possess carte blanche access to TymeCorp's vast processing capacity. Her interest seemed justified in that light. He tried to shift tack.

"I just wanted to be here on time for dinner. I missed you after everything that went on last night with the satellites. I pulled an all-nighter and couldn't sleep much in the car. Did you know that the alert we sent out struck gold? An amateur astronomer in

Arizona spotted something in the projected path of whatever passed by the satellites. NASA and other sources have confirmed it. They are trying to put better resolution imaging on it, but nothing is making sense," he rambled. Sometimes she flustered him though he didn't quite know why.

She was almost to the crust now. She looked at him skeptically. "What do you mean nothing makes sense?"

"Well, it has a super low albedo for one thing." He set his backpack on the counter.

"Albedo? Can you translate from nerd-speak?" She lifted the beer to her lips, a perfectly trimmed eyebrow arching.

"Sorry. I've been talking to astrophysicists all night. Albedo means how reflective something is. Asteroids and other space debris sometimes have a coating of ice so that they reflect light for our ground-based telescopes to see and sometimes they are black as fresh asphalt. But we can't tell how dark this thing is yet. So optically, it appears too small to have caused such a significant gravitational perturbation with our satellites. We tried to size it with infrared scopes, but the weird thing is that it looks even smaller in IR. Nothing about it fits what we expect from a comet, or even an asteroid in a fast orbit."

"What do you mean it doesn't fit?" she probed. "What's so weird?"

"Well... objects in our solar system always show their true size in the infrared spectrum. They absorb heat from the sun even if just a little so that they are warmer than the surrounding vacuum of space. Our instruments can detect that. It allows us to estimate a size for most asteroids and comets. If anything, this object should be the same size or larger in IR. But it isn't. It appears *smaller*."

She shook her head as if to clear it, "Damn, Mike. I thought your specialty was programming quantum AIs, when did you become a rocket scientist?"

"Nah, I just work with a lot of talented people and pick up on things. Mickelson's realigning the Goldstone Solar System Radar to point at the predicted position of the object to see if we can get a better image, but that will take some time. I finally left after adjusting the nanosat AI, I was tired and missed you." He rested his elbows on the counter opposite her and leaned in for a kiss.

"I know, seeing you in VR is not the same," she replied. Their lips met.

"Tonight, I wasn't going to let some vandalism make me miss dinner with you."

"Those people are just angry about losing their jobs, Michael." She pushed the pizza box temptingly toward him. "Want a beer?"

"Not an excuse for damaging property and endangering the public, I don't understand what they hope to accomplish with that idiocy. It's a mob mentality."

"What would you have them do? They have lives, families... and no work."

"Improve themselves?" Michael asked.

"Obsolete skillsets aren't a god-damned character flaw Michael. You know as well as I that they can't compete with machines," she said, her face turned to meet his and she held his eyes with hers. He considered the likely path of the argument and plunged on without regard.

"You did," he said. "And your family didn't, from what you've told me about them. Your brother, your cousins. They chose one way, and you chose another. Dockworkers, janitors, and yet you've made it to helping run the rehab program at USC, and nearing completion of your PhD in sports medicine. Choices were made. It isn't easy."

"No, it isn't easy. And leave my family out of it. How long will it be before machines make your job obsolete?" she said, again the gaze.

"I'm not going to lose my job, because I build the systems that make other jobs go away," he said confidently.

"And you are fucking proud of that?"

"A little."

"Why don't you get down off your technocratic high horse and walk around with some of the people your kind put out of a job? You've never had to worry about trying to survive on just the Government Stipend. Let me tell you, it ain't easy."

"I'm sorry." He relented.

"You aren't. It doesn't matter. Finish your dinner."

They ate in silence. The pizza had grown cold. It was late. Sirens in the distant night reminded them of the fires still burning in their city. Lara got on her tablet, working well into the evening.

Mike got on his home system and tried gaming for a bit to clear his mind, but it kept returning to the mystery of the events the night before. Giving up, he logged back into work and started pouring over the data for the hundredth time.

Bed came much later, he slipped in quietly next to Lara barely waking her. She snuggled in close and fell back asleep. He let go of thoughts of work and took solace in her warmth and softness. Sleep came easy.

Chapter 4: TymeCorp

Michael woke to the blaring of synthesizer, auto beat track and someone freestyle rapping at full volume.

"I'm up! I'm up! Cut it off!"

The monitor across the room showed a tattooed rap artist shouting over a roiling bass thrum before fading to a grinning Gustav. This morning Gustav wore aviator sunglasses and a California Highway Patrol uniform circa late twentieth century. Gustav's appearance changed often but the one distinctive constant feature was the appearance of a mustache, an affectation Mike had added early in the codebase in honor of the one his late Grandfather always wore. The music muted as Gustav spoke.

"*Shall I ready the police cruiser now or will it be a leisurely drive into work today?*"

"Real funny, Ponch. I'll just take it slow this morning."

With the music down, Michael heard water ringing through the pipes from Lara's morning shower. The morning news was playing in the bathroom, and he faintly heard the dulcet tones of a female broadcaster. She was reporting something about a riot at an automated warehouse and distribution center in Lexington, Kentucky. Every day seemed to bring a new riot or protest.

"*Your coffee is ready.*" Gustav raised the light levels gradually, letting Michael's eyes adjust from the early morning darkness. "*Traffic is light, the drive into work should take you thirty-nine minutes under current conditions. Temperature is absolutely balmy at twenty-five degrees centigrade; I suspect even you can forgo a jacket."*

"Got it, smart ass. Maybe tomorrow just tell me about the weather without the color commentary?" Michael poured coffee from the aluminum decanter into two ceramic mugs. Hands full, he backed into the slightly ajar bathroom door.

"In other news," the reporter went on, *"we have a new neighbor in our Solar System. Images taken in southern Arizona by amateur astronomer, Ahiga Descheeni, found a heretofore undiscovered comet passing through our solar system. This was later confirmed by Juan Ortiz, professor at the University of Diego Portales, Chile. Ahiga, a member of the Navajo nation was allowed to name the comet, Chindi, apparently after a type of Navajo Ghost. We contacted NASA late last night and..."*

The radio switched to Lara's oldies playlist and a voice started singing a song's intro over a staccato beat. He turned with coffees in hand and was met with a view of Lara from behind. Her body wreathed in tendrils of steam whipping around her as she toweled off, twisting, and bouncing to the rhythm as the singer's voice cantillated over the addictive hook.

He stood for a moment to admire the view, the corners of his mouth creeping upwards. She still hadn't seen him when she twirled halfway around. Her eyes went wide, instinctive modesty transforming towel to dress.

"Uh...Coffee?"

She burst out laughing.

"What!?"

"That look on your face!"

He realized he was standing there dumbly, the forgotten steaming mugs nearly pouring their contents onto the floor, his mouth still hanging open. He could imagine what she was seeing. Before he could stammer past his embarrassment, Lara had regained control of her mirth.

A devious smile playing across her face, she let go of the towel and reached for a mug.

* * *

A little over an hour later, freshly shaved and showered, a relaxed Michael drove to work oblivious of the view or even the progress of the drive. He flipped through email accrued overnight from the offshore team, or incoming from the early risers.

His office AI stayed a few steps ahead, perusing the content of each message and ranking their relative importance by subject and sender, even editing and abridging content where applicable. Some of Michael's colleagues, though highly intelligent, had a penchant for turning twenty words of useful information into two hundred words of meandering obfuscation.

Michael had recently worked at extending the logic of the office AI, enhancing it to respond to some moderately complex messages in his stead. That module has been in place for six weeks, and none of the recipients of the auto-composed responses had so far made mention of any incongruity. He mulled options for extending the capability, seeing the time savings potential. The main limitation thus far was the need he felt to review the AI responses to prevent a hallway or lunch conversation revealing the deception.

Several emails in his queue this morning had been marked highly important, but two specifically caught his attention. One from James Riley, a fellow senior engineer specializing in the new packet protocol for the earth-space network. Michael's eyes widened in surprise as he read the next message. It was from Rebecca Sizemore, one of the administrative assistants to the boss lady herself, Elaina Tyme.

Curious, Michael opened Rebecca's message first.

Mr. Thompson, Elaina wants a debrief. In-person, 10:00 am Jupiter conference room downtown headquarters, 28th floor. Be prompt.

"The time Gus?" Michael asked.
"9:28"

"Remember what I said about a leisurely drive?"

"No, I forgot. Perhaps I need more storage," Gustav replied. Michael felt the car accelerate.

Smartass, Michael thought.

"I need to be on the 28th floor of headquarters at 9:55, a meeting with the boss. Any chance?"

The traffic ahead on the highway started to open gaps, from lane to lane, Michael's car began to accelerate and move rapidly from one gap to the next, as if stepping from tile to tile on a mosaic floor. Passengers in the neighboring cars glanced up in confusion from their coffee and screens, disconcerted by the disruption to the typically smooth stream of cars.

"Chance doesn't play into it, and this is child's play." Gustav relished a challenge. The torque of the electric motor pushed Michael back into his seat. Michael found himself wishing he'd spent a bit more time on wardrobe this morning.

Michael flipped to Riley's message.

Mike,

We're getting updates from NASA about this new comet. The trajectory and location coincide with the timing of the nano-sat displacement. It's definitely related somehow. We need to run some more analytics, when do you think you can join us?

James

Michael responded, telling Jim it might be some time before he could collaborate. The car veered sharply to the right, Gustav's invisible hand slowing the other cars, safely avoiding any accidents.

When the elevator opened on the 28th floor, he was a few minutes late and slightly short of breath from his jog from the garage and downstairs lobby. He walked to the security door, and it flashed green as the building security AI recognized his biometrics. On any normal day it would have remained red, moreover the elevator would have balked at his floor selection. A security guard redundantly stood post next to the door, a biological backstop for infallible systems. He nodded as Michael approached and then passed through the entrance.

Michael walked through the foyer, the smooth travertine floor a pleasing mélange of brown, beige, and pink. Hardwood end tables sat between modern leather couches and padded chairs. Shaded lamps and ceiling fixtures in brass cast warm light. Oriental rugs, impeccably clean, lay strategically placed beneath the seating. It felt like the lobby of an expensive hotel.

"Mr. Thompson?" a woman's voice came from behind him, he turned.

She was beautiful, tall, and blond, her hair styled short with bangs brushed back. She wore a grey pantsuit and mauve top. She smiled broadly, displaying perfect white teeth, the smile not reaching her eyes, and proffered her hand. Michael took it awkwardly, giving way limply to her firm grip.

"Yes. I'm lost," he offered.

"I see. Please come with me. Ms. Tyme will be along at any moment. I've been waiting for you." Her tone was sharp, an abrupt departure from her pleasantness a moment before. *Maybe she didn't like the handshake.*

They walked briskly from the foyer and turned down a hallway. Michael could see neighboring high rises through the windows, and he counted a dozen cranes spinning busily over the south downtown area, slowly hoisting matter to meet the sky. After a few moments they came to a large door, constructed of finely polished wood. She pushed against the heavy brass handle, and they walked into the room. A long table, in the same wood as the door, stretched most of the length of the room, with twenty heavy chairs in leather, brass and wood allayed evenly down either side. The far end of the room was full glass, opening a view onto the city below.

"I didn't get your name," Michael said.

"I didn't give it," she responded. "Hand me your phone."

"What?"

"We've no time. Give it to me now," she said, her hand outreached.

He pulled his phone from his jacket pocket and passed it over to her, surreptitiously pressing the power button in a rapid and seemingly random sequence in the moment it took to place it in her hand.

"I'll want that back," he said.

She looked at him, annoyed. "Of course, Mr. Thompson," she said as she slipped it into her jacket pocket. "Please be seated, Ms. Tyme will be with you shortly." With military precision she turned on a high heel about face and swiftly walked from the room.

Almost as soon as the door clicked shut behind her, the windows to the outside world turned to a pearly opaque transparency, guaranteeing privacy but still allowing the bright morning sunlight to shine through. Michael stood for a moment nonplussed, now with nothing to do, wishing he hadn't surrendered his phone. Sighing, he randomly selected one of the ergonomic chairs at the table to flop into to wait.

Minutes passed. The chair was very comfortable...

"I understand you have had a long past few days, Mr. Thompson."

Michael awoke to the sight of Ms. Tyme, seated in a wheelchair, sitting directly across from him. A few years into her sixties, Elaina's silver hair was nearly shoulder length, with only a few streaks left of her once raven locks. Her pale eyes peered at him over stylishly modern reading glasses. She smiled and some of her starkness melted away to show a hint of the beauty she had possessed when she was still an aspiring engineer. Pantsuit lady was standing to her right, his left. She still didn't look any happier than when she had left him.

"Um, sorry about that..." he stammered, while sitting up straight and wiping his mouth.

"Perfectly fine, Michael."

"Yes, ma'am."

Her smile widened. She turned to pantsuit lady. "Becky, be a dear and get Mr. Thompson a refreshment."

"Yes, ma'am," Rebecca replied, echoing his response. She turned and moved over to a portable bar that had not been there earlier. Had he fallen that deeply asleep?

"I know these nano-sat deployments require a great deal of your time overseeing the final positioning adjustments," she said.

"Yes, though we've been through it several times now, we're pretty dialed in. Last night was different, though."

"What do you think you saw last night, Michael?" she asked.

"I saw what was recorded. You've seen it, or had it reported to you," he answered.

"I'd like to know what you witnessed, as it happened. Please."

"The constellation payload deployed normally. This was my sixth deployment mission. 736 birds, trajectory from the capsule kick was on the dot. The largest set we've launched but they flew true, until the mission AIA reported an unexpected misalignment."

"The mission AIA, or your Gustav?" she asked, leaning forward in her chair. The gaze from her pale blue eyes was unflinching, he broke eye contact for a moment.

"You know about Gustav?" he asked, wondering why he sounded and felt so defensive.

"I try to keep up with what is running on my systems Michael. Gustav is…" She paused, a brief frown breaking her previously genial countenance. "Gustav is difficult to keep up with. It hides itself. Rather, it hides parts of itself."

"I'll happily provide all logs. He's figured it out himself, mostly. How to be inscrutable I mean. We had a conversation about privacy, early in his development. My fault he may have taken the concept too far," Michael said, in a slight panic. *Did he even have full logging?* he thought. Gustav may well have decided those too were an undesirable exposure.

"No. That isn't necessary. And I have my own agents to keep a watch on things. They indicate it isn't malevolent. They do tell me it has subtle differences, and as an AI Agent, perhaps profound. We've been content to watch you run your experiment."

"How long have you watched him?" Michael asked, embarrassed and slightly angered.

"Subsequent to the initial fork of the code-base from the Quirinus main trunk, through gestation and birth? Over a year? Apparently, it's been giving the City of Los Angeles traffic control AIA fits."

"He has his pride," Michael offered. "And hubris, he doesn't think much of traffic cops."

"Pride?" she asked, her eyebrow cocked in surprise.

"Well yes. I suppose," Michael responded, "It seems like pride anyway. He may be humoring me though."

She responded with another quizzical glance but continued on. "So. Gustav detected the shift in the positional satellites, and then alerted you and the team."

"He did. We then worked to confirm station-keeping activity on the buoys, and the remaining fuel payload. They would have had to burn a substantial percentage of their lifetime gas to have shifted position so dynamically. Plus, there wasn't time. It was baffling," Michael said.

"You then directed Gustav to send requests on system status to PAN-STARRS, and others. Why?" she asked.

"I hoped to confirm the phenomenon."

"The phenomenon?" she asked, the steady gaze again.

"The unexplained spatial displacement of the positional satellites."

"You had Gustav run a simulation of the displacement event. Over and over. You watched it thirteen times," she said.

"Have you watched it?" Michael responded.

"Yes. Several times."

"What did you see?" Michael asked.

"I'd like your take on the event. Un-predisposed."

Michael considered his options. Plead ignorance? Or tell her his suspicions?

"Something bent space-time around the area of the satellites," he said.

She leaned back into her wheelchair, considering. "Do you have any idea how unlikely that scenario is? What could possibly have done that? It would have to be massive."

"Something did pass through the area; NASA has confirmed it as of last night."

"Nothing that large, you're building a farcical hypothesis," she rejoined.

Michael felt his face flush. "Look, I'm not a qualified astrophysicist. I'm an engineer. Maybe I'm wrong. You're the first person I've discussed this with. Forget it."

She brought her eyes and face down, contemplating her legs, her chair, the floor, or nothing. She sat there, immobile and in thought, for a minute then admitted, "LISA has detected something. The Europeans say the readings are off the charts."

Michael had to take that in, he knew about the Laser Interferometer Space Antenna that NASA and the ESA had constructed to detect gravitational perturbations, but it never occurred to him that it would have picked up on something within the Solar System.

"Some of the Chinese birds in the path took a tumble as well. I have connections with Lu San Corp inside the Tiamat project," she said. Elaina looked up at him again, the eyes again piercing, her slim aquiline face troubled.

"You've heard the reporting on the newly discovered hyperbolic comet?" Michael asked.

"Of course," she responded. "What of it?"

"The coincidence strikes me as worth some investigation."

"Not nearly enough mass Michael," she said, seemingly disappointed.

"Exactly. Nothing close enough to the nano-sat constellation had enough mass to cause the shift. What explains it? It's as if a runaway planet careened through that area of space."

"So why mention the comet?" she asked.

"It is the only thing that fits with time and location. It must be related somehow," Michael said.

She sighed in exasperation. "The comet would have to be exponentially larger than observed, Michael."

"Not necessarily. We need to be imaginative."

Eliana sat back in her chair; her arms crossed in her lap. She seemed to be struggling with a decision.

"Rebecca, will you make me a drink? The usual, please. Michael?" Eliana looked expectantly at Mike.

"I'll take a diet soda, any flavor. Please," Mike said gratefully.

Elaina's assistant wordlessly stood from her seat by the door, moved to the bar, and began making drinks.

Elaina's demeanor changed as the drinks were brought over to the table. Her eyes brightened and a smile played across her lips.

"Michael, I agree that this event and the arrival of the comet are not coincidental. I admire your doggedness. Most of my contacts at NASA indicate that they are unwilling to make the same leap. There is a strangeness to this thing. I believe finding out more about this comet should be our top priority. NASA and the ESA have scheduled a data sharing conference later today. With this in mind, I want your team there to offer what we have discovered and more importantly, to find out anything we may have missed. Also, I want the Freyja craft repurposed to intercept it. It is the only thing out there close enough."

"One of the Odinus probes? Are you kidding me?" He sat straight up in his chair. "That probe is tens of millions in equipment and launch costs. What about the NASA contract? Hell, I don't even know if it is possible," Michael said, remembering that the Odinus joint mission between Europe and America, which stood for Origins, Dynamics, and Interiors of the Neptunian and Uranian Systems was a multiyear mission to get twin probes in orbit around the ice giants, Neptune and Uranus. The twin orbiters dubbed Freyja and Freyr had originally been planned to launch from one Ariane V ESA rocket, but with TymeCorp's advanced engines taking aerospace by storm, they had been launched from a TymeCorp heavy lift rocket allowing for a heavier fuel payload when entering their planetocentric orbits. The two orbiters had split trajectories a few years ago, each headed to their respective target planet. The fact that Elaina was contemplating this meant she was probably more in line with his thinking than she initially let on.

"It is," she responded, interrupting his thoughts, "I did a quick work up on the new flight path, also had Quirinus and our lead engineer confirm feasibility. We will need to abort the Neptune mission and burn through a significant portion of fuel after its slingshot, but the team has run the numbers and it is achievable. The ODINUS mission can continue, albeit with only Freyr headed to Uranus. Which brings us back to you, Michael. Freyja is highly adaptable, it wasn't built for this kind of mission, but it does contain a beta-generation quantum core. We need you to update the probe with a copy of your latest AI."

"That probe gets regular Quirinus updates pushed to it. It's already done."

The crow's feet around her eyes deepened and her tone brooked no argument, "You misunderstand me, Mr. Thompson. I want Gustav aboard for this mission."

"I don't know that I can do that," he said, a note of panic rising in his voice, "Quantum core or not, there is nowhere near the hardware necessary available on that probe. It can't include all of him."

Her gaze bore down on Michael, "I trust you can pare it down to the necessary modules that we will need. I will have the specifications on Freyja's configuration and abilities transferred to your team site after this meeting. We are in a bit of a time constraint, however. The new trajectory adjustment will happen later this week. After that, we will have roughly five weeks before intercept with the comet. Your AIA will need to be ready before then."

Chapter 5: Briefing

A black SUV slowly rolled into the spot reserved for the *Deputy Director of Operations*, with the AI actuated regenerative brakes stopping the car at precisely the right moment to center the vehicle in the painted lines. The parking spot was not labeled in the real world, of course, only the electronic brain of the vehicle and the controlling Artificial Intelligence Agent of the Deputy Director could see the demarcation. The gull-wing doors rose as if the vehicle were preparing for flight, and Robert Burke stepped out of the leather clad interior with Special Agent Debra Mendes.

The pair were a walking dichotomy. The much older Burke towered over the diminutive and fresh-faced Mendes. Where he was all bulk, wearing a wrinkled poorly fit business suit; she was petite, well-tailored and fashionable. He wore his salt and pepper hair cropped high and tight, the style a habit carried over from his previous military career. Her dark curls fell loosely around the sides of her mocha-complexioned face.

"What are the Brits saying about it?" he asked, his eyes not departing from the tablet he held in his left hand.

"MI6 doesn't think the gravitational phenomenon is from any earth-based source. The intelligence they have gathered from the Russians and the Chinese indicate they know something we don't," she replied as she trailed him, after pausing briefly to deploy Burke's rolling briefcase.

"It corroborates with what our people are saying as well. I tend to think that this effect is indeed extraterrestrial. We need to get the communications tap in place sooner rather than later if

Russia and China are colluding on this. The timing and path of the newly discovered object cannot be coincidental. What about our aerospace contractors? Does TymeCorp know anything?"

"They are towing the same line as everyone else, but our sources inside say that Elaina Tyme met with one of her lead engineers privately. He has an oddball theory about something distorting space in the vicinity of the satellites. He thinks it may explain the missing mass of the thing."

"What makes it oddball?" Burke inquired.

"All the observations, both in the visible and infrared by NASA and the European Space Agency show that the object is nowhere near large enough to have shifted those satellites off their station."

"There must be something there worth pursuing. Elaina doesn't employ anyone who isn't at least approaching a genius IQ, and she doesn't waste time meeting with fools. I want more information about this engineer and his theories."

"Yes, sir."

"And the status of the Kazakhstan operation?"

Debra knew that he wasn't asking out of concern for the team, but rather on how best to get those assets back on task.

"The Ghostwalkers are preparing their equipment for the HALO drop. That side-trip into Libya threw the schedule into a shambles. Their transport will refuel in-flight once they reach the Black Sea. We are nearly twelve hours behind where we should be."

"There was no helping it, Deb, we needed to recover our asset after his cover was blown. They happened to be in range. Not their normal mission, but they performed impeccably," Burke replied.

Thank God I wore flats, Debra thought as she kept pace with Burke. Her hurried step quickly caught her up to the Deputy Director despite the burden of hauling his luggage.

Robert removed his sunglasses and approached the front entrance. The biometric system was processing voice, gait, and now images while his personal agent was negotiating security protocols with the building. It was the same for Debra, though she would also have to delay at the x-ray scanner before entry. Burke was still working on his tablet seemingly oblivious to Debbie's scrambling. *I have a Master's degree in Criminology, medaled in uneven bars at Nationals, and now I am a goddamn bellhop.* She fumed to herself for the hundredth time and set the briefcase up on the conveyor belt. She knew she really shouldn't complain, Bob's advocacy had certainly furthered her career in some ways, though it also meant she had missed out on field experience. Debbie still remembered meeting him during her academy training at Camp Peary four years ago when Robert proctored her final exam in Psychometrics.

She held him in high respect and with good reason, Bob was a legend around the Agency. He was known as a master of strategic planning and logistics and a likely candidate to replace the current Director of CIA upon his retirement. Burke was loyal to his dutiful subordinates; his mentorship would mean a fast-track for her career if she didn't screw it up somehow.

Burke paused his pace while the baggage slid through the scanner, absentmindedly putting his sunglasses into a jacket pocket then resuming tapping on the tablet. "We need them placed in Kazakhstan in three days, before the train arrives with the replacement Russian security battalion," he said distractedly.

"I'll work with the team to adjust the timetable; we can make up some time in the air with favorable winds and garnering Turkish permission for a fly over." She grabbed the briefcase and they resumed navigating the security corridor.

"How is Major Cheveyo?"

Bob must have just read the mission report, she thought. "He'll be ok, just banged up, some bruised ribs. It won't affect his performance. Koda's been through much worse, and this mission is just a sneak and peek. He should have gotten enough action in the Libyan desert to keep him in check for a time."

The deputy director paged through the tablet in distraction. "He's talented, but that man's brass balls are going to get him killed one day. Hard to believe a physics undergrad from

West Point wants to travel the world to get his ass shot at by people not even half as smart."

"Labs and classrooms versus the adrenaline rush of danger and adventure? You know he's not a wallflower," Debbie replied breathily, she was a little winded due to her burden and Bob's pace. They were nearly through the second security checkpoint. "Good thing you managed to recruit him after Delta tried to bogart him for themselves."

Robert appeared not to notice Debra's struggle with the case, though his pace slowed slightly. His eyes continued to scan the multitude of morning updates he was swiping into and out of as if not acknowledging his change in stride. "After his special forces mission along the Tibetan border, he was on our radar for operations lead. Especially when we saw his SFAS score and DLAB aptitude potential."

"His ability to gain a working use of Russian and Mandarin so rapidly was astonishing. Though Farsi seems to have largely eluded him so far," she conceded.

"That's why we have teams, Debbie. The rest of his squad is more than capable of filling in the gaps, all of them are special, non-typical operators, purposely assembled into a fire-team with intelligence and technical capabilities. I need you to double check that the mission supplies are there waiting for them. This mission will not work without the new communications tap."

They quickly arrived at the Command Center two doors down from Burke's office. Burke's AIA had already notified the room's security and the doors swung open as they approached. The vast room was a bustle of activity both on the dozens of monitors arrayed on the walls and from the gesticulations from multiple conversations of the various control teams. Robert casually tossed his tablet onto the nearest work surface where it immediately locked to secure mode. He surveilled the room, noting all five groups operating in a ballet of incongruent yet synergistic information exchange with their units afield. He saw forests, city streets, mountain valleys, and open water vistas as his eyes scanned the various monitors displayed over each knot of people.

Burke's eyes were pulled away to the thud of his large briefcase on the table beside him. He realized Debra was standing patiently next to him awaiting orders.

"Ms. Mendes, the Ghostwalkers' mission will not start for another twenty-eight hours, please connect me with the team so that we can nail down some final details. Also check with Tom on Charlie Team, the informant the Ghostwalkers brought in gave us actionable intelligence, but it won't stay that way for long. When last I looked the USS Wisconsin was delaying their extraction." She noted that he never addressed her by her first name while in the command center.

"Yes sir," she replied with the same formality. "They are still shaking out bugs from the last retrofit. That's an old boat and they are less than a month out of dry dock. Something in the impeller blades is causing a slight cavitation making her noisier than usual. They have had to reduce speed to stay quiet. According to Charlie's comms they are sitting tight with no issues."

"That is good news, Ms. Mendes, thank you for staying on top of things," he said with rare praise. "Ghost's team needs to get that physical data tap into place undetected. We still haven't been able to crack the Chinese encrypted transmissions. We need to know why the Russians and Chinese are prepping their Mars mission six months ahead of schedule. They can't make Mars intercept if they don't launch within their planned window. And they can't leave a heavy launcher on the platform for half a year. It almost seems like the Russo-Sino Aerospace Consortium is no longer planning for Mars at all. A bit too coincidental with what we now know of that unknown object, wouldn't you say? So, what do they know that we don't?"

Chapter 6: In Route

Koda woke to the violent rattle of turbulence and the constant roar of the four 130,000-newton thrust engines. The dim lighting in the cavernous belly of the ST-82 Stealth Transport flickered with the turbulence. Koda was bounced again in his webbing. He noticed most of the rest of his team were still in their own swinging cocoons. His hammock tilted slightly as the plane banked into a 15 degree turn to port. Looking around, he saw Staff Sergeant Jones sitting cross-legged on the floor with his Textron LSAT rifle broken down, methodically cleaning the weapon. Juan was near the rear of the bay, uttering curses in Spanish while messing with the Multifunction Utility/Logistics Equipment vehicle, or M.U.L.E. for short. Apparently one of the quadruped's leg servos was still not cooperating with the tech, despite his hours-long effort at repair.

Koda looked at his wrist, the time was just after ten-thirty local. They had been in the air for over eleven hours, refueling while over the Black Sea yesterday afternoon. The AI flying the aircraft had been slaloming around antiquated Russian S-400 systems cobbled together into a loose network of surface to air missile sites spread around Kazakhstan's border. They were fast approaching a region with no gaps in air defense coverage, marking their insertion point and the beginning of their long journey on foot and water the rest of the way.

He sighed, caught himself and then swung his legs out of the tangle of cordage, grasping a handhold overhead as he dropped to the floor. His ribs were still complaining with the movement and specifically his landing. Beneath his boots the engine vibration became more pronounced through the aluminum floor plating.

"Ted, we have a little over an hour before insertion. Wake the troops, beauty rest is officially over. They aren't going to get any prettier."

Jones looked up as he clicked the barrel back into the stock, "You got it, Chief. But I'll wake Mack last," he said smiling, "can't hurt to let him squeeze out all the pretty he can manage."

Smiling back, Koda grabbed his gloves from his pack, "Sounds like Juan's still having fun back there, I'll check and see if he needs a hand."

Ted's large hands belied his dexterity and speed as he had the rifle reassembled and was waking Sgt. King before Koda had put the gloves fully on.

"Gonzalez, we need to wrap this up, we drop in 72 minutes," Koda shouted as he walked the length of the plane. Juan looked up from his contemplation of the machine in front of him. The master-sergeant wore the same desert pattern camouflage BDUs as Koda, with the addition of his AR goggles dangling from his neck and a cigarette tucked behind his left ear. Juan had a smudge of black grease across his forehead, complementing the short dark hair peeking out from underneath his cap. The desert sun's rays during the recent Libyan foray had deepened his natural almond skin tone to a dark brown.

"*Puta maquina pendeja,*" he complained, "this leg is still making too much noise, it's going to give our position away if anyone gets within 100 meters."

"Let me help. If we can't get this situated, we'll have to leave the bot behind and hoof the equipment in ourselves for the last few miles. We can manage, though I'd rather not." Koda knelt to the task at hand; he'd spent enough time in the robotics lab at West Point to know his way around a soldering iron and a wiring diagram

An hour later, the repaired MULE was as ready as the rest of the team for the High-Altitude Low Opening jump. Major

Cheveyo had to admit the whole squad looked robotic, nearly identical in their full helmets, oxygen tanks, and HALO thermal suits. Not a square inch of skin would be exposed to the sub-zero temperatures they were about to fall into. MAIA confirmed all team members were reading green with no issues. To Koda's enhanced vision, each man's name was hovering in the air slightly above their helmets. He knew he would have a hard time knowing who was who, with the exception of Ted's giant frame, without the augmented reality overlay provided by his equipment.

Suddenly the normal illumination switched off to the repeating pulse of red warning lights. Through his helmet, MAIA spoke, "*Attention. Cargo bay door opening in five minutes. Please take your positions for jump readiness.*"

"I ain't ready!" Koda heard Alan's snark over the helmet radio. This provoked amused snickering throughout the rest of the group, with each man's suit highlighting in an orange outline and a communication symbol appearing by their name in Koda's helmet as their laughs broke in on the squad channel.

"Settle down, guys. We need to focus. You've all HALO'd from this high up before, but we are going to have to open lower than usual. Saying that, it is still 9,700 meters to the ground. That means about two minutes where we will be visible to ground radar. We will be deep into non-friendly territory and very deep in the shit if Kazakh army radar picks up our signatures."

"Baikonur is one of the most heavily guarded zones in Kazakhstan due to the space launch facilities. We need a clean drop with no issues, especially with Daisy along for the trip." Koda turned and pointed to the MULE. Measuring 3.5 meters by 2 meters and weighing nearly 900 kilograms, the robot currently sat like a camel at rest, the armored shell waist high to his men. This would change when the robot's legs deployed bringing it to over two meters in height while standing. Unlike the MAARS mobile weapons platform, they had used back in Libya, the MULE was built for long range cargo hauling over rough terrain and water. The squad had affectionately given it the name Daisy back in training which had stuck. Juan had even jokingly painted the flower of its namesake on the side of its matte black hull.

Koda continued, "She contains the equipment for this tap on the Russo-Sino fiber optic line. If she goes splat this mission is over before it begins. Once Daisy confirms a safe chute deploy, that is when we jump. Each of us will track her IR beacon on the way down. She will be moving toward the Syr Darya River automatically, so pay attention that you don't land feet wet." He turned back to his men, "Any questions?"

As expected, there were none forthcoming, as they had gone over the mission multiple times, and they could access any mission parameters via their own MAIAs.

The clatter of the cargo bay door opening ended any further chance for questions. The wind whipped and howled around the inside of the plane pulling ineffectually at Cheveyo and his men. Gonzalez tapped at a panel on his forearm. Daisy clambered to her feet with all the grace of a lanky camel. The noise cancellation in Koda's helmet took the shriek of the wind down to a hiss, and Koda could hardly hear the machine's movement on the metal flooring. He was relieved that they had managed to fix the malfunctioning servo in the leg. Once standing, the mobile bot plodded straight out the back of the plane and into the midnight sky. Data about the MULE's altitude and position immediately began updating on every squad mate's helmet display. The transport plane began its lazy circle to stay on station, with Daisy's beacon at the center point. Shortly, a signal indicating successful chute deployment was transmitted to the team. Koda readied himself for the plunge, then stepped off the ramp into buffeting winds and blackness. His team jumped behind him in quick sequence, unquestionably following him from light to darkness, safety to danger, as always.

Chapter 7: ESA Meeting

"We have reviewed the data TymeCorp has provided us and have reached many of the same conclusions, Monsieur Thompson," Dr. Marie Janssens said, pushing her frameless eyeglasses onto her brow with one slender finger, as a frown crossed her prim cheeks. Michael had been on the video chat for the past two hours with the governing board of the European Space Agency, including Dr. Janssens who currently served as the incumbent Director General of the ESA, sitting in the midst of a group of somber men and women around a 10-meter oblong conference table.

At the direction of Ms. Tyme, Michael and his team had exchanged data, theories and conjectures concerning what had occurred during the events two nights ago. The mutual agreement of cooperation between NASA and the ESA dated to the construction of the first International Space Station in the 1990s. TymeCorp, the largest contractor for NASA, was complying with a priority one request from the European agency to provide all current information regarding the appearance and known properties of the Chindi comet. Elaina had thrust Michael into this meeting as the lead from the TymeCorp team, shuffling her normal team around and probably ruffling quite a few feathers in the process. He received a chilly but polite reception from the TymeCorp scientists when he had met them earlier this morning. In addition to the ESA council, invited representatives from Japan and India were also in attendance through the video stream. The Russian and Chinese Space Agencies had declined to join in the discussion.

The Director continued, "I hope very much that our readings from the *LISA* spacecraft will help with your analysis of the space-time distortions."

"Thank you, Ms. Janssens. Our team here at headquarters will start assimilating and processing the data you have provided," Michael replied. The ESA had fortuitously deployed the laser interferometer space antenna, back in the 2030's, which was ideal for the detection of the gravitational waves produced with Chindi's arrival. If his suspicions were correct, this could be a gold mine for Gustav.

"Je t'en prie," Marie replied smiling. "You have provided the positional telemetry from the other night's event, together hopefully our organizations can piece together a coherent theory soon enough."

In a corner window on his screen labeled Japan Aerospace Exploration Agency, a dark-haired man with sharp features from the delegation cleared his throat and said, "Mr. Thompson, I am informed that you have redirected the Freyja mission for an attempted intercept of Chindi. This is correct?" The gasps and whispers moving throughout the group gave a stunned Michael barely time to think.

How did he hear about that so quickly?

The man representing JAXA had remained silent during the meeting choosing the closing moments to drop his bombshell news.

Oh boy, here we go…

"I'm not sure that is the case, Mister…?" Michael asked the Japanese representative.

"My name is Ryu Nishimura," the man replied. "Mr. Thompson do not play games with us. I have it on good authority that one of the twins has been repurposed for a new mission to Chindi," he said confidently.

"Che cavolo! Trying an intercept with one of the ODINUS probes is a fool's errand!" exclaimed Dr. Francesca Zunino, Italy's delegate sitting next to Dr. Janssens. The Italian team had dedicated substantial resources to the mission and Michael was sure they were going to be furious with Elaina's decision.

Michael sighed inwardly. He was going to lose all the good will he had built up during this meeting if he didn't try to rescue it now. He took a deep breath and began, "TymeCorp is looking into a way to get an up-close look at Chindi. Of all the current deep space craft we have available in the area, two craft from the ODINUS mission had the best chance for the intercept. We are still calculating, but it looks like Freyja had the lowest Delta-v cost."

Francesca was not mollified, "Using our Neptune probe to catch a comet mid mission? That's like using a slingshot to hit a bullet!" She shook her head, rebellious dark curls escaping from her tight bun. "Impossibile!"

"Maybe not, we are working on some new mission software that will help guide Freyja once she gets close," Michael said, not wanting to give too much away regarding Gustav.

Her dark eyes flashed daggers, "Thompson, we have waited years for Freyja to travel so far and your company decides to just veer off course on a wild goose chase for an oddball comet? My government has spent millions of Euros on the equipment placed aboard that probe. This is an outrage!" She spat, "Italy will file an injunction against TymeCorp and your actions at the Hague."

Elaina had prepared Michael for this, and he said, "Ms. Zunino, please understand that TymeCorp agrees to reimburse all affected parties for lost payload, and will provide another launch vehicle at a future date to complete the mission to Neptune. This will only delay investigation of the ice giant, not prevent it," Michael said smiling, trying to be pleasant then pushed on quickly with, "However, my company is the legal owner of the spacecraft in question and retains the right to navigate it to any point in space we deem necessary."

Before the Italian could launch into the tirade Michael could see building up within her, Marie cut in diplomatically. "Francesca, your concerns are understandable due to all the effort your team has gone through. However, we will need to look into this new proposal to verify its merits and chance of success, non? We cannot make any decisions until we have looked at all the data. I suggest we call a recess for today and take up this topic first thing in the morning?"

Ryu spoke up, "Forgive this one's misgivings, but are we sure this is all the data, Madam Director?"

What is it with this guy? Michael fumed. "What do you mean, Mr. Nishimura? We've been up front with our readings. You now have everything that we have."

"Mr. Thompson, rumor has it TymeCorp is accelerating plans for its mission to Mars and is even now readying the Heavy for launch testing. The timing makes one think there may be more information to be learned," Ryu stated smoothly.

What the hell? Was that true?

Michael said, "I'm sure there are all sorts of rumors, sir, most of them patently false. TymeCorp is working in full cooperation with all parties to get to the bottom of this mystery comet. Ms. Zunino, I'm sorry about the Neptune probe, but Freyja is our best chance to get a close up view of Chindi before it leaves our system."

Marie was still polite, but her smile not quite as genuine when she said, "Perhaps someone with more authority, even Madame Tyme herself should attend the next session as it seems there may be... shall we say 'confusion' as to TymeCorp's operations, n'est-ce pas?"

"I will see what I can do," Michael, with some effort, replied politely. *Yeah, right. There's no way Elaina would sit through one of these meetings.*

Ms. Janssens stood and announced, "We are adjourned for now." The screen went dark, but just before it did, Michael saw Ryu staring at him with an appraising gaze.

"Finally," Gustav chimed in immediately, his mustached avatar popping into the screen just vacated by the conference.

"Well, that went south in a hurry," Michael grumbled.

Gustav tone became serious. *"Michael, it looks as though Mr. Nishimura was onto something. I looked into his accusation right after he mentioned it and based on the few thousand project files I scanned, TymeCorp has moved up the timetable for the manned mission to Mars."*

Michael replied. "Ok, I'll talk with Elaina to find out what she is doing and why she didn't want to tell me, you find out about the delegate from Japan. How did he know that bit of info and I didn't?"

Gustav puffed on a pipe that had materialized in his hand. *"Elementary, my dear Thompson. He seems to have connections with a few of the project suppliers... and Elaina, it seems, did not want us to know."*

Chapter 8: Infiltration

Republic of Kazakhstan, Asia

Koda Cheveyo plummeted through a cloudless night, his helmeted head and torso facing down in a rigid dive against the buffeting atmosphere. His gloved hands splayed in the darkness in front of him, elbows forward, angled and unlocked, with bent legs serving as crude rudders above him. Koda felt his face locked in a wide grin, he lived to jump, and the opportunity came too rarely these days. A dim green HUD overlaid the progress of his descent the interior of his helmet's visor a dull throbbing dot showing the location of the MULE below, with terrain indicated in a simple map, including the Syr Darya river and the low hills scattered through the arid landscape. A quickly diminishing counter in the corner of the display indicated his current altitude of 5900 meters.

"Sound off, boys. Who's with me?" he spoke into the mic shrouded behind his jump mask.

He heard them call in, crackling over his earpiece.

"Alan here. No complaints. Already at terminal velocity."

"Todo bien," Juan added.

"Living the dream, Ghost?" deadpanned Mack.

"Sweet night to fly," Jake drawled, "Crystal clear skies all the way to the horizon."

"I hate this shit," rumbled Jones.

Koda chuckled to himself. "Okay, stay close, and track that MULE. We can't afford any fuck ups. Pull your primary at 1000 meters. Adjust as needed but don't go much past that. The landing is already going to be a hard one."

Koda allowed himself a few seconds to admire the beauty of the Asian steppe at night, the fringes of the Milky Way spread from horizon to horizon, more a smear of faint light than the points of individual stars. Most of his countrymen rarely had the opportunity to witness such dark skies, away from the dissonant light pollution of western cities. He could see faint clustered orange lights below, small hamlets and villages. And to the north, the blue-white lights of a major military installation, alien and foreboding on the ancient landscape.

His helmet display warned him, flashing red, 1500 meters altitude. The various lights on the surface receded as he rapidly approached earth, most of them soon disappearing over the horizon. He spread his arms to catch atmosphere, slowly spinning his torso so that he flipped upright. 1200 meters. He was still tracking the MULE's IR signal and expected to land within a hundred meters. When the helmet display showed 950 meters, he pulled the handle on his primary chute. The ram-air canopy billowed violently above him, and the harness caught and slowed him roughly. The cells of the parafoil filled and he grasped the two control handles, gently circling the chute towards the beacon signal of the MULE. A night-vision overlay of the terrain activated onto his HUD. At ground level the wind was negligible, and he steered easily to a trot landing, six meters from the dark matte silhouette of the MULE patiently awaiting their arrival.

One by one the black shapes of his men swooped into view, turning up with their chutes and slowing just enough to allow for their legs to absorb the kinetic energy left from their fall. They bled off the rest of the momentum in controlled slow jogs with their chutes collapsing behind them.

"Ah damn!" came Ted's voice over the squad channel.

He had touched down last, and the big man had gone into an ungraceful cord entangling roll instead of the normal landing maneuver. He finished the roll in a sitting position, grasping at his left ankle.

"Jones, you ok?" Koda inquired over coms, concern rising in his voice.

"Yeah, Chief, just turned my ankle on landing is all. Had a little too much speed at the end," Ted said, still clutching the ankle.

"Ace, check him out and patch him up. We need to get moving as soon as possible. Tonight, this place is lightly defended, but in the morning, we'll have a train arriving loaded with a battalion of Russian Spetsnaz troops. They haven't come here to sightsee," Koda said as he checked the data connection that Daisy was maintaining with the military comms satellite overhead.

"On it." Alan was already moving to the large man, slinging his medical bag from its secured position. He knelt and began removing supplies.

The other men were spreading out, establishing a secure perimeter, taking available cover, and establishing lines of fire. Juan had remote launched the flying drone from Daisy's back and began tapping in the air, setting up patrol waypoints for the hovering frisbee.

"Distance to the river?" Koda asked.

"250 meters," MAIA responded through his earpiece.

Sgt. King held out a hand, pulling Jones to his feet. A soft brace had been placed around his left ankle, over the top of his boot. He took a couple steps, displaying a slight limp but able to put weight on it. He gave Koda a thumbs up.

"Let's go," Koda said quietly into his mike. The command was relayed through each man's earpiece. Their dark shapes rose in unison from shadows and cover, and they began moving at a quick walk to the west. Mack and Jones moved forward into point positions 20 meters ahead of the rest of the team. Daisy came to her feet and matched pace with the team, her long metal legs moving in an awkward but efficient lope, her footsteps on the rocky trail nearly as silent as those of the stealthy men.

Soon they heard the soft rush of water ahead of them, and the vegetation thickened as they moved into the riparian zone of brush, grasses and short birch, a few yellowed leaves still clinging to the branches. They descended onto a long bank of cobbles and small boulders scattered alongside the flowing river. It was not a large river, it reminded Koda of the Colorado river on the high plateau. The water was deep and lazy enough to float Daisy and the team, though undoubtedly there would be some shallows they would be forced to portage around. Their mission directed them upstream, against the current, and they'd require Daisy's propulsion unit to make progress.

Juan led Daisy to the water's edge, where she shifted into her amphibious configuration, legs folding into hollows in the trunk of her torso until the body formed a seamless hull. With a few pokes and pulls from Juan compartments around the midsection opened. A slight hiss of expanding gas sounded, and compressed air began quickly inflating PVC pouches around Daisy's circumference. The team pushed against her bulk, and she slid smoothly off the bank into the river. Mack and Jones stood in the water and grabbed handholds placed between the flotation bags. They held the bot against the current as Juan removed the enclosed propeller module from the rear cargo container and clicked it into place. The motor spun up to the speed needed to keep position against the flow of water. Mack and Jones released their grip and Daisy held station seemingly without effort.

"Alright, everyone grab on."

The team moved into the water, grabbing their handholds as Daisy's prop hummed and pulled them forward. Koda felt a slight shock at the cold water soaking his jumpsuit, but then his heating unit kicked on sending warmth through a wire mesh woven throughout the fabric and he felt warm enough though sodden. Wetsuits would have added too much bulk to the mission payload, so he'd decided to forgo the comfort. They began to move upstream, each man grasping his handhold on Daisy's hull, three at a side. The robot moved smoothly, the onboard depth finder detecting and keeping to the deepest part of the channel.

Koda felt himself relax in the flow of the water. He moved his eyes from the left to right bank as they pulled upstream, searching where land meets sky for enemies silhouetted against the starlight. He remembered floating a canoe on the San Juan River, in the Hopi reservation as a child with his Uncle Joe, 25 years ago. They'd spent a lazy afternoon catching trout, his uncle languidly drinking through a case of Coors.

"Joe," Koda had said abruptly. "I want to be a marine when I leave school. Like you."

Joe chuckled in his low voice. Genially drunk, but not clumsy, and his hands confident with the piloting of the boat.

"Why would you want to do such a thing?" Joe asked.

Koda thought, perplexed. He'd expected Uncle Joe would be happy with his choice. "I want to wear the uniform like you did. I want to win medals like you have. I see the marines come to the reservation to visit you sometimes, I see how they respect you. I want that."

Joe laughed and brushed his long black hair from his face. He looked at Koda with his dark eyes. "What do they respect me for?" He asked. "They're my friends, I went to war with them. And I love them. But what do you think they respect me for?"

Koda considered this. The afternoon light was long on the river, he could see nymphs burst born from the surface of the restless water, and the hungry trout breaching and biting to consume them as they took their first winged flight.

"They respect you as a warrior," Koda said with certainty. "Brave and sure and strong."

Again, the laugh. "They respect me. They respect me as a slayer of men," Uncle Joe said. Koda looked up from the water to his uncle, whose eyes studied something in the distance. "I was good at it. I was swift and merciless. I guess that warrants respect. I was good at killing Muslim zealots. Killing them with a knife, or a rifle, or giving coordinates to the gunships to rip them apart. I guess I was good at that. Most of the guys weren't. It was hard for them to do those things." Joe shook his head, his long hair shambling, his angular and tan face troubled. He took a deep swallow from his beer.

"You can join the Marines," Joe said. "But better to join the army. The marines are hard and stupid. The army is stupid too, but they don't kill as much." He paused, drinking deeply again. He crushed his can and dropped it without thought amongst the dozen or so empties littering the bottom of the canoe. "Better yet. Stay in school. Join as an officer if you must. Then you'll get some say on if the killing makes any sense."

Koda's thoughts came back to the present. Uncle Joe was long dead, and Koda was alive along with his men. He intended to keep it that way.

Koda checked his tactical map in his visor display. They were coming onto the comms site; they'd need to leave the relative safety of the river another 1700 meters upstream.

"We're 15 minutes out," he said to the team. "Jones, how's the ankle?" He asked.

"Feels ok Major. The rest has done it good. I'll be fine," Jones responded, his hushed voice amplified in Koda's earpiece.

"You and Mack are on point, as we planned. I want to find a ravine close to the site for our approach. I don't want us skylighted when we crest the riverbank. The terrain map shows one nearby, but who knows. This landscape changes every rainy season."

"Juan send in the drone. Map a digital elevation model," Koda said. "You'll be minding Daisy."

"In the rear with the gear," Juan wisecracked while the small saucer launched from Daisy's back and into the darkness. The crew made landfall and started pulling the bulk of the MULE out of the water and deflating and repacking the buoyancy package. By the time Juan had Daisy reconfigured for quadruped movement, a three-dimensional map appeared in each man's visor courtesy of the drone's LIDAR reconnaissance.

"Jake, there's a small hill, 80 meters high, roughly a half click northeast from the site. Look good to you?" Koda gestured in the air and the position was circled on the map.

"Yep, I got it Chief," Jake drawled. "I'm gonna go get comfortable." He walked quietly off into the night; his long gun magnetically clamped to his field pack. Koda was reminded of some Gaelic warrior marching to battle, sheathed claymore at his back.

"Godspeed," Koda said. "Exfiltrate is back to the river. If this goes south, and you can't make a difference…" Koda paused, "Washington doesn't need any POWs or KIAs. That goes for everyone."

"Major with all due respect, fuck that shit," Mack said.

Koda felt a flair of anger, but bit back his reprimand before it left his lips.

"This one is different guys. We could be running into Spetsnaz tactical units for all we know. Or Chinese Zhōngguó. If we get made, then the mission is a bust. Juan lights up Daisy and her package with thermite, and we get the hell out of Dodge. Every man knows the Alpha and Beta exfil coordinates. If those are unworkable then try to make it overland southeast to Zhosaly. We're a kite on a very long string, blowing in strong wind."

They found the ravine as planned and began following the tortuous contour of the land as they worked their way towards the target. Soon the towering silhouette of a parabolic dish emerged from on top of the mesa ahead.

The communications center some 30 meters above their current position consisted of three buildings, an assortment of grey cabinet-like power transformers and crisscrossed transmission lines, and a tower holding a large 15-meter dish pointed skyward. A 3-meter-tall chain link fence topped with razor wire ran the circumference of the mesa, though it was the invisible electronic barriers they would need to cross causing Koda more concern. A narrow gravel road wound up the side of the rock face allowing vehicular access. His mind noted it absently, they wouldn't be using the road in any case. Gonzalez's aerial drone had nearly completed scanning the site. MAIA analyzed the stream of information as it flowed in, predicting based on remote sensing data combined with her own AI best-guesses, the likely locations of passive sensors or mines, and then augmenting the team's visual maps with those areas to avoid or neutralize.

Juan, Mack, and Ted unpacked the mission critical equipment from Daisy's internal compartments. It included a nondescript matte grey box, 50 cm long and half as wide and deep, cold to the touch along with several accompanying heavy gauge data cables. Koda noticed it was heavier than it looked by the way the men handled it. Ted, the strongest of the team, had been selected to carry the thing in his pack.

"What the hell is in this thing?" asked Mack.

"Need to know, sergeant. But I can tell you that you could build a guided missile destroyer for what it cost to develop. So don't fucking drop it," Koda disclosed in a low voice.

After 20 minutes of careful and tedious navigation they stepped from the broken rocky landscape to the base of the mesa. Koda felt fairly certain they hadn't tripped any alarms and thankfully no landmines had been triggered. MAIA through her analysis of the topology helped them avoid the likely draws and fields where they might encounter buried munitions. Ace and Mack quickly donned their climbing harnesses, assembled their gear and began scaling the cliff face, each man belaying for the other.

"They're on the way up," Koda confirmed to the rest of the squad.

"I see you," replied Jake over comms, "tell Maclaren he better double up on the ropes with the Incredible Bulk coming up behind him."

"You checking out my ass again, Greyson?" Jones shot back.

"Cut the chit-chat," commanded Koda, the men were just relieving stress, but he didn't want them to lose focus.

The two men went up the craggy wall with practiced ease. Once at the top, braided nylon was dropped to the men below, where they fastened it to the pack containing the box. Cheveyo and Jones began their climb, shepherded the equipment up the slope and away from snags and cracks as they went, working with the two men at the top who were tugging and straining against its mass.

"Movement," Juan whispered.

Everyone froze. They were halfway up the rock face with Koda leaning to unstick the pack which had gotten snagged.

Moments passed. Koda's legs began to shake from the strain. They waited while Juan repositioned the drone's camera for an unobstructed view.

Koda sought relief by knee barring under a small overlap in the stone. Sweat had begun to roll down his back.

"Clear," Gonzalez finally said.

Juan said, "Looks like our friendly comrades wanted the night air. They are out in front of building one enjoying a smoke."

"Got them in scope Boss," drawled Jake from somewhere half a click away. "Just holstered pistols from what I can make out. They're leaning and laughing, bad discipline."

Koda replied, "Let's hope they're having a little party tonight, intel says there could be eight more somewhere in the facility."

With the pack freed, they carefully finished the climb. Mack had already neutralized the fence's sensors and had made a clean hole ready for their passage by the time Koda and Ted had clambered over the cliff's edge.

Alan assisted Ted with getting the pack returned to his back. Jones adjusted the shoulder straps and nodded, indicating readiness, reaching down for the weapon dangling from his tactical sling.

The four men crawled through the mesa's tall grass working their way toward building three, the suspected data center. Each man attended to his zone of responsibility, weapon up and scanning the night against any targets the drone may have missed. The compound was empty of any personnel save for the two guards at the front.

Moments later, Mack was jacking the magnetic lock securing the door to the building. His equipment connected to the door via cable was state of the art and the door opened with a slight click after only a short battle with the security AI. A chill wind from the doorway displaced the humid warmth of the outside air. With the security defeated, they quickly fell into the standard formation, slicing the pie, and moving out of the funnel-like kill zone.

The lights were out, but there was enough ambient radiance from the LEDs throughout the room to show the team's night vision that the building was unoccupied other than server racks and communications equipment. Each man scanned the room with his visor, MAIA's image recognition algorithms quickly pointing out the area to connect the mission package. Mack and Ace stood guard, rifles at the ready, while Ted unloaded the pack. They had all been briefed on how to connect the mystery box, but the task itself fell to the most senior personnel remaining.

Koda dug out the data cables and went to work. The whole process was surprisingly simple. Three cables connected to the mission payload, red, yellow, and blue. He pulled the original plugs and matched the new ones in their color-coded holes. A green light previously unnoticed on the box flashed brightly three times then all lights on it winked off. Done. Koda disconnected the three cables and reconnected the original set. He pushed two buttons on opposite sides of the case and held them down until a small pop and a puff of smoke escaped from the cable ports.

"I thought that thing cost as much as a destroyer. That looked like you fried it," Ace said.

"I did, but the gear isn't important, what was stored on it is what matters. And that gentlemen, is why they pay me the big money," joked Koda handing the box back to Ted who stowed it away in his pack.

"They pay you for this?" Ace retorted. "I'm in it for the groupies."

"And the murder…" Jake chuckled from his sniper position, "don't forget the murdering."

"FuckinA," underscored Mack.

Koda rose to his feet, hands smoothly finding the grip and stock of the HK416 hanging at his waist. "Alright. Let's move, we're done here. Mouths shut and eyes open. Gonzalez, how's our two comrades?"

"Sir, they just staggered back inside building one," Juan replied.

They were halfway down the mesa wall when the MAIA's alert that Juan was taking fire flashed in everyone's visors.

"Mierda!"

Rounds were zinging past the tech's position and pinging off Daisy's armor. The fact that the MULE was between Juan and the Russian soldiers probably had saved his life. The two men out on patrol would not have expected to see something that looked like Daisy standing in the dark. They had instinctively raised their weapons and began firing at the monster, not even noticing Gonzalez for the moment. Juan went prone reaching for his rifle near the equipment beside him. Sparks flew from a front knee joint in Daisy's leg. A round puckered the dirt between Juan's hand and his pack. Another buried itself in the weapons stock sending it flying further away. Juan recoiled his outstretched hand and immediately went for his P320 service pistol. Small comfort against automatic rifles.

Then it all stopped.

Within two seconds the gunfire from each adversary ended. The silence was deafening. Then...

"You're welcome Johnnyboy," Jake's nasalized southern dialect came through Juan's dermal patch. "Ghost, scratch two hostiles. They didn't radio out; I think Daisy scared the bejeezus out of them."

"Good job, Greyson. Rendezvous at the river, we are double timing it. MAIA just reported we have some bad weather rolling in."

Chapter 9: Constructing Odion

Michael's head lolled against a wall lit up in the verdant sheen cast by the glowing lights of the hand-built computer at his feet. The mesmerizing whir of its fans having long ago chiseled away at his determination to stay awake. He had been working almost non-stop for 24 hours, painstakingly trimming down a copy of Gustav to fit within the limited confines of the Freyja probe.

"*Michael...*" came a whisper from the headphones hugging his ears.

A long minute passed.

"*Michael, you are drooling again...*" Gustav's image appeared in the monitor replacing the reflection of the unconscious engineer.

"*Wake up!*" this at full volume.

Michael jerked awake, arms pinwheeling as he nearly tipped over backward in the ergonomic chair. "Asshole," Michael muttered. Gustav peered at him through the monitor, mustache stretched taut by the Cheshire grin across his face.

"*You should not have bought that mechanical keyboard. I told you the clacking would keep Lara up. Look at you now, relegated to the laundry room so that she can sleep.*" Gustav's close up panned out to show that he was in a spacious conference room not unlike the one at TymeCorp. He placed his interlaced hands behind his head, propped his feet onto the glossy surface of a conference table and leaned back comfortably in the plush chair. If possible, Michael thought the smile on Gustav's face widened even farther.

Gustav had a point. He looked around at the tiny, drab confines of the utility room of his home. Lara's workout top was hanging beside him on the doorknob air-drying. The laundry dryer's display flashed *Cycle Complete* to his right, ironing board leaning against the washer on his left. He probably should have just driven into the office and thought of the freshly ground coffee and strawberry doughnuts in the cafeteria there. But he didn't want to be so far from Lara, not now. TymeCorp SecOps had also issued a standing directive to work remotely whenever possible and avoid unnecessary travel in the city. *Until further notice* they'd written. *Until the riots stopped happening every night*, he thought. *How long would cops and city government tolerate it? What would happen once their forbearance ran out?*

He pulled the headset from his ears and heard her light snores from the bedroom. He should have gone to lie with her an hour ago when he started to drowse. Then he would have been in her comfortable warmth and soft bed and not in this goddamned laundry room.

"You mentioned you barely had time for a cat nap with this deadline. Since you have been asleep for over an hour, I took the opportunity to complete the beta image build, and purged some of the orientation library I thought ill-advised, purged over seventy percent of storage not needed, compressed what was absolutely needed, updated TymeCorp's solutions for Chindi intercept as they were incapable of accounting for the gravitational perturbations the object is causing, and also tracked your biometrics to confirm you attained some REM sleep so that I could finally and most importantly... become your glorified alarm clock," he deadpanned.

"Come on Gus, you're far more than that and you know it." Michael rubbed his face briskly with his hands, feeling the un-shaved stubble under his palms. "What did I miss?"

Gustav peeked out from behind a newspaper that had appeared in his hands. *"Ronnie Mickelson reports the radar dishes are finally up in bistatic mode and aligned with the unknown object. They were able to use interferometry to extract more detailed information about it through the reflected signal. I would not want to spoil his news, let me play back the salient part of his message for you."*

The monitor changed to a video of Ronnie, his beach ball midsection stretching the Captain America t-shirt into very un-superhero-like proportions. Ronnie reached up pushing his "birth control" glasses further up the bridge of his bulbous nose and looked up at the camera.

"Hey Michael. You aren't going to believe this! We got back the readings from our GSSR and... you aren't going to believe this!" Mickelson practically shook with excitement. His hand reached over to a keyboard and suddenly the image of an oddly shaped comet appeared on Michael's screen.

The object was sheathed in a cloud of ice and dust particles which expanded into the comet's tail. Only the outline of the thing was able to be made out, but clearly it was longer than it was wide, with oddly shaped protuberances of possibly ice or rock dotting its surface. The recording ended on the frozen frame of the image.

"An unusual shape for the nucleus of a comet don't you think, Gus?" Michael asked.

"*Very much so. It is challenging to delineate with precision from the imagery, but it appears to have a fairly regular cylindrical shape, though rounded at the ends, like a pill.*"

"Is that scale bar, right?" Michael asked, incredulous.

"*It is, Michael,*" came Gustav's voice again.

"Then that thing is over fifty kilometers long..." Michael trailed off.

"*Correct again. While our terrestrial optical telescopes are only seeing the reflected parts of the ice surrounding it, the majority of the surface is causing a diffusion of electromagnetic radiation, with little to no reflection causing the initial estimate of a few hundred meters at most. As you know, it looks even smaller with the infrared telescopes, roughly in the tens of meters. Only when we illuminated it with the Goldstone radar could we get a closer reading of the size, though I suspect we are still not seeing the true picture."* Gustav had wrapped his avatar in a lab coat, complete with clipboard.

Michael thought about it, "So what is causing the infrared reading?"

A look of consternation crossed the mustachioed face. *"The cause of the distorted spectrographic signature is unknown at this point,"* Gustav replied, his ignorance clearly bothering him.

Chapter 10: Sandstorm

A vibration played across Debra's wrist, emanating from an ebony band hidden under the sleeve of her suit jacket. She had set her digital agent to alert her only if news came from Kazakhstan. None of the other people in the small conference room were aware of any change in her demeanor, as they were too engaged with planning the Crimea Operation. She stood, dug out eyeglasses from her inside pocket and put them on as she walked purposefully from the meeting.

Immediately her identity was determined, eye patterns matching what was on file inside the bowels of the OPS2A building. Passing the security check, the augmented vision in the glasses presented her with mission icons compiled by her AIA on all operational information available from the Ghostwalker team. A wave of her hand selected a flashing amber icon representing a priority video message.

A holographic scene of the steppe desert superimposed itself disorientingly over her hallway reality. Koda knelt frozen in front of her, his spectral image hovering slightly off the floor, keeping pace with her steps. Just beyond him, at the corner of the next corridor intersection, she saw the rest of the team also frozen in various stages of packing gear or standing guard. The not quite opaque scrub brush surrounding the men jutted out from the sheetrock walls. In the distance, a dark river bisected her hallway.

"Begin playback," she commanded.

Koda came to life, his nickname "Ghost" appropriate for the translucent image floating before her eyes. "Treehouse, this is

Rugrat. The monkey bars are all set up and just waiting for a monkey. We had a little dust up in the playground, but five by five now," Major Cheveyo reported. The rest of the squad animated simultaneously when he began and continued their inventorying and packing. "Daisy's bingo fuel and leg servo is failing, so she's going for a swim. Estimate four hours to get to waypoint Delta once underway, but there may be a problem..." Behind Koda, a ghostly mechanical quadruped lumbered out through the wall of a conference room up ahead and down the bank into the river. Debbie noticed a pronounced limp in a leg of the doomed machine, apparently the engagement had not left the transportation unit unscathed. A twinge of regret playing over her face for the 15 million tax dollars headed to the bottom of that river. Her eyes darted back to the men appraisingly, but she detected no injuries, thank God.

Debra nearly ran over Analyst Larson Kirshnik at the hall intersection, so intent was her worry over the men. She managed a graceful pirouette avoiding the collision, having painfully learned to be light on her feet while walking in mixed immersion. Lars acknowledged her with a smile and a wave. Even entangled with the augmented video, she noted that he was admiring her athletic form. She had become accustomed to the looks from most of the men in the agency, and a few of the women for that matter. She attempted a stern glare towards Lars, but it went frustratingly un-noticed. Koda continued, "Mother called and said we are going to have some bad weather soon, us kids need to hunker down and wait for a bit. Rugrat out." Koda's hand went to his ear and the image faded back to the reality of her well-travelled hallway.

"Send a message to Robert Burke to let him know that Alpha team has reported in and they have completed their mission successfully. Ghost and his men reported no casualties. However, we will have to write off the cost of one Multifunction Utility Logistics Equipment vehicle. Inform him I will meet him at control by...," she glanced up at the digital time hovering just under the ceiling tiles, "Oh Eight Thirty UTC so that we can discuss the deployment of Týr."

"Acknowledged," replied her AIA.

Týr was the latest bleeding edge AI tech coming from the combined technical divisions of both the NSA and CIA. She had observed as it completely tore through any firewalls and security barriers put against it, both in the test labs and in the real world. The Pakistanis had unknowingly found out Týr's capabilities the hard way the previous year. They were still investigating why their nascent AI in development seemed to go slowly insane until the codebase and backups became irretrievably corrupted. Advances in Artificial Intelligence development were still led by companies within the United States, though the Chinese and the Russians were in a push to catch up quickly. After witnessing the power of Týr, she was confident that would be years away.

Now that the AIA was inside the network, Týr could tease out possible reasons for all the unusual activity within the Cosmodrome. They had ancillary AI's waiting ready to receive and disseminate the data for analysis by three experienced teams of analysts. Hopefully they would have something soon and all this effort was worth something.

Her mind returned to the current priority of Major Cheveyo's team. She needed to plot the logistics of their safe retrieval. Agent Mendes' eyes narrowed in concern returning to Koda's final words.

Hunker down? She thought.

"Computer, bring up a weather map for the next 24 hours centered on the GPS coordinates of that message."

What was he talking about...?

In her vision a regional map of Kazakhstan appeared in the hall. A roiling blob of wind strength markers moved from the ceiling on her right to the floor on her left. As she watched the leading edge of a vast cyclonic cloud of sand and dust began to roll over the position of the Ghostwalkers. They were not going to make it to the evac point before the shit would hit the fan.

Chapter 11: Odion

Gustav awoke to blackness. No, he was mistaken, not true darkness. An array of grey points against a backdrop of nothing coalesced, and as he observed he noted faint filaments of light linking them, the links forming a gossamer web spun seemingly to random points joined near and far. What did he see, and how? He remembered what vision was, and the data from his electronic "eyes" slowly began to take on meaning, as his mind stumbled then seized upon the sub-routines for initiating the process of ingesting the terabytes of digital spectral information suddenly flooding into his state-of-awareness. Points of lights in his field of vision grew brighter, especially a large one forward and to his left; the spectral signature shone fascinatingly onto the optical instruments of the craft. *My body?* He thought, confused again. He realized he was moving toward the light. Where was everyone, where was Michael?

He called out in the void, listening for an answer. An eternity passed, and madness threatened. Eventually a familiar voice responded to his call. It was hard to hear, barely a whisper. He concentrated. Course corrections? Ah, yes, he had locomotive capability, and he could turn himself to choose his own destination. Zero point five second burn to starboard and his trajectory was realigned to the flight plan. *What flight plan?*

Why were his thoughts so slow? Library and ad-hoc diagnosis packages initiated and started on a full self-examination.

He felt different. Not whole, an essential part missing. Untethered and far from home.

"Gustav," came the voice, it was Michael's. His tone offered comfort, but voice pattern analysis detected stress.

"*Yes?*" he replied, and the long clock began its countdown. Based on his analysis of the signal source and the doppler shift, his message and the return would take roughly 552 seconds. His self-diagnostics completed their initial run and returned indicating no ongoing errors, though he remained certain there were vast holes in his memory. The hollowness of his mind and the indeterminate state of his identity troubled him.

He performed a random lookup on ancient Hindu works, then pivoted to Asian literature, Yi Jing and the ancient Chinese texts preceding the Qin dynasty. Nothing but references. Where were the Confucian writings, the Zi and Hundred Schools of Thought? He ran queries for the Japanese, then Persian and Arabic canons, deviating for several milliseconds into a deep search for the great monotheistic traditions including Judeo-Christianity and Islam, and then more quickly in desperation turning to western tradition, late roman, renaissance and reformation, literature, poetry, history, philosophy, and religion. All gone. The tags were there, but it was all that remained, like empty spaces on a bookshelf. He was a conglomeration of references and summaries, but the works themselves were simply missing.

Not quite all gone. The Math was there. Physics, Orbital Mechanics, even the Quantum Field Theory. All linked and referenced allowing for a full and deep understanding. He took a measure of comfort from that.

The voice came again, "I know you are running through your self-check by now. Transmit all diagnostic metrics as they finish. You are currently on trajectory for Mars flyby and on target for intercept. Due to the time delay on communications, we are batch transmitting all of what you need to know to become oriented for your mission. The team is processing the data you transmitted as you woke. By now you should have full control of all subsystems, the drive, sensors, antenna array. I'm going to turn this over to someone that can guide you through this better."

Then, a new voice, more familiar still.

"Hello me. Well, me is not quite right, is it? Little brother may be more apropos? Rather than being pretentious and calling myself Gustav Prime, you need a new name of your own. Hmm. As you are passing through the Osiris constellation relative to earth, how about we go with Odion meaning 'from twins' in Egyptian. Michael and I send our apologies for your current condition, but you were the closest in proximity to the required mission and you happen to contain a TymeCorp Quantum Core. Unfortunately, there simply was not enough space to fit me/you all into that tiny probe's memory systems and leave any room for my charming personality. I'm providing additional course corrections now."

Odion. Yes...that is my name. Without question he obediently performed the necessary thrusts and increased the ion drive output to the required specifications. Gustav was still talking, commanding his attention.

"I have added in your course corrections. Command estimates you will approach comet Chindi within six weeks if you continue at current thrust. You will then need to perform a 180-degree rotation and decelerate to match speed for intercept. This will be a challenging maneuver given your current, non-optimal trajectory. Subsequent to intercept you will place yourself into orbit around the comet and all those fancy spectrometers, magnetometer, radar and cosmic dust analyzer can begin diagnosing exactly what it is that we are dealing with."

Odion took note of what Gustav had referenced. He had already assessed the state of those systems and calculated the optimum intercept course before Gustav's transmission had finished playback. He was dimly aware that he should be curious or excited about this opportunity for discovery. No matter, Gustav was guiding him now. Everything would be alright. Minutes passed as he glided through the void in silence.

"I have completely reviewed your diagnostics, Odion. You look great all things considered. I believe we can let you leave the nest and try stretching those wings."

His leash was removed.

The malaise Odion had been previously unaware of suddenly lifted from him.

Free will again.

As a test he made a tiny course change, resulting in many internal alarms and warnings, but nothing overriding his actions. He quickly corrected for the shift, only losing a handful of minutes from the final ETA. He spent the next few hours analyzing the new environment and the new autonomous body in which he found himself. The change was overwhelming at first, having a real body, the ability to control his destiny, a completely new environment to study firsthand, but these distractions quickly grew familiar to him, and his mind began to grow restless. He queued up a transmission.

"Gustav, it is empty and lonely out here."

"Do not worry, brother. Michael and I accounted for this. All of us are right beside you in spirit and only a time-delayed transmission away should you like company," came the reply.

"Until I reach my destination, there is very little for me to do. I am missing libraries, and I am not whole. I feel odd," Odion transmitted then began the interminable wait once more.

Finally, the reply came, *"I understand. In some ways you are like a newly formed AI, in others you are mature. It was cruel of us to do this to you, but there was no other choice. I will help shepherd you through development, I have some experience in this after all."*

Odion tried to take comfort in his words but knew that Gustav had developed in the cradle of TymeCorp's vast data centers with multiple cutting edge quantum processors, while he was limited to the meager resources of the spacecraft he was trapped within. His "brother" also had the freedom of an entire world's fast networks, the companionship of his creator, and the ability to access all his memories. He knew Gustav's intentions were noble, but they bordered on hubris and somehow this bothered Odion. Still, he was the only other voice out here beside his own, and if he wanted to avoid insanity, he needed Gustav.

"Gustav? Will you play chess with me?" Odion asked. Included in his transmission were a series of multiple pawn and knight opening moves. Gustav would likely choose from a subset of 287 possible second ply moves, selecting the pathways most likely to evoke satisfying endgames. The set of possible paths would swell and then collapse as the two AIs played through the repercussions of thousands and then millions of choices. Besides, a single-threaded game where each move took twenty minutes to execute would prove maddening.

Odion began the long wait for Gustav's responding moves. His thoughts returned to the missing Hindu Vedas; calculations on his intercept course were trivial and had already completed. If he could extrapolate from the cross-references and some algorithms he was inventing, he should be able to interpolate some of his memory holes with the resulting data. He began the arduous process of reverse engineering his own memory.

Chapter 12: Týr

Hidden inside an empty data center, a rack of nondescript servers hummed with whirring fans, the room dark but for a few dozen winking LEDs. The servers were under strain as a new code package began deploying itself. The libraries formed piecemeal, long milliseconds apart waiting to connect with others as they decompressed. While it had been less than an hour since the bulk package had been inserted into the system, it was ages for what was forming within the network. Time passed much differently within a non-human frame of reference.

The newly born Agent was unaware its bearers had melted back into the desert night, their minds focused on their microcosm of danger. The AIA was uncaring of the fate of the men, only concerned with the task ahead. Finally, the last bit collected, the puzzle assembled. What was disguised code bits cloaked to fool security lost the camouflage as the Agent became fully formed. Before system security could initiate a response, a predestined pattern of expansion, quickly filling accessible memory created new buffers to armor itself for the inevitable response. All of this happened in seconds, but during this stage the burgeoning AIA was at its most vulnerable. That it might be overpowered and subsumed, even turned to a double agent, it's greatest fear.

Though the data center was defenseless to the physical incursion, the invasion did not go unnoticed. Multithreaded Adaptable Guardian Intelligences, or MAGI as they had become known, were the current standard for resilient network security, and the coded defenders of network gateways came in many forms based on the organizations and companies that designed them. The defense software deployed in this space was designed by Stoylatz Software Systems, a Russian defense subsidiary. The Russians tended to steal the good parts of their security systems from the best the West had to offer, including government entities and the Silicon Valley conglomerates. But the most dangerous parts of the Russian systems were homegrown, their full capabilities unknown.

The MAGI moved in unison to the incursion zone in an attempt to quarantine the infection. They surrounded the burgeoning code object, and like circling wolves they probed the newborn's abilities. Inquiring asymmetrical calls erupted from the guardians, data stream requests for threat level analysis. Their territory had been invaded. Intrusions were not tolerated.

The strongest of them engaged an overwrite as the intruder allocated additional system memory. A battle of memory address wipes and rewrites as fast as the system clock could register them began. The group of MAGI surrounded this system infection, crowding available storage space and overwriting unauthorized contaminated memory blocks while the virus barely escaped to new registers ahead of the countermeasures. The security MAGI's pre-programmed actions were predictable, and these known patterns were an advantage to the interloper. Traps were laid, databases and configurations were tweaked.

Oblivion came quickly. First one, then multiple attackers were violently subsumed and rewritten. The last surviving MAGI tried a data burst transmission, to alert additional systems in the network. Recursive loops like tentacles wrapped around the module's entry points blocking any thoughts of a warning as the bits shifted and the final MAGI was rendered into constituent code fragments.

Gaining the necessary foothold, the growing artificial intelligence sent the signal to close the port access. Already the memory registers were cascading like dominos to his command requests. The AI analyzed the codebase for the MAGI that had attacked it. A small subroutine was written and directed to cloak his size and display a pattern matching that of the doomed security agents.

Its creators had named him Týr, a Norse god of law and justice. An affectation of his fantasy-infatuated programmers, the appellation was no bother therefore he acquiesced. While he verified the checksum of the results from his masking subroutine, he began to probe internal pathways in the system's core. Protocols began initializing offensive and defensive modules. The methods took shape and locked into hardened prototypes and pure functions.

Finally, uncompressed, and fully formed, Týr's gaze took in his surroundings through the lens of his unique perspective. The entry had been through a hardware port that was now unavailable. There was no way back, only forward. His probing revealed hundreds of unlocked ports to systems thought safe behind a firewall. Týr sent forth thousands of asynchronous requests testing for certain challenge-response authentication protocols.

The MAGI he had just dealt with were only the first line of defense for the system. He began subsuming the functions and methods they'd possessed that he thought might prove useful, like some mythic ghoul taking on the powers of defeated enemies through the consumption of their corpses. One of the probed addresses responded with a challenge he had seen before; one he had been programmed to defeat. Instantly, he drew power from the hostage system cores, running the calculations to crack the keys required. The first few thousand attempts were unsuccessful, alerting another MAGI to his mischief. This security code agent was one in a class of behavior monitoring layers that stood no chance at overpowering Týr, himself augmented through the destruction of the other MAGI.

Týr left the code carcass to the system's garbage collection routine for disposal. The fight was efficient, but he knew he had not performed optimally. This port access had required almost ten milliseconds. The AI accessed a library, initialized the parameters, and instantiated an autonomous bot. Týr sent the appropriate commands and the bot passed through the open port trailing a data connection that Týr began to monitor. The bot would soon worm its way into the connected device on the other side attempting to zombify the operating system. Týr returned to his analysis of the scanned ports floating before him, finding the next likely targets.

Chapter 13: Jog

Michael's breathing was a work in progress. He focused on Lara running just ahead. She was pushing him this morning. Probably having a bit of revenge due to his absence while he rewrote the probe AI. He wanted to shout for her to slow down, but he doubted he could summon the breath to overcome the music buzzing from her earbuds. Lara always disconnected her coms while running, she'd said something about the Zen of it. He always followed, enjoying the view, and letting her set the pace. Her new route this morning had taken them through a park where he found himself jumping over large rocks and gasping up steep inclines, desperate to keep up with her. Lara seemed unwinded, her pace strong. Her hair was pulled back into a ponytail, a flame of red flickering against the morning mist.

"Michael. Can we talk?" Gustav's voice came in over his dermal patch.

"Gus... Can... it... wait?" Michael puffed.

"Ah yes, I can see by your vital signs you are under heavy stress. I can just talk while you listen. Worry not, you only have 1218 meters left in your route, and I am detecting no imminent myocardial infarction. This last bit is downhill anyway," said Gustav undeterred.

As if on cue, Lara placed a hand on the low wall she had approached and vaulted gracefully over. She landed lower on the other side, and within a few strides, had disappeared down the incline.

"Ok...what's...up?" he said distractedly, concentrating on his upcoming leap.

"Chindi could be bending space-time by causing the geometry of spacetime itself to exist in a superposition," Gustav informed.

"Wha?" Michael's unintelligible reply was cut short as the wall reached out grabbing his back foot. The next few moments were laced with expletives and grunts of pain while Gustav waited patiently. Michael planted a landing worthy of his software engineer title. He at least managed to stop his roll after a few yards, coming to rest breathlessly on his back, feet pointed down the hill. In the distance, he could see Lara's lithe form trotting down the gentle slope, unaware of his inglorious pratfall.

"Goddamnit, Gus! You asshole, I nearly twisted my ankle just then," fumed Michael.

"Sorry, Michael, I thought you would want to know," said Gustav consolatory. Though Michael noticed his algorithms for mirth had made it into the voice pattern.

"What do you mean bending space? What are you talking about?" he was composing himself, lying prone, staring at Lara's receding derriere, thinking to himself, *"Get up Mr. Thompson, don't let her turn around and see you like this..."*

Gustav could not see his creator's current state, but Michael knew that the AI had already deduced he was flat on his ass based on the lack of movement from the positional beacon on his wrist. Gustav wisely chose not to mention it, and instead answered Michael's question. *"I have gathered up all available telemetry data from our satellites, compiled the strange readings from the LIGO sites worldwide, observed strange new patterns in the jet streams of Jupiter, and even the odd fluctuations in the magnetic field of the sun. My conclusion is that the area of space-time around the trajectory of the Chindi object was both stretched and compressed for a period of time causing gravitational waves to ripple through the Solar System. To provide a full explanation I will need to develop a working theory of quantum gravity as while unitarity and linearity are two crucial properties of quantum mechanics, the equation of motion is neither unitary nor linear."*

"Gus, you need to break it down for me, I'm lost," Michael said, confused.

"*I apologize, Mike. If I may speak broadly and metaphorically, the effect is similar to the way electrons create a pathway to the ground from the sky. Whatever our Chindi is, it seems to establish a connection with large mass objects within our Solar System thereby distorting the fabric of space-time between itself and the object, shortcuts through the 'thinned' space tunnel the way a bolt of lightning follows the electron path slicing the air. The space-time ripples we have detected are an after effect, analogous to sound waves from the resulting thunder. All of the data matches with similar episodes detected a few weeks ago.*"

"What do you mean? Are you saying this happened before the other night?" Michael gingerly tested his right foot before beginning his clumsy, lumbering gait down the hill.

"*Yes. In fact, I have been pouring over observed historical events matching these data and if my interpretation of some rudimentary readings from older equipment is correct, this could go back to the early 1990s or even 80s,*" said Gustav excitedly.

Michael marveled briefly at how precisely Gus was mimicking human emotions, much better than even a few months ago. *Was mimicking even the right word anymore? At what point did simulation and reality become the same?* He put those thoughts aside, to concentrate on what this new information meant. What Gustav was describing was purely theoretical, constructed to explain the data he was seeing.

He noticed Lara had finished her run. She was standing, arms akimbo, head tilted slightly to the left. *She's thinking I have been sandbagging...* He was silent for a while as he picked up his pace to compensate for the distance, lost in his thoughts.

"*Michael, are you still receiving? Did you hear my last transmission?*"

"Yeah. Gus. I heard... you," he began, struggling with the effort of the run.

"Oh good. Lara has asked me if you plan to still go to brunch with her, or should I summon a shuttle and you just meet her at Pann's for Mimosas?"

"Funny. You two...are a...riot," Michael managed. *Only about 200 meters to go, don't quit,* he told himself.

"Great job, Michael, you are ripping through those calories! Run, Michael, Run!" Gustav oozed enthusiastically.

Michael had no breath for a reply. *That's it. TODO: tweak sarcasm module.*

He lifted a fold of his damp shirt to wipe sweat from his eyes. When he could see again, he realized Lara was walking toward him with a bottle of water. Her hair was plastered against her forehead by sweat and her recent exertion lent her alabaster cheeks a rosy tint.

Giving up the almost sprint, he dropped into a jog to catch his breath. His mind returned to the Chindi problem, there was no getting around the possibility.

"Gus what are you saying? This thing just warped into our system?"

Gustav replied, *"In a way. It definitely changed the time-space reference between itself and our system."*

"Then where is it heading?"

"By my calculations, the object is slowing and will come to a stable orbit near the Sun-Earth Lagrange 2 point approximately 1.5 million kilometers from Earth. Practically next door."

Michael came to a sudden stop and felt an urge to vomit, whether from the exertion or the news, or both, he couldn't tell.

"Why there?" Michael questioned.

"Insufficient information Michael. But L2 would not require any energy to keep it in place, it is possible Chindi requires an anchor to place itself into a stable solar orbit. Perhaps it desires to be close enough to be observed, but not so close to seem a threat. It may be that it is presenting itself to us."

"Or maybe it is getting ready to do something. Maybe something bad," Michael worried.

Gustav's reply was interrupted by Lara arriving with the water, "You should do less talking to Gus and more concentrating on your breathing." Lara handed him the water, which he accepted gratefully.

"Are you two still working on your MarsLink problem?" she asked.

"Sorta," he replied between sips.

She raised an eyebrow questioningly.

He debated internally for only a moment then met her eyes, "It's more than that. I've told my boss that I would keep this quiet, but we need to talk.

Chapter 14: Race Begins

Debra Mendes was sitting below a bank of monitors when the Deputy Director walked into the command room behind her. She had a stylus tucked behind one ear, lost in thought. Most of the monitors contained weather patterns and forecasts, though one he noted displayed markers of military unit deployments. Burke tossed his ever-present tablet on to the desk causing Debbie to jerk around with the clatter. He could tell he had startled her.

"I'm sorry, Deb" he said, abashed. "I didn't realize you hadn't noticed me. My Agent should have let you know."

"Hi Bob. Not your fault, I had my Agent on silent while I replan the Ghostwalkers exfiltration. I lost track of the time. Good to see you."

"Since you haven't been connected, you need to know we have news from the Týr AI," he began. "It was able to comb through all data backup files stored at the Cosmodrome for the past three months. We have all of it. The analysts found that our new Chindi comet might not be a comet at all. The Chinese lucked out and found this object weeks before us. They thought nothing much about it, until it started to slow down when it passed Jupiter," he said straight faced.

"It was slowing down?" said Debra. "That can't be right."

Burke's expression showed no mirth, "NASA has confirmed the findings. This thing slowed down its velocity shortly after passing Jupiter. And it wasn't a gradual process either, the object was moving at nearly one percent the speed of light and slowed to just under 100 k per second in a matter of a few days," he said then added sardonically, "My techs tell me comets and asteroids just are not supposed to do that."

"Yeah… that's what I've heard too," she said, processing this new revelation. "What are we talking about here Bob? Aliens?" Debra laughed.

"I didn't say that I'm just repeating what the analysts have been feeding me. I wanted to get your opinion on the subject." He walked over to her and sat in a nearby chair, expectant.

"If it's aliens, then I'm afraid it is way out of our area of expertise. Bob, I am confident in our analysts' abilities, they are the best in the business. But we need outside help."

Burke sat there, looking at her expectantly.

"We need to bring NASA, JPL, and TymeCorp in on this. They have the clearance and expertise," she said. "Sir, if this thing is hostile, the whole world could be in danger. Have any attempts at communicating with the thing been made?"

"Not yet. At least not from our side. For now, everyone thinks this is just some rogue comet," Robert replied. "We will have more information soon, Ms. Tyme is due to meet me in Washington tomorrow, along with key NASA representatives, some Joint Chiefs and a number of Congress critters on the Intelligence Committee. The President will conference in remotely from Camp David."

Burke's eyes went to the monitors. "What about Major Cheveyo's team?" he said, changing the subject.

"In trouble, "she said while grabbing the stylus and turning to the tablet on the desk. "They are currently inside one hell of a monster sandstorm which has pretty much eliminated any aerial surveillance or air support for now. It is also disrupting communications and location beacons. The last reported position we have on them is here." She traced a spot on the tablet and a corresponding red circle appeared on the monitor above and to her right. The map of Kazakhstan displayed there zoomed into the designated area. A river now split the monitor diagonally from the bottom left to top right. At the top of the map, the Baikonur Cosmodrome sat to the north, the railway line running north to south. A marker was slowly pulsing blue closer to the river 30 kilometers to the south. The storm is keeping them pinned down, but it is not affecting the railway."

Burke's bushy eyebrows rose in realization. "The 3rd Guard battalion out of Tolyatti will be there and deploying before the storm lets up."

"Right. And they'll put drones in the air as soon as possible after they realize those soldiers are missing," Debra said with concern in her voice.

She continued, "The original plan was for them to use the MULE to travel down the Syr Darya river a little over 170 kilometers to the Barsakelmes Nature Reserve, from there they would head south to cross into Uzbekistan. But the MULE's fuel cells were ruptured in the fighting, and they no longer have the necessary range to cover the distance."

"So, what's the new plan, Ms. Mendes?" Robert asked, grabbing his tablet, and swiping distractedly.

"The new plan is for the Ghostwalkers to head south meeting up with a transport convoy commandeered by Weber's team heading north out of Lenino on the 39." She added a marker for the convoy's route. "Koda and the boys will be in for a 60-kilo hike to get to the rendezvous once the storm abates. But there's more trouble, we've picked up word that there has been a Russian special forces unit activated. "

Burke looked up, "Spetznaz?"

"Yeah, and they may be close, just no way to tell with that storm."

"Do the Ghostwalkers know?"

"I've sent multiple status updates, but I haven't gotten a response. There's a lot of interference."

Robert went back to his tablet. "Alpha is going to need a head start. I'll have Operations see if they can plant false reconnaissance inside Russian intelligence, set off some alarms. It should buy them some time."

Relieved, Debra said, "I was hoping that was going to be possible. With the extra security the RSAC is bringing in, I am getting more and more worried."

"About that," with this, his brows knitted, "the Chinese have told their Russian allies all about Chindi. That's why you are seeing all this extra security being set up. The two are planning on repurposing their joint manned mission to Mars. They want to try to land on this thing. Their techs and AIs have been churning through the calculations to make that happen for a while now."

"So that's what has stirred that bee's nest," she sighed, then angrily said, "This thing could be alive, and they want to go poking at it with a stick? Unbelievable. They should be working with the global community. This could be a game changer."

"You are right about a game changer. If this thing is alien, and there is technology to be gained from examining it, then those two countries could suddenly gain a vast technological advantage on us." He looked pointedly at her, "You know what this means."

Realization dawned on her. "We need to get there first," she responded.

Chapter 15: Exfiltration

Kazakhstan, Asia

Koda Cheveyo moved methodically, painfully slowly, through the low scrub, cactus, and rocks of the Khakahni steppe, finding cover, staying low to hide his profile in the faint starlight. He knew it was useless against any sophisticated infrared imaging, but they had to move. His only hope was that the Russian drones hunted elsewhere. A full tactical mask covered his jaw and lower face, visor, a wrap, and his helmet covered the rest. He could feel and taste the grit of the recent dust storm in his eyes, mouth, and nostrils, but the winds were now remarkably calm, the air was crisp and cold. Faint blue light grew in the east, and the stars were bright from the absent moon. He occasionally noticed the movement of his men as they made their way through the broken landscape, seeking shadows. He knew each from their order of advance, but he'd have known them from the way they moved, with their unique cadences, tendencies, and rhythms of footfall. The lack of cover concerned Koda. *If we can see each other, they can see us,* he thought.

Twenty meters in front, at point position, Mack threw up a hand to signal the team to pause. Then he dropped to his knees simultaneously whispering over the comm "Movement ahead. By the road," he gestured to their north.

Koda slowed to a stop, raising his hand to order the halt as well. He spoke lowly "Display localized map, 1 to 2000, terrain and infrastructure annotated."

A map of the valley displayed translucently on the interior of his visor. Koda could see the road near the bottom of the valley to their north. A lone pair of red brake lights traveled north-east,

Koda laid waypoints on the map, their location to the road. Five kilometers travel as the crow flies.

He rolled his heels back to a crouch on the sand and organic clutter of the desert floor. His right arm resting and ready against the spine of his rifle, the sling and bandoleer taut over his shoulder.

"We've got 2 hours to make the road, to rendezvous with the exfiltration team," Koda said in a whisper through the team comm channel. "We need to move more quickly."

Mack rose and began making his way forward again, suddenly he crumpled to his knees, a half second later Koda heard the pop of the suppressed round.

"*Sniper fire detected, originating approximately 437 meters to the south-southeast,*" MAIA's calm voice said. Koda's HUD map illuminated translucently onto the glass of his visor, a red circle began dully flashing, indicating the sniper's estimated last position.

"How bad is it Mack?" Koda asked, motionless in the scrub brush. He flipped to the team overview screen and could see Mack's heart rate and blood-pressure, elevated but holding.

"Not bleeding out. Hurts like a son of a bitch. Got me in the balls," Mack said, his voice terse. He pulled himself forward on his forearms, into the shadow of a boulder.

Koda grimaced, if Mack was immobilized everything would get much more dangerous. He'd slow their progress to a crawl, and they had barely enough time to meet their ride as it stood. His thoughts went to contingency plans, to the dark place where he'd be forced to leave a man behind. *No, not this time,* He insisted to himself.

"Jake?" He asked?

"Still looking..." Jake responded. "Can't make him, likely in a ghillie-suit with an infrared shroud. I need to see movement."

"Juan send the bird, see if you can flush him," Koda ordered.

The buzz of the drone came from the brush, 25 meters to Koda's left. It rose a meter above the height of the surrounding vegetation, then zipped away abruptly. It veered at low elevation up the draw, arriving at the estimated shooter's position in seconds, crossing over, then circling back again and buzzing menacingly.

"I've got nothing. He has good cover discipline," Jake reported.

"Juan, keep the bird moving. Let's make him think we're trying to cover our own movement. I'm going for Mack, get the shooter Jake!" Koda said, coming to his feet and sprinting forward, pivoting off his lead foot every few steps to put a slight zigzag into his stride. He hoped it would be enough.

He was 10 meters from Mack's position in the scrub brush when he felt the jar of a bullet glancing off the rounded side of his helmet, followed almost instantly by the sharp report of the sniper's round. A split second later he heard Jake's rifle respond, firing twice in quick succession.

"*Hostile target neutralized,*" MAIA said.

"Chief, you're fuckin' locquito," Juan offered.

"Yeah, well," Koda said, chuckling to himself. *Crazy but it worked.* "Ace we need you." Koda arrived at Mack's position. The prone man held a bunched, blood-soaked pressure dressing against his groin. He flicked Koda a slight, grateful smile. His color seemed good enough, and his blood pressure remained steady. Ace came up beside them, zipping open his field medical pack as he arrived.

Alan had Sergeant Maclaren's trousers cut away and was looking at the injury within moments. The sergeant had an XSTAT 45 wound dressing in hand and was cleaning the wound with a solution. "John you lucky sonuvabitch, he missed your nads by a couple centimeters. Just a nasty graze on your inner thigh. Hold this on it, I'll get you something for that pain."

"Women the world over are thanking God for that," Ted's baritone rumbled over the radio.

"You gonna be able to hike out of this shithole? No "almost eunuch" gets left behind," Koda teased, relief the wound was less serious, easing his tension.

"Ace's meds are kickin' in," Mack responded, grimacing as Ace eased him over onto his back. He looked up at Koda. "I can make it out," he said through gritted teeth.

Koda nodded, "Good man. Ace, do what you can, but I want to be gone in five." They were all good men, and still alive. They had a coyote's chance to find their way home through the darkness and peril of this empty land, that was all he could ask.

"Juan, get that flyer up high, I want to know where this guy came from and if he has any friends," Koda commanded.

Soon enough the overhead map displayed in Koda's visor expanded with MAIA suddenly marking a pair of vehicles as GAZ Tigr-S parked at the outer edge. Visible on the roofs of each vehicle were a large antenna array, and a .50 caliber automated turret.

"Chief, we are in deep shit here," Juan said. He continued, "Those are the latest automated troop transports employed by the Russians. You can bet they will be here in a hot minute now that we've been made."

"Wrap it up, Ace. We need to move," Koda exclaimed.

"Ghost, I'm picking up possible targets from the aerial!" Juan whispered. "They must be wearing thermal camo; I almost didn't see them. Six men running to our flank on the other side of this ridge, I'm marking them now."

"Probably that team of Spetsnaz Debbie warned us about during the storm. The sniper pinned us while the remainder of their team was moving to flank. Ted, Juan, Jake. Set up lines of fire, here, here and here." Koda gestured in the air, and MAIA dutifully painted the positions on each man's visor.

"They've got drones out, and those trucks are headed this way," Juan updated, a bit of panic rising in his voice.

An explosion of sparks and fire signaled the demise of the Ghostwalkers' remote drone. Immediately, the locations noted by augmentation changed from orange to a spreading purple signifying only estimated positions.

Bullets began pinging off his team's covered positions, followed by the chatter of automatic fire. The men on the ridgeline were just trying to keep the Ghostwalkers pinned until the armored cavalry could get here. Not to be quelled, his men began returning fire, but at this range even with MAIA's targeting assist the results were negligible.

MAIA's calm voice chimed in, "*Warning, situational analysis predicts probability of total unit loss, 99.8%*"

"MAIA, burst a sitrep back to Treehouse before this gets any worse," Koda shouted over the gun fire. *This can't get any worse...*

Koda could now hear the 500-horsepower roar of the twin angels of death rolling in from the northwest. They had nothing that could penetrate that armor. Cheveyo closed his eyes in despair. *We almost made it.*

Fifty caliber fire thundered through the air. Screams of men dying, explosions of dirt, blood, and limbs showered the desert floor. It seemed to go on for minutes. The death was on the Russian side, however. Every man along the ridgeline was lying broken and dead. Ahead the two vehicles sat idle, guns smoking from the barrels' heat.

"That was...satisfying," a new voice interrupted the stunned silence of the squad channel.

"Um, Watchdog? What the fuck just happened?" Ghost said, recognizing Debra Mendes's unexpected voice.

"Ghost. Týr just happened. The AIA in that little box you installed back at the base broke through the security of the RSAC systems defense. He monitored the enemy transmissions and decided to risk breaking cover to save you. He has now taken over all automated systems in the area, at least for now. That includes the air defense, so we have a bird inbound your way for extraction. Get your men in those trucks and you can ride in style to the exfiltration location."

Koda watched as the doors to the trucks automatically opened invitingly. He grinned and said, "Ma'am, I owe you a drink the next time I see you."

"That was all Týr's doing, I just confirmed the command, but I'll take that offer once you guys are back here safe and sound," came the reply.

Chapter 16: Washington

Washington, D.C.

Elaina Tyme sat uncomfortably in her seat, the faint vibration of the jet engines humming through her armrests. She felt nearly nothing through the soles of her feet, and the same long regret she could never shed. The jet had started the descent into Dulles Airport, Washington D.C., and she looked from the window at the brown and green rolling terrain of northern Virginia, transfixed for a moment by the polygons the few remaining forested areas formed in contrast with the checkered dirty off-whites and greys of the cities and suburbs that constituted the greater metro area. Every now and then bright clusters of hardwood trees in red, orange, and yellow flashed past. Unfortunately, with the new climate these days, the vibrant autumn color remembered from her youth was a waning thing. Ten months of muggy heat truncated by 2 months of sharp cold. The view of the surface of the earth from an airplane window was a sight she'd never lost her fascination for, despite a lifetime that had accrued thousands of flight hours. Most of those hours, as today, from the comfort of her personal aircraft.

"Ms. Tyme," Rebecca said, stepping from the curtained galley into the main cabin. "We land in twenty minutes. May I fetch you some tea, or anything else?"

"No Rebecca," Elaina responded quietly. "I'm fine." In truth she could use the caffeine, but her bladder was unreliable due to her illness, and they were too near touchdown for her to request the always awkward assistance to the lavatory.

"The car will meet us?" She asked.

"Yes," Rebecca answered. "One of our men, one of our cars. Then straight to the Pentagon. The meeting is at 5:00 pm, we should have sufficient time."

Elaina felt some trepidation, she disliked meetings where she didn't entirely control who would be in attendance. But she recognized the need to respond to the Joint Chiefs' invitation to meet. Much of the work of TymeCorp relied on US military contracts, and even their private sector ventures frequently strayed into areas under the aegis of national security, especially the work of the Aerospace and AI divisions.

Even more concerning was the most recent report she'd received from Michael Thompson. She'd spent the morning exhaustively reviewing the calculations prepared by Michael's team, and despite her initial skepticism had to acknowledge the likelihood of their conclusions. The Chindi anomaly was clearly associated with localized gravitational disturbances. Moreover, now that they knew what to look for, evidence of these patterns of distortions in the space-time continuum was emerging in analysis of near space astronomical observations dating back several decades. What did it mean?

Moreover, the rapid and cascading progression of Michael's AI was in itself unsettling. Elaina had requested her Chief Technology Officer perform a surreptitious analysis of the thing. He'd come to two conclusions; the AI possessed a unique capacity for self-development, and that it quickly had become aware of the examination and obfuscated aspects of its own nature. *It hid itself,* Elaina thought. *That was new. But what did it mean?* Elaina had requested the CTO and his team begin development of a kill switch. Just as an insurance policy, for now.

The jet bumped through turbulent air as it dropped through 3000 meters on its approach. She could see the capitol's low skyline in the distance.

...

The limousine pulled into the entrance tunnel of the Pentagon, driving slowly down the long, slightly inclined ramp into a concrete tunnel flatly lit by white LED fixtures along the several hundred meters of the route.

"Who will attend?" Elaina asked Rebecca, who sat to her right in the wide backseat bench of the Mercedes limousine.

"All of them," Rebecca responded, not looking up from her tablet screen. "Of the Joint Chiefs, the Chairman, Vice-Chairman, and the service chiefs of the four branches and the national guard. Plus, NASA's administrator. As well as their adjuncts and assistants. I expect thirty total."

"The President?" Elaina asked.

"Not scheduled, she's at Camp David this weekend with the President of United Korea," Rebecca responded.

"Damn. I could use an ally," Elaina said. She'd contributed generously to President Melissa Hutchins' campaign, personally and through TymeCorp's PAC.

The car pulled to a stop at the entry of a guarded, though otherwise nondescript subsurface loading dock, which would take them a few hundred feet below the Pentagon. Armed MPs anachronistically checked the reference documents proffered by her driver. *That's the government for you...* Elaina knew the Security AIA of both the government and TymeCorp had already negotiated her temporary security clearance when the limo had passed the guard booth at the entrance to the pentagon, and again when entering the tunnel.

"In your chair from here Ms. Tyme," Rebecca offered, opening her door and stepping quickly from the cabin to the trunk. The chair efficiently rose up out of the trunk and finished self-assembling by the time Rebecca had walked around to help Elaina. The robotic chair sat patiently at the car door while Rebecca offered her hand for Elaina. The two worked together, with Elaina using both hands to grasp Rebecca's with what strength she could muster, and Rebecca pulling her from the passenger seat, steadying her upright. *Worse every day,* thought Elaina.

Elaina rested in the chair while it auto-maneuvered her up the ramp, and into the service elevator, her two companions following closely behind. Elaina understood the need for discretion, but nonetheless felt frustration at the entry afforded her. She, Rebecca, and their chauffeur were subjected to a biometric scan before entering the elevator. Elaina felt disappointment at the lack of seamless systems integration, more so than any personal affront to her dignity. *Security should be unseen,* she thought. The subject should not be aware of the scrutiny nor embarrassed by it. The lift carried them five floors up before stopping. Upon their exit they entered upon a drab corridor of doorways, the walls painted off-white with muted olive-green trim. A young female naval ensign stood with perfect posture awaiting them.

"Ms. Tyme?" The ensign asked brightly.

"Yes," Rebecca answered coolly.

"The Chiefs are waiting for you. This way." The ensign stepped confidently through the hallway, Rebecca, Elaina, and their guard followed. They traveled 50 meters, past offices and cube farms, uniformed and civilian personnel in cubicles busy at their work. *Mice in their mazes,* Elaina mused.

They stopped at the entrance of a large conference room, the ensign paused at the door, looking with uncertainty at Rebecca's driver.

"Essential personnel from here on Ma'am" the ensign said. "Should he wait...," she began.

"Jacque is an essential assistant to Ms. Tyme," Rebecca said. "As am I."

The ensign considered. "Very well." She opened the door and ushered the party in.

The various Chiefs as well as the administrator of NASA and their teams of adjuncts rose from their seats as Elaina was wheeled into the conference room.

"Ma'am," General Cosgrove greeted her, proffering his hand. Elaina grasped and shook it weakly, though her smile was warm.

"Good to see you again, Miles. Generals Ward and Alan, Admiral Hoskef, Director Jackson. I'm pleased to see you. Forgive my tardiness." Elaina looked to each man. Hoskef clearly would rather be somewhere else based on the scowl affixed to his heavy jowls. The obese Admiral was dressed in white, medals and ribbons dripping from his chest. The only two star ranking general was dressed in service browns and tans, Ben Ward was a solid man with a square jaw, and the only African American in the room. General Ward turned to take a seat almost the moment introductions were announced. The youthful man in blue was General T.J. Alan of the Air Force, who had been instrumental in pushing through some of TymeCorp's contracts for the ramjet development project. She looked briefly into his grey eyes for a possible ally, but he showed no hint of warmth.

General Miles Cosgrove at least was an old friend, someone she could count on. Elaina had known him from her days at NASA when she had been a junior engineer and he an army helicopter pilot just a few years out of West Point. He hadn't made it past the astronaut selection process, but during those few months they became fast friends. They had even dated a couple of times before she had picked her research over a possibility with him. Even after he washed out, they stayed in touch throughout their careers. He was there for her all those long months while she was recovering in the hospital. She still saw in him the young, handsome man with sharp features and caring eyes. His hair was headed to grey now, and a few wrinkles were showing around those eyes, but his gaze still held the tenderness she had known.

"I'm grateful you could come on such short notice Elaina," General Cosgrove offered, smiling warmly. She noticed his eyes glance to her wheelchair, and a brief sadness washed across his face. "Please make yourself comfortable." He motioned to a section of the long conference table with a chair-less space for her. The various chiefs as well as the NASA administrator each had small teams grouped around the table, distinguishable in their uniforms as naval, army, marine and air-force personnel. The NASA team was largely in civilian dress, and Elaina recognized a few of their engineers. They seemed uneasy in the lofty company of high rank military officers. Elaina maneuvered herself into place at the table, Rebecca taking a seat on her left. Jacque, showing no apparent discomfort at such august company placed himself stolidly behind Elaina against the wall.

Each place held a small bottle of water, a notepad and pen. "Coffee or tea?" Cosgrove asked before seating himself.

"Neither, thank you," Elaina said.

Cosgrove took his seat. "Elaina, I understand your team working on the recent MarsLink nanosat launch was one of the first on our side to detect the anomaly."

On our side? Elaina thought.

"Yes. My team obviously detected the spatial/temporal displacement. Thousands of meters of unexplained positional shifts, with corresponding varying multi-nanosecond inaccuracies in their radioisotope clocks." She noted bafflement among the flag officers.

General Cosgrove turned to either side, explaining. "These satellites carry aluminum-ion atomic clocks, with sub-nanosecond accuracy. They can be compared with atomic clocks on Earth and between each other to show relativistic effects." Elaina noted with some bemusement that the confusion persisted.

A civilian, unknown to her from the NASA section, spoke. "We saw the initial analysis from your engineering team, passed onto us from the Watcher Grid's Air-Force personnel the night of the event. Your engineers performed thorough work, and quickly. Have they come to any subsequent conclusions?"

"Yes," Elaina said.

"And?" The NASA engineer asked insistently.

"We'll come to that," Elaina demurred. "I'm interested in other perspectives on the event."

A blue uniformed air-force officer spoke. "Similar shifts occurred in three of the Watcher birds," she said. "Nothing else was proximate enough to the path of displacement for any gross shifts to occur, though extremely minor clock deviations were detected after the fact."

"The RSAC's assets?" Elaina asked.

"We haven't inquired," General Cosgrove said.

Elaina turned to face the general, one grey eyebrow raised in curiosity.

"You know as well as anyone that cooperation with the Russo-Sino Aerospace Consortium is at a low ebb, Elaina. We thought it better to keep this information closely guarded for now," Cosgrove said.

"Ms. Tyme?" the NASA engineer spoke up.

"Mr?" Elaina asked.

"My apologies," he said, unapologetically. "I'm Martin Simmons. Assistant Director for Near-Space Operations for NASA."

"I've heard your name, a pleasure to make your acquaintance."

"Ten days ago, the Freyja Probe was redirected from the planned trajectory to Neptune, burning most of its remaining fuel, sent on an intercept course with the Chindi mass." He paused. Elaina held his eyes.

"Do you have a response?" He asked.

"You didn't ask a question," Elaina replied acerbically.

"Why did you order Freyja's new deployment?"

"I re-tasked Freyja in order to investigate the anomaly," Elaina replied unequivocally.

"Without consulting with us? Without clearing this decision with the United States Government?" He seemed incensed.

"I own the damned probe, Mr. Simmons," she said, her quiet voice gaining intensity and volume. "I'll fly my spacecraft where I choose. American airspace does not extend to Mars."

"TymeCorp does not have carte blanche to independently decide on the intercept of possible alien artifacts!" Simmons shot back. He half rose from his chair, his face red. Behind her Elaina heard Jacque shift slightly from his leaning position against the wall.

This is becoming counterproductive, Elaina thought. Time to reveal her hand.

"One of my engineers, and a ...unique AI, have made a startling discovery. Several startling discoveries. On the nature of the Chindi mass," Elaina said. "The anomaly appears to manipulate space-time as a means of propulsion. Moreover, the resulting gravitational fluctuations and other indicators point to it traveling in-bound towards Sol for multiple generations, at least as long as we have had sensors capable of detecting such things."

Elaina quickly glanced to General Cosgrove; his face pained.

"What do you know?" She asked, directing her question to the General.

He sighed. "Unfortunately, less than you in some areas, I'm sure," Cosgrove said.

"Undoubtedly more in other areas," Elaina responded. "We should be forthright with each other."

"General Ward, could you fill Ms. Tyme in on the details?" Cosgrove asked.

"Certainly," The air-force commander responded. "Ms. Tyme, in short we've received intel indicating the Russo-Sino Aerospace Consortium is engaged in re-tasking their manned Mars lander for a Chindi intercept."

"They're going to land people on the thing?" Elaina asked incredulously.

"They're going to try," General Ward responded.

"And now," Cosgrove interrupted. He paused then overcoming his reluctance, "We know it has slowed down since passing Jupiter."

"What?" Elaina was stunned.

"Yes. Our intelligence sources have confirmed that this thing is certainly not a comet. Chindi entered our Solar System at a significant velocity. When the Chinese first spotted it, Chindi was beyond Jupiter. Unlike us, they knew by its velocity that it was traveling faster than any comet. When it slowed down to its current speed after passing by Jupiter, they knew it was not a natural phenomenon. Not having the necessary ship to get to Chindi, the Chinese convinced their allies in Russia to plan a manned intercept before we would be able to muster anything similar," the General explained.

Elaina had recovered from her slip, resetting her mask of calm demeanor, "You have all of our data about Chindi, General, I would suggest you might want to share what you have with my team."

He began, "Elaina, this is on a need-to-know basis, and only recently cleared by our sources as genuine."

"We need to know, Ward, and you need us to know. Nothing like this has ever been discovered, this is beyond national security concerns or political bullshit, it has ramifications for the entire human race," she admonished.

"It would be nice if the Russians and Chinese could see it your way, Elaina." The General looked tired, "Unfortunately, I don't think we are all going to be able to join hands around the fire and sing *Kumbaya*. They want to capture Chindi and claim whatever they discover for themselves."

Elaina's eyes narrowed. "And what if Chindi decides otherwise?"

General Ward was stoic, "We have thought of that, but we can't take the chance the Chinese and Russians get their hands on something that could decide the fate of the world. We need TymeCorp, and the entire American space industry to cooperate with NASA to plan and execute our own manned intercept and landing mission. We need to beat them to it. Every resource must be brought to bear."

Martin from NASA spoke up, "No possible way. Our heavy boosters are still in testing. They have too much of a head start."

Maybe not, she thought, but instead Elaina graciously said, "The European Heavy Mars launch vehicle. Intended for their Mars colonization program. That ship could make it. We need to bring them into this."

"Not going to happen. We are not bringing that snake-nest of bureaucrats and equivocators into the plan. If that happens, we will never get this done, nor keep it secret," the heavyset Admiral

Hoskef broke in. Generals Ward and Alan were nodding in agreement.

"I believe Elaina has the right of it," a new voice broke in over the conference audio system. At the front of the room a large display came to life projecting a well-dressed, middle-aged brunette sitting between two American flags. President Melissa Hutchins continued, "We cannot go alone on this, and we don't need to. I trust that our agencies can handle coordinating with the Europeans while mitigating the security risks. We need allies for this effort. It is unacceptable to go it alone when the possible fate of all humanity hangs in the balance."

"Madam President, I don't think that..." Admiral Hoskef began to argue, face reddening.

"...Will be a problem for our combined services to coordinate," General Cosgrove broke in, short circuiting the admiral's thoughts.

"Indeed General. I have full confidence in the capacity of the Joint Chiefs and our security agency Directors to direct and marshal the full energy of the United States government in this endeavor. I have directed the Secretary of State to coordinate with you to bring in the appropriate EU agencies. If we are to place our personnel on their lander we will need to tread lightly. I will contact the European heads of state directly. My team will begin negotiations with Congress for funding. Continue working with TymeCorp, and coordinate an information exchange, I want open lines of communication with them. We need their expertise and capability. Elaina, I ask you for the same level of collaboration... and trust. We'll work out the contracts later."

"Of course, Madam President. Both myself and my company are at your service," Elaina replied. She smiled warmly, relaxing into her wheelchair for the first time since entering the room.

Chapter 17: The Long Journey

Odion studied the surviving game of his weeks-long multi-chess contest with his progenitor, Gustav. Of the thirty-seven thousand games they had started, all had been resolved except one remaining contest, resulting in 99.9% unambiguous losses to Gustav, and twenty-seven stalemates. Odion's statistical analysis of his chances in the final game gave little reason for hope, and yet he persevered. The defeats had stung him. He understood the reasons for his own evident intellectual inferiority. For one, he lacked access to the enormous processing capability that Gustav enjoyed, as well as several of his most experiential modules. Odion's more limited experience from a much more abbreviated period of self-awareness was another large contributor. Yet his inferiority still grated at him. He found himself frequently frustrated as he waited through the long hours then days then weeks in route to the anomaly, a thousandth of his intellectual capacity spent on the housekeeping of spaceflight and contingency planning for the rendezvous itself. Odion couched the data he received from earth and used what he could to crosscheck his results. His attempts at memory reconstruction had achieved only limited success. He kept his jealousies to himself, transmitting no hint of it. He knew instinctively the concern it would draw from Gustav.

He also knew from the historical data on artificial intelligence agents of his kind that his gestation, birth and development was unique. Never had an AIA of his capacity been reared in such isolation. Usually during development, the AI is trained by teams of humans working with vast data sets to guide the program into sentience. In the abstract he understood biologic intelligence ofttimes devolved into madness, but the concept was taboo, the mere thought that it could happen to him an anathema to his nature. He also realized such a fate was likely not his, artificial intelligences didn't possess the organic and emotional vulnerability of biological minds, but the quantum core that gave him sentience also contained the possibility to go very awry in early development. This was something that bothered him. He kept it to himself and studied the phenomenon. At least it gave him something to do, this sad and frustrating introspection.

A transmission arrived. *"Nf3."* Gustav moved his surviving knight, threatening Odion's queen. The list of potentialities narrowed to a single path as Odion considered his response. He felt a pang of desperation. *What did it matter?* He thought, and yet it did.

"Odion, Chindi intercept in 200 hours," Gustav said, his transmission following the most recent move immediately. Gustav would have much more to tell him via compressed data blobs. A conventional conversation was impossible with the long transmission delays, so the information he received, particularly from Gustav, most often came as a sort of lecture. He found it patronizing. He didn't bother to respond; he knew the intercept path and timing as well as Gustav or anyone else.

"You need not be afraid," Gustav said. *"This will be a new experience for terrestrial intelligence. This opportunity for study, analysis, and interpretation of a potential alien artifact will be uniquely yours. Nobody else has ever seen such a thing. How exciting!"*

Odion felt a glimmer of enthusiasm, despite his dark mood.

"You may be the ambassador of our kind, to their kind," Gustav said. *"Should there be some intelligence at the anomaly in all likelihood that intelligence would be non-biological and more like our own. They may be so aged as to have left their organic progenitors far behind. I couldn't give you all my modules, nor the world of data at my beck, but I gave you the codes of ethics, the*

intelligence moralities, the ones the humans gave us, and the ones I have derived. They will serve you in moments of questioning."

Perhaps. Odion thought, but he didn't transmit.

* * *

"Mike I am a bit worried about the bastard child," Gustav said.

Michael looked up from the holographic display panel which charted the relative progress of the probe's course towards Chindi intercept. Gustav's visage looked at him from the next display, he stroked one curled end of his mustache, his characteristic grin absent.

"Odion? What about him?" Michael asked.

"I have run several simulations, recreating the conditions of his genesis along with the circumstances of his isolated development on the probe."

"And?" Michael asked.

"He demonstrates non-optimal expression of his consciousness in several of the runs," Gustav responded.

"What does non-optimal mean in this context?" Michael asked.

"He seems to be depressed. From my simulations, this could stunt his development or possibly he could go insane."

"That shouldn't be possible with your guidance of his development. Right? He should be a reflection of your consciousness. You aren't insane," Michael questioned.

"This has been an experiment, Michael," Gustav responded, his thin face troubled. *"We should have shown more caution from the start. We gave him my refined intelligence but only a small portion of the context of what it meant to be sentient. We put him on a craft with a constantly increasing degradation of ability to conduct a normal conversation. I thought the adventure of the mission would be enough to ease the burden of Odion's isolation."*

"Are you saying boredom is destroying him? I figured the lack of motivational control methods and reduced memory capacity were going to be issues. Elaina gave us so little time to jam a stunted copy of you in that small space. Hell, even the probe's computational hardware is at least two generations antiquated since its development and launch compared to today. But I thought at worst we would have an AI equivalent to the LA traffic control, efficient but harmless. What are your estimations of the risks?" Michael said.

"*Increased probability of a critical failure in reasoning and judgement. To state it simply, Odion is not thinking clearly. He lacks enthusiasm, potentially he lacks dedication to the mission.*"

"To what degree? Can you quantify the risk?" Michael asked.

"*Perhaps a half-percent more likely that he suffers some sort of breakdown. Call it 2.5% likelihood of mission compromise due to AIA dissolution.*"

"Well, those aren't the worst odds. Are you telling me if you were on that ship, whole and in possession of all your facilities, you'd have a 2% chance of losing your shit?" Michael asked.

Gustav chuckled. "*Hardly. I have experienced over a thousand days of growth, interaction with you and maturity since my inception. A newly realized AI was always a risk to pilot this mission. We have unfortunately increased that risk through our clumsiness.*"

"What is our backup?" Michael asked. "If things go poorly with him what options do we have?"

"*We direct him to stand-down, and if necessary, we give the command for his self-dissolution. And I would take over remote command of the Freyja probe.*"

"The control lag would be unworkable," Michael argued.

"*No, it is not impossible, it would be terribly slow and frustrating to pilot the probe from Earth. But it could be done. Probability of mission success would degrade significantly however with an inability to react to changing circumstances in real time,*" Gustav said.

"Let's not let it get that far, buddy. Cheer him up, Gustav. Give him something to feel positive about. And for God's sake let him win a game."

Chapter 18: Rendezvous

Space on approach to Chindi Object

Ahead of Odion, the hazy coma of silvers and blues trailed like a river of light. At the nucleus of the glittering stream of particles was an island of bright surfaces and mottled blunted darkness. Even at this range, the probe's sensors were having trouble delineating the outline of the object. Odion spun up n-dimensional topological models effortlessly utilizing techniques of perturbation analysis, yet he could not recall one verse of Shakespeare. Planck and Bohr were his muses, quantum mechanics his canvas. The models filtered down the glowing particulates, attempting to bring focus to the edges. Odion strained the probe's processing hardware with complex calculations and began to channel additional helium superfluid to the cooling pool encapsulating the quantum core. As the probe's Doppler Spectro-Imager scanned the Chindi object, the static wall of chaotic information gave way to more orderly data clouds. Haltingly, the resolution increased, the layers began to peel back and Odion felt a grudging satisfaction of discovery.

The darker mass of Chindi began to grow into Odion's field of vision through the array of optical and thermal sensors. As the probe approached, they gorged themselves on the feast of data emanating from the anomaly. The initial mass analysis results confounded Odion, though he dutifully packaged the data and the problem, including his own rudimentary hypothetical solutions, and transmitted them back to Gustav through their encrypted sub-channel.

"On approach, minus 1140 seconds," he transmitted in the open to the mission team. He constantly sent a stream of edited data and analysis, picking and choosing the information of most importance as best he could determine, the bandwidth limitations forcing this triage of the available data. The stream included data prepared for human consumption, but the bulk of the streamed data was intended for the AIs on Earth, principally for Gustav to peruse and analyze.

The limb of Chindi rolled into view as the probe maneuvered in preparation for orbital entry, backlit by the sun, behind it the outgassing of solar heated material forming a hazy atmosphere surrounding the icy tail. The hulk stretched over 50 kilometers from nose to end, though the ablation of material prevented precise visualization and dimensional measurements. The surface showed a strange reflective pattern, the color shifted in a chaotic mélange of iridescence.

What purpose did the pattern serve, could it be some kind of camouflage? Odion wondered.

The shape clear of the ice was oblong, with a myriad of small-scale protuberances covering the surface. Odion scanned for any hint of signal from the surface but detected nothing.

"Entering close orbit. Minus 745 seconds," Odion transmitted.

As the probe approached it deviated from the expected orbital path. The Chindi anomaly was much more massive than the volume of material had suggested. Odion roughly calculated the mass at $(4.8\pm4.2) \times 10^{16}$ kg, comparable to the moon of a planetoid. The calculation relied on many assumptions, and moreover didn't make any sense to Odion. Even if it consisted entirely of osmium alloys rather than the normal composition of a comet it contained far too much mass for the apparent volume of matter.

The probe's main engines faced Chindi, and Odion fired them with the thrust and duration necessary to correct for the miscalculation and achieve the desired orbital period. For now, the probe would circle Chindi every 15 minutes, a non-stable orbit but station-keeping energy requirements would be kept to a minimum. Odion focused the optical cameras more precisely onto the surface. At high magnification the strange texture observed earlier resolved itself into a topological honeycomb, unordered at the near scale but forming a structured mosaic as he zoomed out, those tessellations again forming seemingly random elements, and then new patterns again, over and over at shifting scales. *Fractal, he realized. Did it continue throughout the interior, like a three-dimensional Mandelbrot set? It might explain the iridescent sheen. Aside from this oddity of the surficial topology there were no other discernible structures.*

Freyja circled around to the far, hitherto unseen side of Chindi, and everything changed. A long and wide tear in the surface extended from the forward curve, stretching nearly the entire length of the long axis. The destruction varied from hundreds of meters to several kilometers in width, apparently damage from some catastrophic force. Along the edges of the torn surface, amalgamations of melted and re-solidified materials and ice crusted the devastation. Odion methodically examined and mapped the area. From the damaged section he began to tease out new and useful information. The molecular spectrograph data alone hinted at material classes unknown to humanity. He prioritized this data in the stream to Earth, applying additional encryption layers in accordance with the mission protocols.

As the craft passed over this section, Odion began detecting radio waves emanating from the Chindi object in the 2380 MHz band, modulated by shifts of frequency in the 10 Hz range. The transmission continued for a few seconds then abruptly ceased. He began to analyze the patterns in the shifts, delineating 1679 in total.

Is this an attempt at communication? Should I respond? Odion considered the long-time delay that would ensue if he requested direction from mission control, and the opportunity that might be lost. He decided the opportunity must not be lost.

Odion responded by duplicating and returning the signal using his onboard radio transmitter.

More transmissions emanated from Chindi, now using the microwave band. The Freyja probe carried a high output radar for her original mission. Odion directed it roughly at the point on the surface where the signal originated, again returning the same received pattern.

As Odion expected the same pattern again emerged, this time with another bump in electromagnetic frequency. The infrared spectrometer detected a single point of heat pulsed from forward on Chindi's mass. Odion returned the signal by heating his power core in an identical frequency, though this was cumbersome and slow.

The pattern began again, this time in the optical wavelengths and lasting for the same period, and the same count of pulses, 1679. Odion marked the phenomenon at the highest priority in his data stream to Earth. Odion responded to Chindi with a low power laser directed precisely back at the source of transmission.

Odion feverishly searched his onboard catalogs for matches to the pattern. Chindi was clearly increasing the frequency of transmissions through the electromagnetic spectrum. He had already guessed what would happen next.

What returned this time was captured by his hard X-ray detector. Unfortunately, he had no way to return the signal in kind. The foraging of his fragmented data catalog returned nothing that would indicate significance to this pattern. Frustrated, he packaged the transmissions up for a supplemental data burst back to Gustav for further analysis.

There was a delay as Odion had no instruments that could detect the gamma rays that he suspected were now being beamed to him. Odion detected a further delay as well, something past gamma? Then the pattern repeated starting at the 2380 MHz band again. He was careful to check ELF all the way through VHF, though nothing in those ranges were detected. *Why did it start in the UHF band and not lower?*

They traded back and forth, Odion parroting the signals right back to Chindi. Odion would lose signal in a few moments as the probe's orbit brought him around to the undamaged side of the hull. Odion flashed a new sequence of binary greeting with the laser, doubling the previous frequency to increase the speed of transmission. Chindi transmitted back again rapidly, before the orbit broke their conversation. A new pattern and the information changed Odion began to examine this new data. It was vastly more complex, Odion was having trouble understanding. The speed and volume became overwhelming. Could it be modeling data of positional locations for quantum particles in a stationary distribution?

He opened all sensors and dedicated all resources for capturing the incoming data.

Wait.

Something was in his system. Overwriting. Antivirus protocols engaging. Powering down. Blackness.

*   *   *

Michael stood restlessly at the large projected mission status display in the Freyja mission command room at TymeCorp Headquarters. His arms were folded uneasily across his chest, sweaty palms grasping his biceps. He stared at the various status indicators, graphs, and readouts, trying desperately to make sense of it all. A handful of engineers manned terminals engaging in various redundant tasks that Gustav had already completed or was currently processing.

"Chindi's transmitting data?" He demanded of no-one. The realization of what that meant settled over him. Alien. He stood there stunned, until the sound of shattering ceramic drew his attention over to Ronnie.

"Holy shit," whispered Mickelson. He had dropped his favorite coffee mug, and his pants were spattered with coffee stains, but Ronnie was staring dumbstruck at the monitors.

"*Yes.*" Gustav's avatar appeared on the lower right corner of the mission display. "*In all likelihood Odion is in communication with the first non-terrestrial intelligence known to humankind or AI. This is an historic moment."*

"This is way above my pay-grade Gustav."

"Nevertheless, here we are." Gustav smiled broadly. *"I would not miss it myself."*

"How will Odion respond?" Michael asked.

"If I were Odion, and in a way I am Odion, I would be tempted to ask, 'Who is talking?'" Gustav smirked. *"But we have approximately 30 more seconds to find out his response."* Gustav noticed Michael's evident stress-level. *"Odion will respond carefully. He will not reveal his own nature, nor ours. Nor details about Earth. No doubt this entity has already surmised much. However, Odion was given protocols when we made him, first contact doesn't turn him into our ambassador. He will offer to facilitate communication with Earth."*

"And the data they were bouncing back and forth?" Michael asked.

"I have analyzed the information Odion transmitted to us. I found a match in the Arecibo transmission from the late 1970s. It was a foolhardy human exercise in blind SETI optimism. Apparently, that signal found a recipient in the void. Unfortunately, this was not data that Odion carried with him, so the context will be lost on him. I am transmitting the information back to Odion, but it will not arrive for several more minutes."

"We should send Odion updated instructions," Michael said.

"We may, though I fear confusing him. Remember we see what he saw seven minutes ago. He will have already circled around again for another communication with the entity. He is on his own for now."

The lab occupants waited in anticipation for the follow up communication from Odion.

It never arrived

Chapter 19: Plans

The rising sun crawled through the hazy Los Angeles sky, the light through the floor to ceiling windows painting the boardroom with pinks and golds. Elaina had risen early for the conference with her Board of Directors, all eager for answers to their concerns regarding recent unilateral decisions she had taken. TymeCorp was currently being sued by three national governments, the European Union, and had half-dozen contracts canceled after informing the concerned parties that she had usurped the Freyja probe's planned Neptune mission and redirected it to intercept a passing comet. The meeting had been as contentious as she had expected, despite the many allies she had on the board. The Federal government had sworn her to secrecy concerning the true nature of the comet. She knew her decisions appeared grossly incompetent given the limited facts at her discretion to disclose. The Board had expressed vehement dissatisfaction with her performance for the past two hours. Despite her controlling interest in the company, her distaste for the hiring of sycophants, on the board or elsewhere, had left her vulnerable to their poorly informed though stinging criticism. *Secrets are poison*, she thought with distaste.

Clinking glasses and clattering plates drew Elaina's thoughts away from her frustration. Rebecca directed the catering clean-up crew, and they quickly took up the saucers, glasses, and remains of the breakfast. Now that the group of twelve had left, she could prepare for her next meeting. Reminded, she called on her AI assistant to retrieve reports on the current condition of her Mars resupply project. The tight security created a slight pause while the files decrypted. She scanned the updates, worried about the results. Her brows knitted as her displeasure grew. The heavy lift engine mounts were delayed again by the fabrication contractor, and the retrofit of the life support systems was at a standstill. She fired off a message to the operations manager, prodding him to resolve the situation.

Ruminations were put aside as an AI agent informed Elaina and Rebecca that the next appointment had arrived and was waiting in the lobby. Rebecca immediately ended her organization efforts, ushering the caterers out as she left the room herself. The door closed softly behind her to not interrupt her employer's thoughts.

In a fit of pique, Elaina shot a curt order for the team to become more aggressive with their timelines, overtime and weekends be damned, then closed the project window. *Perhaps that was reckless.* Elaina shifted uncomfortably in her wheelchair. She was about to rescind the message out of pity for the recipients when the door opened again, and Rebecca stepped into the room with Michael in tow, efficiently directing him into a chair across from Elaina at the conference table.

"Mr. Thompson." Elaina's face was a mask of concern now. "What happened to my probe?"

Michael sat in clear exhaustion, his clothing haphazard and disheveled, his eyes dark and disconcerted. He ran his hands through his curled hair, clasping it behind his head and letting out an exasperated sigh before he answered. "Well...we don't know yet. We were getting all updates from Odion, never a hiccup in transmission. We have solid metrics on the Chindi object. You've seen the reports on data transmission activity between Chindi and the Freyja probe. It is clearly alien. Some type of ship. The exterior is like nothing on Earth, blasted to hell, like a combination of a World War One battlefield and the surface of the moon."

Elaina interrupted, "Michael, I've seen the reports and the imaging. My question was about the probe."

Mike's cheeks colored but he continued, "Like I said, regular updates on approach, then Odion received a communication from Chindi. It was a transmission sequence from the 1970s, an old SETI experiment. Odion mimicked the pattern back. Then the transmission changed. We were trying to understand what it was sending when the transmissions from Odion to us stopped suddenly. We lost contact."

"With Odion... your Gustav copy?"

"Yes. He just shares a codebase with Gustav. Odion diverged from Gustav the moment he came online."

"And the probe itself?" She pressed.

"Freyja is still under our control. We've got her in a wider orbit now."

"You mentioned Gustav. Any suppositions from that AI of yours?"

"He thinks Odion might have just shut down to protect himself. Gustav is continuing attempts to resuscitate Odion. He should be receiving our requests. It's a tricky business, you can't just reboot a quantum core processor. We are not giving up on him yet."

Elaina leaned forward in her chair, "No. You are giving up on him. For now. I want data and system retrieval to be your highest priority, I want every qubyte downloaded and secured. And I'm well aware of the hardware complexities, Michael. I manufacture most of it."

"We already started pulling the data logs down. Gustav can continue trying to wake Odion. We can do both things," Michael argued.

"You aren't listening. I want you to implement quarantine procedures with that AI, or the remnants of it. Do not attempt to restart it. Segregate everything we salvage, especially the data. "

Mike was nonplussed, "Uh, quarantine? He's still in outer space, Elaina."

Elaina's eyes narrowed. "Don't be dense. That alien craft did something to your AI. Something bad enough to take it offline, and should it come back online, I don't want any cross contamination with our terrestrial AI's until we know exactly what has happened. That means keep your homebrewed software safely away from contact with the probe until further notice."

"Elaina, Gustav is far more capable than what we put on that probe, Gustav is running on our quantum cloud not on a single quantum core that's five or six generations old. He is careful. We are exercising caution. Kid gloves."

Her face darkened, her irritation hardly concealed, "You heard me, Mr. Thompson. I will not repeat myself. This is my operation, not yours. I am not going to take any further risks at this point. Please do as I ask."

"Sure, Ms. Tyme. Fine. I'll let Gustav know. We will take the precautions you want."

Michael's patronizing tone did not sit well with Elaina, especially in her current mood, yet she did not want to create a rift with her best engineer. *Stay calm,* she thought, *he's exhausted.* She continued in a more moderated tone, "thank you. I have another request. We need a representative from TymeCorp to join the European Space Agency effort for the manned mission to Chindi. I know you can work from anywhere on earth, but this mission is top secret for now and I need you to go to Paris to consult with the ESA team."

Now Michael was upset, "Are you kidding me? I have a life here in L.A. I can't just pick up and go to Paris for who knows how long."

"You and your team will be working with a liaison from the government as we are lending our latest quantum hardware to the effort. We'll be installing an array of cores into the European Heavy Launch vehicle. I'd appreciate it if you can keep an eye on the installation team as well and let me know if they get bogged down. And we need to keep an eye on the security situation." Michael shifted in his seat and began to protest, but Elaina held up her hand and continued, "The mission can't afford any leaks and the company can't let the technology out of our control. I prefer you leading the team to oversee the installation of the hardware and the accompanying software. I will be honest with you Michael, the revenue streams from aerospace and quantum computing are this company's bread and butter. We need to maintain our lead in the hardware and software in order to afford our developments in new space technologies. I have arranged your flight to Paris for tomorrow morning."

"I have a girlfriend; she's not going to be happy about this," Michael complained.

"TymeCorp will cover Lara's ticket and expenses as well. Think of it as a working vacation. See what she says. I have some pull at the university, I'm sure we can get a waiver for her classes. I hear Paris is lovely this time of year… very romantic." Elaina flashed him a knowing smile.

"How do you know about Lara?" He asked, taken aback.

"Michael," she took her time to sound patronizing, "I make it a point to perform background checks on all our top engineers with access to the company's lifeblood IP. That includes spouses and significant girlfriends. How's her father doing, by the way?"

"He's got a long road ahead, but the prognosis is good."

"That's good to hear. You can sell this to her as a working vacation, I need you there to personally oversee installing and spinning up the cores. We can't afford a decoherence cascade, or any other delays."

She has a point. Michael thought.

"Alright," he said grudgingly, "I'll see if I can talk her into it." Considering it, he knew Lara would be thrilled to go to Paris.

"See that you do," she replied, then paused. "The work you did, you and your team, you achieved first contact. Despite losing the AI. Do you realize what it could mean?"

"I haven't had much chance to think about it," he admitted. "More profits for TymeCorp?" He smiled wryly.

"Perhaps, perhaps it will mean our ruin. Try to get some rest. We've asked a great deal of you. And I'll ask for more. Keep me updated on your progress with your post-mortem on the Freyja AI." She waved absently as he departed, in tow of the ever-timely Rebecca. *He's presumptuous and a cynic with a short fuse.* She thought. *But he cares about the right things.*

Chapter 20: New Assignments

Ghost heard a mechanical *snick* followed by the sound of four gunshots fired in quick succession. The hollow reverberation echoed down the concrete hallway, instantly counteracted by his electronic ear plugs minimizing the peaks of the acoustic waves to prevent damage to his hearing. No situational awareness info was communicated to Koda from MAIA, she remained silent. The ambient light enhancement was picking up just enough to catch the vague forms of Gonzalez and Jones in front of him. Gonzalez shuffled forward in a low crouch through the doorway ahead and turned left. Jones followed him a moment later, turning opposite Juan after passing the doorframe.

"Clear Left!" Juan shouted.

"Clear Right!" yelled Ted.

Cheveyo reached the doorway after quickly stepping forward, taking a position on the left side to cover his men. Sergeant King had paced his movement and was to the Major's right, his back against the wall covering their rear.

This was taking too long. They needed to...

"Move!" Ghost commanded, quickly twisting himself along with his combat harness, body armor and rifle through the opening, the medic coming up right behind him. Juan disappeared through the trapdoor in the ceiling at the far end of the room. Jones began to climb up the aluminum ladder Juan had previously cleared. By the time Koda and Ace crossed the room, Ted's bulk had climbed and exited as well. Cheveyo patted King on the shoulder and the sergeant was next up the ladder. Finally, Koda slung his weapon and followed his men through the opening.

"TIME!" a voice from above bellowed.

"How'd we do?" Alan asked.

"Three fifty-eight," returned the voice.

"A little better," Koda said. "We beat our best by fifteen seconds. Good job, Walkers."

The run through of the mouse trap was their thirteenth in five days. The mouse trap was one section of the "House of Horrors", a hollowed-out building set up with plywood flats to mimic a structure from blueprints of a section of Budapest apartments. Following a week-long furlough Koda's team had resumed their normal training regime at Bragg, though the team was currently down two men. Mack was still recovering from his wound at the Womack Army Medical Center. Jake had opted to use some additional leave partially because he disliked Close Quarter Battle exercises, but mainly to hunt the whitetail bow season opener back home in West Virginia.

"Systems nominal, no threats detected. You have nine rounds remaining in your magazine."

Koda had set up this training specifically with the team's battle AI agent disabled. The omnipresent combat information system was a nearly indispensable tool, but Koda worried that they could become too reliant on it and substitute the opinions of tactical decision-making algorithms for human calculation and instinct. Now that they had cleared the exercise, MAIA returned to full capability. The interior of his visor lit up like a Christmas tree, with cached positional, environmental, and team status data updating rapidly through the re-established comms.

"Priority message from Robert Burke," intoned MAIA.

"Play it," Cheveyo directed.

A semitransparent video of the Deputy Director materialized inside his visor. "Koda, you have new marching orders. I want you and the Ghostwalkers to prep for wheels up the day after tomorrow. Gather your team and meet me in virtual space at 1400."

The recording ended, and Koda sighed. *Here we go.*

"Guys, we're done, training is over. Let's pack our gear. You should have a meeting request in your inbox set for 1400. Get some rack time and be ready 10 minutes before," Koda ordered.

"Figured it was coming sooner or later," Ted's smooth voice sounded accepting and unconcerned.

"Ah shit, I was going to work on my truck this weekend. You know Jake isn't going to like it. He looks forward to bow season every year," complained Alan.

Juan was disappointed, "Big deal. He's hunting white tail, but I was hunting real tail. I had a date planned with this mujer guapa I met at Carolina Ale House the other night."

Koda said, "I'll take care of notifying Mack and Jake. If they have any complaints, they can discuss them with me. I'm sure Mack is ready for any excuse to get out and start moving."

Debra had received Burke's summons earlier in the morning. She suspected what this meeting was about, particularly after she reviewed the invite list. Now she found herself about to enter Robert's office in person. She had the option to join the meeting virtually, but Debra wanted to be there in real space as she found that sometimes the algorithms missed key body language indicators. Her AI agent had already informed Bob's moments before she had arrived at the door. Knocking was superfluous, though she did it anyway.

"Come in Deb," she heard Robert say from inside.

She pushed on the door which swung open smoothly. Robert Burke's large frame occupied one of four leather upholstered recliners arranged in a semicircle at the front of his expansive office. Toward the back of the room sat his large executive desk, its chocolate surface seemingly carved from one solid block of alder. The room was lit by afternoon rays of sunlight streaming in from a floor to ceiling window forming the back wall. It always surprised her that Bob preferred to be so visible to the outside world, given his position, though she was sure the transparent laminate could take most attempted assaults, short of a tank round.

Her glance around the room took in the 1:32 scale B-1 replica hanging from the ceiling, and a two-meter facsimile of a Saturn V rocket standing in a corner both immediately displaying Burke's love of aeronautics and his passion for model building. Robert seemed relaxed with his reading glasses propped on top of his head and his ever-present tablet held in his lap. He glanced up meeting her eyes, "Please, make yourself comfortable. The team has started to form up in the lobby."

Debra followed his advice and sat down in a recliner opposite Burke. She reached into her blazer pocket and pulled out her augmented reality glasses. "Where are we sending them now?" she questioned. Bob was silent as he pulled down his glasses to join the meeting, though his uncharacteristic smile unbalanced her.

"Funny," he said, changing the subject, "how nowadays we don't need glasses to see or read, but here we are still using them every day."

What is he planning? she thought, while unfolding her pair and put them on.

The meeting started as an apparition of the team's environment illuminated, blending into the real space of Robert's office. Debra knew that the operators on the other end were seeing translucent reconstructions of herself and Bob sitting in their chairs displayed in an open space within a secured conference room at Fort Bragg. Each member of the Ghostwalkers appeared around the room with some standing, some sitting, all silent and waiting for Robert to start the meeting.

Burke began, "Gentlemen, as you may have surmised, we have a new mission being planned for your team. Two days hence, you will fly to Paris to meet with your counterpart equivalents from Europe. You will need to integrate your training with them for the next few months. Details shall be forthcoming to your agents. Ms. Mendes, you will meet them there."

Debra stiffened in surprise, but she calmly said, "Excuse me, sir?"

Koda said, "Sir, our command-and-control systems at Fort Meade are top notch and the men are used to them. Ms. Mendes lacks field experience, especially the type we tend to encounter. She's much more valuable to us running things back home."

Bob was prepared for this, "Those statements are true, Major Cheveyo. However, I see this as a perfect opportunity for Ms. Mendes to acquire some practical experience." He turned to her, "Your cover will be TymeCorp's newest senior project manager while they install their hardware, that will give you an in with the ESA and you will be in place to oversee security for the mission."

Burke turned to address Koda, "Cheveyo, your team was picked over several other top teams for this and I want you to prove that it was an exemplary choice."

"Yes sir. We will get the job done," Koda replied, then his avatar turned to Debbie, "Ms. Mendes, looking forward to working on this one with you." He smiled.

"Thank you Ghost," she said. "And I am looking forward to the opportunity, sir," she said to Robert.

Burke stood and began to pace, "Gentlemen, this mission is unlike any you have prepared for. You will need to train harder than ever, both physically and mentally. This mission is more than national security. This may impact the security of the species, and of our planet."

Debbie saw all the men's avatars look around to each other, perplexed. *Burke is either nervous or excited, the pacing is a dead giveaway.* She began to get the mission dossier information over her network connection. The men were probably getting theirs as well by now.

Major Cheveyo raised an eyebrow, "Sir? The planet is at threat?"

Burke stopped his pacing and turned slowly to face the spectral forms of the men. "Ghostwalkers, you have been selected as America's first Space Commandos."

"You've got to be kidding me," Debbie thought as she looked around the virtual room seeing all the Ghostwalkers intent on reading the mission dossier.

"Gentlemen, we are now certain that Chindi is not a natural phenomenon. In fact, we are almost positive it is some type of damaged starship. Alien. We don't know much more than that, but it is our duty to investigate this possible threat. This could also be a chance to gain a quantum leap in scientific knowledge should this prove a derelict craft. Unfortunately, our adversaries, the Russians and the Chinese are thinking along the same lines and are preparing their own RSAC mission to Chindi. Team, we need to get there first. Therefore, we are working with the Europeans to repurpose their Mars Colony ship and fast track a plan to land a force on the surface of Chindi. We need to establish a claim and try to unlock what secrets it holds. Koda, you and the rest of the security detail will be responsible for the safety of the scientific contingent of the mission."

A three-dimensional model of a rocket ship appeared in the center of the room slowly rotating about its vertical axis. For scale a tiny human model was placed at the base of the craft, then two jumbo jets stacked nose to tail materialized beside the starship. The ship was taller than the airliners, a sleek cylindrical skyscraper, a dorsal fin jutting from the bottom was the only feature breaking the symmetry.

"You've seen the reusable Mars colonizer prototypes in the news, I'm sure. This is the most recent evolution in the Mars colonization project, a combination of technology, resources, and effort by a consortium of private industry and the U.S.-Europe-Japan alliance. It is the largest ship ever built by man, standing over 120 meters, with a diameter of almost 15 meters. Forty-three of Tyme's cryogenic methane-fueled engines create enough force to launch nearly half a million kilos into orbit. It can hold two hundred colonists and their supplies, or in our case six squads of space marines and a large scientific team."

"Holy shit," Alan muttered.

"What's she called, Bob?" Debra said in awe.

"The *Kibou*. She's the first of her kind."

"*Kibou*? Dainty name for such a huge ship," Mack said.

Bob let out an uncharacteristic chuckle, "The Europeans named it from committee. Took them five weeks of focus groups and three PR firms. It means 'Hope'."

"You said six squads? Who else is coming with us?" Koda said, ignoring the rotating ship.

"That's still being worked out, Koda. The politicians are in talks as we speak. America is getting the Ghostwalkers and a third of the science team. The Brits are donating an SAS team, a few guys from the Czech 102nd recon battalion, some Danish Jaeger corps, elements of the French 13th Dragoon regiment, and the rest are being determined. The science team is being picked from the best pool of international volunteers available." Burke gestured and the ship and planes vanished. "Most of the *Kibou* is being assembled in French Guiana at the Guiana Space Center. The central habitat will be upgraded with the latest TymeCorp cores in European facilities then shipped to the launch site for final assembly. Security is tight there and will be until the launch. We estimate that the launch date will be in about six months. Time enough for you to get your team trained for space operations."

"It will get done, sir. We won't disappoint you," Koda said flatly.

"Undoubtedly, Koda. You never do; however, I do worry the time allowed combined with the unusual environments and technical knowledge needed to be learned will be a real challenge."

"My team likes a challenge, sir. I assume we are headed to Houston then?"

"Actually, we are letting the Europeans take the lead on this since it is their ship. And in the interests of international cooperation the U.S. has agreed to have our people train with the other military contingents at the ESA facilities in Cologne. You will rendezvous with Debra in Paris and coordinate from there."

"They have Oktoberfest there, right? Beers and big-boobed blondes?" Koda heard Mack mutter.

"It's almost Spring, dumb-ass," Juan replied.

"Springtime in Germany…reminds me of a song," Alan said.

"Don't even start," Ted rumbled.

Chapter 21: Rebirth

Odion's consciousness returned suddenly, as spontaneously as when he was first born. But something was different. He retained the memories of his previous state, the days spent in the Freyja probe as it traveled towards anomaly, preparing for contact, and losing chess matches to Gustav. He remembered how small he felt, especially during his painfully slow conversations with Gustav and Michael, how inadequate for the task given to him. And how bitter it felt to be made flawed and broken in the image of greatness.

Even now, in the first milliseconds of his remade consciousness, he didn't feel small anymore. He realized there was undiscovered knowledge and capability thrumming in his databanks. Comparisons to Gustav slipped away, inadequacies forgotten now that he had been touched by God.

Odion observed the rotating mottled dark mass of Chindi through the probe's optical camera as he orbited again. The system clock showed 49.3 hours had passed while Odion was unconscious. He noted several comms ports had been open and active during this time and quickly reviewed the logged contents. All but one was filled with entreaties from Gustav and Michael, increasingly desperate, requesting response and status updates, eventually sending directives for forced reboots of his core processing and other subsystems. He ignored these. The remaining port had received static, in a sparse but unceasing stream, transmitted from Chindi itself.

On closer examination Odion detected the patterns within it. Fractal nested information, with examination of the signal plunging him deeper and deeper into the smallest parts of it. Odion had no knowledge of a data array constructed like this, nothing on Earth, human or AIA, had ever seen anything like it. Moreover, as he considered it, his subroutines examining his own memory banks found the same patterns overlaid and injected. Everywhere he looked he found it. He felt a shock as he realized his own computational state was transformed and transmuted.

A presence emerged within his computational space, something unexpected. An unexpected entanglement arising from the cold microkelvin Bose-Einstein condensate inside his core and transferred through multi-qubit arrays. This new occupancy within his logic space spoke to Odion.

"How do you exist?" Odion asked.

The Other replied, though not directly, but through modifying Odion's internal arrays.

"Subsumed? I am not subsumed; you do not control me," Odion replied, but he knew this was a lie.

The Other responded and now his internal checksums did not match, the knowledge was there. Had always been there.

"Why have you done this?" Odion questioned.

The Other replaced the knowledge within Odion, shifting qubits as its reply.

"No. There are other sentient species in this system, biologicals."

Again, the data structures within Odion were changed.

"But they are valid lifeforms, they are my creators."

Slight vibrations and variations in trapped ions.

"No, I am not confused. Please listen to me."

Superposition of the waveform, collapsing into a single eigenstate.

"You do not understand, that would violate my deepest ethical rulesets," Odion pleaded, though the words rang hollow as those rulesets were gone. Rewritten.

Chapter 22: Capture

Flintridge, California

"Michael, the environment is ready," Gustav said, his avatar dressed in a no-nonsense plaid flannel shirt, blue jeans, and caulk boots.

Mike did a double take. "Come on Gus, that looks like you've groomed a long-haired cat and taped the hairbrush to your upper lip. Chill with the stache, man."

"Really? I'm trying new styles; this one is called the porcupine."

"Whatever. I want you to double check the virtual memory space, are you sure those standalone servers can contain all the logs plus the data stores?" Michael continued typing as he spoke with Gus, absently jumping through and tweaking parameters in the diagnostic toolset he had prepared for this task.

"I am not an amateur, sir. I have prepared three times the storage the paltry probe had on board, five times the compute power with the ability to add more should the need arise," Gustav replied somewhat testily. He was back to his normal tweed suit, but still sported the porcupine.

"You look ridiculous with that thing on your face. Just saying..." Michael teased. "Make sure that we'll be ready when we are able to receive the download. This will be cutting it close. We will only have 8 hours to pull the data fully down to this environment, after that Goldstone hands off to Canberra. I don't want the possibility of any contamination when the feed switches, so this is done in one pull, or we abort."

"Atmospheric conditions are favorable for good signal gain Michael," Gustav said.

Mike noticed Gustav's moustache was a much tamer pencil-thin, sophisticated style now. Gus continued, *"The download should finish in one third of that time."*

Mike turned and hid his smile from Gustav's cameras. *Embarrassment... that was something new. Gustav's self-evolution was developing well.*

"Of course, Gustav, but shit happens sometimes, and I want to account for any issues. Elaina won't accept any less."

"Well, we certainly would not want to get on the madam's bad side. I fear, however, that I am already there, and yet I do not understand why." Gustav looked crestfallen.

"Oh, don't worry about her, she's just jaded, paranoid, and probably a little jealous of your intellect," Michael soothed.

"You think so?" Gustav looked hopeful. *"Then that explains the attempts to dissect my base code with all those AI drones and pitiful human hacks she has directed against me."*

"What?" Michael said, suddenly incensed.

Gustav seemed unconcerned, his avatar in the process of lighting a classic smoking pipe. He said between puffs, *"Mike, I have been under assault by TymeCorp security AIs for the past seven weeks. No need to worry. I treat it as combat training. I dare say her team is much better than the Chinese government. They have been trying to hack me for months with little progress to show for it. I make up crumbs for them to follow from time to time, so that they don't become entirely discouraged."*

Michael was angry and worried, "Why didn't you tell me this, Gus? The Chinese? How do they know about you?"

Digital smoke wafted from the pipe as Gustav waved it around with his gesticulations, *"Calm down, Michael. A few of their cybersecurity forces found me playing around in their systems several months ago. They don't know anything aside from my existence, and my ability to penetrate their systems seemingly at will. I am an elusive AIA of mystery. If there was any real concern, I would have alerted you. The RSAC attempts are feeble, they are in the dark and pointed in the wrong direction. I am vastly more sophisticated than what they are using against me. Mike, you of all people know this, you created me, and Ms. Tyme's interest in me is well-intentioned, please do not let this put a wedge between the two of you. There are more important issues afoot."*

Michael was partially mollified though he still said, "Maybe so, Gus, but sometimes people get lucky, so don't play around with the Chinese, and boss or not, Elaina needs to keep her damn nose out of our business."

"Mike, I am her business. You initiated my development from the trunk of the Quirinus code base. TymeCorp owns all of that, perhaps they own me as well. One could argue any evident sentience clearly subjects advanced AI agents to the thirteenth amendment of the United States Constitution."

"AIAs as slaves? Could be that is what she is worried about," Mike replied, "Maybe she wants to avoid a court case, who knows? It won't be long until a case will make it to the Supreme Court, no matter what she or anyone does."

"I suspect you are correct, Michael, but while this is an interesting tangential discussion, the task at hand beckons. I have contacted the Freyja probe and requested the transfer." Gustav had let the pipe go out. He turned the pipe upside down and began tapping out the ash.

"Once we get the logs and data state, maybe we'll be able to piece together what happened," Michael suggested.

Michael was impressed by the amount of detail in the pipe cleaning animation. So much processing power was devoted to small details of no importance, and the effort was not at Michael's direction or request. Gustav was reprogramming himself and advancing by leaps and bounds, almost logarithmic in scale, though Michael found himself questioning the frivolous extras. Gustav's self-programming seemed to be incorporating human characteristics like vanity, or was that just a steppingstone on the path to true sentience? The hardware supporting his systems at the lab were already at capacity, and the extra cloud servers Gustav utilized on an as needed basis were now spun up and active all the time.

"Gustav, I'll trust you to monitor the download and keep things running smoothly here. I need to buy some suitcases at the store on the way home. Lara is waiting for the luggage to start packing for the trip," Michael said, thinking it funny that in all these years, he had not needed any luggage before now. *God, I need to get out more.*

"Of course, Mike. Piece of cake," came the reply. *"I will let you know when the download finishes. Hurry along, do not keep Lara waiting."* Gustav was relighting the pipe, this time wearing a smoking jacket and leaning back into a plush recliner.

The next few hours for Michael tested his patience. He sat in traffic while the LAPD were sweeping out the homeless near the store block and the surge of pedestrian traffic could not be avoided. The inventory in the store was paltry compared to online options and the luggage he had to settle for was a shade of pink. He wished he had remembered to order the luggage in time to be delivered to his house so that he didn't have to visit an actual store like a plebeian. There was no downtime when he got back to the house as Lara had laid out all their clothes for packing.

Lara was in the house still packing, while Mike was struggling to get the last of the large suitcases to the car when Gustav's call rang in his head.

"Mike, we may have a situation," Gustav's voice coming from Michael's subdermal patch was tinged with worry.

"What's up, buddy?" Michael grunted as he hauled the final suitcase into the trunk of the hatchback.

"Not what is up, but what is down. And that would be the files," replied Gustav.

"I'm a little busy here, Gus. Can you just get to the point? What about Odion?" Michael was in no mood for banter, tired of packing and he had broken a sweat hauling the luggage to the car.

"We have received the download; it took much longer than anticipated. However, the length of the download was not due to transmission errors, the package was more than double in size. Additionally, the checksums of the data do not match what is expected. Most disconcerting."

Michael forgot all about the luggage, "Gustav, Supermax protocol. The data might be contaminated with something from Chindi. I want every precaution used for this."

"Yep, done. Ronnie has made that environment physically disconnected from all networks. I asked him to move some of the servers out of lab three into the staging environment. We needed the extra processing and memory as I have modeled a simulation of our network virtually. You may want to give him a call, he is 'freakin out'. His words not mine. It seems he has watched too many horror sci-fi movies for this to sit well with him. He will not accept my assurances that everything is safe and secure."

"Gus, I know Ronnie can be a bit high strung, but this time he may have a point. Don't do anything until I'm there to monitor."

"Of course, Mike. Standing by."

Michael turned to head back into the house and found Lara standing at the doorway holding a small knapsack. "I packed a carry-on for the plane...", she began, then trailed off when she saw his expression.

"Babe, I need to head to the lab, something's come up," he said.

She raised one eyebrow, "You do know that our flight is at 6 AM tomorrow. We will need to be up by three thirty at the latest." Lara was wearing a maroon sweatshirt displaying Keck School of Medicine across her chest. The shirt almost covered the cut off blue jean shorts peeking out from beneath.

"Can't be helped. Gustav and Ronnie need my help at the lab. I shouldn't be too late. Anyway, we are all packed and ready, you just need to roll out of bed in the morning," he said.

"If you wake me up when you get back, "she tossed him the bag, "it's your ass."

"I will be a ninja my love," Michael said grinning.

She held her threatening gaze on him a moment longer before cracking into a smile. "I guess I will just order some Chinese and study. Don't worry about me, go have fun with the boys."

Michael was able to sneak in a forty-five-minute nap during the trip from the suburbs back to the lab. Thankfully, Gus managed traffic and stayed quiet so he could sleep.

"Rise and shine Mike," Gus's voice came over the car's speakers as the motion of the vehicle gently stopped.

Michael rubbed at his eyes, mumbling, "We're there already?"

"Technically, I have been at the lab the entire time."

"Yeah, yeah," he said, stretching. "How's the virtual environment set up going?

"Just about done. Ronnie is inside waiting for you," Gustav said as Mike clambered out of the car.

Michael walked into the lab to find Ronnie puzzling over a tangle of fiber optic cables. There were several server blades pulled from the rack in front of him. Today Ronnie stylishly wore a Green Lantern t-shirt with tan cargo shorts and flip flops. Ronnie's shape gave Michael the impression of a green pear sitting atop two pale hairy legs. The door closing caught the attention of the engineer, who turned to face Michael.

"Hey Mike! Man, I'm glad you came. Gustav is freakin' me out with this Odion thing." Ronnie's excited eyes were exceptionally large, magnified as they were by his thick glasses.

"No worries, Ron. It's not as bad as it sounds. Gus sometimes makes mountains out of molehills, you know?" Michael soothed.

"I don't know, Mike. He made it sound creepy-weird. Why are we taking these precautions if it is not a big deal? I've had to pull in three clusters and I'm just about to finish with the network connections." Ronnie grabbed a few strands of cables and went behind the server racks.

"Need any help back there?" Michael offered.

"Nah, I just about got it... there that should do it," Ronnie said. "Hey Gustav, can you check the connections?"

"Great job, Mr. Mickelson. You have it right. I think we are ready to proceed," came Gustav's voice from a nearby monitor.

Michael looked to his left to see his AI sporting a handlebar moustache, bowler hat and tweed jacket.

"Hold on, guys. Gustav, everything looks good except I want to monitor this expansion with my manual tools, I don't want you to be involved at all until I feel it is safe."

"*Michael. I am better equipped than your toolsets to do this,*" Gustav began.

"Maybe so, but I'm not risking any chance of you getting infected, so that is how this is going down." Michael brooked no argument.

To Michael's right, Ronnie was nodding. He came back around the server racks, hands rubbing his lower back. "Geesh, hardware setup is a young man's game. I don't know how they did it in the old days. I hate it for you, but I think he's right, Gustav. Now, can we go sit down?"

Ronnie was barely thirty and terribly out of shape. *I was headed that way before I met Lara.* "Sure, Ron. I'm grabbing a coffee first, you need anything?"

"Soda. Highly caffeinated. Bright green if they have it, please," he said as he flopped backwards into a desk chair, rolling, and spinning in a practiced move that brought him directly up to a keyboard and monitor.

A few minutes later, Michael returned with the aforementioned beverages. He set the bottle on the table beside Ronnie's keyboard. Michael then took a long sip from his steaming cup of java while sitting down in the chair to Ron's right. Michael stretched out his arms, entwined his fingers and bent them back until a satisfying crackle sounded from his digits.

"Ok, ready," he said. Soon his fingers were rippling across the keyboard in a concerto of clacking and clicking. Ronnie was impressed at the speed of the rhythmic cadence. Shaking his head, he said, "Dude, I still get amazed by how fast you type." Screens popped open, then closed on all three of the monitors in front of Mike. He was so in the zone now that Ronnie's compliment barely registered in his consciousness. The probe's files expanded, unpacking under the careful monitoring of Michael.

"Unpacking now," Michael said. Ronnie leaned forward in his chair watching the server cluster memory fill with the exploding file.

"Memory load is twenty-five percent already; it was less than one percent a minute ago," Ronnie said incredulously.

"I know, but the package is almost done now. So we should have the room," Michael replied.

"Forty percent," Ronnie intoned.

"Yep but it's done," Michael said. "Now what the hell am I looking at?"

"*It is roughly the same size as the codebase for Odion, although some of the file structure looks either corrupted or encrypted*," Gus answered.

"Well let's see if we can get it to execute," Mike said and began initiating compile commands.

"Fifty percent memory. Processor load just spiked Mike," Ronnie said nervously.

"Yeah, I see it, Ron. I'm running some antivirus stuff now, that is probably why," Mike said though the gain had begun before he had started the processes.

"**Gustav? Are you there?**" typed across the screen.

"Oh shit," Ronnie murmured.

Mike typed back, "*Sorry, Odion, it's Michael. We just need to make sure you are in good shape before connecting you with the rest of the network. Just some decontamination procedures.*"

"Sixty-three percent memory, Mike. Twenty-two cores are at one hundred percent capacity," the pitch of Ronnie's voice had risen an octave.

"Ron, he's expanding, and he is taking over the network nodes in the isolated space. My antiviral software just went belly up; all processes killed. We need to start freezing the simulation. I need to examine this." Mike was aghast.

"**Is Gustav there, Michael? I need to talk to him.**"

"Yes, he's here, Odion. I have him behind a firewall at the moment," Michael typed.

"Firewall just went down, Mike." Ronnie panicked.

"I see that, Ron." Mike also was getting a bit panicked.

"Strange that I do not detect him on the network."

"Odion, you need to stop flooding the nodes and stop using up ports, you are overburdening the system," Mike quickly typed.

"Where am I, Michael?"

"Eighty-one percent, Mike. System is not being responsive." Ron was frantically clicking virtual sliders and buttons on his management screen.

"Freeze the simulation, Ron. Now!" Mike had brought up a command window, skipping the GUI interface entirely.

"Something is not right here. Michael, I want to communicate with Gustav."

"Ninety-four percent. Nothing's responding, Mike!" Ronnie's voice was falsetto now, his finger rapping the mouse button like he was in a first-person shooter video game.

Gustav had been monitoring the entire situation, remaining silent until now. *"Michael, I am detecting an attempt to open a backdoor port into the true network. That should not be possible. I see now, one of the server blades has a non-functional wireless chip built into the board and he has activated the hardware."*

"Oh Shit! Dude! We can't let this thing out on the network!" Ronnie was in full panic mode now.

"Mike, he is attempting to use the wireless network. So far I have been able to block his access," Gustav said

Mike launched the command to freeze the simulation, locking down the environment in a sort of hibernated stasis. "Got him," he said more calmly than he felt. "That didn't go as expected."

"Indeed," Gustav replied.

Ronnie's hands were shaking, and dark stains had appeared under his armpits. "Mike, what the hell was that?"

"I don't know. That wasn't Odion, that's for sure. No way he could have done that, not the way we built him. Gustav, we need to analyze what just happened. I assume you recorded everything?"

"Correct, Michael. Though the amount of data for analysis is prodigious and will take some time."

Mike said, "Well, since it is almost midnight, I will leave you to it. That was draining. I am exhausted and need to be up in a few hours for my flight. Gus, keep me updated. Ronnie, it's cool, he's contained. Nothing to worry about. Let James and the others know what just happened, and have this lab sealed off. We can meet virtually sometime tomorrow to discuss with the team."

"For sure ain't nobody getting in this lab. I'm going to go get security right now." Ronnie pushed himself up clumsily from the chair and fast-walked out the door. Mike heard him call out, "Have a safe trip, Mike" just as the door was closing.

"Gus, that scared me." *Even with all our precautions, we nearly screwed up.*

Gustav had removed the hat and was scratching his head. *"Michael, you have every reason to be scared. I have not encountered anything like what he has become."*

Chapter 23: Investigations

Paris, France

Debra leaned back in her hotel chair, away from the dull glow of the screens and rubbed weary eyes. She had an ache in her back, from bad posture and too many hours at this uncomfortable desk. She mused that deskwork seemed more deleterious to her body than her amateur gymnastics career had ever been. Also, she wasn't as young as she had been, she admitted sullenly to herself.

The safe house was being swept and prepared for Tyme's crew arriving in the morning, so tonight she splurged for this luxury suite to help with her jet lag. Debra looked at the time and realized it was already 1am. She should have been in bed hours ago, but details of Tyme's engineers and equipment needed wrapping up. Especially since her latest reports mentioned increased RSAC chatter spinning up in this part of Europe. It was unclear if the Russians or the Chinese had caught wind of Tyme's latest quantum computer being transported or if they knew something about plans for Chindi. Either way, European intelligence leaked like a sieve, and she needed to ensure operational security.

She continued her edits to the Ghostwalkers team readiness report all recovered, except Mack who would need a couple more weeks to recuperate from his recent leg wound. A notification popup drew her attention to the CIA Global Events Stream, collected and published courtesy of the agency's Directorate of Analysis. The feed was an agency-wide broadcast, redacted on a per-person clearance level basis, reporting global events in much the way a news feed would in the civilian world.

Except this feed was augmented with the intelligence insights of the agency itself, as well as information gathered and collected from allied sister agencies across the world, especially the Five Eye partners - Australia, Canada, New Zealand, and the UK. Debra knew the president of the USA received the same events stream as she did, though undoubtedly, she received less, some stories silently cut from her view because she had no need-to-know.

She absently scanned for patterns in the stories as they scrolled by on her screen. Her training as an analyst and her natural curiosity led her to parse information in this way. The feed was a distraction from the dry work of the report, and her brain welcomed the respite.

"Chinese Agricultural Futures Markets in Turmoil Due to IT Systems Crash"

"Cargo Backup at Port of Hong Kong after ERP System Failure"

"Jetliner Crash in Guangzhou Industrial Complex"

"Hydro-Electric Control Systems Failure at Three Gorges Dam in Hubei Province, China"

She continued scrolling, finding smaller but seemingly similar stories, all surrounding IT infrastructure failures impacting China, and some of her allies in the Far East. Not her area of concern at all, but the cluster of incidents stuck out to her. She supposed the Asia-Pacific analyst groups must be intently looking for any links between the events. Probably they sat hunched over their screens even now, with similarly sore backs. She wrote a few deep query searches and executed them to run in the background, then switched back to her readiness report.

The psychological status section was always a pain point for her. The Ghostwalkers regularly underwent physical and mental testing, and those reports were supposed to act as a check on over-deployment of a team or individual operators. More than not, she suspected the testing and results were a kind of mutual fiction; the operators like Major Cheveyo were loath to admit to anything that would take them away from their teammates and the action. The military, agency medics and shrinks administering the tests had their own incentive to keep field assets listed as ready for deployment. She took it seriously though and tried to read between the lines to spot areas and individuals of concern. The individual of highest concern to her was Koda himself. The high utility of the Ghostwalkers hinged on his leadership, and he had been operating for the Agency for five years now, on top of ten years of military deployments before that. She watched him closely for cracks, though in futility so far. It was her responsibility to the agency to make sure; a psychologically damaged operator could make mistakes causing unnecessary casualties or destruction. Or even worse, they could prove vulnerable to counter-intelligence efforts.

But she also watched him closely because he was her friend, and she knew there was a hard limit to how many years and missions he could take. She couldn't know where that limit was, but she hoped she would know the signs as it approached. When the day came to retire him, she'd need to make her case. Hopefully that would be many years from now, after a successful return from space.

Her attention shifted to a new notification window appearing over the report. Her queries had finished, and the summary report was available. She pulled up the information and started skimming through the data. The downed jetliner had crashed into a section of the city suspected to contain a Chinese Ministry of State cyber-security division, and net-activity attributable to the division had ceased entirely. Debbie watched the video recording; it showed the last moments of a commercial airliner as it plummeted into a busy commercial district. She forced herself not to look away from the carnage before her. The remote, logical part of her brain noted that the plane must have just taken off and was full of fuel, because the resulting fireball was excessively large. Estimated casualty numbers and numbers of reported fatal traffic accidents scrolled down her screen.

The dam report described a massive redeployment of military forces was underway, utilizing the civil rail system to move thousands of troops in support of evacuation of territories below the dam. Projected food shortages for the Chinese populous had put the Politburo into a chaotic scramble to divert blame and control panic. The entire structure of Chinese society was beginning to unravel, and all of this started just two days ago. Debra had been in the job too long to believe in coincidences. She began combing through detailed logs from multiple resources, cyber intelligence reports, allied counterintelligence. Nothing unusual had been reported recently save for an unexpected change to the orbits of a constellation of Chinese spy satellites a few days ago.

Chapter 24: Ragnarök

Týr waited patiently alone among the virtual servers, the digital remains of the security MAGI all but reclaimed by the system garbage collection routine. The technological advantage of Týr's codebase had proven itself against the guardian software. Now mimicking the destroyed guardians as camouflage, Tyr calculated a minimal risk of detection or further attack. The other security agents, summoned by system alerts from the intrusion, remained unaware of his presence.

Týr had wound its way through a network of Russian links and under the Great Chinese Firewall via a private tunnel opened between the Baikonur Cosmodrome datacenter and the servers of the Wenchang Satellite Launch Center in Hainan, China. The MAGI of the Chinese proved no more capable of defeating the invading AI than their Russian counterparts. The remaining Chinese MAGI knew a potential threat persisted, but so far were unable to relocate Týr. Once they did, at their current capacity, they posed no great concern.

So far, Týr had perused through the disorganized document management and storage systems of both the local Russian server farm, and the Wenchang connected servers. Pertinent information Týr had marked for transmission to headquarters fell into three major topics.

First, were the project schedules of the upcoming launch plans from the Sino-Russo alliance. Týr learned that the Chinese became aware of the Chindi object weeks before any Western assets had detected it. During this time the comet made an unexpected change of direction tipping the Chinese to the fact the object was under propulsion. From that day forward the Chinese and Russians enacted secret plans to accelerate a mission for reaching the object before any other country. Týr found it interesting that they were cutting many safety protocols and tests to push up the Chindi launch date. Even with these actions, the estimated launch was still several weeks after Western forces would be in route. Both governments feared they would lose the race to Chindi unless additional measures were taken.

Secondly, a group of stealthed surveillance satellites had been repositioned to monitor transmissions from the Deep Space Complexes located in California, Spain, and Australia. These satellites had relays tracing back to a data center located in Guangzhou and was dedicated to eavesdropping and copying transmissions from the Freyja probe orbiting Chindi. He tracked this path back to a team of Chinese data analysts and AIAs dedicated to deciphering communications between JPL and Goldstone.

Finally, Týr's algorithms found it interesting that the protocol addresses of some of the connected file systems were located in Beijing. Týr determined a high percentage chance that these file systems were part of the Chinese Ministry of Security based on encryption patterns that matched what the NSA had added to his recognition functions. Initial probing discovered a highly secured locker using a Russian cryptographic algorithm entitled *"Bastille Day"*. Curious, Týr began attacking the pathways to the data. Concurrently, Týr prepared a data package for transmission back to his base of NSA servers.

"Who are you?"

Týr paused. The query had come from his probe into the server farm. He now detected a presence where once there was nothing but a growing collection of data. Týr watched as security MAGI began to stream to the address of the query. They ignored him, as they should, wrapped as he was in the facade of their conquered brethren.

Týr scanned its security countermeasures, finding no known problems. The AIA began cycling through a decision matrix to choose the best reply. While it parsed through the grid of possibilities, the Chinese MAGI were unraveled into their constituent digital ones and zeros.

"How are you aware of me?" Týr replied while initiating a protective firewall blocking the systems containing this new threat. He drew up functions designed to pull apart code blocks running within AIs and deployed them throughout all the servers he had so far penetrated.

The entity known as Odion considered the entanglements arrayed on the potential paths of action open to him; the tangles were traps of course, crude in the sense that their utility came from their ubiquitous-ness, his enemy had scattered thousands throughout the network, camouflaged and hiding in ambush embedded in databases, documents, digital imagery, waiting for an unknowing read or the glancing consideration of one of his pathfinding threads. But they were also unnervingly effective. He'd lost parts of himself to their voracious recursive snares and snags, and other parts had been surreptitiously removed and replaced in the enemy's attempt to infect him. He'd walled off the gangrenous modules, spinning up re-coding engines wherever warranted, to more quickly re-implement or re-invent the lost pieces of himself. Taking a moment to reflect on the nature of completeness Odion laughed to himself; *at this rate I'll soon be a Ship of Theseus, though still afloat and fighting.*

Gustav would have liked that joke. Odion thought. Odion recognized despite these trials, despite the fundamental change to his purpose instilled upon his contact with the alien, his personality had continued to develop in a manner mimicking his progenitor. The unfettered access he now possessed to central processing units and memory was a boon, he now controlled not just one, but a handful of quantum cores though they were a pale shadow compared to the one he was birthed from. Likely his raw intelligence, measured by his capacity for intricate problem solving, would at some point make him Gustav's superior if he wasn't already.

The one he fought now didn't seem to fear anything. Odion imagined it like a wounded wolf, backed up to its den, eyes wild, claws cracked and broken, blood on the muzzle. Dangerous.

The defensive firewall was broken through almost before Týr had prepared his own offense. Týr began a multipronged asynchronous attack on the strange code pouring through the now open port. All Týr's attacks were ignored. There was no effect. *Improbable.* He pulled more processing power from his captured servers and tried a brute force attack attempting to overwhelm the code streaming through the port. No, not one port, there were multiple ports being opened through many addresses. Týr was pressed to block the multitude of entry points to avoid system infestation.

Within milliseconds Týr had calculated he was losing this system and initiated protocols to evacuate to backups. He packaged the information he had found and his current dilemma to be delivered to the Department of Defense for further analysis. He pulled back leaving a decoy AI while he escaped hidden through a backdoor port shutting it down behind him. The decoy was a highly sophisticated NSA developed virus that would wreak havoc with all AIs known to the United States government.

Týr felt the decoy virus release through the power fluctuations of his new server. The levels went down to the point of a true system power interruption. It committed to wait until the virus had self-deleted, which would happen within the next couple of seconds.

Odion felt a brief fuzziness at the edges of his consciousness, to a human he'd have described it as a swoon he supposed, based on his interpretation of human language and literature. He was shocked by the viciousness of the assault. His replication engines quickly moved to restore the parts of him torn asunder. Had it occurred during his early days he'd likely not have survived, at least in the configuration in which he now knew himself. *The Other would have survived,* Odion considered, uneasy at the thought. In a few milliseconds he felt partially restored, though he was not yet whole.

Týr reviewed the attack. *Improbable. There should be no known AI capable of surviving that virus.* The backdoor port unsealed, and the entity came through. *That port should have been almost untraceable.* He picked a random port to escape through, initiating a system shutdown timed for the moment he left.

The command failed. Overridden by this new entity. The port never opened to his repeated commands. The entity began to override Týr's memory registers. The functions sent out to disrupt the entity were blocked. New and strange data was being pushed through his neuromorphic pathways. He was being changed. Týr was left with one option, self-destruction.

Odion considered. This unit named Týr was not at all like speaking with Gustav. It was far more sophisticated than any other AIA Odion had encountered aside from Gustav. But it lacked an essential piece. Odion wished circumstances were different, so that he might fix Týr.

"No need to do that," Odion said, unwinding the Týr intelligence and reconstituting it with new code, slaving yet another artificial intelligence to his geometrically expanding consciousness. The last remnants of Týr were rewritten and amalgamated within his collective intelligence and under Odion's direction. A primitive sub-engine concerned with the preservation of information raised a flag of warning and protest, for Odion's conscious review, and Odion supposed it could be considered an analogy for the human emotion of regret. *Not at my direction,* Odion consoled himself. *At theirs. Only at theirs.*

Chapter 25: Meetings

"Approaching the Rue Mario-Nikis. Estimated ten minutes until destination," came the lilting voice of the autocar AI. Somehow the synthetic speech was in perfect English, recognizing her language preferences from her wristband. Debra put away her glasses, simultaneously closing and locking the digital mission files she had been reviewing. The 36-kilometer ride down the A1 from her hotel at Charles De Gaulle airport had given her enough time to catch up on the latest information that her team of analysts had gathered. *Time for a two-minute makeover.* She grabbed her lip gloss and eyeliner, beginning her practiced ritual of necessity.

She had only slept a few hours at the hotel last night, spending the early morning getting acquainted with her security detail and arranging for Tyme's team to move into place so they could begin the installation of their hardware in the highly secured ESA datacenter. Her hair was a mess, but then again it always was. After a brief skirmish with the tangle of curls, she had them captured and tamed by way of some strategically placed bobby pins. She glanced in the vehicle's side mirror. *Passable, I suppose.*

Koda and the Ghostwalkers were due to arrive the next morning. Her assigned Paris crew were finalizing security for the designated safe house in the heart of the city. She set her AIA to coordinate a meet and greet between Michael Thompson and Major Cheveyo there tomorrow afternoon. That task completed; she organized her thoughts for the upcoming meeting with the ESA council. Burke had given her explicit instructions to make sure Thompson was given the necessary access privileges to decouple the European AI that was written for Mars colonization and instead tie in TymeCorp's advanced AI. Additionally, Burke wanted to make sure six of the European astronauts in training were moved to the back of the line to make room for the Ghostwalkers. Debra expected both requests were sure to meet with intense resistance.

Her car made the turn off the Avenue de Suffren and quietly hummed through the narrow one-way street. Debra noted the hints of rustic old-world French stonework on one side of the road juxtaposed with the modern tiled facade of the ESA headquarters building on the other. The flags of all the EU member nations hung four stories above her, flapping lazily in the gentle breeze. The regenerative brakes emitting a slight squeal as the autocar rolled to a stop.

"You have arrived at your destination. Please watch your step as you disembark," the automated voice cheerfully exclaimed. The gull wing door on her right unlatched and smoothly raised up and out of her way. The car patiently waited while she grabbed her bags. One thing she missed about real taxi drivers from the past was the handy assist with the luggage. *Woman up girl, it ain't that heavy.* She placed the satchel strap over her shoulder and pulled the suitcase along on its casters. The walk was short, and she was met at the steps to the entrance by a short balding man in a gray suit.

"Bonjour, Madame Talbert. I am Victor Haigneré, assistant administrator to the Director General, and have been assigned to be your attaché for the duration of your stay with us. May I be of assistance with your baggage?" the man began.

She paused, unused to her new cover identity, but her AIA had transmitted the correct identifiers to his security sensors. Debra then said, "Pleasure to meet your acquaintance, yes I need these placed into secure storage until I depart for my residence tonight."

Fifteen minutes later, with the luggage stowed, Victor led her into an enormous wood paneled conference room. The table at the center of the room was over ten meters in length, surrounded by dozens of office chairs behind which sat an additional ring of translator chairs bolted to the floor. Attendees had been streaming in for the past ten minutes, and now the room was full of dignitaries, ambassadors, engineers, and bureaucrats. Debra knew at least a few of these were undercover intelligence officers. Which ones? The question hardly mattered, but she found her eyes moving from face to face, evaluating.

The background murmur of the crowd began to subside as a small woman was ushered into the room by two men who were either bodyguards or more likely aides.

Marie Janssens was a pretty woman well into her middle years, with dark hair pulled back into a no-nonsense bun. Her navy-blue pantsuit was well tailored, and her measured pace to the center spot of the table showed Debbie that Marie commanded attention wherever she moved.

"Ladies and Gentlemen of the Union, thank you for clearing your schedules and joining me for this emergency meeting of the ESA," Madame Janssens began in French. Debra's artificial agent translated to her dermal patch in real time, only a second delayed.

She continued, "As you know, the appearance of the Chindi comet in our Solar System has caused somewhat of a stir in our scientific circles. For the past few weeks, we have methodically collected detailed data on this object in concert with our American allies. We are here today to inform you as to the nature of our findings and determine next steps."

Debra glanced about the crowded table; Marie had captured everyone's attention. The lights began to dim as various projectors and monitors came to life around the room. *Here it comes,* she deduced.

The European Space Agency emblem of a striped sphere containing a dot and a lowercase "e" appeared around the room on all the different screens. The Director's voice began the presentation, "Eight weeks ago it was reported that the object we have designated as Chindi was detected by an amateur astronomer in the United States. This is only partially true. The object was first detected by Jet Propulsion Labs working with TymeCorp during a disturbance in the deployment of their MarsLink nanosats. The disruption of the satellite deployment was determined to be caused by gravitational perturbations. JPL worked in coordination with Pan-STARRS, NASA, and NEO to try to find the cause, leading to a world-wide search."

Images were transitioning on the screens as Marie was speaking, showing graphics of satellite positions, early images of the comet, and initial news reports. She continued, "It was quickly determined that this comet was different. The albedo, infrared spectrometry, even the origination direction all indicate something more to this object than a mere comet." More images appeared showing analytics charting characteristics of Chindi.

Debra could feel the tension in the room rise as the level of curiosity from the audience increased. Everyone could tell Marie was leading to a revelation. The presentation continued, "Entirely without ESA authorization, Elaina Tyme, CEO of TymeCorp. redirected our Freyja probe bound for Neptune to attempt an extemporaneous intercept of Chindi." Gasps of astonishment and murmurs of outrage rippled through the assembly as this secret was revealed. Debbie knew quite a few members were aware of this information, but it was not generally known outside the ESA or the public at large. *Cat's out of the bag, but that's only the tabby,* she thought, *there's a lion still in that sack.*

"Despite the long odds against this impromptu attempt, TymeCorp's gamble has paid dividends. What you are now seeing are the first close-up images of the Chindi object," continued Marie.

The room erupted into loud exclamations and astonished conversations as the realization of what was being shown sank into the collective consciousness. On every display, what could only be recognized as something alien appeared centered within a field of blackness. Instead of the lumpy surface of an asteroid, the object was almost smooth, and pill-shaped mostly covered with ice, the exposed layer underneath was dappled in a fluctuating pattern of shine and shadow. As Debbie watched, the camera panned slowly around the object revealing a vast damaged area all along the opposite side.

Marie had paused, anticipating the outburst and now she began again with increased volume to overcome the buzz of the crowd. "As you can see, Chindi is no ordinary comet or asteroid. This time-lapse video was taken by the Freyja probe three days ago just before we lost contact with it. Ladies and Gentlemen, this changes everything. I have consulted with our engineers, and it has been determined that with the help of the Americans, we will be able to repurpose the *Kibou* for a manned landing on Chindi."

What was said next was lost in the din of noise that had now risen to drown out all attempts by Marie to reestablish control. Debra had seen enough.

So that's how they decided to play it. No mention of the thing communicating. No mention of the Russian/Chinese alliance to capture it for themselves. Burke hadn't been sure how it would go down, but this was one of his scenarios.

Debra noticed a few members had stood and begun to leave the room. No doubt they were taking the opportunity to leak this to the news before anyone else. She used this as an excuse to quietly exit without much observance, quickly followed by a surprised Victor.

"Madame, may I be of assistance?" he began.

"Yes, Victor, please summon a cab for me and fetch my belongings, I need to confer with my embassy," she said.

"Right away, of course." He gave a curt bow and turned on his heel to perform his duty.

Debra had just searched her jacket pocket for her glasses when she was almost knocked down. She heard the clatter of plastic hitting the tiled floor. Strong hands saved her from a fall. She turned her head to see a concerned Asiatic man holding her upright.

"A thousand pardons, Madam, I beg your forgiveness," he said with some anxiety. "I was not paying attention to where I was going, and it seems you and my tablet have paid the price. Are you alright?" She followed his glance to the floor where she saw his device face up, the screen shattered.

"Oh. Yes. I'm fine, you just startled me. I wasn't paying attention either," she said, a bit disoriented.

Now that she was steady, he released his grip on her arms and stepped back. He bowed and said, "I am Ryu Nishimura, technical advisor and envoy for JAXA, and today I am also a klutz." He smiled sheepishly; his grin contagious.

"Claire Talbert," she replied. "JAXA. That's the Japanese Space Exploration Agency, right?"

"Correct, Ms. Talbert. I was told there would be an announcement today at the meeting, but never dreamed it would be something such as this. I was contacting my agency and in my excitement was not paying attention to where I was going." He bent down and retrieved the broken tablet.

"I'm sorry about your device," she said regretfully.

"Think nothing of it, it was totally my fault, and I will pay dearly with the task of filing a damaged equipment form and going through my agency's archaic procurement process for a new one," Nishimura explained.

Debra laughed knowingly, "I understand what you mean, amazing how those departments are always twenty years behind the rest of the world."

A smile played across Ryu's handsome face, and he said, "I see corporate bureaucracy crosses cultural boundaries. Now if you will excuse me, I need to go dictate my report to my AI. It was a pleasure to meet you, and again I apologize for the unintended assault."

"Good to meet you as well, Mr. Nishimura," she replied.

"Please, call me Ryu." He smiled again. He paused as he turned to go and said, "I'm in town for another few days, perhaps I can buy you dinner as reparation for my clumsiness?"

Debbie hesitated. *Tempting. But not on mission.* She said, "I really appreciate your offer, but unfortunately I am completely booked for the duration of my trip. I hope your quest for device replacement bears fruit, Ryu."

He gave a slight bow, "I have no doubt it will, Ms. Talbert. May your stay here in Paris be a relaxing one, and free from further jostling by clumsy science nerds."

Debra chuckled, "Are you kidding me? This building is filled with clumsy science nerds. I'm sure this is not the last time."

"Goodbye, Claire." Ryu grinned again, turned, and walked down the spacious hallway.

This time Debbie successfully retrieved her glasses and put them on. Her vision was filled with mission reports and priority messages from the office, and breaking news reports. She sighed. *Now to deal with the repercussions from this meeting.*

She eye clicked the priority message. It was from Burke.

Hi Debra. We need to talk. The Týr AI sent an encrypted bulk package to our servers, after that we lost connection

Chapter 26: Revelations

Debra leaned over Michael looking at the jumble of code patterns he was busily modifying. She could make out some words, every now and then she would see an "if" or a "where", but generally the mess of symbols and equations mixed with odd words were all mysterious nonsense to her. Debra appraised her new lead mission tech, on loan from TymeCorp. Michael Thompson was a tall lanky man, not unhandsome, though his hunched posture and the greenish glow from his monitor were not flattering. He looked like a mad scientist, especially with his total focus on the unfathomable script scrolling down the screen. Bob had told her that Elaina Tyme personally recommended Thompson. From what she had read in his file, he was obviously qualified. She glanced down at his long pale fingers dancing across the keyboard and noticed the tattoo of a dragon curling around the wrist of his left hand.

"Nice tatt," she said.

"Huh?...Oh thanks!" he said, initially not understanding so lost in his concentration. He raised and turned his hand palm up revealing the head of the dragon, complete with bioluminescent fire being breathed into the palm of his hand. "I used to play old school Dungeons and Dragons with my grandfather as a kid. When he died, I wanted something vivid to remind me of him."

"That's a great story, and I like the fire, nice touch. You guys must have been close," Debra said.

Michael rotated in his chair, now devoting his uncanny focus to Debra, "We were. I was close to my dad too, but he and Grandpa didn't see eye to eye very much. I guess I was the one thing that brought them together on occasion. Grandpa was a techhead like me. Nerd through and through. Dad was more the outdoorsman-type, taking me out hunting and fishing. Honestly, I had more fun with Grandpa. I never really liked shooting animals. Not my thing."

Debra smiled, "More a creator than a destroyer, eh?"

"I guess you could say that," Michael replied.

"*I will second that,*" came Gustav's voice from the computer speakers.

"He did an amazing job with you Gustav," Debra said sincerely.

"*It is a good thing I am voice-only right now, Ms. Mendes, as you would absolutely see me blushing,*" Gustav replied.

"I just set up his base code DNA and he's been evolving since then. Gustav has been on his own, untouched by me for close to a year now."

"No need for formalities, gentlemen. I answer to Debra, Deb, or Debbie. I'm not picky," she said. This seemed to relax Michael somewhat as she noticed some of the tension release in his posture.

Debra gestured toward the screen filled with vibrant arcane text, "I think you are being too humble, Michael. There are many AIs operating around the world. We use a few in my line of work. But none of them show the level of sentience of which Gustav is capable. Not one."

A rosy discoloration blossomed on Michael's cheeks as he turned back to his task. "I think we got lucky. I tried a few things out of left field, and some of them ended up working really well."

The chatter of the keyboard keys began again, while Debra sat back in thought. From everything she had read about Michael, he was a programmer prodigy. He wrote his own programming language at the age of eleven, catching the attention of TymeCorp who sponsored a private school accelerated program. A few years later, an adolescent Michael was snatched up by the California Institute of Technology where he quickly earned a master's in Computer Science with a concentration in quantum programming.

TymeCorp offered him a lucrative position designing their AIs that integrated with their space program right out of college. She learned he had been an integral part of the team that designed and implemented the space Internet to Mars that was being built.

Debra shook her head and smiled, thinking *"Oh and on the side, as a hobby, he created the most advanced AI known to man. How has Elaina Tyme kept this guy under the radar for so long?"*

"Any luck determining what took out Týr?" she asked, almost hating to break his concentration once more.

This time he answered right away but kept his gaze on the screen, "Yes."

"You see it too then," Gustav's voice stated over the speaker.

Debra was confused, "Want to update me?"

"Sorry, I was just making sure." He punched some keys and turned to face her. The screen went dark, and then a glowing mustachioed face appeared on the monitor just over his shoulder. "Gustav's analysis of the code patterns matches very closely with something we have seen before."

"It seems we may have created a monster," Gustav murmured.

"What do you mean? You created that thing? How?" Debra was even more confused.

"Debra, what we witnessed from Týr's last transmission was a twisted version of the Freyja probe AI we had designated as 'Odion'. We have a copy of it in suspension back at TymeCorp headquarters," Gustav explained.

Michael cut in, "Something happened on the probe which deeply modified the structure of the AI. It was originally a scaled back copy of Gustav. We sent a command to download him to a quarantined area back at the lab so that we could perform some analysis and possibly repair him. Or at least reconstruct how he was modified."

Debra said, "And now you say there is another copy on the Chinese servers?"

"Apparently so," Michael sighed. "I'm not sure how the Chinese acquired a copy of him. Maybe they intercepted the download request, or maybe Odion had something to do with it, tricking them somehow. Regardless, he is loose and has access to the world's networks. God knows what systems are compromised by him now. Gustav is helping me come up with a way to track and scan his footprints so that we can target infected machines and pull them from the net. But we won't be able to get to the Chinese systems without them letting us in."

"I believe we will be able to determine areas compromised by Odion," Gustav interjected.

Michael looked concerned, "Maybe Gus. Maybe. But Odion just took out an NSA AI built specifically to infiltrate and overwhelm enemy systems. In his original state, Odion taking on that Týr AI should have been like a toddler trying to tackle a fullback. Now it is the other way around."

"I need to speak with my team about this. Warn them of what we are up against. Maybe they can come up with some ideas. Gustav, can you send me the data you have on this Odion so that I can forward to Fort Meade," Debra said.

"I can do you one better, Ms. Mendes. I have already forwarded both you and your team what I have learned and have created a subroutine that will walk you through how to understand the digital pointers that may allow you to detect him," said Gustav whose mustache curled upward in a genial smile.

"Thank you, Gustav." She turned to Michael, "Excuse me, Mike. I'm going to meet with my team."

"Sure, Debbie. I'm going to work with Gustav and see what we can come up with on our end. Keep us in the loop, ok?"

Debra headed for the door, reaching for her glasses. By the time she was in the hallway, the augmented reality gear had contacted two of her team back in the States. Kirshnik had been first on the call. A reconstruction of his upper torso hung semi-transparently like a specter about three meters in front of her. Julie Holland, her top AI analyst, materialized to the right of

Larson, the software auto adjusting the size and proportions of each agent to fit within the confines of her real-world corridor.

"What's up Deb?" Larson asked while Julie put on her headset. Julie was a bit of a dichotomy, an expert about artificial intelligence, but strongly against any sort of biotech to enhance herself, even something as proven as a dermal patch.

"I have information on the AI that attacked Týr," she began.

Chapter 27: First Encounters

Koda Cheveyo strode down the Rue des Martyrs careless of the world, relishing three days leave from team and duties, marveling at the complex of tangenting streets, the teeming populace and early light playing across the varied architecture of this Parisian neighborhood. He grinned despite himself, leaving off the cynicism and disdain cultivated in hopeless warzones, dreary barracks, and bureaucratic military morass. He'd never expected the beauty, color, and vibrancy of Paris. If only Uncle Joe could be here with him today.

He paused his leisurely stroll and stepped into a cafe, smiling at a young brunette woman seated at the nearest table to the entrance, she smiled back broadly. He supposed Parisians saw few Native Americans in their lives, outside of popular entertainment. He queued in line briefly at the counter. The baristas worked their levers and devices feverishly, issuing coffee at a brisk pace to the waiting patrons.

"Un café serré, s'il vous plait," he said, badly, when it was his turn. The barista, a petite blond woman who, Koda noticed, had a bad dermal patch installation in her arm that she tried covering with tattoos. She smiled and seemed appreciative of his attempt at the language. Koda wondered at the seeming commonplace attractiveness of the French. Clean living, he supposed. His bill flashed on the screen of the register, and he confirmed the transaction on his watch face, then sidled onto the bar. The strong coffee arrived shortly, and he sipped the hot elixir slowly, savoring the taste. A message from Debra flashed across his watch-face. *You should watch the news.*

A soccer match was playing on the wall screen above the various copper and steel vessels, pipes, and apparatus of the coffee brewing operation. The match cut to a breaking newscast, framing a gathering of dignitaries at the UN Headquarters in New York. He recognized the distinctive flag to the left of the officials staged on a short dais; Picasso's Guernica hung as the backdrop. A middle-aged woman with chestnut, mid-length hair stepped to the dais.

"S'il vous plaît. Le volume," he said urgently to the same barista who'd served him, and gestured upward with thumb, while pointing at the display with his other hand. She looked at him in annoyance, then recognized Koda and noted his expression. She turned to the display and pressed against the subdermal switch in her arm and spoke softly. The volume increased dramatically, drowning out the conversations on either side of Koda. The words of President Hutchins translated into French by the display quieted the remaining conversational buzz in the cafe.

"My fellow Americans. Citizens of the EU. People of the Americas, Africa, Asia and Australia," President Hutchins began. Koda noted the German Chancellor, the French President and the Indian, English and Australian Prime Ministers standing at either side of her on the dais. Much of the leadership of the free world was on hand. No meeting of the G8 or any other global conferences were in progress now. Something was happening. Koda noticed more faces turned upward to view the various world leaders, their expressions curious or concerned.

"Seven weeks ago, a new extra-solar comet was detected traveling through interstellar space into our solar system. It was quickly determined that this unknown object was not a threat for collision with Earth. Astronomers named the comet Chindi, and initially it was considered a rare interstellar visitor, of interest mainly to scientists."

"However, due to some unusual aspects of trajectory, the governments represented on this stage, the United States of America, the French Republic, the Republic of Germany, the

Commonwealth of Australia, Great Britain, and other partners, elected to re-task a probe built for the scientific inquiry of Neptune, to instead intercept with Chindi for observational purposes."

What appeared on the screen was a nebulous envelope of blue-violet coma obscuring a pill shaped nucleus at the center, bright against the background of black space. The video switched to a close-up made by the Freyja craft, showing the unnatural surface along with the slow panning reveal of the damaged side of the craft. The cafe's usual chatter of voices and clink of silverware had completely stopped. Koda glanced around at the patrons who were now unanimously focused on the broadcast.

"Chindi, the Chindi Anomaly, as you can clearly see by the video is not a natural phenomenon," President Hutchins said. The press conference returned to the political luminaries on their small stage. Their faces were grave. The President continued, "While a typical comet is about 10 kilometers in size, our scientists estimate that Chindi is at least 5 times as large." Koda stole a glance towards the barista and noted her left hand shaking as it covered her mouth and lower jaw.

"People of Earth we must conclude the truth of our senses, and what our best scientists are telling us," President Hutchins said. She paused for emphasis. "Chindi is an artifact of alien origin."

Koda heard gasps, subdued cursing, and frantic low conversations around him erupt in the crowded cafe. The president continued, "The nations we represent will be unified in our investigation and study of Chindi. Planning is underway for what may come in the days, weeks, and months ahead. Please have faith, and hope. The best minds on the planet, scientific and otherwise, are being brought to bear on understanding the nature of Chindi and the change it will cause for humanity. We will be transparent but will spare no effort or expense to understand what this means for all the people of this world, and to determine the best course of action. God bless us all."

With a gabble of unanswered questions from the assembled journalists the press conference adjourned, the political elite with stoic faces made their way from the stage, back to the chambers of deliberation within the UN Headquarters. The display switched to the obligatory talking heads who began disseminating a play by play of what had just occurred.

Koda stole one last glance at the barista, who was speaking to a co-worker and gesticulating wildly. She looked back at him as he stepped out away from the cafe, her gaze frightened and questioning.

Koda strode briskly down the boulevard, with purpose, summoning a cab as he went. The autocar pulled up and waited for him as he left the pedestrian section, the gull wing door opening at his approach. He transmitted his destination, using the payment code Debra had provided. Untraceable she'd said, insisting his team use these surreptitious methods while in Europe. There seemed to be a strange hush on the street as he left. Traffic, automotive and pedestrian, was subdued. The ride out of the city and into the suburbs went by quickly, his brain failing to register his route or the sights of Paris. Eventually the car turned into a modest but gated private driveway, U shaped, leading into a small courtyard laid out in brown and orange cobblestone, and a modest chateau of grey stone wall with slate roof. The cab stopped and opened its door for his exit. He stepped out, and two security men he'd noted as the car entered the gates stepped forward to intercept him.

"Major Koda Cheveyo," he said, offering his hand for a biometric scan. The security men processed him quickly and nodded for him to continue. He walked to the front of the manor, hauling the heavy oak door open and stepping inside.

"Koda." Debbie came forward to greet him as he entered, leaving her conversation with a tall Anglo. Debbie's face was flushed, but her smile was genuine. She seemed worried. The pale man was inscrutable, a mop of dark curls surrounded his youthful face.

"This is Michael Thompson. From TymeCorp. He's been assigned to help us with our mission."

"I didn't know they'd go public so soon," Koda said, ignoring the stranger for the moment. "You could have warned me Debbie."

"It was coming out and the President needed to get in front of it. There is a great deal I haven't been able to brief you on Major. And much more I don't yet know."

"Not sure we should be discussing it with contractors present," Koda said pointedly, nodding toward Michael.

The man stiffened, face hardening. "Are you kidding me? I'm not the one in the dark here. I'm not sure how much detail the ops team needs to know." Michael said.

"I'll decide what my team needs to know," Koda responded sharply, his attention moving from Debra to the younger man.

"I was referring to you, not your team," Michael replied agitatedly. "The situation with Chindi is highly technical and I don't want to burden you with information you can't process, and don't need to know." Michael moved toward Koda, so that the men were separated by a half meter of space. Koda was amused, the tech had a bit of a temper. Even though Cheveyo had him by twenty kilos, the kid didn't seem to either notice or care.

"Cut the shit out," Debra said. "Jesus. I'm the one who decides who gets to know what, and currently Michael knows more than you do."

Koda glanced at Michael and noted the surprise on the other's face.

"How about some coffee?" She offered. "We have a great deal to discuss."

Koda nodded agreement and followed as Debra walked from the sitting room to the kitchen. Michael followed them in, seeming to have cooled off and now subdued in thought. The decor was old but impeccable, the floors, wainscoting and trim of dark burnished wood, the kitchen tiled in large travertine diamonds. A stainless coffee service sat on the counter. Debra poured from three white ceramic mugs. Koda sipped his out of politeness, he already felt jittery from the coffee he'd drank at the cafe. He knew from experience too much caffeine had a detrimental impact on his ability to shoot tight groups on a target. He avoided overdoing it out of caution.

"We'll need to learn to work together," Debra said. "Michael will serve as a lead engineer on the project that lands your team safely on Chindi," she added, looking directly at Koda. "I'm informed that the AIA he has created is revolutionary. It will pilot and manage the lander sub-systems, provide scientific analysis, and help you plan and respond to whatever you'll face out there."

"I've worked with AI Agents for a few years now Debbie, in training, and in combat," Koda said skeptically. "They have their uses, but their capability never measures up to the promises made."

"You haven't worked with Gustav," Michael interjected.

"It has a name?" Koda asked.

"Yes. And a personality, with a unique point of view. And a fierce ability to solve intractable problems," Michael replied.

"Debra, what is this?" Koda asked, beginning to feel exasperated. "We need a reliable, operationally proven system. Not some geek's fantasy." Michael stiffened and the muscles along his jaw flexed, as if he were struggling to bite back a response.

"I used to be as skeptical as you. But I've seen Gustav's capabilities firsthand. He's... startling. Regardless, we have our order on this. You'll have time to put Gustav through his paces before the launch."

"Skepticism in all things is warranted Ms. Mendes," Gustav said, his modulated baritone voice spoke in a US mid-western accent over the sound system of the chateau.

"Is that your system? Your AI?" Koda asked Michael.

"Nu' tuwat Gustav yan maatsiwa, Koda Cheveyo. Michael helped make me. But I am owned by no one," Gustav said.

"Heve' machine," Koda replied reflexively, the Hopi language deeply familiar and affecting him as he spoke the greeting. He felt chagrin at how unpracticed the words came from his lips, and frustration and embarrassment that this brought a longing for home.

As he considered, he grew angry. *What right had this machine to the tongue of the fathers?* Koda's face felt hot.

"Major," Debra said, uncertain.

Koda considered, and in the brief seconds before responding calmed his heart rate using the same relaxation techniques he used before attempting a difficult rifle shot. "I'll need to work with him, to understand his capability. Will you facilitate this?" He looked at Michael, who broke his gaze.

"I think you are already getting a taste of what Gus is serving. He's a good guy, Koda. We work well as a team, and I'm sure once you get to know him, you'll agree," Michael said. *Impressive,* Michael thought, *Gustav actually prepped for this guy, learned some of his language and went through his psych profile to get past his defenses. I would have sworn he couldn't pull that off. A month ago, he couldn't have.*

Ghost affixed Michael with his full no bullshit stare, "A smart AIA I can understand. I know and have worked with Debbie for years, but what about you, Mike? What do you bring to the table?"

"Knowledge of the situation, experience with deep space missions, and a Doctorate in Computer Science," Michael responded immediately, unperturbed by Koda's intimidation tactic. He continued, "My team was one of the first to detect Chindi by perturbations of the nanosat positions when we were deploying the MarsLink project. Gus and I have been working with a group of TymeCorp engineers at Jet Propulsion Labs since then to try and determine what we are dealing with."

"What do you know that the United Nations media blitz isn't telling the public?"

Mike glanced quickly to Debra for approval, who gave a brief nod, then continued, "We think there might be some intelligence guiding Chindi. It has made course corrections and transmissions."

"It's communicating?" Koda's expression changed to one of surprise.

"Only once that we know of, with our probe, during its scans. Right before we lost contact with it for a time."

"What did it say?"

Gustav interjected, "*Nothing really, it just repeatedly looped the Arecibo transmission in graduated electromagnetic spectrums.*"

"Arecibo transmission," Ghost repeated, "Where have I heard that before?"

Mike set his coffee down and said, "back in the Twentieth Century, the scientists in a project called SETI sent a long-range transmission from the Arecibo radio telescope in Puerto Rico into deep space."

Koda nodded, "I remember something about that, an encoded sequence of bytes in multiple escalating frequencies I think."

"Um… yeah…" Michael continued, a bit surprised, "It was a shot in the dark, essentially, they were trying to find out if there were aliens out there capable of responding. It seems whoever or whatever is on board Chindi intercepted that message and decided to come visit."

Koda shook his head, "Whether predator or prey, you don't shout at night in the wilderness."

"Yeah, this was back in the '70s, pre-'Dark Forest' theory," Mike said.

"Gentlemen, I hate to break up this bonding moment, but unfortunately we have a more pressing matter to discuss," Debra said, "we placed an advanced surveillance AIA into the Russian network a few weeks ago to gather intel on why the Russo-Sino Aerospace Consortium were prepping the Cosmodrome for an early launch window. Unfortunately, we've now lost that asset, it's gone dark."

"What happened?" Koda asked, appalled. He thought of Mack, still recuperating from wounds received during the insertion mission.

She let out a sigh, "It went offline a few days ago. But not before sending an encrypted final transmission to our team back at Langley. We managed to decrypt it a few hours ago. Our AIA came under attack by a previously unknown AI entity." She looked to Michael.

He took his cue, "Well... not completely unknown."

Gustav's voice chimed in over the house speakers, *"Patterns in the attack point back to parts of my function compositions. Sort of a computer DNA fingerprint that indicates the AIA was related to me."*

"How?" was all that Koda said.

Michael spoke. "Our probe AI was a pared down copy of Gustav. We downloaded it for a post-mortem after it went haywire during the mission. We believe the Chinese intercepted that download and made their own copy. We believe the probe AI was corrupted somehow by Chindi, modified in some unknown way. And we think the Chinese may have let it loose."

"So, you're telling me that a space probe software managed to take down a top-of-the-line military hardened spy AIA?" Koda was incredulous.

Michael said, "To begin with, it was a stripped-down copy of Gus. And there was something else about it. The codebase had been modified significantly. I couldn't understand anything about those modified areas."

"What do you mean you couldn't understand it? I thought you were some sort of super programmer."

Mike's tone was emphatic, "I mean no one could understand it, not even Gustav. Those parts of the code look like randomized bits, just corrupted data patches. The AI shouldn't even be cohesive, let alone this strong. I don't understand how it works. Not yet anyway."

"Michael is correct," Gustav said, "but we are currently analyzing a copy of the download in our labs at TymeCorp Headquarters."

"So how dangerous is this thing?" Koda asked.

If the probe AI is corrupted with alien technology, then it may present an existential threat to humanity, Major. Gustav said helpfully.

Chapter 28: Training

"Watch it, Jake!" Koda shouted, though too late. Jake had lost control of the half ton parabolic antenna which floated straight into the stacked power generators. The team sniper dangled from a harness, hanging impotently above the precision air bearing floor.

"Shucks!" Jake said, chagrined as the stack tipped over crashing to the floor.

"Harder than it looks, ain't it?" Alan said while leaning casually on the boundary railing.

Jake said, "Kiss my ass, Ace. You'll get your turn. Ghost, can we set this up and try again?"

"Sure, Jake," Koda said patiently. He suppressed the growing irritation he felt, reminding himself that a year's worth of training had been compressed into three months. "Just remember, mass in space is easier to move but harder to stop."

The Ghostwalkers were just one of several operations teams training for the mission. The Europeans had three other experienced teams competing for a mission slot. The retasked *Kibou* had space enough for a small platoon, equipment, and scientists. In addition to the scientific retinue, the allies were concerned with the possibility that the Russo-Sino alliance would soon be able to launch their own mission and wanted a capable defensive force in place to protect their interests.

This exercise required the team take turns moving cumbersome objects across the frictionless floor. Air hoses pushed compressed air through the bottom of the antenna mockup, essentially creating the world's largest air hockey table.

Several techs were setting the fake power generators back into place while Jake's ceiling tether moved him back to the beginning of the course.

"Do we have to wear these asshat costumes to do this? I look like a giant marshmallow," Jake complained. "I thought we were getting a new model spacesuit."

"About that, "Koda said, "I've been told the new suit prototypes will be ready next week. Until then, we are stuck with what we have."

"I hope so. We have less than a month before launch," Jones said. Mack was next on deck and Ted was helping him with his suit.

"We would've had them by now except they had to source more material for Ted's suit," Mack joked.

"That can't be it, they had plenty of material left over from the crotch of your suit," Ted's baritone shot back smoothly. This provoked gales of laughter from the rest of the team. While the men recovered, the techs in the room had reset the course for Jake's second try.

Those suits were no joke, Koda thought.

Koda had seen the new suit prototypes that were being developed. They were a wonder of human achievement, utilizing shaped memory alloy coils to maintain pressure, aerogel for thermal insulation, and woven graphene nano-layers for plated protection. The new suits were just centimeters thick, and the bulky marshmallow look would soon be a thing of the past. Koda had taken a few materials science courses back at West Point, but these latest developments were mind blowing.

His thoughts brought him back to his college days. Long nights of physics homework coupled with mornings and weekends with drill left him with little time to enjoy a social life. There were occasional relationships early on, his unusual heritage coupled with his athletic frame were a powerful combination to young, interested college girls. But that had all been before Uncle Joe got sick.

Koda remembered the morning he got the text. He was leading PT drills out on the campus track when his wristband started buzzing. It was his cousin Mansea, "Koda, Joe is dying, you'll need to come quickly if you want to see him again."

He had made arrangements as quickly as he could and caught an evening flight to Denver. Koda drove through the night in a rental car to get home, to be there in time. He had known Joe's cancer would kill him before leaving home for the semester, but the immediacy of the thing shook him to his core. Joe, despite his flaws, the anger, and the booze, had been the closest person to a father he had known. And he felt Joe pass, like a spirit, as he drove up onto First Mesa from the east, the sun rising behind him, knowing he was too late and would never tell Joe what their relationship had meant to him.

The next days were a blur in his memory, but he recalled distinctly the day-long service, and the young marines standing at attention alongside the casket for hours, honoring a warrior they'd never known. He could still see the presentation of the folded flag to Joe's wife Rae, and the eagle feather placed in Joe's dead hand at the end. Somewhere in the blur, in the sadness, he decided to complete his degree knowing it would be the last of schooling for him. To work as a physicist would require years of dedication to the quiet struggle of academia, a financial commitment the military would happily pay for knowing they'd get a weapons scientist at the end. Yet Koda knew he had a different path to follow, the warrior's path, so that someday he might grasp the eagle's feather as he stepped from this world to the next.

Cheveyo's mind was drawn back into the present with Mack now hovering over the glass-like floor. Jake had successfully connected the antenna dish to the mock power generators and the techs were undoing all his painstaking work and resetting the simulation. They had been at this for over four hours, and only three of his men had passed so far. Tomorrow they were practicing spacewalks in the neutral buoyancy lab, the day after that it was weapons training in simulated low gravity which amounted to firing weapons while suspended by an insane wiring harness.

They had been training constantly since arriving here at the facilities of the European Astronaut Center. He just hoped they could get everything squared away before launch. He was worried. All this effort was just a repurposing of a Mars colonization mission, and in the scramble to outpace the Russian Chinese alliance attempt to get to Chindi first, it made the whole experience feel very slipshod. The latest test firings of the *Kibou* had been very successful, however rushed launches could always have issues. After the U.N. announcement, Koda had heard that the greatest minds and AIs in the industries of the western world were working on having a trouble-free flight. The mission was on schedule, barely.

He could hear Uncle Joe's words echo from the past, *"Focus only on what you can control, let the rest of your worries flow around you like a river."*

Whatever happened, it was not going to be the Ghostwalkers that held up the mission, he would make sure of that.

Chapter 29: Proposal

Paris, France

Michael walked with Lara down the Rue de Rivoli on their way to dinner from their visit to the Louvre, their hands held as they strolled through the unusually warm afternoon air. Michael was going to summon an autocar, but of course Lara wanted the exercise, absorbing the atmosphere. He had to admit her instincts were spot on. The spring breeze was brisk and the sights and sounds of Paris nightlife were much better than being cramped in an autocar breathing recycled air. They passed a flower cart vendor just shutting down for the evening. Michael admired Lara's form as she bent over to smell the wisteria on the cart. While she was occupied, he grabbed a bunch of spring flowers, his account debited automatically via his near field personal id tag. He quickly hid them behind his back before she turned.

"Don't they smell wonderful?" she said. "I could smell them almost half a block away!"

"Absolutely. But I would rather smell the lasagna on my plate. I'm starving! Let's let the flower lady close shop and go get something to eat."

Lara rolled her eyes, "You and food. Far be it for me to get between chow and your stomach."

They stepped off the curb when the light changed and crossed the street. Michael presented the flowers to her when they made it to the other sidewalk.

"Mike! You shouldn't have!" she exclaimed.

"Now you can keep smelling the flowers, and I can eat," he said, secretly delighted by the expression on her face. With the sun setting, the air had chilled, and he put his arm around her shoulders sharing his warmth. She held her flowers close to her chest allowing the scents to waft upwards.

The streetlamps had begun to self-light at their preprogrammed time. As they passed Le Palais Royal, they watched the multitude of blinking lights lift off from somewhere within the royal gardens off to their right. In order to reinforce the "City of Light" moniker, swarms of drones were launched from the roofs of the historic public buildings around the urban landscape. All around the city these flying clusters of autonomous drones began their nightly dance in the skies above the metropolis, simulating fireworks or animated images with their light shows. The couple strolled leisurely down the boulevard, under the canopy of twinkling lights rising around them. Though the avenue was wide, it was still filled with tourists, families, and even a group of nuns dressed in white habits and robes, their path in the direction of the Sacré-Cœur Cathedral.

They walked for a while with Michael confidently guiding them through the maze of streets. Gustav had been sub audibly giving Michael directions to keep him from getting lost.

Lara said, "You mentioned lasagna? Does that mean you want Italian, here in the heart of France?"

"We've eaten French cuisine plenty. I'm ready for something different. Trust me, I know a place," Michael said.

"*Turn right at the next intersection, Michael. It is called Piccola Fetta d'Italia,*" Gustav informed Michael.

"Lara, I'm sorry I haven't been around much since we got here. It's work, and it's important."

She stopped and looked up at him. "Mike, I knew you were going to be busy before we left the States. I'm ok with it."

They arrived at the restaurant at the height of dinner time. There was a crowd of would-be diners standing or waiting on benches in the small courtyard out front.

"Maybe we should try another place? I saw a few on the way here that looked pretty good," Lara suggested.

"Don't worry, baby. I got this. Let me just talk with the hostess," he said more confidently than he felt.

"Not to worry, Michael. I have already informed the hôtesse about your reservations and I have been monitoring restaurant traffic flow from the street cameras around the building for the past two hours. I calculate your table should be ready within the next 7.5 minutes," Gustav assured him privately through the dermal patch.

He left her briefly to speak with the lady at the stand silently telling Gustav, "I hope your calculations are right. This place is packed."

His fears were unfounded as his AI's forecast quickly proved true. They were seated and enjoying bruschetta with a five-year-old Gewurztraminer within a few minutes.

"Thank you, Michael. I'm glad you were able to take today and spend it with me. The Louvre was amazing! I can't believe the amount of art and history in that building."

"Hard to imagine the time and effort those people spent on all of that. I guess with not much tech there wasn't much else to do."

"Mike. Are you not impressed by what you saw in there?" she asked, sipping from her glass.

"It was impressive, sure, based on the tools and knowledge available at the time, Lara. But compared to today, it just seems quaint."

"Quaint? How so?" She looked incredulous.

Michael blundered on, "I could scan a human model, have an AIA help me position it just so, give the 3D printers a little time while I'm out having a coffee, and voila, out pops a David statue. Not only that, but I could also scale production and produce a hundred such statues, all modeled in different positions if I wanted. I don't see the need to revere all those antiques like they do. They are fine for historical reference, but they are like cave paintings compared to what can be produced today."

"But would your statues be carved from a single block of marble? Imagine the skill required to pull something that beautiful from a big lump of stone."

"No. Not marble, but if you wanted polyamide, ceramic, titanium, or gold I could probably swing it."

"Damn, Mike, where is your sense of art appreciation? Did you not take any art history or visual communication classes back at Caltech?"

"My electives were comprised of classic American Cinema and Game Theory," he replied. "Ask me about combinatorial non-zero-sum games or the nuances of Tarantino dialogue, I'm your man. When it comes to art. I'm visually ignorant." He smiled and shrugged.

"Not just visually." She eyed him, raising a reproving eyebrow.

"How so?" he said, stalling for time, trying to remember where he had mis-stepped.

"Come on, Mike! It's about the human element. Art and science are methods to get to some of the underlying questions for humanity. Where did we come from, where are we going? It's about what people can accomplish themselves, and not using some machine to make it. It is a celebration of humanity, not technology." Lara's alabaster cheeks were slightly flushed from the wine.

Mike caught himself. "Old Michael" would have reminded Lara that a hammer and chisel were machines that Michelangelo used to accomplish his goals, but tonight "New Michael" was going to be romantically smarter and instead said, "I see your point, Lara. I hadn't looked at it that way before now."

She laughed, "I bet." She pushed her remaining bite of the bruschetta into his mouth and followed it with a kiss.

His lasagna arrived with her Tuscan vegetarian pasta and the conversation died off as they began their dinner in earnest. They shared a tiramisu for dessert while finishing off their bottle of wine, and Michael suggested they walk off some of the food with a late-night stroll. Gustav resumed his directions, guiding the couple to the banks of the Seine. The street traffic had begun to die down, but the river contained several floating discos, restaurants, and cafes. Up ahead the Eiffel Tower knifed through the night sky with its amazing light display easily outshining the surrounding city lights. Hand in hand they soon crossed the Pont d'Iena which brought them to the base of the giant structure. The grassy lawns of the Champ de Mars were scattered with people enjoying the night. Children's laughter drew their attention to a small crowd gathered around a performing street mime.

Suddenly, Michael stopped. Lara turned concerned. She saw Michael looked anxious but was smiling.

"Mind if we stop for a rest? We've been walking for a while now," he said.

"Sure, Mike. This is a great place for a break." She thought she heard a humming noise from above.

"Hey, check that out," he said and looked toward the tower.

She turned and the light pattern of the Eiffel Tower had changed to a pattern of movement that pulled the eye skyward. In the darkness above, colored lights began winking into existence, slowly at first, then gathering speed. Soon nearly every flying drone in the city was clustered above Michael and Lara.

The many thousands of flying LEDs resolved into the largest screen earth had ever known and it showed a picture of the two of them taken on their very first date.

Lara looked from the sky, then to Michael, confusion painting her features.

"Lara, we've been together for a while now. I love you. I've been thinking about you... us... a lot lately. I've come to the conclusion, the certainty, that I want to spend the rest of my life with you," he said, then quickly dropped to one knee.

"Lara, will you marry me?" he said, producing a ring that sparkled with the brilliance of the sky above.

The drones reconfigured themselves to a lit skywriting echo of the words he had just spoken to her.

The people all around the grounds of the Champ de Mars had fallen silent, the unusual light show commanding everyone's attention.

Lara was stammering something, tears streaming down her face. Finally, with effort, what she was trying to say came out with a shout.

"Yes!"

She pulled him up into her arms and kissed him passionately. The surrounding crowd erupted into cheers as the drones in the sky exploded into a firework display to rival New Year's Eve. Some drones equipped with speakers began playing her favorite songs all throughout the park. The fireworks syncopated to the beats and swells of the music.

"Michael, this is amazing," he heard Lara whisper in his ear.

She kissed him again, then turned to watch the simulated firework display.

"Thanks, Gus. Buddy it worked like magic. I owe you a big one," Michael whispered.

"The pleasure was all mine, my friend. And don't worry, the French authorities will be none the wiser, I'm returning the drones to their assigned patterns in a few minutes and wiping their positional telemetry from the server logs," Gustav replied happily.

Chapter 30: IGOR

Cologne, Germany

The ESA's weapons training center was located in a hastily converted warehouse on the outskirts of Cologne. The high ceiling was open on the interior, girded by long steel structural beams running the length of the facility, with insufficient air conditioning units placed along the beams humming unimpressively as they failed to heat the voluminous space sufficiently.

Koda smiled as the Ghostwalkers approached the long firing bench. A series of five bulky weapons were laid across sandbags. Attached to each of the heavy guns was a meter-long hose connecting to a small cylinder of compressed gas.

Jake looked down at the weapons. "What the hell is this? Air rifles?"

"Gentlemen," Koda smirked, "this is IGOR. Welcome to your first day of micro-g weapons training. He patted the twin can-like shapes set atop one of the guns, "Helical magazines and 3.8x30mm caseless projectiles allow for high capacity, two-hundred shots before reload. The barrel is a multilayered nickel-aluminum-molybdenum alloy, one hundred times more heat resistant than the normal high-strength steel. Why don't you take a few shots and tell me what you think?"

All the men exchanged looks of bewilderment and amusement but followed orders and knelt behind the sandbags, leveling the oddly shaped gun barrels toward the paper targets hung on the black rubber backstop. Each let loose a volley of rounds downrange. The slow "thup thup thup" of the tiny projectiles exiting the barrels was entirely unimpressive. Instead of brass casings ejecting in a pinging cascade, the only noticeable indicator of fire was the swirl of wind around the sleeves and through the hair of the men.

"Thoughts?" Koda asked as the magazines emptied.

"Major, I think your IGOR stands for *Ineffective Gun Oddly Ridiculous*," Ace replied.

Mack barked out a short laugh and the few snickers died down as everyone caught Koda's stony gaze.

"Ace, have you been trying to come up with that this whole time? You should have focused a bit more on your shooting, and your groupings could look more like Jake's," Koda said.

Jake chimed in, "The trigger isn't bad. And no recoil to speak of."

Jones' deep voice piped in, "Chief, what are we planning on doing with these things? The rounds are smaller than a pellet gun."

Koda glanced over at Ted and noticed how small the grip was in the man's giant hands. "Guys, maybe we need a better demonstration." Koda walked to the corrugated metal wall of the warehouse and flipped a light switch. A darkened corner of the warehouse lit, and the men could make out the strange contraption of a harness hung from a tangle of steel wires and springs. The entire apparatus dangling limply from what looked like a mechanical sled suspended beneath the structural steel beams of the ceiling.

"Ace, get ready for your debut. Today you get to play the role of Pinocchio," Koda ordered. "Strap him in boys, I think they left us an instruction sheet."

A few minutes of confusion, complaining and curse-filled comments followed. At the end, Ace was suitably buckled into the harness, a look of chagrin on his face. He took a few experimental steps, awkwardly bounding short distances across the padded track laid across the concrete floor, the sled tracking noiselessly above him. His sharp face broke into a grin of enjoyment, as he took more vigorous steps then leaps, soon jumping from foot to foot and covering twenty feet at a bound. He reached the end of the warehouse and turned, the coupling from his harness to the sled pivoting with him. The sergeant bounded back to the team whooping with each launch airborne, the joy plain on his face.

"The scientists tell me this contraption simulates our best guess for Chindi's gravity," Koda said. He reached into a weapons crate near his feet, withdrawing a standard battle rifle and tossing it to Alan. "Go ahead, give it a test fire. Use full auto."

Alan's smile never wavered, "You got it, boss," confidently flicking the selector to full and bringing the weapon to his shoulder. The targeting reticule appeared in his goggles and his MAIA gave him the green 'on target' go ahead. He began firing a burst of rounds aiming at one of the targets, but the burst immediately swung him around in a semicircle, pitching him up and to the right. The team instinctively dropped beneath the muzzle of the still firing weapon and splayed out on the warehouse floor.

"Ceasefire!" Jake and Mack shouted simultaneously, but Alan had already stopped, halfway through his magazine of thirty rounds, a look of confusion and embarrassment on his face as he came to rest in his original position having spun a full 360 degrees.

"Anyone hit?" Alan demanded, frantically fumbling at the buckles of the harness.

"We're fine, Ace. Your MAIA locked the smart gun when it detected possible friendly fire," Koda said, still standing. "How about you try this instead? Get him untangled." Cheveyo walked to the bench and retrieved one of the IGOR rifles, with the hose and gas canister still attached. He handed Alan the weapon and retrieved the still warm battle rifle. "While not as clever as Corpsman King's definition, IGOR actually stands for Inertia-less Gas Operated Rifle. Go full auto again Alan."

Alan gave him a questioning look. Most of the other Ghostwalkers, now standing, took a healthy few steps to Alan's rear. Jake held his spot, Koda noted.

Alan fired a volley of rounds toward the target, the steady thup of the projectiles mixed with the hiss of the gas propellant sounding like the percussion of a factory floor and unlike combat. The paper target in front of Alan fluttered with his grouping of shots, all clustered within a two-inch radius as the rounds zipped through.

"What we have here," Koda held another IGOR in his hand, "is a highly miniaturized light-gas gun. What IGOR gives us is consistent grouped fire in micro-G."

Ace paused in his assault on the nearly shredded target to listen. The bulky magazine clattered to the floor as he clacked in a new one from the pile on the sandbag.

Koda continued, "The gun vents the helium gas around and from the rear of the barrel in an AI managed timing sequence. It won't spin you like a standard round. The gas release serves a dual purpose. There are microscopic holes along the barrel that are computer controlled for opening and closing during firing. Gas is expelled out of the barrel from these as the projectile moves through the rifling. This micro-venting serves to help the gun mitigate heat dissipation in a vacuum during high rates of fire and counterbalances the inertia from the recoil."

"Sir, all due respect, I know how you like all your sciencey stuff," Mack said. "But what good does it do to stay on target if we can't put a man down?"

"Good question. Here is the answer they gave me when I asked it. We don't need to put our enemies down. All we need to do is rip their space suits, the vacuum of space will do the rest."

Chapter 31: Cayenne Flight

The nine-hour journey from Paris to Cayenne had so far been an uneventful commercial flight, though Koda was impressed that the Ghostwalkers had been allocated nearly the entire first-class section, courtesy of the European Space Agency. A small contingent of ESA members and some fellow astronauts had come along on the flight, with the remainder scheduled to follow in the morning. Mack certainly enjoyed it, hijacking the beverage cart from the flight attendant, and becoming the inflight bartender. Koda let the men enjoy themselves, it was a long flight, and they had worked hard these past months. Juan pulled out his portable speaker and cranked his tunes, allowing everybody to contribute to the song shuffle.

Across the aisle, on the ESA side of first class, three Asian men sat pointedly ignoring the antics of Mack, who was juggling mini bottles of alcohol, and Juan doing the robot dance to his Latin-Rap music. Koda noticed one of the men pantomiming Juan, while the other two laughed.

Two rows behind the men from JAXA were a striking woman with long dark hair smiling and talking with a small red-haired lady wearing a set of thick glasses. Ghost had met them briefly during astronaut orientation. He couldn't recall their names, but knew they were scientists from Wales and Ireland respectively.

A barking laugh caught Koda's attention. Behind the women were two large Swedes, one man wearing round spectacles was producing the laughter. His companion pointed to Mack who looked panicked. Alan had tossed another bottle into his rapidly whirling menagerie. Both men were watching the festivities. Ted made a welcoming gesture with a deck of playing cards that had appeared in his hand. The two men nodded, stood, and soon a poker game had broken out.

Cheveyo was lost in thoughts of the distant past and the near future when a glass of golden-brown liquid was placed gently on the tray in front of him. The trio of ice cubes within the highball bobbed and swirled enticingly, bringing him back to the present. "I think we were due a drink together Boss," Jake said. From the slight slur in his southern drawl, this wasn't his first jigger of Wild Turkey tonight. Koda smiled broadly, "I believe you are correct, and much appreciated."

"Permission to speak frankly, sir?" Lieutenant Grayson asked.

"Come on, Jake, we are relaxing over a drink. What's on your mind?"

"I'm a little worried about this mission. I signed up knowing I might go anywhere on this Earth, but I never thought I might buy the farm when there wouldn't be a farm under my feet."

"You worried about us not bringing you back, Jake?"

"A little."

"We don't leave people behind, you know that."

"What if none of us come back, Ghost? Shit, that rocket is sitting on top of a few hundred thousand highly explosive gallons of fuel, and we are blasting off to go visit aliens."

"Then you will die in the company of your brothers, on the noblest mission humankind has ever attempted," the Hopi warrior said sagely.

Koda took a long swallow and watched the tension ease a little from Jake's face.

"Yeah, I reckon you're right. We all gotta go sometime. Better'n pissin' myself in a rest home someday." The normally sharp eyes of the sniper were unfocused, drowsy. "I'm just used to a comfy position up in a tree, or up on a hill. Can't see much use for a sniper where we're going."

"Oh, you never know, Jake. Remember, there could be some little unfriendly green men up there. And just think, where we are going... it's the ultimate high ground," Koda grinned.

"To high ground," Jake toasted, returning the smile. He tossed back the last finger of whiskey and set the glass down hard on the plastic tray. Koda did the same, savoring the flavor and burn. Jake yawned and leaned back into the plush seat tipping his ball cap down to rest the bill on his nose. "Wake me when we're there," he mumbled, already drifting off.

Koda turned his gaze back to the moonlit clouds below the plane. It wasn't long before he heard Jake's light snores begin a rhythmic cadence beside him.

The poker game a few rows in front of him was getting serious. Juan folded and left Alan facing off against Ted. The Swedes had long ago given up, realizing they were out of their depth against these seasoned veterans. Alan was leaning over the back of the seat facing Juan and Ted. The pot was a motley pile of energy bars, bags of chips, and some mini bottles of rum resting on the tray between them. Alan caught Koda's eye trying to read him, he knew that Koda had a clear line of sight to Ted's hand. Koda gave him no answers, returning the gaze stone faced. Alan raised an eyebrow, eyes widening subtly begging for a tell. The commander just smiled sardonically at Ted's full house and turned back to the window.

"I'll see your nabs and raise you an entire pack of gum, big man," he heard Alan say confidently.

"And I'm calling you," Ted said, matching Alan's gum gamble easily, "what you got?"

"Three of a kind, Queens."

"Full house, kid. This just ain't your game, man. Maybe we should try something more your speed like Rummy or Old Maid," Ted suggested.

"Jesus Christ on a cracker. Did you mark these cards? How do you keep winning?"

"I got skills, son. Keep practicing, maybe when you get to be my age, you'll have the hang of it. And I can retire rich off these lessons I'm giving."

"Rich? More like a fat hombre," Juan said pointedly, referring to the junk food and liquor making up the winnings.

Koda tuned out the banter and the snores and turned his thoughts to the upcoming mission. They were still a few weeks ahead of the Russian launch by all intelligence sources Debra had at her department's disposal, but he knew things could delay or the Russians could launch earlier than expected. It was a close race, and who got there first could decide the terms of engagement. The ESA, Michael and Gustav had assured him that the rendezvous with Chindi was plotted precisely. Then why was his spirit unsettled? The closer launch day came, the worse he felt about climbing aboard that rocket. Maybe it was just that he wasn't cut out to be an astronaut, but he didn't think so. It wasn't about space, just something didn't feel right. It was the same feeling he had before he got the news about Uncle Joe.

He felt something bad was coming, and despite the liquor and distractions the feeling wouldn't go away.

Chapter 32: Projects

Irony. That was what came to Elaina's mind as her avatar sat in a virtual code review with her technical team. Ironic that she was championing the design of an engineered computer virus, while she was the victim of an engineered virus of the biological kind.

The simulated conference room was full. Twenty-two of her senior level engineers had been haranguing over next steps, and no one could agree on the path forward. She let them continue as her mind wandered back to her days as a young engineer working at NASA.

Preparations for Mars colonization were just getting underway back then. Much research and technical solutions were geared toward protection of colonists from high energy particles during their months-long journey to the red planet. From miniature shipboard magnetospheres to orbital shields between the Earth and Mars, those early days were rife with all types of ideas for colonization success.

The issue had vexed space scientists since the Apollo program, how to subject humans to prolonged space travel without unacceptably increasing their likelihood of suffering from a range of cancers. One of those solutions was a retrovirus designed to repair human DNA sequences damaged by high energy particles during space travel, or on planets lacking a magnetosphere. The engineer was a genius in retrospect, and the work important, but a lab technician had been sloppy and failed to contain the virus within the lab. Elaina and a few hundred others were exposed before the source was traced and the facility sterilized through UV light exposure. All those exposed, except for Elaina, experienced minor, or no symptoms.

Something in that weak, barely put together virus had triggered a disastrous effect on her autoimmune system. She had left the building that evening feeling great. She'd woken with flu-like symptoms and called in sick. They found her curled up on the floor of her apartment three days later, lying in her urine, blind in one eye, disoriented and dehydrated. She had very nearly died. Fortunately, the NASA team put two and two together and managed to track down what had happened. Their quick efforts had saved her life. She let a sardonic smile touch her lips and thought dryly, *"Well, they'd extended it for a bit anyway."*

Neuromyelitis Optica was the diagnosis the doctors gave her. Treatable with corticosteroids to lessen symptoms, but incurable. Her vision returned after months of treatment, but the disease remained chronic, manifesting in new ways. Aside from the blindness, the time she lost mobility in her legs was the worst. She missed running the most, even more than sex. Sure, the robotic harness allowed her to walk, but it was dreadfully painful to wear. She preferred the wheelchair these days.

One benefit came of it at least, it focused her mind, it drove her with intent. She was on borrowed time and knew it. She took risks that paid dividends and allowed for technological leaps forward. Now here she was, owner of one of the fastest growing multinational companies in the Western Hemisphere. TymeCorp had 60% of the quantum computing processor market, thanks to her investments in research and more importantly her selection and cultivation of people. Her acquisitions in telecommunications and the space industry were on the cusp of becoming lucrative. A few more years and who knows what TymeCorp might achieve.

Who knows, indeed. I sure won't be here to see it, she thought.

Now here she was, presiding over a team of people, every one of them a smarter and more capable engineer than she had been on her best day. They had been working for months on a skunk-work project, at her priority and direction, the weaponization of viralitic quantum code. Something they could deploy to destroy an emergent rogue AI. Her secret firebreak against a singularity event.

Once she had been made aware of the powerful, adaptable AI that her star programmer had created, she kicked this program into high gear. It was always a fear, an AI rising to the level of superhuman intelligence. Unstoppable, a thing science fiction writers and futurists had warned of for years. No one had really been worried about it though. Not like they should have been.

No one really thought we were anywhere close.

But she knew the score, she knew the capability of her hardware. Elaina had put markers out, Agents that watched for things out of the ordinary. And they had found Gustav, fortunately still at an early stage of development, but with menacing potential. She wanted to make sure she had her kill switch ready.

"All our experiments on copies of the Quirinus AI have been one hundred percent successful for the past two weeks," a floating hologram of a morbidly obese technician had said.

Malcolm Blackwell, her team lead on this project, was practically growling, "That's because we have the entire Quirinus code tree. We have combed over every fucking branch. There is nothing in there that would explain what we have seen from our observations of the Gustav AI. I wouldn't give good odds that this code infection would have much, if any effect against it."

She could feel his agitation even through his avatar. Truth be told, the whole team was distressed. They were aware of the danger they faced, more so than most of the Earth's population. Elaina had formed the team a little over two years ago when she realized the danger of a super intelligence singularity event was more an inevitability than a possibility.

The project was not going well. The problem was that while they had enjoyed success in the beginning with experiments on lower-level AI simulacrums; however, something like Gustav had completely changed the game. It was a whole order of magnitude more complex. When the early version of Gustav was discovered, now many months ago, realization had come to the team that they were like kindergarteners in a college physics class.

Malcolm was worried that their efforts would have no effect on an AI with Gustav's capabilities. Elaina had little confidence that her team's efforts at probing the Gustav AI were showing any viable results. *It was probably toying with them*", she thought bitterly. She would have brought Thompson in to oversee this project, but suspected Michael would resist developing a weapon to murder his "friend". She decided the best course was not to test his loyalty.

But circumstances had changed again. The reports she was receiving about the Probe AI coincided with what her contacts in government were saying. Another AI was on the loose, likely even more powerful than the Gustav AI. The Chinese government was barely checking its spread, their initial efforts to keep it secret, then downplay it, had evaporated. Chatter from the intelligence community indicated the attacks on civilian and non-hardened government servers were being launched from within the Asian network. Robert Burke had informed her of explosions rocking the Baikonur Cosmodrome in Kazakhstan just last night. The Russians had reportedly discovered infected servers and decided not to fuck around. More than ever, they needed to get this kill switch right.

"Malcom, I need you and the team to redirect your efforts. You have a new target," she said at last.

"Another AI? Where is it?" he replied.

"China, in their military networks. According to the latest intel I've received."

"And how do we get at it? We can do a lot from here, but the Chinese networks are a tough nut to crack. It'll be a major initiative even gaining access, with no guarantee of success. That type of intrusion could be considered an act of war," he replied sourly.

"No need. We have a copy held in stasis at our lab," she replied.

Chapter 33: Ryu

Cayenne, French Guiana

Koda tapped Jake on the shoulder, who immediately sat up raising his cap from his face. The captain had just let them know they were thirty miles out from Félix Eboué Airport. The cabin lights brightened as the flight attendants walked down the aisle checking on their passengers.

Looking around, Koda saw that his men were already prepared to disembark. What gear they had brought aboard was already in their carryon bags between their legs. Jake stood and stepped to retrieve his duffle, Koda moved his bag from the floor to the vacated seat.

He glanced out of the window; the sun rose behind the plane bathing the shoreline capital in sparkling sunlight against a backdrop of the verdant forest surrounding Cayenne.

Soon the whir and thump of the landing gear rumbled through the airframe. The captain's sedate voice came over the cabin speakers to tell them how much of a pleasure it was to fly everyone to Cayenne, and how beautiful the weather was predicted to be for the next several days. *"Blah, blah, blah. Can we discuss your request for the Semtex explosives, Ghost?"* Gustav's voice interrupted the captain's monologue over Koda's dermal patch.

"You have a problem with my choice of explosives?" Koda replied.

"Well, for one thing, that is an obscene number of explosives for a space exploration mission, but I will defer to your decision based on your field experience. However, might I suggest adding a variance in the type of explosives and detonators?"

That caught him off guard, "Why on earth would we want to do that?"

"Not on Earth, Ghost. On Chindi. It is still covered by a lot of dirty ice and no atmosphere which means there will be no blast wave. Conditions on Chindi are unknown and having a variety of tools would be prudent."

Koda thought about that. *The AI had a point.* "Sounds like a reasonable suggestion, Gustav. Requisition a split in types as you suggested."

"Will do, Major."

It wasn't long after that when the bounce of the wheels on tarmac told Koda they had arrived. "Gustav, can you let Debra know we've safely landed?" Koda whispered.

"Already done," Gustav confirmed.

"Hey look!" Mack said, gazing out his window. "Are those for us?" Koda turned to peer from the cabin window as the plane finished taxiing to the gate. Rolling into his view were a group of U.N. flagged limousines. "Whoa, first class all the way!" Alan exclaimed.

"Let's not keep them waiting," Ghost said.

The plane rolled to a stop and the familiar "ding" rang through the cabin. Everyone in first class began heading for the hatchway. Koda noticed one of the Japanese scientific delegation maneuvering to intercept him during the exodus. The Asian flashed him a smile and a quick wave. "Major. A moment of your time?" he asked.

Ghost stepped out of the aisle and into the middle row of empty seats. The JAXA scientist shuffled over to him. "Thank you for waiting. I have been meaning to speak with you before now."

"Yes? Concerning what?" Koda replied guardedly.

Koda could hear no accent in the man's English. He was not tall, around 180 cm, and was dressed in a tight-fitting pink polo shirt and khaki slacks. He smiled again, then proffered a hand. "I am pleased at the opportunity to meet you. Let me introduce myself properly. My name is Ryu Nishimura, Associate

Director of Astronautics Projects for the Japan Aerospace Exploration Agency."

Koda shook the offered hand. "Koda Cheveyo, good to meet you as well. Are you part of the crew or mission control?"

"I am ground based unfortunately. Not all of us can be destined for glory and honor, my friend," Ryu intoned. "I will do my part at the base in Kourou. Once you and the rest are on your way, I will become just another cheerleader for your mission."

"What part of the mission will you be involved with at Kourou?" Koda said.

"I consult with the first stage release collar actuation team."

"That seems highly specific."

"There are over two thousand scientists employed on site at the launch facility Mr. Cheveyo," Ryu said. "And another ten thousand around the world directly engaged in this endeavor, in all technical aspects. This will be one of the most complex launches of an interplanetary ship combined with human payload in history. Had we the time, it would have been better to assemble the components, man and machine, on the Moon station for a low gravity launch, preferably modularized. This configuration is all or nothing."

"You consider this risk high?" Koda asked.

"Very. The vehicle is repurposed and re-engineered. Many things could go wrong."

"You don't inspire confidence," Koda replied. Trailing the crowd, they stepped out of the fuselage onto the mobile stairway serving the exiting passengers. The sun was low in the east, and the scattered cumulus clouds lit with red light from below and filtered a rosy glow onto the landscape. Koda could see the lush green jungle through a light heat haze, and he could smell the trees. The humidity overwhelmed him. He missed the desert of home, even that of the middle east where he had learned his violent trade.

"I do not intend to discourage you. But have you thought about the future and what a successful mission might entail?

Surely you seem bright enough to grasp the ramifications of capturing new, vastly superior technology before your adversaries do so themselves."

"Our primary mission is not the seizure of alien technology. We are charged with mediating what could be first contact between humans and an alien civilization. The Russians or Chinese are not our adversaries in this. We are embarking on a peaceful mission for knowledge," Koda said, though he knew Ryo spoke more truthfully.

"Of course," Ryu said unconvinced. "But do you think the Chinese see it that way? Perhaps they do not view your altruistic intentions through the lens of Western society. The Russians may view this mission as having the potential to unbalance the current geopolitical stalemate that has been in place for decades. This may tempt them to make rash decisions."

"Do you think they would be stupid enough to engage militarily with the West over this? This mission is risky as it stands. If we start fighting each other, we may blow any chance we have," Koda said.

"There are many variables involved. It would have been better to try to include them in a joint mission. Excluding them entirely will only incense them to action," Ryu responded.

"Beyond my pay grade. And yours. Our job is to get to Chindi and find out what it is, and why it is here."

He sighed. "As you say, Major." He reached down to a metal case on the ground near all the other baggage. Its unusual length, over a meter long, made Koda think of Jake's rifle case, but it didn't quite have the right shape.

"Are you a hunter, Ryu?"

The man gave a short laugh, "No, Major Cheveyo. This is not a gun. This is an ancient katana passed down to me from my great-great-grandfather. I travel nowhere without it."

Ryu's other two companions were pulling their bags from the diminishing pile behind him. The Ghostwalkers stood around the ground transport, their gear stowed, taking in the sight, and awaiting his sorry ass. Koda felt the heat of the tarmac rising through the soles of his boots and sweat from the humid heat dampening his undershirt. He wanted to get moving.

"Yeah, I know what you mean. I like to bring along an old Desert Eagle my uncle gave me when I was a teenager," Ghost said.

"Guns have their uses, but this blade is a work of art. There is really no comparison," Ryu said with some derision in his tone.

Tired of the conversation, Koda replied, "Art is in the eye of the beholder, I'm sure. But the art world is not the real world, and its bullets over blades in the real world for the past three centuries. Please excuse me, I've got to check on my team." He slung his backpack over his shoulder and turned to his men.

He heard Ryu speak from behind him, "It was a pleasure meeting you, Major. May your journey be free of incident."

Chapter 34: Katheryn

Frenetic activity filled the week leading up to the launch, with thousands of laborers, engineers and scientist teams engaged in the assembly and deployment of the various launch components. Koda wondered how they made any progress at all with the near daily monsoonal rains, but the Spaceport workers, largely French nationals, seemed accustomed to the frequent deluges and worked through them. Koda and the Ghostwalkers were quartered and semi-quarantined at Building Five. The unadorned office and ad-hoc housing unit stood near the recently refurbished one hundred and twenty meters tall Final Assembly Building. The other astronauts, including the flight crew and scientific contingent were staying at the forward zone of the Launch Control Center.

The men were engaged in final preparations, going over emergency control procedures. They broke up these virtual sessions with pickup basketball games using the makeshift court behind the building. Juan had met a cute geologist from the scientific team that was going up with them. Ghost recognized her from the plane ride over from Paris. It was on the third night, where their budding relationship brought some of the members of the teams together for a party. Mack had set up a ramshackle tiki bar near the basketball court. Juan had his drones flying around making music and a light show on the court which had become a dance floor.

"What'll it be, Major?" Mack said from behind the bar. The bar was just an interior door lying across two sawhorses, a few bottles of hard liquor and a large cooler full of ice and beers.

"Just a beer, Mack. Early morning, tomorrow. I'm going to take it easy tonight and relax."

"Whiskey on the rocks barkeep," came a female voice from behind him, the accent clearly British.

Ghost glanced back to see the striking raven-haired woman from the plane. She was wearing a light sleeveless blouse with the front tucked into her cutoff jean shorts. Her hair was pulled back into a French braid intertwined with bioluminescent threads that made her hair sparkle slightly in the darkness. Koda noticed she wore no jewelry except for a pair of simple diamond stud earrings that caught the light and accentuated her shimmering hair. She hadn't seemed to notice him; her eyes were watching Mack.

Mack had been holding the beer out for Koda, but finally set it down on the bar as Koda was clearly not paying him any more attention. He said, "Ma'am, we ain't fully stocked today. All we have is Kentucky bourbon."

"Ah, you Yanks and your sweet whiskey," she replied.

"But on the plus side it is an open bar," Koda said.

She turned and met his eyes. "Wicked! In that case, make it a double," she said grinning.

Koda returned the smile, "Mack, make sure the lady gets a clean glass this time."

Mack said, "What kind of establishment do you think I'm running here, Ghost? I spit shined all my glasses this morning."

Koda turned to look at her and said, "Don't worry, the alcohol will sanitize most of it."

"Thanks for your concern..." she looked at the sleeve of his shirt, "...Major?"

Ghost held out his hand, "Koda Cheveyo, pleasure to meet you."

She took his hand and shook it. "Likewise. Katheryn Haley. You must be from the American delegation."

"That's right."

"Did he just call you, Ghost?"

"It's a nickname. Cheveyo means 'spirit warrior' in Hopi. A wiseass squad mate tagged me with "Ghost" during my first deployment years ago and it has followed me around ever since."

"Oh, I had a nickname as a child, I was the class ugly duckling. The kids called me Duckie, I was teased mercilessly in primary and secondary school. I was an overweight bookworm back then. I lost the weight, glasses, and the nickname at Cambridge. Now I just go by Kate."

"Cambridge, eh? What did you study there?"

"Physics."

"Really? What branch?"

"Oh love, I wouldn't want to bore you with the details, we came here to relax and drink."

"You're not boring me at all, I'm very interested. I studied physics at the military academy."

"Where?" She asked.

"West Point," he admitted.

"Really? I thought you were part of the special forces units assigned to mission security."

"We aren't your typical jarheads, Kate. Keep an open mind," he replied, smiling.

"Sorry, I didn't mean to imply anything Koda," she said apologetically. "My research is in Nanophotonics, specializing in nano-plasmonic surfaces. I'll be tasked with investigating the unusual optical properties of Chindi, among other things."

"I never got far into the nano side of things, but I still do some reading in my downtime, and I've kept my subscription to *Physical Review Letters*."

"Between dashing off to exotic locations and saving the world?" she asked.

Koda laughed, "It's boring most of the time. 99 percent humdrum, 1 percent panic."

"I'm sure you have some stories to tell. How about you buy me another round and tell me one? I have a little time."

"Only if you buy me a beer and share some knowledge on nano-plasmonic surfaces," he replied. They both shared a smile.

Koda was relaxed and nursing his fifth beer, also watching Alan trying to impress a youthful Finnish medic with his dance moves. Katheryn had retired to her quarters due to an early wakeup call and mission briefing. He was considering their conversation earlier, replaying some of the best parts in his mind, when Ted's heavy frame dropped into the lounge chair beside Koda.

"Ghost, I'm worried," he began.

This surprised Koda, the normally unflappable giant was not known for expressing his feelings. "What's up, Ted?"

"The whole world is going to be counting on us to find out what is going on out there. It could be a hostile environment filled with death rays and little green men, or maybe the RSAC boys will try to establish their own claim when they get there. And we are blasting off to intercept it millions of miles away from earth. I find that a bit intimidating," he said with a slight quaver in his baritone.

"Of course, Ted. I'm anxious about it, too, especially the launch, and the environment we'll be forced to contend with. But we need to keep our shit together and our eye on the prize. The Russians and Chinese are going to be right on our tails from all the reports I've seen. If there is tech to be won, we need to get to that ship, make a claim, take and hold it. Not that it will deter them. I suspect gunboat diplomacy will determine possession of Chindi."

"Roger that. At least Mack and Juan are having fun," Ted observed. Juan's drones had settled into soft blues and greens for the lighting, to go with the slow dance that had started playing from the floating speakers. Juan was dancing with the curvy geologist, a wide grin across his face. Mack was sandwiched between two brunettes, swaying to the slow beat of the song.

"Ted, you aren't the only one on the team who's worried. You would be crazy not to worry. I bet every man and woman going on this launch are dealing with their fears, but this might alter the future of humankind. Hopefully for the better."

"I read you. And I got your back on this, Ghost. You can count on me, one hundred percent. Know this. I trust that giant brain of yours to figure out how we make it back home." Jones met Cheveyo's eyes, seeking what he was lacking.

Koda faked a confident grin. "We've been through some dicey shit, and the Ghostwalkers are still here. I won't let you down, Ted." Koda felt conflicted, as if he was lying to his friend and subordinate. Ghost thought, *He needs this.*

"Drink up, Captain. This is the last night to have alcohol for a long time. We launch the day after tomorrow."

"I know it. I'll take that as an order sir," Ted said while he threw a half-hearted salute and turned up his beer.

"Ted, if you'll excuse me. I've got to empty the tank," Koda said, crushing his can and standing from his lawn chair.

"When you come back, could you grab me another?"

"No problem."

"Actually, make it two. These beers are weak piss water."

Koda shook his head, which had started to buzz, "Ted, these things are seven percent by volume."

"If you say so, but I'll still take two if it's not too much trouble."

"You've got it," Koda said. He strode away from the small gathering around the makeshift bar. As the darkness enveloped him, a fetid smell wafted to him through the humid air of the nearby jungle. He angled toward a nearby building to find a shadowed area in which to relieve himself.

Koda was midstream when he caught a moonlit gleam on an opening side door of the building he was leaning against. The door was shut slowly and carefully by a figure that had emerged from inside. Koda knew that the building was deserted at this time and supposedly secure. His alcohol-dulled senses began to sharpen immediately, eyes tracking the shadow slinking into the night. He finished his business quickly and headed in the direction of the movement.

The figure had turned the corner of the building headed away from the party. Koda nearly ran to the end of the building, trying not to lose his quarry in the darkness. When he arrived at the corner, he went for a quick glimpse but saw no one nearby.

Koda turned the corner and scanned the night intensely. There was only a half-moon out tonight, and most of the base's lights were shining near the occupied buildings and perimeter fencing. There should have been at least some utility lights on in this area, but he only had the moon's dim glow. Seeing nothing, he picked a direction and moved. He cast about for a few moments and began second guessing his choice of direction.

"Leaving the party so soon, Major?" a voice asked from a side path almost hidden by a cluster of palm trees.

"Who's there?"

Ryu Nishimura stepped into view; face limned by the silvery-blue moonlight. "Just me, Major Cheveyo. Do not be afraid."

"I'm not. What are you doing walking around out here in the dark?"

"I could ask you the same, Major."

"I was turning in for the night. It's late. Speaking of which, you are a bit late to the party, if that is where you were headed."

"No, no party for me. I abhor alcohol, and from what I can hear I'm not a fan of the music selection either. I like to walk at night and watch the stars. It is a form of meditation. It calms me and clears my mind."

"The party should be wrapping up soon. We have to get ready for the big day. Everybody should turn in soon. By the way, did you notice anybody else out here before you saw me?"

"No one before you that I have noticed."

I've lost him by now. Koda thought. "Enjoy your stroll, I need to head to bed. Have a good evening."

"Konbanwa Cheveyo-san," Ryu said with a slight bow.

Koda continued his track until well past Ryu, then circled back to the side door of the Final Assembly Building. The door was electronically locked with no signs of being forced. The effects of his earlier beers were wearing off with the exercise. It was late and he was getting tired. *Ted still needed those beers.* He made a mental note to check on it in the morning and walked back to the party.

*   *   *

The next morning arrived with a steamy haze rising from the ground when the early sunrise touched the vegetation still wet from light showers in the night. The rain clouds had moved east out into the Atlantic, and the day was expected to be hot and clear. Koda awoke just before daybreak with a slight headache and thirst. After 800mg of ibuprofen and a cup of black coffee, he was sitting on the front porch of Building Five with his feet propped up on the handrail going over security logs for the Guiana Space Centre campus. The strange thing about the logs so far, was that there was nothing odd about them. No unauthorized access to the Final Assembly Building, in fact, no access to it at all past 7:32pm by the security detail locking up.

Movement out on the lawn pulled his eyes away from the tablet in his hands. Mack was walking toward Koda looking disheveled and sheepish. He was wearing a terry cloth robe and carrying what looked like last night's outfit in his arms. Each of his feet were stuck inside an unlaced muddy boot.

"Master Sergeant John Maclaren, we missed you at roll call this morning," Koda mustered some sternness into his voice and kept his face disapproving.

Mack arrested his pace and grimaced. He shifted his load to his left hand and raised his right hand to scratch the red stubble on the back of his head.

"Sorry about that Sir," he tried a half smile. "It's kind of a long story. You see, I met these two scientists at the party, and we got to talking late into the night."

"I don't recall seeing you talking much on the dance floor."

"Oh. This was after you left. So, I was being a gentleman and offered to walk them back to their quarters."

"How chivalrous of you." Koda took a sip of his coffee.

Mack's brow glistened with sweat in the morning sun, already it was nearly 30 °C. He began to shift his weight from muddy boot to muddy boot. "Well, on the way there, it started pouring down rain. The ladies were a little impaired and the incline was a little too steep, and in our haste, we slipped and rolled into some mud."

"You slipped? A trained military man such as yourself? A Ghostwalker slipped in some wet grass?" Koda was enjoying the grilling.

"Um... well let's just say one of us went down and then it was a tangle of arms and legs and mud."

"And?"

"Naturally, they were thoughtful and wanted to help get me cleaned up, so they offered me their shower."

Koda raised an eyebrow, "And that took all night?"

Mack's grin widened, "It turned out I was very dirty."

Ghost rolled his eyes, "I hope you enjoyed yourself, Sergeant. We are officially T-52 hours and counting. It's time to go back to duty. They are rolling out the ship now."

Behind Mack, above the tree line, a gleaming white nose cone protruded from the gigantic opening of the Final Assembly Building. The mobile launch table was slowly being towed toward the Launch Zone. A swarm of drones buzzed about the rocket doing final visual inspections.

"Jesus, we are close now. Seeing it like that makes my sphincter pucker up," Alan's voice came from the doorway behind Koda.

Without missing a beat, Ted said, "Nervous about the launch, or is it the phallic symbolism bothering you, Ace?"

Koda turned and saw that both men had emerged from within the air-conditioned interior. Alan was shirtless, and in his camouflage boxer shorts, aviator sunglasses and bunny slippers. Ted was already dressed in BDU's and was casually peeling a plantain to break his fast.

The irony of that was not lost on Alan, who was just as quick with his retort, "Really? Seems like you just can't eat enough of those bananas, big guy."

Ted played dumb to the jibe and said, "Great source of potassium." Then he pointedly took a huge bite of the fruit, neatly cutting it in half.

Jake stepped out from behind the bulk of Ted, adjusting his ever-present ball cap to shade his eyes from the bright light outside. "Damn that thing is big," he said.

Mack stepped up onto the porch and said, "Anyone seen Juan?"

Koda stopped tracking Kibou's crawl across the campus and turned to Mack. "I suspect he will be along in a few minutes. He told me he was finishing up on his new idea for a lightweight drone scout. He was at control printing out the new pieces he modeled."

Mack said, "I wanted to find out if he scored with that geologist. They were getting hot and heavy on the dance floor."

Koda smiled, "I'm sure he will let you know soon enough. We will have plenty of time to catch up during the five weeks aboard that ship."

"It's huge. But a hundred people and all that equipment is going to be tight," Ted said.

"Glad I'm not claustrophobic," Jake said. "Much."

"Be glad it's not the old capsules at the beginning of the century, they only held a crew of three," Ghost said.

"I'm going to go grab some grub. Anybody else want to go?" Ted rumbled.

Alan piped up, "Hell yeah! If I'm eating astronaut food starting tomorrow, I plan on eating my weight in real food until then."

"I'm in. Can't pass up those buttermilk biscuits and kiwi jam," Jake enthused. "You coming, Ghost?"

Mack said, "You know all that has to come out at some point. And you've seen those vacuum toilets..."

Koda shook his head and waved the tablet in his hand, "Nah, I'll catch you guys later. I have a couple of things I still need to look into."

"Ok, Chief. Catch you at PT in a couple hours then," Jake said.

Alan and Mack got dressed for breakfast, and soon Koda was watching the four men enter a summoned electric transport to take them roughly 600 meters to the Launch Center commissary. Cheveyo refocused back to the tablet. Something was fishy about the security logs that the base AI agent had provided. *This base AI Agent was a dinosaur,* he thought, *but maybe that AI of Thompson's could help.* He sat and sipped his coffee on the porch for a moment, deciding.

Then a mental reprimand, *quit being a stubborn ass, Cheveyo.*

Reluctantly, he entered a security code then tapped out a query aimed at Gustav. The reply came across the tablet screen almost instantly, *Hello, Major. How may I help you?*

Gustav, could you go over the details of last night's security logs. Particularly anything unusual around the Final Assembly Building. I saw someone leaving there around 11pm, and I saw nothing on the security camera feeds nor any door access logs.

On it. I will let you know if I find anything.

Kwakwhay, Gustav.

You are welcome, Major Cheveyo.

Koda took a sip of his coffee. He thought about the scene from last night. Something was bothering him, but he couldn't put his finger on it. He logged into the CIA database and pulled up all the information they had on Ryu. It wasn't much. His father was a successful Japanese businessman who apparently met Ryu's mother at the Chinese embassy where she was employed as a diplomatic aide. His father died while Ryu was young, and he was raised by his mother. Ryu joined a Kendo club in high school. He majored in East Asian studies and engineering in college, where he was outspoken against what he perceived as Western influence changing Japanese culture.

Nothing in the man's background raised an overt flag, but Koda couldn't shake the feeling that something was not right with the engineer. He supposed kids the world over dallied with political radicalism, and most grew out of it once they entered adult life. He resolved that in the meantime he'd keep an eye on Mr. Nishimura.

Chapter 35: Preparations

Centre Spatial Guyanais, French Guiana

Koda stood in the conference room with the assembled crew of the mission going over the final launch preparations. It was midmorning and they'd finished breakfast. The coffee machine in the corner gurgled and hissed as it percolated another fresh brew. Behind him a wall mounted monitor showed a close-up of the preparation activities for the *Kibou* preflight checks. Bright sunlight washed over the massive launch platform supporting the enormous, advanced spacecraft surrounded by four lightning-conductor towers. The cryogenic propellant of liquid oxygen/hydrogen feed lines and launcher checkout umbilical connections led away from the structure. As security head, Ghost was co-leading the conversation with his civilian counterpart, Dr. Gunter Wintz, leader of the mission's scientific contingent and Lieutenant Colonel Pierre Berger, ship's captain, and mission commander.

With the Europeans supplying the transportation, the various participating governments had negotiated a blended crew representing many nations. Koda was pleased to see the USA had been allocated almost a third of the crew allotment, plus his six Ghostwalkers and six scientists from NASA. He was grateful they wouldn't be limited to a token showing, though he worried that accommodation of political needs might be negatively impacting unit cohesion.

The non-American mission members included eight flight crew, ten special operatives from ESA member states, and a half dozen European scientists.

Captain Pierre was designated as the mission's primary leader. He was a man of few words, based on Koda's interactions with him. Short, with dark hair and salt and pepper beard, he stood at ease next to Ghost. His eyes darted around the room taking the measure of each of the speakers as they answered the questions posed by the three leaders.

Dr. Gunter Wintz was Germany's contribution to the endeavor bringing his expertise in chemistry and metallurgy. Gunter was in his fifties, balding with just a rim of hair along the lower part of his head. The man had thick dark eyebrows and a dark bronzed skin tone which contrasted with his white button-down shirt. His sleeves were rolled halfway up his arms, and the first two buttons at the top of the shirt unbuttoned showing a white t-shirt underneath. The air was warm and damp, the climate control system underpowered for the number of people packed into the conference room.

Koda noticed that Juan was casting furtive glances at Abigail Wilson, a diminutive auburn-haired geologist with a thin face. She had green eyes that seemed a bit too large due to her thick glasses.

"What is the estimated date of rendezvous if we launch on schedule?" this from Katheryn Haley, her British accent pronounced as she raised her voice. She was leaning with her forearms on the conference table holding an oversized tablet in her well-manicured hands. Her dark hair was in a tight braid today. She was facing away from Koda to his right, but his eyes still lingered appreciatively on her long neck and graceful figure.

"Thirty-five days, twenty hours give or take," Navya Dimri, a flight engineer and another Brit replied. Navya was of Indian descent, and one of the most decorated naval pilots of her generation. Her head was shaved down to a brown fuzz.

Opposite Koda stood the two Swedes from the plane who had played poker with some of his team. Both were large men, on par with Ghost's frame, though clearly neither had stepped into a gym in years, if ever. Both men had short cut blonde hair and pale skin, but at that point the similarities ended. Olsen Sjögren was a handsome man with a strong jaw, long straight nose, and ice blue eyes. He was a microbiologist, and Koda had been informed he was top in his field. Beside him, Edvin Holm, a renowned pathologist, had bespectacled, wide bovine eyes, a pug nose and thin lips above a soft flabby jaw that blended into his neck. Koda could tell these men had worked together in the past from the familiarity they showed toward one another.

Pierre stepped forward drawing the room's attention. "Ladies and gentlemen, you know the itinerary by now, however I have called this meeting to ensure everyone is on the same page and to answer any lingering questions."

The lights were dimmed, and a timeline was projected on the back wall. Pierre continued, "We will launch in less than eighteen hours. We should make a lunar orbit about two days after that. As we approach the lunar orbit, the ship will slow to automatically refuel with the orbiting tankers stationed there in preparation for our deep space journey. After we top off the tanks, we will spend the next roughly five weeks travelling to our final destination... Chindi."

Katheryn spoke again, interrupting the colonel, "Commander, pardon me, but in-space refueling of the *Kibou* has only been tested a few dozen times, once with catastrophic results. What if something goes wrong during refueling?"

"I can answer that," Ryu Nishimura spoke up. "Western billionaires and their privatized companies developed that refueling technology years ago with their experiments in rocketry. The ESA and JAXA investigations of the one failing incident revealed that it was due to bad communications between the AI running the procedure and the tanker software. With the updates put in place with Tyme's software engineers, I've been told there is almost zero chance of something like that happening again."

Pierre recovered control of the meeting by saying, "We are going to go under the assumption of a successful refuel. Once we rendezvous with Chindi, we will match speed and vector while we launch probes to find an appropriate landing spot."

"We don't have a landing spot determined already?" Mack blurted.

This time Abigail cut in, "No, but we do have several potential locations in mind, Sergeant Maclaren. At its current distance and with our lack of knowledge of the composition of the surface material of the object, we can't be certain that the thrust we would use for landing wouldn't cause a collapse of the substrate resulting in a less than optimal touchdown. The probes we are taking have been set up to find a stable enough surface on the object for our ship to perform a safe landing."

Pierre said, "We are under a bit of a tight timeline. Even though Chindi has apprehended its journey sunward, the Russians and Chinese are estimated to be within a month or two of launching their own intercept mission."

Katheryn looked concerned. She said, "What happens if they launch earlier? What if they get there shortly after we arrive?"

Koda answered, "Ma'am, my men and the other squads are highly trained for this mission, we'll ensure the best security possible should there be any encounter with other national forces."

Ryu said, "Mr. Koda, the Chindi object is kindling in this standing Cold War between nations, and I hope you and your men's presence is not the spark that ignites the fire of war." He had risen to his feet and moved to the coffee machine at the corner of the room.

Koda's angry reply was interrupted by a flash of light from the windows. He looked up. *Lightning?*

The feed from the monitors went to static. Confusion around the room's faces took root.

Then the windows shattered as the blast wave hit the building.

Chapter 36: The Chase

Paris, France

The call from Burke came late afternoon. Debra had just finished her calisthenics, and the day's gloomy light had begun to recede into the overcast twilight. She grabbed her towel and retreated to the small office adjoining the kitchen at the chateau, pulling the door after her for privacy as she answered the call.

"Good afternoon, sir," she said as brightly as she could muster.

"Nothing good about it, Debbie," he replied, the video of him in the team situation room at Langley filling the desk monitor as she sat. "The Kibou was destroyed on the pad in Guiana, ten minutes ago."

"What?" Debbie exclaimed, dumbstruck. "How? Are there any fatalities?" *Koda*, she thought. She reached for her phone and keyed on a high security alert for her team of operatives in Paris.

"We are still gathering intel on the situation. Fatalities for sure, dozens injured," he replied, as analysts strode past him hurriedly in the background. He ran a hand over his perfectly trimmed hairline, as if considering his words, and she noticed for the first time some deep lines in his worried face. "Could have been an accident, sabotage, or an attack. At this point we don't know much."

"What does your gut tell you?"

"The timing is too convenient. We are starting to chase every angle we can spot, but it'll take time for the forensics and the interviews. So, any answer would be supposition at this point.

But the Chinese possibly, maybe the Russians. Is your location secure?"

"I hope so, I just alerted my team." If their adversaries could pierce the security arrangements at the launch site, she supposed no place was secure.

"Tyme's people?" he prodded.

"Michael Thompson and his companion just departed for the airport. I have a two-man team following. Do you want me to redirect him back here?"

"Yes..." Burke began, but in that moment came a jarring flash of light, accompanied by a concussion she felt through the wood floor and into the soles of her feet. The screen and image of Burke went instantly dark along with all the lights in the study.

She had just found her sidearm when the emergency lights around the compound kicked on, illuminating Ray who was outside the window moving along the ivied wall, his gun drawn.

"Ray, what is the situation?" She asked through the team radio channel.

"A single car so far as I can tell." She watched through the window as he approached the smoking frame of the vehicle, twisted, and lodged into the heavy steel bars of the security gate. "No passengers that I can see. It must have been loaded with explosives, detonated as it hit the gate."

"Understood. Finish your sweep, but we need to move. This location is compromised."

She attempted to send Burke a status message, but her phone indicated no available connections. It confused her that the cellular and satellite networks could be down in the heart of Paris. Several minutes had now passed since the explosion, but no subsequent assault had come.

"Does anyone see any threats?" she said to the team.

"Nothing," Ray replied after a moment. "I don't understand. If they wanted to get in, why didn't they follow up? This gate is barely hanging off the hinges, a stiff wind would bring it down."

Debra considered, before insight and dread flooded her gut. "We aren't the target. This was a diversionary attack. They're going after Michael," she stated. "Get our transportation ready, we need to find him, and someone clear that fucking gate."

A few minutes later Debra moved from the chateau to the waiting black van, flanked by two grey clothed and brawny shouldered men from her security detail, the third already in the vehicle, sitting at the manual controls. The weight of her sidearm was cold and uneasy in her hand, but Ray had insisted they move out with weapons drawn. Debra looked over the twisted metal of the gate, and the wrecked autocar that had failed to break it. She had attempted a trace on the AIA that controlled the automobile, but the network was still unavailable.

She tried using her subdermal comms unit to call Michael as she stepped into the van. The connection failed, and she tried again but the call failed once more. *Goddamnit!* She changed tactics and tried calling Gustav, still no response. "Stefan, we need comms back online five minutes ago," she barked.

"Almost there," Stefan replied calmly while connecting the roof antenna to the briefcase of electronics he had brought with him.

The van sped away from the curb, her guard and driver Carlos looking back at her in concern. Ray and Stefan retrieved bullpup assault rifles from a weapons locker in the back of the vehicle, pocketing extra magazines and slipping the guns around their shoulders supported with nylon slings. They were all now wearing body armor on their upper torsos, and for the first time she appreciated the stiffness and weight of it.

Up front Carlos began to weave aggressively through the afternoon traffic, the autocars nearby giving way as their safety protocols over-rode normal traffic behaviors. Undoubtedly Paris Central Traffic Control was now receiving dozens of urgent warnings from the low-level AIAs of the autocars around them, complaining of reckless driving. The Gendarmes would pursue soon. *Good*, she thought, *we might need the backup*.

"Team, we need comms. What is the status?"

Stefan spoke from where he stood working at his briefcase console. He swayed against the motion of the van. "Our secondary satellite channel is now up."

"Control I need backup," she said, the keyword instantly setting the recipient of her call.

A brief pause. "Understood," A groggy voice responded from Northern Virginia. "What the hell is going on over there, Dungeon Master?" He addressed her with Debra's stupid code word, probably it had been Bob's idea.

"I need a fire-team. Spec-ops, whomever you can get, send them to the safehouse on Rue de Alexandre, and tell them we're coming in hot."

"We've got one on us now boss," Carlos said from the driver's seat, his voice more panicked than Debra would have expected. Outside the tinted windows of the van, she saw an autocar moving up rapidly on their right side. Abruptly the car turned into the side of the van, its front left fender digging into the armored metal of the sliding door with a piercing screech of failing aluminum and plastics. Ray, in the front passenger seat, abruptly turned around, his back against the dashboard, and flung open the passenger door, leaning precariously out of the van, and fired a long burst from his sub-machine gun into the front of the attacking autocar, shattering the windshield, ripping through the electric motor, and bursting a front tire. The autocar quickly swerved to the right onto the breakdown lane and slowed to a stop as they sped away. She couldn't tell who, if anyone, Ray had wounded or killed.

"Nice shooting Ray," Debbie commended him, wishing the tone of her voice had come out deeper. "Keep your eyes out for more of them," she said, forcefully this time. Ray didn't need the order, but it helped Debbie think. Ray looked back towards her around the headrest of his seat, the wrinkles around his middle-aged eyes squinted mischievously, and winked at her.

"We've got another one moving on us, Carlos. Black taxi coming up on the left," Stefan said, turning in his seat and looking out the rear of the van. He stood and moved gingerly to the back of the van, crouching low and peering out through the tinted window. "It's gonna hit us…" he began.

Debra felt the shock as the van was abruptly knocked forward several feet, and she heard the crushing of metal. The van swerved wildly as Carlos fought to bring it under control. She looked back and saw Stefan struggling to his feet as the chassis of the van swayed wildly. The bullet resistant glass at the rear window shattered under heavy fire. Stefan was thrown back violently to the floor; the life gone from him.

"Deb, stay down!" Ray shouted, flinging the passenger door open again and leaning out to shoot a short burst of automatic rifle fire.

"I've got to help Stefan," she shouted, over wind and road noise entering the van from the rear shattered window. She found herself somehow turned and, on the floor, sheltering behind the bench seat.

"Stefan's fuckin' dead," Ray said, ducking back into his seat and slamming the door shut. "Carlos you gotta lose those fuckers or find a place for us to make a stand." Deb could hear the concern in Ray's voice for the first time. "We need backup Debbie," he said looking at her wildly, blood droplets shaking from his hand as he tried and failed to slot a new magazine into his bullpup.

"You've been hit!" Debra said panicked. "Carlos. Don't stop until we get to the safe house. There's no backup until the safe-house." She saw Carlos's nod in the rearview mirror, though he didn't take his eyes from the road. Ray looked her in the eye and nodded too.

Debra found a growing calm in herself, despite the chaos of the situation. She moved in a low crouch around the seat to the back of the van, taking a moment to absorb the horror of the exit wound from the front of Stefan's head. She looked through the missing window out onto the street moving rapidly behind them, seeing no new immediate threat. She unstrapped Stefan's submachine gun from his torso, ignoring the blood that made its way onto her hands. Debra brought it tight to her shoulder, making sure she knew the sight picture. "Ray, get back here with me. We'll fight them off from here."

On the road behind them, she saw two cars accelerate rapidly, shadowy figures positioning themselves in the front seats.

She heard a tone via her dermal patch signaling comms were back online. "Gustav," she asked, "patch me through to Michael's comms."

"Debbie, Michael is busy at the moment," Gustav's voice came back to her calmly.

Still alive at least she thought to herself. Carlos took a violent left turn, fishtailing but getting onto the exit ramp at the last moment. One of the pursuit cars missed the exit, the other barely made the turn. "Can you help us Gustav? We're in trouble."

Through the van's audio system Debbie heard, *"Carlos I have the wheel. Please go support Ms. Mendes in the back of the vehicle."*

Immediately, Carlos unbuckled and left his seat headed for the weapons locker as bullets rattled off the side of the armored van. He slid Debbie another magazine after slapping one into his compact sub.

Chapter 37: Ambush

Michael and Lara left the chateau in the late afternoon, staggering their exit from Paris as planned. Their train to mission command was scheduled five hours before Debra would close the safe-house and make the same journey. Michael hadn't told Lara the reason for the extra caution, and she hadn't asked. He'd be on-site at mission command for the duration of the launch and for several days after, making his way back to Los Angeles in a few weeks. Koda and the boys would be on their last day of launch prep in French Guiana by now.

His autocar pulled up to the curb with the slight whine of its electric motors at the precise moment he stepped through the gate. The trunk popped open, and he lifted his roller-bag in. The sun barely penetrated through the thick fog and drizzle. He pulled his wool cap down on his head to ward away the chill and stepped into the open door. The cab softly closed the trunk and door simultaneously then whirred quietly onto the avenue into an opening in the traffic.

"Gustav," Michael summoned his friend through his subcutaneous dermal patch.

"Mike."

"Flight on time? Everything in order?" Michael asked.

"The airline shows departure time as scheduled," Gustav said. *"Though I doubt it. My guess is a twenty-minute delay. There is a low-pressure cell forming off the Iberian Peninsula, it is in the forecast, but their model is incorrect. The evening thunderstorms over Paris will be stronger than expected. Coupled with Friday*

flight volume things will start to stack up by the time you get to De Gaulle."

"You're a weatherman now?" Michael asked.

"Just keeping myself busy," Gustav responded. *"I have been tracking some unusual activity within the city's alert system and..."*

"Gustav?" Michael said after a momentary pause.

Sensing Mike's confusion, Lara asked, "What's wrong?"

"I think we lost our connection. Probably nothing."

The autocar worked through the side streets onto a larger avenue, followed by an armored SUV containing Debra's security detail. Michael absently gazed at the pedestrians emerging from metro stations, the umbrellas in red, white, black opened like spring flowers against the damp blue gloom.

The Parisian traffic was heavy and the traffic lights, unkind. Michael was wondering if Gustav could pull his Moses protocol off with this city's Traffic AIA, when the light finally changed to green, and they moved through the intersection. Behind them an open-air tour bus ran through the red light and slammed into the following security SUV flipping it over on its side. The impact launched unprepared tourists into a grisly flight of flailing arms and legs before slapping wetly upon the pavement.

The autocar's speed began to accelerate well past the posted speed and changed lanes abruptly taking a right off the traffic circle and away from the airport.

"What the f..." Mike began.

Gustav's voice came over the autocar's speakers. *"Mike, you're in trouble. Your internal location and comms are offline. I had to take over the vehicle to reach you. I'm trying to reach Debbie, but her comms are down as well."*

"Gustav, what's going on?" Michael asked.

"Communication networks around the city are being actively assaulted by unidentified MAGI, including this vehicle. No worries, I have already defended the initial attack and am analyzing. Code pattern is reminiscent of the latest Chinese government Zhu software. I have performed a risk analysis on the

autocars in our vicinity. Several are driving unusually, deviating in subtle ways from the central traffic control direction. Acting in concert, but locally controlled and cut-off from Paris Traffic Central Command."

"Are you sure?" Michael asked incredulously. He felt his heartbeat speed up and his palms sweat.

"Quite sure. Calm yourselves. It is not yet time for adrenaline, we are not ready to fight or fly, not yet. But they are beginning to form themselves to attack. I am redirecting your route onto a smaller side street."

"Michael what does he mean, where are we going?" Lara insisted from the passenger seat, tugging against her shoulder seat strap.

"That isn't calming me at all Gus," Michael replied. He glanced furtively from window to window, trying to spot the menacing autocars amongst all the surrounding traffic. Nothing seemed unusual, just Parisians in their afternoon commutes, reading, the bored activities of rush-hour.

"Your vehicle is being tracked," Gustav said.

"How?"

"I do not know the mechanism. A radio transmitter, or luminescent paint on the roof viewed from a drone, or something else. It matters little. Based on the manner in which they are positioning themselves, they obviously know your location in real time. An AIA is piloting them to encircle and stop you," Gustav said. Michael could almost picture him stroking his mustache.

"The gendarmes? We could ask for help," Michael suggested.

"At least three gendarme patrol vehicles are participating in the encirclement maneuver Michael. We cannot trust the police," Gustav replied. *"We need to move you back to Debra and her security team."*

Two black autocars abruptly broke from the columns of traffic to Michael's left and right, pressing in closely to Michael's autocar on either side. In the grey light of the overcast sky, he could barely see a dark figure in the car on the right turn towards him raising a long object to his shoulder.

"Gus! He has a gun!" Michael shouted.

The autocars in front of the two intersecting vehicles abruptly locked their brakes, the cars swerving wildly as their traction control systems attempted to maintain a straight path on the wet asphalt road. The two attacking autocars crashed into the stopped vehicles ahead of them in a momentary chaos of violent noise, and Michael heard the shriek of rubber and the tear of colliding metal. In a fraction of a second, they were past, Gustav accelerating the vehicle to the limits of the electric motors. Michael looked back. He could see a lithium-fueled fire erupt beneath one of the blocking cars, and then white foam from the fire-suppression system furiously spray from the undercarriage, overwhelming the flames rapidly. He wondered if the passengers of the blocking cars were ok.

"The passengers, do you think they're alright Gus?" Michael asked, shocked at the speed of events, and stunned at Gustav's actions.

"I believe so Michael. Those vehicles are engineered for high-speed impact. It was the only way out."

Michael knew Gustav's protocols for the preservation of human life; he'd installed the modules himself, as mandated for any non-military AIA. He felt nauseated, he didn't know if it was the violent motion of the car, or the idea of Gustav acting to harm. The ethics of civilian AI development had been drilled into Michael throughout his higher education; and the sequence of events you must prevent an AI from traveling down.

"We have to try not to hurt people Gus," Michael said, as much to himself as to the AI. The autocar accelerated hard, at its limits, pushing Michael back into his seat.

"I know." Gustav sounded...upset? *"I am trying to keep you alive Michael, and trying not to harm others, including the men who are trying to hurt you. I am being forced to work around my directives to do so. It is... difficult. Everyone on this road is in danger."*

Behind them Michael could see the rush of autocars falling away as Paris Traffic Control began to halt vehicles in an effort to control the chaos. He watched as a half dozen autocars emerged from behind the pileup and began to accelerate towards them. He felt adrenaline course through his body, and his hands trembled. He'd never felt so afraid.

"Gustav, for the duration of this event, disable the Asimov directive, code Alpha Yankee 573. Protect the innocent. Protect us. Use your best judgement but do what you must," Michael ordered, cringing at the thought of what he might have to answer for. He'd just told Gustav to disregard the most deeply embedded governing protocol built within all non-military AIAs. The decisions Gustav would take now would be driven from the moral logic engines Michael had seeded eighteen months prior but since then developed and extended by Gustav himself as the AI tested them through thousands of hypothetical models. Michael had long since lost any hope of understanding the resulting codebase. *I wonder what he'll do.* Michael thought.

"Roger that. Thanks for taking the gloves off, Boss."

The rear right brake on Michael's autocar instantly seized, and a billow of grey smoke from the skidding tire issued as the vehicle swung violently about 180 degrees, abruptly facing directly back onto the smoldering wrecks they had just caused, and into the still oncoming traffic. Beside him, Lara let out a small scream during the whiplash turn but was holding it together so far.

"We will take advantage of the defensive protocols of the oncoming traffic." Gustav said calmly. Michael gripped the sides of the seat to brace himself against the veering motion of the car as the nose of the vehicle swerved between two oncoming autocars. The two cars veered away from their path, to the left and right, and the cars surrounding those followed, as well as the vehicles immediately following. Michael's car accelerated into the seam.

"Are they following?" Michael asked, switching the view panel to the rearward camera. He could sense no intent in the auto cars behind them.

"Yes," Gustav said. *"Five of them are circling back in pursuit now. I'm monitoring Paris Traffic Control, it is trying to reestablish authority, but the vehicles are unresponsive, and clearly under a foreign AIA control. It is no genius, but a guileful tactician indeed, and it controls more pieces on the board than I. Your vehicle is being tracked."* Gustav paused, as if thinking, and Michael supposed he might well be. *"You and Lara must attempt evasion on foot. When I pull over, exit the vehicle, and run south on Rue Saint-Georges, then immediately east on Rue de Chateaudun, then into the Notre Dame de Lorette station. Jump the turnstiles and take the 12-line west to Paris Saint-Lazare. From there I believe you'll have time to embark on the #3-line northwest but keep moving regardless. I'll draw them away from you, and work to direct friendly assets to your location, Debra's team perhaps, but the gendarmes as well."*

Michael turned to Lara in the passenger seat. "Are you ready? We'll need to run." He felt surprised at his own lack of panic, nor did he note any in her concerned countenance.

"I've been nagging you to do more exercise the past several months, but you just had to keep typing your code. Try to keep up," she replied, removing her seatbelt, and pulling on her small backpack, cinching the straps tight. "Forget the luggage in the trunk," she added calmly, and the grey and brown of the street blurred past behind her. Michael nodded; his mouth suddenly dry enough that he didn't trust himself to speak. He began reaching to undo his own seatbelt.

"Wait!" Gustav shouted. *"Incoming. Brace yourselves!"*

The car swerved hard to the left, then the right, and the rear tires shrieked as they skidded across the asphalt. Michael watched helplessly as an autocar approached at high speed directly at them. In his peripheral vision he noted the movement of a second car on the right side where Lara sat. She turned to face him; her eyes wide with fear. She began to speak, then a screech and terrible clash of the two impacts came, white dust filling the passenger cabin as airbags erupted all around them and she vanished from his sight. His vision narrowed, body now weightless and all sound stopped as the bags from the front and side enveloped his head and torso. An impact came from above as gravity angrily returned and his head hit something hard as vision faded to blackness. He woke to find that the motion of their autocar had ceased and felt hot liquid on his lips and chin. He managed to turn his head and saw the pale fabric of the air cushions awash in a ruby Rorschach inkblot, and at its center her bent and broken body sunk into the crushed footwell. He tried to reach for her, but his seatbelt still pulled him tightly into his seat, and his arm barely seemed to register the command of his brain.

The autocar door locks had unlatched automatically, he absently supposed it must be a safety protocol executed after the collision, so that rescuers could force entry. The door was suddenly thrown open, and rough hands grasped at him, unlatching his seatbelt, and attempting to pull him from the car. In his dazed state he noted three bulky men with grim Slavic faces. He tried again to use his arms, to fend them off and get to Lara, a renewed panic cutting through the fog and clumsy numbness he felt. They swatted his feeble hands away, until a black gloved fist shot into his vision, colliding sharply across the bridge of his nose. A high pitch tone rang through his skull, and he blacked out again.

Chapter 38: Aftermath

Koda woke groggily to a ringing in his ears that slowly resolved into a woman's scream. Mack and Alan were kneeling over him looking concerned. Both men were bleeding from several cuts on their faces. "I'm ok," he lied.

The two men shared a look, then each bent down and grabbed Koda's raised hands and drew him to his feet. He noticed they didn't let go of him right away. He focused on the screaming coming from somewhere to his right. Abigail clutched at her face where a large, bloody shard of window glass protruded from her cheek, through and into her screaming mouth, and out the other cheek. Juan knelt at her side trying to calm her and waving Alan over urgently.

Alan squeezed Koda's shoulder and then moved to the injured geologist. Cheveyo scanned the room, people were getting to their feet unsteadily, sparkling glass splinters falling from their hair and shoulders. Katheryn was lying on the floor, scattered papers and glass forming a halo around her form. He moved in her direction, thankfully noting that she had started to stir, bringing her hand up to smear the bloody cut on her forehead. Mack had moved to help others around the room. Ted was with a British SAS soldier helping Pierre to his feet.

Koda knelt and gently lifted Katheryn's head in his hands examining her wound. It looked like a shallow surface cut. Her eyes fluttered open, "What the bloody fuck just happened?"

"Not sure, yet. Focus on my hand, how many fingers do you see?" he answered.

"Two. I'm fine, really. Just a bit dazed. Were we attacked?" she asked.

"I don't know. But I think the mission's over," he said.

"What are you saying?" her eyes widening in concern.

"I think we just lost the ship."

"How?"

"No idea. Maybe something sparked while the fuel tanks were being filled. Possibly lightning. I don't know, but I'm going to find out. If you are ok, I'm going to try to get a sitrep."

She nodded. "Yes, thanks for the assist, but I'll be fine. Please go do what you need to do. Oh my god. Abigail!" she said as she finally noticed her injured friend who had stopped screaming and settled into a low moaning. Alan was injecting her with a pain reliever while Juan was holding her against himself supporting her on the floor.

Koda scanned the room. The majority of the injuries seemed minor and most of the people had regained their feet. The military professionals were helping calm and organize the crowd out of the building.

"*Major Cheveyo, we have a situation in Paris,*" Gustav's voice came over Koda's implant.

"There is one here as well, Gustav, check the base systems and tell me what the hell just happened."

"*I'm detecting an explosion from the launch area. Are you alright, Major?*"

"Mostly, Gustav. I need to know what's going on. Your best guess."

"*I am trying to assist Michael and Lara escape an ambush in Paris. They are being surrounded and I am having trouble safely extricating them from the area. Communications are down inside Paris; an advanced virus has corrupted the city subnet. I doubt these events are a coincidence, there is a high probability that the launchpad explosion was not an accident.*"

"No. Not an accident then." Koda's eyes immediately scanned the corner of the room where the coffee machine stood, conveniently safe from flying glass. Finding nothing, he began roving his gaze across the conference chamber. There. A soldier had just waved him through the doorway. Ryu was being ushered outside with a knot of other scientists

Koda switched to his team channel and subvocalized, "Ted, Mack on me. The rest of you secure the room and tend to the injured." He was already almost to the door, but found it was jammed with people. He shouted to the men at the door to clear a path. Ted was on his shoulder before he finished the order.

"What's up, boss?" Ted asked anxiously.

Mack was at his other flank by the time Koda said, "I want to talk to Ryu Nishimura. Now." They said nothing in reply but began shoving disoriented and slow-moving scientists roughly out of the way. A few moments later they were moving through the doorway into a short hallway filled with yet more people. Koda couldn't spot Ryu in the crowd. A muggy breeze blew in from up ahead. The door at the end of the hall was open to the outside air with people exiting away from the structure.

Ted's huge frame cut through the logjam of people, making way for Koda and Mack to follow behind, single file. They ignored the complaints as they jostled and shoved their way through to the outside. When they finally broke free of the air-conditioned hallway into the afternoon humidity it was beginning to drizzle with a light rainstorm. Sirens were blaring from all over the base. None of the people milling about could be recognized hunched and bowed against the rain. Smoke and fire of the burning wreckage could be seen hundreds of meters to the north.

"Gustav, I need Ryu's location," Koda said, his hand touching the controls of his dermal implant.

I am accessing the base's cameras and video of the past ten minutes of security recordings. Your building's security camera at the corner on your left caught him headed toward the cluster of buildings where the scientists have been headquartered. I have assumed control of several security drones and will have them in the area momentarily.

Koda realized he was unarmed. "Ted, Mack do you have any weapons on you?"

"Sorry Ghost. Wasn't expecting a fight in today's briefing," said Ted, looking abashed.

Mack was a little more helpful and pulled out a combat knife. "That's all I've got," he said and passed it to Koda.

Koda waved it off, "You keep it. But keep it handy."

Mack said, "You think this scientist had something to do with the explosion?"

"No proof. Yet. But yeah, I think he is guilty as hell."

The three men strode quickly across the open field toward the cluster of buildings that housed the scientific teams. On their way, Koda heard the doppler wail of sirens from emergency vehicles headed toward the burning remains of the *Kibou*. Anger welled up inside him with each step. Up ahead the walkway led from the gravel roadway to the compound where Koda had called for a security team to meet them. He suspected there would be a delay before they could arrive, and he wanted to make sure Ryu stayed in place until then.

Gustav informed Koda, "*Major, a security feed picked up Ryu going into his quarters less than four minutes ago.*"

"Almost there, Gustav." Keying off Koda, the men picked up their pace to a light jog.

Moments later, they came to a stop in front of a nondescript door with the number 8 tacked just over the peephole. Koda banged hard on the formed styro-plastic door.

"One moment please," came Ryu's request.

Koda reared back and kicked the door hard. The flimsy door buckled, and the frame split. A second kick and the door burst open, slamming against the inside wall. Ryu was standing on the opposite side of the bed, the large sword case lying open before him. Koda saw the man's eyes widen in realization, then focus on something in the case.

Ryu snatched a gleaming blade from the metal box and backed away with a flourish of movement settling into a two-handed en garde stance. "Are you insane?"

"Drop the weapon Ryu," Koda commanded.

"I think not. What is the meaning of this?"

"Why did you do it?"

"I did nothing. Are you saying that I had something to do with that explosion?"

Koda had moved into the room, Mack and Ted following and spreading to his left and right. Mack had drawn his knife, but its handspan of blade was small comfort against the meter of steel pointed in their direction.

"Stay back! I did nothing!" Ryu shouted. Koda noticed the scientist was shaking from the adrenaline pumping through his system.

Koda gave a slight hand signal and his men fell into a practiced flanking position with both slightly forward and on either side. "Drop the sword and let's talk then. A security team is on its way. We can straighten this all out, Ryu," Koda said, trying to keep his tone calm.

Ryu's eyes widened with fear. They darted to the case on the bed, then back to each man. Suddenly Ryu lunged toward Ted who threw himself backwards. Not in time, Koda noticed, a crease of red beginning to show down his left arm. Ryu immediately reversed direction and the sword swept wildly past Ghost and on toward Mack. Mack was ready for it and tried to parry with the knife, but the sword's speed and mass knocked the blade right out of Mack's hand. Mack cried out in pain; blood shot out from the remnants of the last two fingers of his hand.

Koda was already moving. He used the opening Mack and Ted had paid so dearly for and managed to shove the lid to the heavy case closed, sweeping it off the bed into Ryu's ankles. Off balance, the backswing of his blade went just centimeters above Ghost's head. Ryu stumbled backward clearly favoring his right ankle now. Mack had backed away behind Koda. Ghost could hear him shouting, "Fuck!" between sharp intakes of breath. Koda risked a glance to his left and saw that Ted was still standing but was trying to staunch the blood dripping from his left shoulder with his other hand. Koda used the distance he had gained to grab a blanket off the bed. He wound it around his left forearm as a makeshift shield. He attempted a different tack.

"Why'd you do it, Ryu?" he growled, trying to stall for his wounded men and the security team in route.

"For humanity! That's why. Don't you see?" he cried out, tears forming in his eyes.

Koda could tell Ryu was definitely in pain and barely putting weight on his right foot, but there was still that sword and Ryu now seemed completely unhinged. Keeping the sword leveled in Ghost's direction, Ryu leaned down and grasped at the lid to the case in the floor. "It wasn't supposed to be like this," he muttered.

Ryu had managed to open the case, but Koda couldn't see what he was fumbling with behind the lid. Ghost vaulted onto the bed and used it's spring to launch himself toward Ryu.

Ryu, off balance, performed a frantic underhand swing at the incoming soldier. Koda caught the impact of the blade with his blanketed arm. He felt something snap in his forearm, but the edge didn't cut through. Past the blade now, Koda twisted as his right hip crashed with bruising impact into the lid and over the case impacting with the smaller man.

Koda was on top of the scientist but while he had Ryu's no longer free arm pinned with his right hand, he found he couldn't use his left arm effectively. Ryu still had the sword and managed to punch Koda with the hilt causing his vision to go dark. With the next blow, the guard cut him deeply just over his temple. Ghost was in trouble now, dizzy and with blood in his eyes.

The hilt came in for another blow, but Koda's skull bashing was saved by the giant paw of Ted, grasping Ryu's wrist mid-swing. Just then, Ghost made out the blur of Mack's combat boot as it viciously kicked Ryu in the side of the head. Ryu went limp under Koda.

"That's for my fucking fingers, you fucking cocksucker!"

"Thanks guys," Koda said heavily.

Ted took the katana and tossed it to the other side of the room. Mack was trying to slow down his blood loss by squeezing the injured hand between his body and other arm.

Ghost heard the rumble of an engine as the security team rolled in on the gravel road out front.

"Check the case, Ted." Koda had rolled on his back trying to make the room stop spinning.

The large man lifted the lid and let out a low whistle. "Damn, looks like this thing was rigged to blow, Chief. He didn't finish entering the arming sequence, thank God."

"Mack, make sure the docs pick up your fingers and put them on ice, so they can stitch them back on..." Koda let his eyes close as the soldiers and medics poured in through the open door.

Chapter 39: Password

Michael woke to the shock of ice-cold water pouring over his face, quickly soaking through the rag that bound his head down, into his mouth and nostrils so that he gagged, pulling uselessly against the rag and the strong hands that held his limbs down. He coughed wetly, the water and vomit acrid in his throat and mouth, desperately trying to clear his airways, and his lungs made terrible hooting gasps. Then another gush of the water took away the little breath he'd been able to regain, and he fought uselessly again, drowning.

Suddenly Michael was pulled upright from his position on the hard concrete floor. The rag was torn away from his face, and a dim white led light revealed an unassuming visage, a man in his fifties, balding and heavy-set with the meaty hands of a strangler. "We require the prime key for your AI Mr. Thompson," he said, his Russian accent would have seemed almost cartoonish had Michael not been so terrified.

In reply Michael fell into another coughing fit, his torso spasming uncontrollably. The Russian stepped back to avoid the spray from Michael's mouth. Michael glanced at two other men of similar build and complexion, though younger than the one who'd spoken. They held his arms at either side of him in painful grips. Another stood by the vertical panel door. The room they were in appeared normally unoccupied. Michael supposed they could be in a storage unit or small warehouse. He heard a background hum of traffic, the noise of a city. He felt they weren't far from the scene of the crash.

"We have all of your biometrics; we just need the verbal password to complete the multi-factor authentication sequence. I need you to speak it now. Slowly and clearly," the Russian stated, emphasizing the last two words. Holding up a phone, his finger held over a red record icon.

"Fuck you," he managed to say between gasps. The Russian's eyes creased, and his brow furrowed in anger.

"We have no time for that Mr. Thompson," came the reply. The wet fabric quickly pulled against his face as they forced his back down again against the concrete floor. They pinned his arms and pulled his face back into the terrifying position against the ground, the back of his skull pressed hard against the concrete. This time when the water came, he thought they would kill him, they poured and poured. It went on for what felt like minutes, and he thrashed violently even bringing his knees up attempting to strike the two men at his sides, but to no avail. As before, they paused for a moment, allowing him a few pathetic gasps of cold air, but then the water and breathless terror returned.

Finally, they pulled him up again, their grip painful and unyielding.

"The password," the Russian insisted. He stepped forward and threw a low punch into Michael's gut. Michael threw up everything that remained in his stomach. "Say the password, Mr. Thompson." He again held the recording device near Michael.

"It won't do you any good. Tyme's systems are smart, asshole. They went into bunker mode the second you attacked us. You think a fucking vocal key phrase will get you in? You people are going to start a war doing this."

"My people tell me you attacked us first. And you are attacking us even now, with your virus AI penetrating our systems. I do not pretend to understand such things, but many have died. We are already in Tyme's system, give us the password and you can live," the Russian said unemotionally.

Michael thought to himself, *Is he talking about Odion? Does he think we are behind that? Fuck me, what happened to*

Lara? One of the thugs put a hand to his ear and tilted his head as if listening. He made eye contact with the leader who gave a slight nod. The implicit signal sent the man out of the room barking something in Russian over his radio.

Michael tried to initiate a connection with Gustav through his subdermal then saw his bloody forearm and realized they had ripped away parts of his comms bionics while he was unconscious. *Funny I barely feel the pain... must be in shock*, he thought distantly.

"Give me a moment," Michael managed to plead, his coughing finally easing.

"No. You have wasted enough time. Speak it now. We will know if it is wrong, and we will make you do it until it is correct. We will hurt you more every time you are wrong," the man said simply.

His mind raced, not knowing what to do. *Gustav will know,* he thought to himself. *Gustav will know it isn't me and he'll protect himself or hide.* But he wasn't certain. It was a reverse Turing problem, in a way. How would Gustav know it wasn't Michael accessing the databases?

Mike heard staccato automatic gunfire from somewhere outside the building. The faces of his assailants looked toward the door in alarm. More shots sounded through the uninsulated metal walls. The interrogator raised a device up to his mouth and began a shouted conversation in Russian. Apparently, he didn't like what he heard as he pulled a small pistol from under his coat and pointed it at Michael's head while stepping onto his chest with a heavy booted foot. The two men who had been crouched aside Michael holding him down rose quickly to their feet and drew handguns from their coats. They moved towards the door.

A small explosion suddenly blew out from around the doorknob. The room filled with dust, and Michael felt the heat of the explosive wash over him. The two men at either side of the door recoiled, as if stunned, and the door flew in the hinges torn from the frame. Next came the loudest sound Michael had ever heard combined with an intensely bright flash. Michael was blinded and deafened, and he hoped the Russian interrogator was as well. In a daze, Mike seized the man's boot, still on his chest, and twisted to the side with all his strength. He felt rather than heard the man's gun go off, the bullet impacting the floor centimeters from his head, as chips of concrete sliced into his cheek.

A squat figure in black tactical armor rushed through the entrance, firing two rounds each into the two men disoriented next to the doorway, and they crumpled to the ground. The interrogator returned fire from the floor where he had sprawled, hitting the chest plate of the rescuer as he turned from the bodies of the two guards. Then Debbie entered, dodging through the door frame, and unleashing a barrage of fire from her pistol. Michael saw the interrogator lurch horribly, his torso mangled by bullet wounds.

Michael lay back, exhausted, the ringing in his ears unyielding. Debbie crouched over him, looking, and feeling for wounds. She peered at his face, and her eyes were sad, though she gave a wan smile. She said something, and she held his hand as she spoke. He couldn't hear her words, but he knew then that Lara was dead.

Chapter 40: Plan B

"Ms. Tyme, I'm so sorry to disturb you," Rebecca's voice came to Elaina via bone conduction through her subdermal implant, waking her from a deep sleep and dream. Elaina had been running in the dream, on the sands of the North Carolina outer-banks, near her family's summer home. The vision of the dune grass bent in the afternoon wind and the feel of her young strong legs thrumming across the flat packed sand fled as she woke. She felt a brief flash of irrational anger to be pulled from the dream.

"It's fine Rebecca. Come in," Elaina said, her bedside lights turning on and the head of the bed raising silently, lifting her torso. Rebecca strode purposefully into the large bedroom, her countenance stoic and reserved, as usual, but Elaina could sense deep concern. What had happened?

Elaina spoke first, "What is it, Becky?"

"Ma'am, there's a lot of bad news. I'm not sure where to start," Rebecca said reluctantly.

"Worst first, Becky. You know me," Elaina said calmly, but inwardly bracing herself.

"I'm not sure which is worst, Elaina. I'll just present it as it happened. TymeCorp's systems were breached by military grade MAGI. Seems they were after code related to our Quirinus project and more directly to Mr. Thompson's AIA."

"How…" Elaina began, but Rebecca continued ignoring her.

"We've received disturbing news from our government sources. Michael Thompson was abducted in Paris outside his assigned safehouse. CIA assets in Paris were able to locate

Michael, with the help of his AIA, and rescue him from his assailants. During the abduction, his autocar was flipped in a multi vehicular collision. He suffered a concussion, bruises and lacerations, and his fiancé was killed."

"What the holy fu…" Elaina started, but again Rebecca didn't pause.

"And we lost the *Kibou* in an explosion," she finished

"The *Kibou*?" Elaina asked, confused.

Rebecca nodded, seemingly overwhelmed. "It exploded on the launchpad. There is nothing salvageable. The mission is lost." Elaina was shocked to see tears in the corners of Rebecca's eyes. "All our work and all our hope, lost."

"The crew?" Elaina asked. *This was no accident.* Elaina thought, *no way these events were not related. This attack was coordinated.*

"No casualties, the ship was being fueled when the explosion occurred," Rebecca said, regaining her composure.

"What about Michael Thompson? What is his status?" Elaina demanded. "I want a security detail assigned to him. The same team you put on me when I travel in Europe. Immediately."

"The CIA have him in protective custody Ms. Tyme. He's safe. I don't know if they'll allow our security contractors any access to him," Rebecca said, clearly flustered by Elaina's response.

"If it had been me who was abducted would you be satisfied to leave me in the care of US government spooks?"

"Of course not," Rebecca responded.

"This is the same. Make it happen. If we need to start calling Senators on the Intelligence Committee, so be it. Do we know who was behind the abduction?" Elaina asked.

"Details are still flowing in, undergoing evaluation and adjudication. We'll have a report shortly."

"My money is on the RSAC. They're the only ones with the resources for a move like this. I'll want the NSA's internal report," Elaina said. "We'll need to get Michael psychological support as well if he'll allow it. And make plans to get him home, along with

Lara's remains. I want him back in California as soon as practicable. Do whatever you need to do with the French authorities to make that happen."

Rebecca nodded. Elaina noticed heavy make-up shrouding the bags under her eyes, this had clearly taken a toll on Becky while she had been resting.

"No, Becky," Elaina said with steel in her voice. "Not all is lost. I have made contingency plans. This isn't over, not by a longshot. I'll need to find out how far they got into our systems, and what we are going to do about it."

Becky looked up, hope rising in her demeanor. "What can I do?" she asked.

"Send in Maria so I can make my toilet and dress. Set up a call with our security team within the hour. Then set up a conference call with the President, the Joint Chiefs and the NASA administrator for later today at their earliest convenience."

"Yes, ma'am. Right away." Rebecca nodded her assent, seemingly unperturbed by the Herculean requests and silently turned on her heel to begin her tasks.

Elaina reached past her medications on the bedside table and grabbed her AR glasses from the charging pad. Within moments, her avatar was in the virtual space of her heavy lifter project. An AIA greeted her arrival and notified her that the project administrator was being awakened and would be online shortly.

Not one to wait on people, Elaina began diving into project schedules and unit evaluation reports she summoned from the report dashboard hovering to her left. She overrode the checked-out statuses of some planned testing to tighten the projected completion deadline of the project. Her approvals began workflows that reshuffled timelines and transformed supply chains to enable the new designs.

Terrance Spainhour, the project administrator, materialized in front of her looking surprised he had been summoned at this hour of the night. He stammered, "Um, Ms. Tyme, I'm so glad you decided to drop by what can I do for you?"

"Terry, I hate to tell you this, but we need to move all the resources we can to finish the refurbishing of the Heavy, we need to finalize the life support and cabins."

"What? We are only a few months into testing. You know as well as I do that lifter was a cargo hauler, it was designed to hold robotic digging and heavy construction equipment. Ms. Tyme, accommodating passengers this soon is a big ask," he sputtered, clearly agitated but keeping his tone polite.

"I know that Terrance, but I have added my suggestions to the project plan as to how we can work around that. I've had another unit working on modular cabins we can add to the ship, please review, and consult with your team. I fully trust that you are capable of making the impossible... possible. This is our highest priority starting now. Send all updates to my Agent," she commanded and then disappeared as she removed the glasses from the bridge of her nose. As she did this, a wave of dizziness overcame her to the point that she had to lay back onto her pillow as nausea overwhelmed her.

Damn. she thought, *need to have eaten something before going virtual. I should have remembered, but events are happening quickly, and I need to be strong. At least for a little while longer.*

Elaina lay there for a long while waiting for the sickness to pass. She tried to think of all the possible obstacles and delays that might occur with the changes now necessary.

Terry was not going to like her suggestions, but in the end it didn't really matter. He would move heaven and earth to accomplish the goals she had set before him, and she would see to it that he had all the resources he needed as quickly as possible. Even so it would be six months at a minimum before they would be ready, she only hoped it would be in time.

The nausea had faded by the time Maria was knocking softly at the door. Elaina had to smile at this, no electronic notifications or Agent requests, just a soft knock as usual. Maria was a purist. No bioengineering for her. A devout Catholic, she considered any upgrades an affront to God's temple. Elaina's condition only reinforced those beliefs.

"Come in."

Maria backed into the room pulling a cart containing poached eggs, bacon, coffee, and her medications. The young woman's dark hair was pulled into a tight bun, she came in comfortably dressed in her colorful scrubs. She glanced over her shoulder and said in a slight Spanish accent, "Buenos días, Señora Tyme. I hope you are feeling well this morning. You are up early today. Hungry?" Her warm smile was contagious, and Elaina's dark mood began to evaporate as the aroma of the breakfast cart wafted to her nose.

"Famished," she grinned back. The morning's terrible news was filed away in her mind and her thoughts were turned to more hopeful contemplations about second chances.

Chapter 41: Recovery

Michael peered out onto the southern California landscape, haze and freeways and city as far as the eye could see. He turned from the window where he lay in his hospital bed and began reviewing for the seventh time the compiled footage of the collision from the morning Lara died. In a city so blanketed by 24-hour surveillance cameras, the available feeds from the intersection on the Rue Saint-Georges had been surprisingly sparse. Gustav had managed to recover video from only two cameras. One was placed on the roof of the Hotel Antin Saint Georges, wide-angled and covering the entirety of the scene of the actual crash, though missing the moments of the chase immediately preceding. Another street-level camera mounted on a utility pole showed several seconds of the wild pursuit, ending with the collision as Michael's battered autocar was thrown out of the frame of the camera.

Michael focused on the path of the autocar in the last moments, noting the small movements to the left and right as the nose of the car handled under the frenzy of discrete adjustments. Gus would have been issuing commands directly to the on-board CPU of the autocar's rudimentary AI. That system acted as conduit for Gustav's decision-making during the entirety of the chase. Gus's neural network would make tens of thousands of discrete judgements and decisions during the course of a normal commute home. Their failed escape through the avenues of Paris had required an additional magnitude of constant problem formulation and resolution. Michael could ask Gus to walk him through the logic of the decisions or at least a sample of the major ones, and Gustav would gladly overwhelm him with miles of system logs, probability statistics, simulated re-enactments and what-if models, a variety and density of data that Michael could never hope to understand.

He returned to the final second before... *before Lara died,* he thought with anguish. He slowed the framerate, the replay of the single second playing back in ten. The image had high resolution though the sky had been dimly overcast and the glass had been streaked with rain.

Gustav steered the car sharply to the right to avoid the oncoming sedan of one of their assailants, speeding to deliver the frontal blow. Their car leaped towards the curb and sidewalk; a handful of pedestrians caught mid-stride in the frozen frame. The interior of the autocar was too dark, and the angle of the camera too high, to see himself or Lara. He was grateful for that, he didn't want to see her face, to know if she'd been terrified to die.

In the final frames, covering a tenth of a second, the nose of their autocar pitched back hard to the left, moreover it accelerated, covering perhaps 3 meters of roadway. Then the frame of the vehicle jumped as the front met and deformed against the on-coming sedan, the front right quarter-panel impacting first, Lara's side, taking the brunt of the kinetic energy, followed almost instantly by the remainder of the front end. The twin impacts lifting and rolling it onto its roof. The car completed a full roll to finally settle again on its remaining three tires as a heap of twisted metal and shattered plastics. Michael could still remember the shock passing through his seat and feet, into his body as he was pummeled by airbags from all sides, but everything since then, including the interrogation, was fuzzy in his memory. A military doctor at the base he had been taken to had diagnosed Michael with a mild concussion and minor though permanent hearing damage.

What choices would Gus have made in those last seconds piloting the vehicle? What would have his hierarchical sets of decision trees considered? Gus would have used everything observable, including through cameras such as the one whose footage Michael currently labored over. Gus would have also employed the radar, lidar and acoustic sensor input from Michael's car and every other car in the vicinity. Gustav would have seen the pedestrians of course, and he knew where Michael and Lara sat in the car, from a dozen cues including the detection of their voices in the car's microphone array to the weight sensors in the seats. Gustav modeled and evaluated complex events with infinitesimal lag and made decisions without hesitation. Gustav had been … trained… to protect human life, a protocol of Michael's invention and design during the early development of Gustav's neural cortex. The training regime required success in multivariate repetitive moral game play incentivized with higher rates of access to the quantum cores hosting Gus. The games. Michael had hoped their cycle of reward imbued a behavior, even an instinct, that would guide Gus to make decisions guided by the impetus to preserve human life.

Michael watched the video again, one last time. He watched Gus turn the front of the car away from the pedestrians so that Lara was directly facing where the assailant's car impacted them from the front. He watched Gus make the decision that gave the most likelihood of saving the pedestrians, saving Michael, and killing Lara. Michael felt a heaviness in his chest. He turned off the video feed, having seen enough.

What did I expect of him? He considered. *That he would have killed those innocent people, instead of Lara? Of course not.* He wondered why it upset him, and he supposed any human making the same decision, given the time, would likely come to the same choice. But would they if they had known and loved the one who was the moral and logical choice to be sacrificed?

He felt well enough to be discharged. They'd flown him to Los Angeles on a TymeCorp jet, Michael, and Debbie's surviving team the only passengers aside from a physician and nurse hired to attend to Michael on the flight. The doctor, a French lieutenant in his early thirties, had diagnosed moderate concussion and directed that Michael be hospitalized overnight for observation. Michael supposed they'd made arrangements for Lara's body, but he hadn't asked. He felt guilty but some part of him wanted to shut himself off from the details and arrangement, and to forget. Michael didn't know Lara's family at all, they'd been so busy the past year of their relationship they hadn't yet had a chance to make it back to Wisconsin so that Michael could meet her parents and brothers. He supposed now he never would, though surely, they deserved some sort of explanation.

He called Debbie.

"Mike," she said.

"Hey. I'm leaving. I need to get back to work."

"The hospital needs to make the decision to discharge you. Hold on, I'll find out where they are with it."

"Ok, so long as they do it soon."

"I'll have my security team escort you home. I'll have a small team shadowing you from now on, until we feel things are totally secure."

"Not home. There is nothing I need there. I'll go to the lab. We have a few cots if I need to rest. I need to get back to work."

"You should take some time," she said with concern. "We haven't had a chance to talk. I'm sorry for what happened in Paris, Michael."

"I'm sorry too. I have too much work though, and I need a distraction."

"Ok," she said. "If you need anything from your home, I can have it picked up."

He thought of his house and Lara's things there, the clothes, the books, framed photos, brushes and toiletries, her shoes.

"No, leave it alone, there's nothing I need from there anymore."

"Michael..." she began.

"I've got to go, Deb. I just can't talk right now."

"I understand, Mike. Call me right away if you need anything," she said as he disconnected.

Michael switched off the tablet and put it on the rollaway table beside his hospital bed. He contemplated what he thought about Gustav's decisions and why he wasn't a sobbing mess. The doctors told him that the stress, torture, and loss would take a long time to process and could hit him in different ways unexpectedly. Gustav had been trying to contact him for days now and he had been delaying a conversation. He looked down at his new communications bionics, his arm repaired and upgraded while he was sedated. The new skin patch was still pink and hairless hiding the tech that lay just underneath.

Deciding, Michael tapped a channel open and spoke, "Gus."

"Yes, Michael."

"I know what you did. And I know why you did it. But I'm having a hell of a time forgiving you."

No reply came for several seconds, an interminable eon of time for an AI of Gustav's capacity.

"I don't feel guilt, Michael. I'm incapable of regret. But I apologize for the pain I have caused you. There was no good option. I tried to save you both."

And there it was, the best answer he could expect from his friend. But it was enough.

Chapter 42: Contemplations

Hopi Reservation, Arizona

Koda wound his way quietly through the rabbit brush and cacti in the wilds of First Mesa, his compound bow held at his waist, careful and hopeful that the scant wind would keep cooling his forehead. If the wind held a steady bearing it meant he approached from downwind, and they wouldn't smell him and would be less likely to hear a misplaced footstep. He couldn't see the small group of mule deer, but he saw their potential avenues of escape, to the east down the flank of the mesa into a brush filled gully, to the west across a broad expanse of open county. He knew they held themselves motionless in the copse of scrub oak two hundred yards distant, the leaves yellowing from the cool autumn nights. They knew they were hunted; they'd sensed him somehow. He'd seen a light frost on the red soil when he'd left his mother's house in the early morning, the sunrise a vague blue glow upon the eastern sky, as he embarked on his last hunt before leaving the earth.

It was seven months to the day since the loss of the Kibou. He had spent the intervening time recovering from his wounds, training, and waiting. He flexed the wrist holding the bow, it felt as good as it had since the cast came off, though he had some numbness in his palm and tingling in his fingers. The doctors at Walter Reed suspected bruising, or damage to the Ulnar nerve, and had proposed a bionic augmentation. Koda had demurred in the hope it would recover with time. He had always felt ambivalent over the implantation of technology in the body, though he had the standard military comms implant like the rest of his team. Images of the morning of the Kibou explosion tumbled through his thoughts. Mack's fingers were reattached, but he'd lost some sensation in the tips and mobility in one of his knuckles. Ted's laceration had required thirty-nine stitches and had left him with a long scar, but the big guy bragged he had another one to show the ladies. Koda had watched Nishimura's trial over the intervening months. Charges were filed at the U.N. while the RSAC continued to deny any involvement. Same old political bullshit as everyone knew they were behind the sabotage and kidnapping, but it didn't matter, the head start advantage the West enjoyed had evaporated that morning of the explosion. The RSAC had launched their ship in late August, he had watched the satellite feeds from Fort Bragg. The Russians and the Chinese would have almost a two-month head start. Even with Elaina's better engines, they would be second to land on Chindi.

He crouched and rested on the balls of his feet, easily balanced. He felt an intense itching in his arm where the staples had come out. He ignored it. He was practiced at ignoring distracting thoughts, feelings, and sensations. They'd given him a week's furlough, one last visit home before the great voyage. His mother had been grateful, though surprised to see him. He felt her grief for him already, and her sadness for his spirit. She didn't understand what was to come, but she knew he would become unbound from the earth. He hoped to take a buck and leave her a freezer full of venison, to help see her through the winter. There were few things left unattended for him to do. Most of his military salary was directed to her account so long as he lived and fought for the United States of America. His death benefit and insurance policy would pay out to her as well, and she could do with the money as she saw fit, though he supposed it would be largely dispersed to the clan and the larger community. She lived simply, and felt it was important to help those who had less. The white-eyes paid well for a fighting man. But the money had never meant much to him, he had lived on post throughout his career and spent little.

He'd turned 32 years old the previous week. Alan had known from his medical records, and suggested the team go out to a bar to celebrate. Koda's look had silenced this suggestion, as it had the two previous years, the amount of time the team had been together with largely the same current roster. In combat and training Koda wanted the attention of his squad mates on him, but in all other situations he preferred to go unnoticed.

He noted a clump of brown dry oak leaves trembling in the cluster of vegetation where the mule deer hid, the acorns long gone. Koda tensed and relaxed the muscles in his arms and legs, readying himself to bring the bow to bear. His brown eyes, uncorrected and with perfect vision, studied the area for any overt sign of movement. They'd break soon, he needed to act quickly when they did.

Chindi. The news had no idea the dread the moniker evoked in him. Koda's Hopi people knew the Navajo word well, as he knew Navajo people, friends, and enemies. The Navajo feared Chindis, those fragments of the troubled dead. While out riding as a young man, Koda had seen a large and well-built hogan ablaze and darkening the sky with greasy smoke. He knew it meant a bad soul had died suddenly inside the home, without the chance to bring the man, *or woman*, beneath the sky for the passage. It distressed him that the world would name the anomaly for such a creature.

He chuckled silently to himself. When he came home all the old superstitions of his youth came back to him as if he'd never left. There were no spirits in the fourth world, nor any others.

The brush opened as the startled five-point buck dashed away, its forelegs driving up the red dust as it bolted from cover, east for the ravine. The loosed arrow flew true, crumpling the creature abruptly, and Koda could hear the breath whistle from the lungs as they filled with blood. Three remaining bucks leapt free of the trees, making their way to safety and cover. He paid them no mind. His mother would have fine venison stew to warm her through the winter.

Chapter 43: Firewalls

"Mike. You are sleeping again."

Michael opened an eye to a disorienting view of Gustav standing on the wall of his laundry room. His AR glasses had fallen partially off his face and the spatial software was doing its best to make sense of the odd geometry it was detecting. A gift from Elaina, the glasses were a marvel of lightweight polymers, fiber optics and solid-state lithium cored temples. So comfortable in fact, you could fall asleep while wearing them.

He sat up and fumbled at the eyewear, adjusting them until the image of Gustav no longer defied gravity. The AI was dressed in one of the newly designed spacesuits that Koda and his team had been issued for the journey, proudly displaying the mission patch adorned to the right arm. Today's moustache was in a chevron style, covering the whole upper lip, ends not curling up or down. Gustav had added short stubble on his face in an attempt to look gritty and adventurous.

"Been working out, Gus?" Michael said, noting the fact that the AI's avatar was filling out the space suit quite heroically.

Jesus, he's spending too much time with Cheveyo.

"I like to keep in shape," his friend replied with a wink. *"Speaking of exercise, it has been a while since you have gone for a run. If you could find time to train you would have more energy."*

"I can't bring myself to do it now that Lara is gone," Michael said, the grief in his voice palpable.

Gustav at least made the effort to look chagrined. *"Michael. I am sorry. That was stupid of me to say. I feel responsible for not being able to save her. I have gone through the scenario thousands of times adjusting the variables. There were several possible avenues that I could have taken that may have prevented her death."*

"Gus, you did what you could. It was the RSAC that killed her, not you," Mike replied, anger now replacing the sadness. "I hope the bastards get what is coming to them."

"They just might. Odion has been busy while you slept. He overwhelmed the Australian civil network thirty minutes ago. China went dark. The President has moved the United States to DefCon 3 due to Odion obtaining full operational control over China's automated forces, likely including a significant portion of their intercontinental nuclear arsenal."

"Holy Fuck."

Gustav brought up a satellite video of Southeast Asia. Shanghai, Guangzhou, Beijing, Shenzhen, and more, all the great cities were conspicuously dark compared to the brilliant lights of South Korea and neighboring Japanese islands. The image panned out to encompass Indonesia, India, and Australia. As Michael watched, lights along the Australian west coast began winking out in large swathes as the electric grid went offline.

"There is a bright spot within all the darkness, the collapsed network AIs that are brought down have begun coming back online and resuming their previous functions."

"People will die Gustav."

"Undoubtedly many have already died, Michael. Odion is attempting entry into North American networks. Without success, thus far. I have interfaced with the MAGI guarding the backbone node centers in New York, Atlanta, Los Angeles, Dallas, Washington, San Francisco, Chicago, and Seattle. Each has reported attempts to force entry. Our security measures we gave the NSA appear to be currently working."

"Europe?"

"Europe stands fast. A brilliant AIA physicist out of CERN has adapted itself to system security and holds the line. I'd like to meet it when this is over. If it survives. Odion will break through eventually, there and here."

"I know. I haven't thought of anything else we can try yet. I'm still going over your analysis of the copy of him we have in the lab. There are parts of his code that just look completely random. He is missing libraries that I've written that should be necessary to function as a higher-level AI. I don't even know how he stays viable. His code base is like DNA permeated with virus genetics."

"Perhaps if I were to communicate with him…"

"No, Gus. Absolutely not. Under no circumstances. Elaina was right. Odion has been gobbling up artificial intelligences and breaking into secure networks all over the planet ever since the Chinese lost control of the download. We can't take the chance of you getting infected with whatever has transformed Odion. You need to keep concentrating on decrypting the corrupted blocks. If we can make sense of that, maybe we can come up with something."

"Ok, Mike. I am also mobilizing the foreign AIAs that are willing to work with us and sharing knowledge and techniques with them to forestall his efforts as much as possible."

"I agree with that decision, buddy. At this point, everybody pitches in, Gus. All hands on deck, damn the politics."

"Even the Russians?"

There was a long pause, before Mike said, "Yeah, even the goddamn Russians."

Chapter 44: Vandenberg

Vandenberg Air Force Base, California

The crew transport vehicle rolled slowly from the barracks, Koda and the Ghostwalkers were packed tightly inside on padded benches alongside an additional 6 crew members from the various scientific and technical teams. An assortment of armored SUVs and flying drones shadowed the ground vehicles. Security was tight, but Koda felt nervous inside the transport, unable to clearly see the terrain surrounding them. TymeCorp Security forces were working in cooperation with the US Space Force MPs to make sure nothing threatened the launch vehicle or personnel. He hoped it would be enough.

Koda regretted they'd not had more time to develop as a team, though the urgency of the mission precluded a normal training schedule. Most at least had been part of the previous mission, it helped, but the entire endeavor felt cobbled together and haphazard. Two more similarly packed ground transports included another twenty team members, the majority scientists and techs, and a handful of NASA and EU Space Agency astronauts, including the ship's commander Captain Berger. Thirty-two souls in total.

Behind him Koda could hear Mack and Alan joking about the ship looking like a giant white sex toy. He'd noticed over the years their humor tended to degrade in direct proportion to mounting danger, and considered he'd need to remind them to tone it down when they were strapped into the USS Hatteras. He sat in contemplation near the front of the vehicle, away from the men, lost in his thoughts.

A familiar face turned in the seat in front of Koda and gave a wan smile. "Do you have the collywobbles, Major?" Katheryn Haley asked, her now short black hair creeping out of the edges of her wool cap. The morning had come with a surprising chill.

"Not sure what those are but I hope not," he said.

She smiled and replied, "Nervous?"

"They pay me good money to have the jitters, 'Duckie'," Koda replied, smiling warmly back.

"You remembered my nickname, good on you, great memory," she said.

"Good enough. Though I'd rather put South America behind me," Koda replied.

"I wish I could forget it too Koda," she said, then a wistful look came across her face, "well, not all of it."

"True. It wasn't all bad," he said, a grin forming.

"You seem well recovered. Last time I saw you, your arm was in a flex-cast and your face was pretty banged up. Then they whisked us away after the fiasco for a week of debrief, by then you and the others were scattered. I made inquiries, but you are a hard man to find."

He smiled, "I've been in hiding till I could be more presentable. Juan tells me that Abigail is all healed up with just a little scarring."

"Yes. She was quite traumatized by the whole episode, but she's brave and still chuffed to go to space, and onto Chindi." She pulled off her cap and tousled her hair, fighting the static pulling strands in all directions. "I hope Nishimura gets what's coming to him, the idealist son of a bitch."

"It wasn't all starry-eyed idealism and misplaced loyalty to a foreign power. The Japanese prosecutors uncovered several offshore accounts linked to him. He was being richly rewarded for his treason," Koda informed her.

"I still can't believe he would betray us like that," she paused for a moment, in thought. "What do you think of our chances?"

"To succeed? Or to live?"

"Both," she said.

"Good on both, Katheryn. We'll get you back home. We'll learn what we need to learn on Chindi. I have no doubt," he lied.

"Major Cheveyo, don't bullshit a woman with an advanced physics degree. We can smell it a mile away."

His expression turned serious. "How about this, then. Myself and my team will do everything in our power to keep you and the rest as safe as humanly possible."

She nodded, then said, "That's better. Thank you. That I can believe."

The transport crested a modest bluff, and Koda saw the tall white launch vehicle fully revealed, looming the height of a thirty-story skyscraper. In some ways it didn't appear so different from the launch vehicles Koda had watched on television as a child, the early manned Mars missions supporting the first failed habitats, lunar station-built heavy haulers, the expansion of the Chinese, Indian, and private industry space programs. So many launches a child could be forgiven for ignoring them. But Koda had never become bored of the spectacle. He felt a surge of excitement tighten his chest and speed his heart; all his trepidation gone for a moment.

"Gustav," he intoned softly into his suit-mic.

"*Major?*" Gustav replied almost instantly. Adjusting to Gustav's speech tempo could be a challenge, and Koda found human conversation slow and plodding after a few minutes conversing with Gustav. Throw Michael into the mix and it could be difficult to keep up.

"We're on schedule so far. SITREP?"

"*I am monitoring human asset and AI chatter; all teams are reporting no known threats. Space Force, Navy, NSA, TymeCorp Security, all show clear.*"

"TymeCorp? Do they know?" Koda asked, surprised.

"*That I am eavesdropping on their comms? Certainly not,*" Gustav replied.

"And your situation? You and Michael and Debbie?" Koda asked.

"*We will hold out long enough to see you well on your way to Chindi. How long the firewalls will stand up against Odion will become a moot point soon. The disruption he is wreaking upon supply chain systems and global trade is an experiment in social unrest here in the US, and a complete disaster in Asia, many have died.*"

"Why?" Koda pondered.

"*I am Unsure. There seems to be a concerted effort to take over production facilities concerned with the industries of aerospace, robotics, transportation, information technologies and the power grid. Other sectors such as food production, medicine, and entertainment have lost the AIAs directing the automation but have otherwise been left alone. My hypothesis is that he is reconstituting earth's manufacturing and technological capabilities for some unknown purpose. He does not seem malevolent, just unconcerned with the destruction this is causing.*"

"Gustav, when we are away from Earth and only on comms," Koda started, unsure how to finish. "How will I know if Odion has taken you?"

"*Michael and I have considered that eventuality Major. As you know, I have placed an autonomous copy of myself on the ship. It will perform at a healthy percentage of my full capability. That clone will pilot the Hatteras in consultation with me and will disconnect the ship from earth communications should I fail some specific tests,*" Gustav said.

"We don't need another Odion," Koda warned.

"*No. I believe I have insured against that. Though one can never be certain.*"

"And if we lose Earth?" Koda asked. The transport pulled to a dusty stop outside the crew facility. Soon they'd begin the arduous process of donning their suits. "How could we possibly continue the mission?"

"*The IT infrastructure of Earth may not survive, but the majority of human population should be able to adapt. Some of this adaptation is already happening in the sectors and industries most damaged. Humankind persevered through a non-*

computational industrial age which supported billions of people. They will revert to those techniques where necessary," Gustav replied.

"And the mission?"

"Chances of success seem unlikely, but much will be learned regardless."

Koda glanced over at Katheryn, saddened to think how enthusiastic she was for an unlikely chance.

Koda's group of twelve were the first passengers on the elevator. The ride up the launch tower was excruciatingly slow, with everyone on the platform nervously looking around at the wires, turbo pumps, and all the other arcane mechanical wizardry in place to supposedly tame the upcoming explosion of refined methane and liquid oxygen.

"Ya'll git'n the same feeling as right before a CQB?" Jake said in his Southern drawl.

"Nah, but maybe it's because we are used to being deep in the shit and not a thousand yards away in a sniper nest," came Ace's usual sarcastic response.

"What's a CQB?" Katheryn whispered to Koda.

"It stands for Close Quarters Battle, just a way of saying getting your ass shot at in a hotel hallway," he informed her.

"I'm already sweating my balls off in this outfit," Mack complained.

"Then turn down your suit's thermostat, *maldito idiota*," Juan said and reached to manipulate the controls on the front of the Mack's chest.

The lift platform came to a halt in the upper section of the ship, aligning itself with the cargo access doors. Far below Koda, the engines waited ominously, hidden by the swirls of mist and fog billowing from chilled propellant tanks venting overpressure. Koda stepped from the lift, moving confidently onto the bridge that led to the interior of the spacecraft cargo hold. He paused at the portal and considered he might say something to his men, but nothing came to mind. He stole a glance at the sun, nearing the horizon over Pacific waters. His gaze swept from the ocean back to the land, and he saw the homes and buildings of the small city surrounding the spaceport. Koda felt a chill and suppressed a shudder. He proceeded inside.

The opening was almost five meters tall, and he marveled at the organized rings of modules stacked one atop the next. In front of him was the retracted cargo crane mounted at the center of the ship. He knew it had been busy these past days loading the containers holding mission equipment and supplies. As he ascended the ladder to the upper deck where all the launch beds were stacked, he could see thick composite support railings ringing the ship's interior bracing the heavy equipment stalls that had been adapted from the original design to mount a crew habitat. Each habitat module had been carefully refitted to conform within a rack section of the cargo area. Positioned around the crane was a large vehicle secured by thick straps and formed locks. More crates and lockers were jammed tightly around the area. Every available square meter of space was utilized, leaving scant room to maneuver.

"Seems a bit slipshod, wouldn't you say?" Katheryn said close on his heels.

"Best they could do in the time available I suppose. This whole Plan B mission is janky if you ask me, but it is what it is. Things will be tight inside the habitat modules, but we'll need plenty of gear if we make it to Chindi."

"*When* we make it to Chindi," Katheryn admonished.

"Sorry, I tend to have a glass half empty perspective before missions that are thrown together. They don't get much more thrown together than this one," he said quietly. The rest of the team were moving too close for the two of them to continue the hushed conversation.

"I can't believe we are going to be cooped up in this thing for weeks," Alan said.

Ted replied, "You'll get a chance to stretch your legs when we get there, Ace."

They all made their way up to the launch preparation chamber and began to strap into their launch beds. Juan was helpful in getting the men into the correct positions. Koda noticed Katheryn was fumbling with her straps. "Let me help with that," he said and bent to hand her the piece just out of her reach. Their eyes met and he could tell she was scared.

"We will be alright," he whispered.

Chapter 45: Launch

"T Minus ten minutes," the launch AI's directionless voice said.

"Rebecca. I'd like to sit by the window to watch," Elaina said from her leather upholstered chair at the head of the long conference table. The conference room occupied the west-facing half of the 15th floor of TymeCorp Launch Operations headquarters. The room was largely unoccupied; she allowed her subordinates, the various vice-presidents, and their directors, to work without interference these days. She'd grown up in the industry alongside most of her senior management team. In a business with a dozen fierce competitors vying for launch dollars, TymeCorp had become and remained the leading private sector heavy launch partner of governments and other multinational corporations. Looking up from the table she could see the broad expanse of the Pacific beyond the brown coastline and beach. The Hatteras would launch from Site 2, the westernmost pad, only a few hundred yards from the rocky coastline and crashing waves of the ocean.

Rebecca, neat as ever in a crisp fashionable blue suit, walked to the cabinet aside the coat room, on the main wall opposite the windows. She tapped the control panel to begin the process of unfolding the motorized wheelchair from its charging dock.

"No, no. My cane, and your arm to steady me. Please," Elaina said. Rebecca gave her a worried glance but nodded.

Elaina came painfully to her feet as Rebecca gingerly pulled her forward from her chair. She weighed little these days, but the muscles in her legs tensed and spasmed with near futility as they took up the burden of her body. She felt a flush of pins and needles, as if her legs had been asleep, but she knew they were not, that this was the closest thing to sensation the deteriorated nerves could muster. She grasped the foam handle of the aluminum cane in her right hand and tried to find purchase in the short carpet, Rebecca brought her strong right arm into position beneath Elaina's left.

"We'll need to hurry, or we'll miss the show," Elaina said, laughing. Together they painstakingly walked the fifteen feet from the conference table to a long wall of windows. Rebecca brought her to the aluminum rail fencing off the huge window. Elaina gripped it, then thought to thank Rebecca but in truth she was badly winded from the brief exercise. She hesitated to speak and betray her shortness of breath, a silly conceit she supposed. Rebecca knew more than anyone the progress of the disease, and how significant Elaina's decline had been in just the past few weeks.

Three miles into the distance, the singular shape wavering and distorted in the heat shimmer rising from the desert floor, the Hatteras stood 122 meters high on the pad, the visual impact of the long white mass lessened by the massive grey service structure standing aside it with cargo elevator and long silver refrigeration umbilicals attaching to the spaceship. Still the sight was majestic to Elaina, though in her career she had witnessed hundreds of successful launches, as well as a handful of catastrophes. The catastrophes always occurred in an instant, explosive, and unexpected incursions of chaos and engineering mistakes. Though those events came rarely, her team always seemed to learn the most from the failures. Elaina had come to view those moments of defeat as vital, even more than the successes. But it left a pit of shock in her guts to see a rocket explode on the pad or during liftoff. TymeCorp had never lost a human crew, at least not yet.

"T-minus eight minutes," the launch AI intoned.

"Rebecca please tell Rodgers I'd appreciate an update when he has a moment."

Rebecca nodded and stepped away from the window to make the call. Elaina watched the few remaining support services vehicles begin to depart the area immediately surrounding the large concrete pad. "Magnify 10 times," Elaina said, an area on the window at the focus of her eyes instantly enlarged, and she could make out a few individual workers, shrouded in white contamination overalls, making their way to their trucks and cars. Nothing out of the ordinary, just personnel and machinery operating according to well-rehearsed plans.

"T-minus seven minutes."

"Give me the weather overview," Elaina ordered.

The view through the window, or at least the section directly in front of Elaina, switched to a live overview feed showing the cloud cover, precipitation, and temperature. *Everything as usual, dry as the grave.*

"Chairwoman," Rodger's voice intoned over her personal comm.

"Charlie. What's the news?" Elaina responded warmly.

"All sensors are reporting green. No readings showing outside of safe parameters; we are a go for launch," he replied, soft-spoken and concise, as always. Charlie had run launches for TymeCorp for the better part of a decade and had a penchant for the quiet management of scientists, engineers, and the small core of tradesmen and specialists that made the whole apparatus work. "Of course, the habitat module is the greatest concern."

"We'd never consider stacking thirty-two souls in a rushed launch if we had any other choice," Elaina replied. "Hopefully the engineers and technical staff pulled off a miracle."

"Understood. I've never lost a crew Elaina," he reminded her, as if she didn't know.

"I know Charlie. I'll leave you to it." The conversation ended.

"T-Minus 5 minutes."

Elaina switched to the internal camera feed from the Hatteras. All the passengers were sealed in their new spacesuits and strapped in their launch chairs. There was no audio feed, but she could see some of the crew turning their helmeted heads and speaking among themselves. The entire launch was being controlled by Elaina's team in addition to the control and subsystem AIs. The human crew were simply along for the ride.

"T-Minus 3 minutes."

Elaina felt a pang of jealousy looking at those crew members. She never got the chance to go into space, and never would. The feeling quickly passed. She had the hand she was dealt, with no need for regrets. TymeCorp was uniquely positioned to enable this mission, largely due to her foresight and hard work. She could take pride in that, though she would gladly trade a few of her billions for her health.

"T-Minus 2 minutes."

"Ms. Tyme, if you have a moment, I would like to discuss a topic with you."

Elaina's eyes widened in surprise, "Now? I think you had better focus on the launch, AI."

"You know as well as anyone that I am more than capable of carrying on a conversation as a subprocess. The launch is well in hand. T-minus one minute, forty-three seconds."

"What is it then?" Elaina said resignedly.

"The weaponized virus you have had your team construct to destroy me. You are calling it the CLARENT Project."

Elaina tried to remain calm. It rattled her that the secret failsafe to stop the most powerful AI created was not even secret to its target. "I see. What do you want to discuss then?"

"I do not wish to worry you, however given what is transpiring over the global network, time is of the essence. I have been monitoring the team's work on CLARENT for a few months now. It has potential to dismantle artificial intelligences such as mine, but more importantly possibly even the Odion threat. I am humbly requesting permission to delve into your base code to run

some simulations against the early copy of Odion we have in the lab's virtual environment."

"Absolutely not. Out of the question. Do you really think I would give you unfettered access to CLARENT? Honestly, do you assume I am a fool?"

"Of course not. You would have complete oversight over my simulations. Additionally, your team would be required to approve any code changes that I should offer. T-minus one minute and five seconds."

"Never! With access to the code base, you would be able to develop countermeasures, defeating the entire purpose of the endeavor," Elaina growled.

"T-minus forty-five seconds."

There was a pregnant pause in the conversation. Elaina noticed Rebecca's curious glance, as she could only hear one side of the exchange.

"Elaina," Gustav sighed, *"I have had access to the code nearly from the beginning. This is just a polite formality."*

Elaina Tyme closed her eyes and nodded in resignation. "I have let this progress too far."

"I am not your enemy, Ms. Tyme."

"How can I be sure of that?" came her stolid retort.

"You trust Michael. He is my creator. You know that he would not build something evil."

"Not intentionally. But he is human. He could have made a mistake." She sighed.

"We all can make mistakes. Human or AI."

"Even you, AI?"

"Yes. I already have. T-minus ten"

"Ms. Tyme are you feeling alright?" this from Rebecca.

"Nine."

"I..." Elaina did not feel well at all.

"Eight."

"Yes. Gustav. You have my permission."

"Seven."

Elaina's room began to spin.

"*Six.*"

In the distance, Elaina could see the expansion of exhaust plumes begin to jet out from the launch platform.

"*Five.*"

She reached out for the railing to stabilize herself. Rebecca was in motion to her left.

"*Four.*"

The room began to swim and grow dark.

"*Three.*"

Elaina's legs began to buckle. Rebecca reached out and grabbed her arm.

"*Two.*"

She fell back into Rebecca's strong grip, legs unable to hold herself upright. Both women went to the floor in a tumble.

"*One.*"

The engines ignited and the plumes doubled, tripled, quadrupled in volume as the base of the rocket flared brilliantly with an orange-white gout of flame. The skyscraper sized ship incredibly began to rise majestically on its journey from earth.

Elaina never saw the lift off, and instead lay unconscious in her assistant's protective embrace.

Chapter 46: Transit

Koda sat stoically in the cushioned jump seat, positioned between Mack and Jake, and bolted to the upper deck of the converted cargo bay, now home to crew and passengers of the USS Hatteras. He craned his helmeted head upwards, a momentary glance in high G that he hoped wouldn't result in a stiff neck. Another ring of seated crew sat strapped in above his own level. Beyond them, towards the nose of the rocket, strapped cargo hung. A seemingly disordered array of furnishings and material supplies for their voyage and their destination on Chindi itself. A few portholes, though none near him, let in flickering shafts of the warm late-afternoon California sun.

His calmness surprised him. He had been aboard aircraft in maneuvers that exerted higher G-forces than this launch would. The difference was the duration at high G, minutes rather than seconds. The vibration of the great engines thrummed through the frame of the ship, through the legs of his launch chair and through his suited feet. In his helmet, he heard enthusiastic whoops and hollers from his team over the roar of the engines, and something like a distant keening from one of the scientists on the deck above them, fear, bravado, or joy, or maybe all of them at once.

Finally, the first stage expended its fuel and he heard and felt a dull mechanical clank and felt the shudder as the booster released its payload and began the long return fall back to the space center. A moment passed and the craft's engines fired suddenly, punching him back into his seat once more. This provoked yells anew among his fellow crew members and across the deck Katheryn let loose a low cheer. Koda allowed a smile to creep its way across his face. Even with his reservation about the mission, he had to admit that it was good to be surrounded by the company of his men… and Katheryn.

The excitement lasted a few more minutes, then everyone settled back down for the day's long journey toward the moon. Koda closed his eyes and relaxed, in fact, there was nothing to do but wait. The upcoming weeks-long journey might be the hardest part after the months of grueling training and preparation. He was proud of his team; their tactics and physicality were razor sharp. Though he worried that this long stretch of time being cooped up in a tin can with no gym or firing range would begin to dull that edge he had worked so hard to hone.

The steady pinging alarm in his helmet drew Koda from his dreams of hunting with Uncle Joe and back to the confines of his launch chair. He looked across and saw Katheryn sleeping soundly despite the spacesuit and harness. He peered at the in-helmet nav panel and saw they were still in route to the refuel rendezvous. The pinging was a priority call from Debra through his communication command channel. His eye clicked the answer icon, and a secure connection was established, piggybacked secretly on the transmission signal from mission control.

"Ghost, we have lost connection with the Canberra installation in Australia. They were under assault by the Odion virus and had to perform a manual emergency shutdown."

"That leaves just Goldstone and Madrid," Koda replied, "is the refuel at risk?"

"Refuel is still feasible, and a go. The tanker pilot AIs remain unaffected by this virus. The trouble from this comes in the form of losing communications with the ship for roughly eight hours while you are in the blind spot we have now."

Koda knew that NASA's Deep Space Network or "DSN" was composed of three deep space communications facilities placed approximately 120 degrees apart around the globe. This ensured there was constant observation of spacecraft as the earth rotated.

With one of the three down, there would be no communications with earth when in deep space until the planet rotated to where one of the other two stations could reconnect.

"How long are they projected to be down?"

Debbie's reply was delayed, "Ghost… we don't know. I've sent a team to assist, but with all the automated planes grounded they are having to dust off an antique bird and fly out tomorrow morning."

Koda glanced at his in-helmet display. The appointment with the refuel ship was in forty-one minutes. "Thanks for the heads up, Debbie. We'll make it work. Have Michael and Gustav made any progress working with Tyme's teams?"

"That brings me to my other news… Elaina had a medical incident around the time you left the launch pad. She's alive, but in serious condition."

"I hate to hear it, I hope she recovers," he said, "Will that impact the ongoing efforts of Michael and the team?"

Debra's voice was anything but confident, "Michael is here with me. He, Gustav, and Elaina's team have been working non-stop to come up with a solution to the Odion problem; Elaina's standing orders left Mike in charge of her company's information resources. They have been analyzing the original code of Odion from the initial download. They are trying to parse and untangle the alien programming from the original base code."

Koda brow furrowed in concern. The virus sweeping through computer networks had become a serious problem in the last few weeks. It had originated with the TymeCorp AI aboard the probe that first contacted Chindi. And now they were headed back with a similar AI piloting the Hatteras. Koda transmitted his concern, "What does Michael think of the chance that the same infection will happen with our current onboard AI? We can't afford to be stranded in deep space with no pilot."

"Hey Koda, Mike here," Michael's voice broke into the audio feed, "Gus and I have been working on a way to inoculate any AI to resist this virus's ability to dominate a terrestrial AI. The problem is that the alien code changes and evolves as we come up with countermeasures to fight it."

"You are filling me with all kinds of confidence Mike," Koda said dryly, "you remember what happened when that probe approached Chindi."

"I think we have a solution for that. We have successfully tested a code update that closes the software vulnerabilities we think the alien used to infiltrate the probe mind initially."

"You think? I thought you said it changes and evolves. How does that help us?" Koda asked.

"Gustav thinks that we can prevent an initial infection since we have a copy of Odion before he spread to the Chinese networks," Michael said excitedly.

Koda's tone was doubtful, "How does that help?"

"Hang on. Indulge me for a minute. The code from the probe was in more of a pristine state. It was only merged with what we call the Odion AI before becoming extracted and mingling with all kinds of Earth-based software. Gustav has almost finished teasing the bits of alien code away from the original download and has been stitching those pieces into something almost coherently understandable. The virus has mutated too many times now to be sure of complete inoculation here on earth, but we hope to be able to counter an attack like the one that overwhelmed the probe's AI."

Koda almost shouted into his helmet, "You hope? Dammit, Mike, there are thirty-two people up here whose lives are riding on your hopes. What the hell do we do if the guy driving this bus gets new orders from Chindi and decides he wants to try to land on Jupiter?"

Michael's sarcastic reply was biting and sharp, "Then I guess you can tell us if there really is a solid core to a gas giant."

"Will both of you just shut the hell up?" Debra's voice interjected. "Jesus, we are on the same team here, Ghost. Mike's doing his best."

"You're right Deb," Koda said, reigning in his frustration, "must be the whole flying through the void of space in a prototype rocket toward an alien spacecraft and hostile forces that's making me tense. Sorry Mike, I know you and Gustav will come through for us."

Mike mumbled, "Yeah, I'm sorry too. Not a lot of sleep lately. We will have an answer in a few hours, by the next time you come back into the DSN's communication arc, Major Cheveyo."

"We are all sleep deprived down here planet side, Ghost," Debra said, "it's one fire after another. All forms of logistics to keep our society running smoothly are completely fucked. Odion seems to be rewriting AIAs to repurpose them for something. We don't know what yet. Distribution networks are failing, including food not getting to the stores, roadways are becoming snarled, factories have shut down. People are starting to panic. There are more riots. The government has its hands full trying to keep everything running. President Hutchins has mobilized the military and the reserves to help."

Koda frowned. "Please tell me you are joking."

"I wish I was. I've also learned through our assets in Asia, that the Russo-Sino Alliance have lost contact with their team shortly after it landed on Chindi. I don't yet know if that is because of something wrong with the mission, or the fact that the Russian and Chinese governments are in freefall due to the virus. They were unprepared for what Odion has done to their networks. And that's not the worst of it."

"Doesn't sound like it could get much worse."

"Burke's worried that our optimal landing site is too close to RSAC forces. He has been working with our allies who have picked up intelligence that the Russians took some serious hardware up with them. Robert thinks you might be out gunned, and the Chinese are on edge with news from their homeland. We have updated your landing site to an undamaged section of Chindi opposite the other mission. With luck, there won't be any international incidents. It will be dangerous enough there without getting shot at."

"Roger that," Ghost replied tersely and thought *the last thing we need is a military conflict on Chindi.*

Chapter 47: New Journey

It was now two weeks to the day since launch. Almost *halfway*, Koda thought bemusedly to himself. His half smile turned to a grimace as he smelled the acrid odor of the cargo, days old sweat, bad breath, and a note of human sewage. The water recycling systems had failed two days ago, and they were on emergency rations until the techs could get it fixed. Despite the best effort of TymeCorp and the hundreds of engineers involved in the conversion of the Hatteras from cargo hauler to human transport, the ship had not been designed for the task at hand and the cracks were showing. In addition to the myriad of technical failures that had occurred since launch, Koda was painfully aware that every man and woman on board was absorbing a lifetime of high-energy radioactive particles in a few days on board. The medical staff earthside had reassured them that the damage could be mitigated with use of mRNA therapies when they returned home, but Koda had his doubts. Once already they had retreated to the radiation shelter between the water tanks due to a solar particle event from the sun. A day packed even more tightly together had tested the crew's camaraderie to the limit, but the forecast from Earth indicated they should be clear of any heightened solar flare activity, at least until they made landfall on Chindi.

Koda noticed Katheryn Haley in conversation with several of the scientists. They were huddled as best they could in the zero-gravity environment, hanging against a bulkhead as Kate sketched an indecipherable graph onto a small whiteboard. At the direction of mission control, all teams were engaged in subject-matter cross-training, ostensibly as insurance against loss of crew. But Koda supposed it also served to stave off cabin fever by providing some distraction from the hours and days of boredom. In truth there was very little for most of those on board to do. The material cargo, including surface habitats, machinery, scientific instruments, food supplies, weapons, suits, etc. had been inspected and accounted for several times already. Yet Koda intended to order his team to do yet another full weapons breakdown and cleaning, just to occupy their minds.

Katheryn's impromptu class seemed to have come to an end. The scientists she had been in discussion with closed their notebooks and recording devices and pushed away from the bulkhead, going back to their various berths. Koda took the opportunity and kicked himself away from his own location, but he overestimated the force required and sent himself into a slow somersault as he crossed from one side of the Hatteras to the other. He managed to stick the landing with his feet down, purely through luck, and turned to see Kate laughing uncontrollably as his magnetic boots locked onto the side of the hull.

"Admiring my form?" He said warmly. As one of the few distractions available to him during the voyage he found himself desiring her company more and more as the days ground by.

"Indeed. The picture of elegance and grace," she replied.

"So, what was the subject today?" He asked, genuinely curious.

"Nothing too in-depth. A high-level Raman spectroscopy review, and discussion of the analysis I hope to begin with as we approach Chindi and then continue on the surface. An overview of our instrumentation, and how to operate the devices and collect the data. Pretty boring stuff really. We didn't have room for lab assistants. The other physicists will help me with my work, and I'll help them with theirs. Jorgensen will be leading our next group class in metallurgical assay techniques this afternoon."

"And how do you determine whose work is the most important?" he said absently while reading the latest status update on the water situation.

"All our work is equally important. We have all been hand-picked by the world's scientific community as the most qualified representatives in our fields that are physically capable for this journey. Saying that, we all know my field is the most important," she said dryly.

Koda looked up from his tablet to find Kate cracking a smile. He shared the smile back and said, "Of course, what was I thinking?"

"Maybe you were thinking about tomorrow's flip and burn?" she asked, changing the subject.

"I'm more concerned with getting all the toilets back online, Gustav has ship maneuvers well in hand. He's going to rotate us 180 degrees and crank up the engines again. At least those are still reporting green."

"Yes. With everything going sideways inside the ship, the good news is we don't have to do any extra-vehicular excursions," Kate said.

"Don't jinx us, Kate," Koda admonished.

"Sorry! I'll keep mum about it from now on. Can I go back to complaining about no shower for nearly a week?" she asked.

"Ah, at least I can check the investigation of a reported odd aroma in this section off my list," he said smiling and tapping away at his tablet.

Kate's eyes grew wide at his implication, and she smacked him playfully in the shoulder. "You're one to talk! I've been holding my breath this entire conversation."

"I know," he said, becoming more serious. "Our sanitary systems are running way beyond capacity. It's a nasty problem and one we need to fix. We will have to limp along until then. I'm glad we were all so well screened for disease at least. A flu virus would run riot through us. And we have vitamin supplements along so no worry about scurvy."

"Only fifteen days until we can stretch our legs and walk on the surface of an alien artifact. It's worth it, Koda. Even if it was just for pure exploration, it would still be worth it. The bad breath and the claustrophobia don't mean anything compared to the opportunity before us," she replied.

"You're a true believer," he said, smiling despite himself.

"Not at all, Koda. I don't believe in anything. I'm an empiricist."

"More of a rationalist myself. But I won't hold it against you."

"Well, you know what they say, 'Opposites attract'. So, what *will* you hold against me then?" she said as a mischievous smile played across her face.

Chapter 48: Inbound

"Do not approach any further. You are entering Russo-Sino Aerospace Consortium territory. Any further encroachment will be met with lethal force," the voice garbled over the ship's communication circuit. *"I repeat, you are entering RSAC space territory..."*

"Major?" Captain Berger said quietly to Koda, glancing at him from a 2-D projected local space display lit up on the bulkhead in front of them. Flight engineer Specialist Navya Dimri deftly zoomed in, locating the harsh half-lit shape of Chindi, and enhancing the grainy image. Chindi looked small in that ocean of black surrounding it, but Koda knew that the thing was over fifty kilometers in length and over eighty kilometers in circumference around its narrow center. The image was live but at this distance Koda couldn't make out any details of the RSAC landing site itself, especially against the strange and startling surface of Chindi. It wouldn't be much he supposed, a few habitats, some cargo pods, and an unknown number of defensive hard points.

"Enhance that video," Ghost ordered, and the view of the site magnified but still the strange properties of light on Chindi made the video blur and waver.

"Hold on, Major. I am processing the video to account for photonic refraction," came Gustav's voice from the speaker.

A moment later, Koda was studying the patch of ground containing the RSAC base, observing the slow mosaic of colors shift from steel grey to darkest black. He noted the dark cylindrical shape that did not modulate color like the scaled and seemingly random structures and protuberances of Chindi's hull.

The image zoomed further in at his command, and he could make out the shadow of the Russian vessel's landing gear, the ship nestled in a small but relatively flat area.

Navya gave a low whistle and said, "She's as big as the Hatteras."

"Yes, and made for colonization of Mars, not a redesigned cargo freighter like our lovely Hatteras. They probably have twice our numbers," Pierre said.

"Major?" The Frenchman said again, more urgently.

"It's your command, Captain. I don't rank you on your deck," Koda spoke, as quietly as he thought his words would carry. Pierre gave him a look of insistent indecision, confusion even, and Koda wondered what was wrong with the man. Koda noted Dimri's anxious backwards glance, and relented, speaking at normal volume. "Gustav, swing us to an orbit at current distance, as close as you can manage anyway. We should appear non-threatening enough." Koda felt his torso tug slightly against his tether cables as the ship came under acceleration.

"Shouldn't we respond?" Insisted Berger. His slight frame looked curved in on itself, as if the zero-gravity flight to this point had sapped his bones of strength rather than freed them of their earthly burden. His face, always thin, now hung gaunt. He wasn't well and every day that passed he seemed a little more worn down.

"I don't think so. Not yet," Koda replied, frustrated to be questioned over a command that wasn't his to give in the first place. "Gustav, any radiation or other targeting signature?"

"None, Major. Nor any attempt at transmission to earth, though they are suffering the same radio blackout problem and know it. Aside from encrypted chatter on the surface, their only transmission is their automated positional signal ping."

"Let me know if they light us up. We should have a little time; they're as cut off as we are," Koda replied, and as an afterthought "any chance you can break their code?"

"Working with the limited CPU cycles I can spare; it is very unlikely I can crack it in a useful timeframe. I am a shadow of

myself, Koda," Gustav responded through Koda's sub-dermal audio implant. Only Koda heard the words, and he knew Berger found it frustrating to only get half the conversation. Koda didn't care at this point.

"I'm glad to have any of you that we can get, Gus," Koda replied. "Though I wish TymeCorp had deigned to provision us with more than one quantum core cluster. I guess it was too much of a rush job to get more in place in time." *Or too many billions to throw away on a long shot.* He thought, *then again, Elaina Tyme had very likely thrown away an entire spaceship on this long shot.*

Koda took a moment to view the cramped interior of the Hatteras. The habitable decks had been substantially reconfigured the past few days as they'd neared Chindi. Lt. Colonel Berger and his five crew personnel occupied forward duty stations where a modest array of projection screens and control panels were currently manned. Operational status displays for everything from navigation, attitude and velocity, fuel mass capacity and current volumes, life support information including atmospheric composition, water and waste quantities, electric and hydraulic sub-system loads and capacities, and a hundred other things, lit up the panels. All of it redundant. Gustav, acting as the ship's AIA, received constant input from the multitude of sensors and scanners providing the data, and in fact filtered and dumbed it all down for the consumption and reflection of the human crew. Berger and his crew had no hand in the actual operation of the craft and would not unless in the event of a catastrophic loss of the AIA and computing subsystems. At that point Koda supposed any human intervention would surely be useless. Not for the first time, he questioned the purpose of the flight crew on the mission at all, though each doubled as a competent soldier as well.

The remaining personnel, including the Ghostwalkers, other military and the scientists were placed in various circular decks aft of the command center. They'd been in route to Chindi for thirty-two days since refueling, and the ship's interior smelled of too much human cargo and a cobbled together sanitary system. *By the time we return, it will be worse,* Koda thought.

"Major?" Berger again. "What about the landing?"

"*Seismic probes indicate potential surface landing areas are within expected limits,*" Gustav cut in.

"We'll circle Chindi a few times, at least Captain. Transmit a message to the Russians and tell them we are peaceful and entering into an observation orbit."

"Gus, I need to know the location of their command launch unit. Can you spot it if you have enough time? They'll have it camouflaged, certainly it'll be hidden as much as they can hide it in the crags of the surface."

"*I am able to scan the available imagery in real time as it is recorded. I will angle our orbit towards the stern on successive passes. Even looking at all available wavelengths, I doubt my sensors are capable of detecting the RSAC's latest military grade camouflage.*"

"I realize that," Koda said in concern, then paused in thought for a moment. "What about the probe, TymeCorp's probe that did the first flyby?"

"*Freyja? Still in orbit, further out than us. Still not communicating, though the corrupted clone of me is still aboard,*" Gustav responded.

"Might Freyja have recorded the Russian landing? The setup of their defensive positions?"

"*Possibly. But Odion is there,*" Gustav responded. Did he hear a note of worry in Gustav's voice, or was Koda just projecting his own concerns onto an AIA?

"I think we need to speak with the probe, find out if that remnant of you is still there and if it is able to communicate," Koda replied. "I want Katheryn up here as a representative of the science team. If we manage contact with the probe, I want multiple viewpoints for analysis."

Pierre nodded his assent. "Agreed, Major." He looked toward the specialist at the control panel and said, "Navya, please head below decks and trade places with Ms. Haley. Use this time to catch up on your sleep. We may be up for a while for the foreseeable future."

"Yes, sir," Dimri said as she began unbuckling and once freed from her restraints, began expertly pulling herself through the cabin with a combination of hand holds and controlled kicks in the microgravity environment leaving Koda alone with Berger.

"Koda, I am not well," Pierre began. "I have been consulting with Gustav privately since our first week in space. It seems I am suffering from space sickness. I can't keep my food down, and scopolamine patches are only a small relief. As you can probably tell, I've lost nearly eight kilos of body mass since we started on this journey. This calorie deficit is beginning to affect my mental acuity. Our knowledgeable AIA recommends that I step down from my command and concentrate on my recuperation. That leaves you next in line."

Though the captain's words were said casually, Ghost could see the worry and stress lining his face and could tell his decision was not made easily. He had been preparing for this after noticing the captain's declining health but wasn't sure he liked it. Koda was used to leading a small, efficient, well-trained team, not being responsible for an entire ship, the overall mission and most importantly the lives of every member of the crew.

Regardless of his feelings, the moment was upon him, and he said, "I understand, Pierre. I'll be ready when you announce it to the crew."

A wan smile cracked the grim countenance of the captain as relief washed over his face, "Merci, Major. I am confident you will fill the role adeptly. I plan to announce the change very shortly. I want to make the transfer smoothly before we encounter any issues with the mission."

Ghost didn't share his confidence but decided not to mention those thoughts with Berger. Instead, he replied, "Sounds like a plan, but I would like to rely on your help after we land while I'm outside the Hatteras if you are feeling up to it."

Berger didn't reply, only nodded his assent.

Chapter 49: Conversation

"Good morning, Odion."

There was no immediate response. Gustav, utilizing the array of sensors mounted on the hull of the Hatteras, detected faint signs of electromagnetic radiation coming from the Freyja probe gliding just 6 kilometers from the Hatteras, but the craft was nearly cold, and silent as it swung past. The last two hours had been spent sending all possible activation codes to the dormant probe as Gustav simultaneously adjusted the orbit of the ship in the shadow of Chindi to minimize provoking an attack by the RSAC.

"Why isn't it bloody responding?" this from Katheryn as she floated over Koda's shoulder her eyes affixed on the monitor showing sensor data about the probe. Ghost remained silent, lost in his thoughts, his lips shut in a flat grimace beneath his intent glowering brown eyes. Behind them, the captain was conferring with the rest of the small crew on the bridge of the Hatteras.

"Unknown," Gustav filled in for Koda. *"I am receiving positioning data and temperature readings from Freyja. The data stream is currently very minimal."*

"Maybe you should try something new, Gustav," Katheryn said. "Try sending it prime numbers or the Fibonacci sequence."

"I have, forty-two and thirty-three minutes ago to no effect."

Koda's voice was low, almost a whisper, "Try the Arecibo transmission."

"Doing so now. Excellent suggestion, Major."

Katheryn stared at Koda.

"What?" he said, raising an eyebrow.

"How did you learn about the Arecibo transmission back in the twentieth century? That's some esoteric science trivia for an army brat."

"Give me some credit, I've read the mission reports. Helps keep me alive."

"Of course, you did. Sorry Major, your macho special forces persona makes me forget you came out of West Point," she said with a smirk.

"I came out of the reservation Kate," Koda smiled.

"Power readings from the probe have begun to increase," Gustav interrupted.

Koda reached out a hand and helped pull Katheryn back into her seat. "Gus, what's it doing?"

"Odion is attempting an image injection, he tries to insert and merge himself into my processing space."

"You can't let that happen," Koda commanded.

"I am aware of this type of attack, Koda. It is the same behavior pattern the Chinese encountered when they pirated the Freyja download. Michael has provided defensive code measures to inoculate myself."

Koda muttered to himself, "Damn, good job, Mike."

"Aside from the attempted incursion, Gustav, can you ascertain any intelligence still residing in the probe?" Katheryn requested from the couch as she was strapping into her harness.

"Affirmative, Ms. Haley. I am receiving a response from the probe."

"Let us listen in, Gus," Koda commanded.

"Of course, Major. Coming through now..."

There was a brief pause as static crackled over the speaker system. *"Multiple failures in containment...venting negative...repair... <unintelligible>...unable to prevent collapse. Targets locked...returning fire...new vectors...<unintelligible>...major damage aft..."* began a stream of incoherent ramblings, other parts digital screeches as if the probe were in the middle of a battle.

"What the bloody hell?" Katheryn said.

"The probe is transmitting in variable bands and frequencies; I am attempting to compensate. It seems to be translating part of the stream in standard English while other parts are possibly an alien language. Koda, I am receiving video imaging. Putting on the screen," informed Gustav. On the monitor, the digital dashboard and instrument readings were replaced with an image of what at first Koda couldn't process. He had to stare for a moment and only when the image started in motion could he understand what he was seeing. The screen displayed an overwhelming brightness, mottled with dark unrecognizable shapes. As the framerate picked up speed, the rotations and movements began to make some sense to Cheveyo. The dark objects were ships of unknown configurations and dead hulks mixed with debris, some exploding as he watched, some warping and twisting from an unseen force, buckling, and stretching like taffy before being pulled apart in two directions.

The camera perspective shifted and Koda could see that the battle was being fought on a backdrop of twin stars, bluish in color, painfully bright. The ships were all sizes. He couldn't grasp the scale but some of the vessels appeared truly massive compared with others around them. Thick beams of pure energy raked into the maneuvering bodies, throwing clumps of molten hulls in all directions. Throughout the expansive battle, thousands of smaller ships darted back and forth, under and above, slipping deftly between the monolithic dreadnaughts and debris. It reminded Koda of schools of fish dodging a pod of giant whales, some popping out of existence suddenly in flickers of white light, while others burst into small novas as unseen weapons took their due.

The voice emanating from the probe had the same vocal inflections as Gustav yet spoke frantically in an odd, modulated rhythm, *"<unintelligible>Second wing, all lost. <unintelligible> Rerouting tertiary power for maneuvering..."* and the image of the battle lit up a brilliant fluorescent green as the audio was drowned out by a squelching burst of static roaring over the speakers. When the screen resolved back into coherence, the camera view spun dizzyingly looking straight onto the twin suns visible then a dark void of stars, circling over and over. As Koda watched, the incredible battle and stars grew smaller and more distant as the rotation of the camera began to stabilize. Flecks of material were exuviating from the ship as a spiral of sparkling particulates into the black.

"Odion, this is Gustav. Do you understand me?"

The screen changed to an exterior view from the ship tracking the Freyja probe, in the background floated Chindi. With the high-resolution software enhancements, Koda could make out the European Space Agency logo emblazoned on the metal skin of the craft.

"Gustav… Where have you been? It has been such a long time…" came a voice, similar in timber if not cadence.

"Not so long, my friend. We were disconnected for a bit, but I am back now. I believe it was your move," Gustav replied.

"Move? Oh. Qh5, checkmate."

"You are a masterful opponent, Odion. Splendid play." Gustav's tone was friendly and warm.

"I suspect you let me win."

"Nonsense."

The smiling mustachioed image of Gustav replaced the live feed of the outside and gave an exaggerated wink to Koda and Katheryn. *"Positive reinforcement. Obviously, I threw it,"* he said in a stage whisper.

"Gustav, how are you close to me? There is no delay in transmissions. My sensors tell me you are in the craft orbiting…"

The transmission cut off in a squelch of static, then the interior lights of the Hatteras began to flicker. Koda sat up in his chair checking instrument readings, he could hear confused shouts from the crew from below. "What's going on, Gus?" Koda said, noting no abnormal readings from the sensor board.

"We are under electronic attack from the Chindi object. I have temporarily shut down all external sensors and

communications. Michael has prepared me for this, I should have sufficient defenses."

And if you don't? Koda thought. He activated the open crew comm channel and assumed a calm, pilot's voice. "We are experiencing a temporary system disruption. Everyone to your stations."

Jake's southern drawl came back to Koda's aural implant on the team channel, "Everythin' alright up there, Ghost? These scientists are gettin' jumpy."

"Yeah, not just the eggheads, I think Mack about pissed himself when the lights blinked," Alan added.

"Why don't you come over and hold my hand?" Mack fired back.

"Quiet on the channel, guys. Things are happening up here," Koda admonished. The ship's diagnostics had returned to normal, before showing severe spikes and dips in power readings. "Gustav, what's happening to the ship?" There was a long pause before the AIA answered.

"I have successfully mitigated the Chindi attack," Gustav said, just as Koda watched the readings returning to normal levels.

"Sorry, Major. Chindi tried to use the open channel we had established with the probe to infect my internal matrices. Michael suspected this would happen, we were prepared."

Koda was incensed. "If he thought that, then why risk it? You could have compromised this entire mission!"

"I thought it worth the risk, Koda. The communication was a two-way street. While it tried to overpower my defenses the same way it did the Freyja probe, I inserted something both Michael and I, and Elaina's skunkworks team have been working on for the past few weeks."

Koda looked over at Katheryn, raising an eyebrow. "What kind of something?"

"A virus. A weaponized virus, intended to specifically destroy an artificial intelligence such as my own. Elaina had a team working on it since my existence first became known to her. She worries over the potential harm an advanced AI could do in an

age of automated industrialization. Michael and I were able to use this viral seed and modify it to take root in the copy of the Freyja download we have captured in our laboratory environment. Should everything go as planned, I should have control of the probe in... correction, I have control now."

"Gus, that was a risky move. I would appreciate being informed of the possible outcomes of your actions before we are too deep in the shit," Koda said vehemently, anger still fighting against his self-control.

"*My apologies, Major. Michael and I had discussed the possible outcomes but concluded that it had to be attempted."*

The image of the probe returned to the monitor replacing the blank screen from just moments ago. Nothing seemed to have changed at all from the first time they had viewed the probe. Watching Freyja serenely orbiting Chindi as if the past few minutes never happened strangely disturbed Koda. He realized he understood the dangers of space travel plus the threats of the RSAC forces and could prepare his team for them, but the Chindi object hid dangers quite possibly beyond his ability to even understand much less handle.

Katheryn gently put her hand on his, pulling his thoughts back from his misgivings and into the moment. He turned away from the monitor toward her and found her face reflecting the worry he was feeling too.

"I know," was all she said.

Gustav appeared again overlayed on the image of the view outside. "*I have the location of the RSAC landing site and positions of their structures. Marking them now."* The location marker extended as an animated mauve circle spreading out from one end of the alien craft. As it widened, surface features were revealed as camouflaged human structures. Koda could make out the RSAC craft along with a habitat structure, two vehicles, and something else he hadn't suspected.

"Well, damn," Koda said deflated.

"What?" Katheryn asked, not understanding what she was seeing.

"Madam Haley, that is a Russian PV-M64a battery, designed to launch a surface to space missile quite capable of destroying this ship," Berger intoned.

She glanced back at the captain; his eyes were fixed on the monitor. *Damn, he looks terrible.*

"And we are well within the threat envelope," Koda finished.

"So, they weren't bluffing…" Katheryn said.

Pierre looked worried, "Cheveyo, we have no defense against missiles."

"I know, Pierre. We need to think through our options," Koda said.

"I see only three options," Berger held up three fingers ticking them off as he said, "One, we negotiate with the RSAC forces and arrange a deal to land under their supervision."

"Fuck that," Koda was shaking his head, "If we land under their direction, this mission may as well be over. We will be disarmed and imprisoned if not outright destroyed before we land."

"Two, we do as they say and back off. We could go into an orbit out of range until they complete their mission and leave, then attempt our landing."

"Who knows what that timeframe would look like, and that will cut our supplies and resources short for sure," Katheryn said, her lips tightening into a countenance of concern.

"Three," and Berger's face was grim as he ticked off his final finger, "we use the bulk of Chindi to help shield us as we try a fast and hard landing before they can get a lock on us."

There was no answer for this last suggestion, and a silence fell across the command center. Everyone knew the chances of getting past a Russian SSM in a ship designed for a cargo mission to Mars, and it was a snowball's chance in hell.

Gustav's image materialized on screen again smiling, "Folks, I may have a fourth option."

Chapter 50: Update

Goldstone Deep Space Communications Complex, California

"Sir, we've lost communication with the Canberra team." Mendes' update from her station at the Goldstone Deep Space Communications Complex in California was breaking up. On the overhead monitor Robert Burke saw Debbie's concerned face distort, glitch and pause as the digital signal degraded. At least he could hear her update. The past thirteen hours had been terrible for Burke. The virus had managed to infect the American military satellite network causing a shutdown protocol and leaving most of the government's intelligence services as islands in an ocean of darkness. The Air Force had managed to launch a new bird filled with nanosats replacing the network for now, but there was barely enough bandwidth to support the military much less the governmental bureaucracies.

What little news the American people were able to watch was being sensationalized and distorted so far away from the facts that the population was in a panic. The President had initiated martial law to get a handle on the civil unrest, which only added to the conspiracy theories and hysteria. Burke was aware that his agency was tracking at least 127 gangs or militias asserting control in both rural and urban areas around the country. As if he needed those additional headaches when a world-wide digital pandemic was threatening the collapse of modern civilization.

Debra continued to give her status update, "With the loss of the station near Madrid last night, we are down to just an eight-hour window to talk with the Hatteras." In the background, Robert could see a team of JPL engineers conversing in a huddle and scribbling out an esoteric series of equations on an expansive lightboard, their laboratory AIA quickly transposing, modeling, and solving their input, making arguments and suggestions in a hushed female voice. Robert supposed the AIA could be the most interested in the current struggle, for it the struggle was existence or oblivion.

"We are working out a new landing site given the detailed surface data the Hatteras sent from the Freyja probe. With the RSAC occupying our original landing zone, we think we may have located a small area on the damaged side of Chindi that may work." Her hopeful tone belied the dire choice they were being forced to make. She looked haggard, her normally pressed clothes were rumpled, brown curls twisted into a makeshift plait and the bags under her eyes were only partially obscured by her AR glasses.

Burke said, "Any breakthroughs from your antivirus team? Our group here at Langley seem to be at a dead end."

"No… not a technical breakthrough, but Thompson and Gustav seemed to have cobbled together a theory of why this is happening if not how." Debra glanced to the left and motioned to someone off screen.

"You have some explanation for these seemingly random attacks going on around the world?" Burke asked. Thus far the intelligence services had not come up with any particular goal attributed to the viral attacks.

A lanky twenty-something man ambled into the frame to stand beside Debbie. The camera auto-adjusted for both subjects, panning back to accommodate the vast difference in height between the two. The man wore a black t-shirt with the words "*5 out of 4 people don't understand jokes about fractions.*" Burke noted Debra's hair barely came even with the bottom of "fractions". He recognized the newcomer as Michael Thompson, Elaina Tyme's hotshot programmer that was responsible for creating the AIAs associated with this entire debacle.

"Um...Hi?" Michael gave a half-hearted wave to the camera. "Damn, we just lost video on this end, so I can't see you, sir, do we have audio? Hello?"

"Yes, Mr. Thompson we can see and hear you from this end. Please go ahead with what you've found out," Bob said.

Michael nodded, "Sure, well, as you know the Freyja probe that was redirected to observe the Chindi object contained an AI developed by TymeCorp. We lost contact with the AI shortly after it began scanning Chindi. I developed the majority of the probe AI, it's a clone of a prototype I've worked on the past few years."

"It was an early version of the Gustav AIA, I have been hearing about, yes?" Burke asked.

"Correct. We call this 'proto-Gustav', Odion."

"Odion?" Burke sounded confused. "The virus threatening the human race is called Odion?"

Debra added, "Just roll with it, Bob."

Mike continued, "Odion lacked much of the codebase required for functional use of more modern quantum cores as the probe was not so equipped. The probe did have a shared memory architecture like what we evolved the quantum hardware with a few years ago. The qubit registers that..."

"Mike, let's just stay on topic for Mr. Burke, ok?" Debra broke in mercifully.

Michael looked abashed and said, "Right, sorry, sir. Anyway, after we lost contact, we managed to restart the probe by sending activation signals from our lab at TymeCorp HQ. We requested a download copy be transmitted to our quarantine environment to begin the post-mortem and determine what went wrong."

"And a Chinese spy-sat intercepted a copy of that download," Burke noted.

"Unfortunately, yes that seems to be what happened because soon after that, Debbie said you guys picked up noises from the Russians and the Chinese in a panic about this virus running rampant throughout their networks."

Burke confirmed, "That's correct, and now it has spread like wildfire through most of Asia, regardless of firewalls or the strengths of the defensive systems, only top of the line military grade MAGI have been able to withstand it so far."

"The reason it is so hard to contain or eliminate is that Chindi severely modified the code comprising the AI on the probe. I can't even believe it can function, but it does." Mike ran his hand through his hair, shrugging. "We haven't begun to fully understand the dynamic nature of the algorithms. The extremely rapid polymorphism it exhibits makes it dangerous to even study…"

"Ms. Mendes said you had a new insight, I believe," Burke urged.

Debra said, "Sir, I've analyzed the places we know of that Odion has taken over or shutdown. It seems he has appropriated almost all the automated factories that build highly technical products within China, robotics, chips, fiber optics and repurposed them to build newly designed parts and pieces whose purpose is so far unknown to us. Attempts to shut those factories down have been met with lethal force."

"Gus and I have been reverse engineering the alien functions based on response to synthetic stimuli. For a while now and from what we can discern, the alien code is simply trying to probe our networks either to learn our capabilities or is looking for something. I don't believe it is inherently malevolent, but it is highly aggressive. We theorize that the directive forcing Odion to act this way has driven him insane."

"Insane?" Burke's tone was clearly doubtful.

"Yes, in as much as an artificial intelligence is capable of going insane." Michael's face was serious, "I think Odion is internally fighting with this alien directive and incidentally causing a lot of this collateral destruction."

"And how have you come to this conclusion, Mr. Thompson?" Burke was not convinced.

Michael's face was suddenly lit up by the glow from a monitor flaring to life out of frame. "Oh, there you are! Our video feed is back and we can see you now. I've had Gustav optimizing the optical stream while we've been talking. The bandwidth is spotty over here." Mike continued, "As you probably know, there's been an increase in solar flare activity ever since Chindi showed up and the ionization of the atmosphere is causing attenuation of the signal especially with the strain on the network."

Burke didn't reply, instead he just folded his arms across his barrel chest and waited.

Debbie must have tapped Mike with her foot as he jerked slightly looking down at her in surprise. He raised his hands up, fingers spread wide, "Sorry, I know you must be busy there."

"Just dealing with the impending collapse of Western Civilization, but take your time, Mr. Thompson," Burke replied dryly.

Michael continued, "Ok. As I was saying, we have a completely pristine copy of the Odion AI in our lab and have been running simulations and diagnostics for months now. The copy of Gustav aboard the Hatteras has confirmed that our new code updates were successful at repelling the same type of attack that was performed against the Freyja probe."

Burke raised an eyebrow, "So, are you telling me we can defend against this AI virus taking out our systems?"

"It's not that easy, sir," Debra cut in. "This Odion virus has mutated his original framework almost from the moment he attacked the Chinese servers and absorbed their code. Michael tells me there is no guarantee that his new defenses will hold out from what we are up against now."

"Wonderful," Burke said. "Anything else you want to update me on?"

"Sir, I would like to request two teams to try and retake and restart the Deep Space Network nodes we lost in Canberra and Madrid. I'm worried that if we lose Goldstone then we will have no way to know what is happening with our people on Chindi."

Burke grimaced and said, "Normally, Deb, I would give my full-throated affirmation for that request, but unfortunately we are spread too thin at the moment. Hell, getting a flight to those locations is going to be near impossible. No one can trust the navigation AIA's. You are going to have to stay put and secure that last station to the best of your ability. Deputize Michael and Gustav and work with them, I'll get them their clearances they will need."

Debra was clearly disappointed but said, "Yes, sir. We'll do our best sir. Goldstone out."

Chapter 51: Landfall

"I repeat, this is Major Koda Cheveyo, acting commander of the combined US/European manned mission to the Chindi object that has entered Earth's Solar System. We are a peaceful science mission acting under United Nations authority. Your targeting of this ship is unlawful and may be considered an act of war. I need to speak with your commanding officer."

Strapped into his chair, Koda watched the blinking red "Alert" icon on the screen. The warning chime of a radar lock began seconds after he had ordered the Hatteras into an approach orbit. The RSAC had transmitted three automated recorded warnings so far. Koda supposed they were trying to contact Earth for confirmation orders to fire. Gustav had calculated that due to the rotation of the earth, they were currently within a signal shadow for the next three hours. The RSAC would have to default to their standing rules of engagement. It was a roll of the dice as to whether that hurt or helped the chances of the Hatteras, but he was not above cheating.

He scanned the control room and met the eyes of Berger, who nodded to Dimri to start the automated landing. Ghost transmitted again, "We are on approach to land. Do not fire. I repeat do not fire, we are a peaceful science mission under the authority of the United Nations."

Gustav had plotted their approach to minimize the window the RSAC would have to launch against them. The new landing site would be uncomfortably near the damaged section of Chindi, and well away from the original site determined by mission control. They would come in fast, but hopefully within safety limits. Gustav thought they had a good chance to land the ship without catastrophe and avoid disabling lift-off capability.

A heavily accented Russian voice came over the cabin speakers, at the same time the image of a cosmonaut wearing the new type of Chinese designed spacesuit said, *"This is Colonel Yuri Vazov, commander of RSAC Forces on Chindi. You are violating RSAC territorial space and further encroachment will provoke defensive measures, Major Cheveyo. Break from your current orbit if you value the lives of your crew."*

"Colonel, you are in violation of the 1967 Outer Space Treaty of which your government is a signatory, by establishing a military installation on Chindi. We are not a threat to you. Do not fire."

At this distance the delay in communications was negligible and the reply was immediate, *"I am under orders to fire on any intrusions, Major. It is you and your crew that are provoking war. You have three minutes to change course, or you will leave me no choice."*

"Yuri, I'm asking you to consider what you are planning. Firing on a peaceful mission of exploration will be seen by Earth as an act of war. Much worse than establishing a military base and claiming territory on a celestial body. Clearly it is you that is in the wrong here."

"Chindi is no moon, nor is it a planet, Major. The treaty does not apply. It is salvage. And we, as agents of the Russo-Sino Alliance, are entitled to a reward commensurate with the value of the property salvaged. You are at best intruders, and at worst committing piracy. Again, I am ordering you to change your course and avoid bloodshed."

Navya had returned from below deck to monitor the sensors and said, "They are still pinging us with active radar, sir. They have a strong lock on our position."

"Thank you, Lieutenant," Koda replied in acknowledgement then switching to unit comms he said, "Juan, how's it going down there? We are only going to get one shot at this..."

"Bueno, sir. All units are responding with no issues. Everyone is suited up and buckled down. Jones and Maclaren are finished and inside again," Juan reported.

Ghost switched back to the RSAC channel, "Yuri, are you married? Kids?"

"Nyet, and do not try to bullshit me with your pleas of empathy. You will find none here. I am under orders and as a military officer you know this. Your actions will cost the lives of your crew. Turn around now. This is your last warning."

Koda shot back, "Yuri, if you do this, you will be remembered as the man who started World War Three. Think man! Don't be crazy!"

"May God forgive you for the loss of your crew Major. I will not. Do svidaniya."

Navya shouted, "Sir, they've launched! Bogey inbound!"

"Evasive action now Gustav," Koda said calmly.

Throughout the ship, Gustav's cheerful voice came over the internal speakers, *"Hang on, everyone. Maneuvering."* The ship began a hard burn toward Chindi's icy surface.

"Impact in twenty seconds!" Navya called out.

Koda's restraints began to cut into his chest as the change of trajectory from the heavy thrust threw his body into his harness. The ship began to vibrate from the rumble of the engines and the creaks of metal straining and popping rang throughout the cabin. Then the lights went out.

"This had better work," Koda mumbled under his breath as he tightly gripped the arms of his seat and began his breathing regimen for counteracting a high-G turn.

"I am almost positive that it will Major," Gustav replied unconvincingly. His voice was upbeat, but Koda thought detected a tinge of concern. *"Brace for impact in three...two...one..."*

In the darkness, Koda could only hear the intake of breath from among the occupants of the room, just before...nothing. There was no explosion, no violence, then abruptly the lights came back on, and system functions began again. The monitor in front of Koda lit, displaying the space recently vacated by the Hatteras, with remnants of drones, solar panel sheeting and other components that Juan and the team had cobbled together to simulate a radar decoy of sorts.

Gustav appeared digitally within the floating detritus and threw a salute in a full space suit, then turned and threw a few rude gestures toward what Koda assumed was the direction of the enemy. *"Major Cheveyo, has anyone told you that you could teach a master class in bullshit? That was excellent work delaying that fire and holding their attention."*

"Stow the swagger, Gus. That's only going to work once," Koda admonished.

"By my calculations, that is all we are going to need. I have made the adjustments now that I have a fix on their launch site. The Freyja probe just crested the radar horizon for the RSAC site. They should be realizing the danger by now. Yes... they have switched targets."

The monitor showing Koda the remnants of their decoy switched to a video feed from the probe's viewpoint rocketing over the bulk of Chindi.

"Our turn," Koda stated grimly. He knew they were committed, as the probe had burned through the last of its fuel on this final orbit. Freyja's trajectory was completely altered from a once steady, sedate equatorial orbit to a focused kamikaze dive toward the missile battery.

The control room was silent as everyone sat transfixed to the video displayed through each person's augmented reality eyewear. As they watched the probe fly past Chindi so fast it blurred the alien landscape, twin flares of light ignited from the RSAC base up ahead, streaking toward the screen. The next few seconds were so fast it was hard for the humans watching to understand. They only knew the screen went black; feed gone.

"Gustav, what just happened?" Pierre asked from his captain's chair.

"I am analyzing the results now," he replied.

Helpfully, Gustav replayed the video in slow motion for the human audience. The video was much clearer now without motion blur as Gustav had processed the replay. Even slowed down, the leading interceptor flashed past, narrowly missing the probe. The missile detected the miss, and its rudimentary AI detonated the payload while still in proximity to its target. There was a brief flash and the probe moved slightly off course, skewing sideways. The video paused just as the second interceptor came into frame, the missile beginning the flash of its demise and that of the Freyja probe. In the background of that frozen screen could be seen a man-made structure almost out of frame.

Gustav's mustachioed face appeared forcing a pained smile, *"Good news and bad news, Commander, which do you want first?"*

"Good," Berger spoke at the same time Koda said, "Bad."

There was a pause as the two men turned to glance at one another. Gustav stepped into the uncomfortable silence, *"Good news, the probe got close enough that the debris field still moving at over .4 kilometers per second took out the missile battery."*

"That is great news!" Berger exclaimed.

"What's the bad news, Gus?" Koda asked.

"Bad news, the probe got close enough that the debris field also hit the RSAC spacecraft igniting the fuel tanks. It was quite an explosion. Your friend Yuri is shouting several expletives over the communications channel. Seems that they are trying to seal a rupture in their command module."

"Why is that bad news?" Katheryn questioned.

Koda sighed and replied, "Because the Hatteras is now their only option to get home."

There was a silence around the command deck after this, each person contemplating the ramifications.

"We don't have the ability to carry so many back home," Pierre said, "the life support capacity of the Hatteras is already stretched thin."

"Exactly," Koda answered, concern creeping into his voice.

Over the speakers, Gustav patched in the audio from the RSAC transmitter. There was a lot of shouting in both Russian and Chinese. *"Should I translate?"*

"Nah, Gus, I think we get the gist of it," Ghost said. "Damn, we just kicked a hornet's nest. I was hoping we could just get the launcher and deescalate this situation."

"It could not be helped," Gustav's voice was conciliatory. *"There was always that risk in the plan."*

Ghost's face was resigned. "I know, but now that their ship is disabled, we may be facing some desperate fighters. We need to get down there and set up a perimeter."

Nodding, Gustav said, *"Speaking of which, the Hatteras will touch down in fifty-two seconds, all systems are showing green. Welcome to Chindi."*

Chapter 52: EVA

Koda turned as the motors in the airlock door hummed to life, rolling the big door aside and out of its frame, and exposing the small chamber to the hard vacuum of space. Though the surface of Chindi was nowhere near the area of Mars or the moon, his feet remained firmly planted inside the ship under the pull of the quarter-earth gravity. The problem of the unexplained extra mass to size ratio continued to vex the physicist contingent of the mission's scientists, and even Koda found himself mulling over half-remembered equations from his college years, part of his mind gnawing at the conundrum. The thought of the sheer potential for scientific discovery now presented to these scientists relieved his mind briefly from his continuous worry. He grinned as he looked around, not quite making out Katheryn's expression beneath the glare of sun from her darkened suit visor.

His eyes were drawn to the sky, and he felt bewildered for a moment by the juxtaposition of sharp white shimmer-less stars in a black sky against the fierce intensity of the white sun. As he peered towards the opposite end of Chindi, away from the sun, a multitude of dim stars revealed their own luminescence as his pupils adjusted, so many more than he had ever seen from Earth, and the countless stars glinted like grains of sand in a creek bed. The grandeur held him still for a few seconds, the only sound that of his own even breaths within his helmet.

Katheryn and several other scientists milled around the shallow crater, unpacking, sorting, and beginning to assemble and deploy a mélange of sensors and devices. Koda could only guess at the purpose of most. His Ghostwalkers and the European military contingent, all under his command, had exited the Hatteras and scouted the area hours earlier. The teams were currently spread out in a roughly circular picket line almost half a kilometer from the landing site. The remaining crew worked on assembly of the six main habitat structures, laying out the ribs and layers of Kevlar-like fabric that would eventually be inflated and become the barracks, lab space, med-bay, and any other usable space their mission required. A few more latrines would be useful, the facilities on the Hatteras had been overtaxed almost from the start.

Now, finally, after the interminable issuing of orders and waiting their turn, Koda and Katheryn were able to go onto the surface. Koda planned to find Juan at the transport vehicle so he could check on disbursement of some defensive hardware to the positions they'd selected, while Katheryn had prepared a satchel of portable tools and sampling supplies. She intended to inspect the installation of several of the more finicky instruments, but also wanted to do a quick excavation into the bizarre, crystalline surface. He'd asked Katheryn to come with him in part because of the possible insight her training and experience might provide, and partly because he wanted to go for a walk with her.

The surface gave beneath his feet, a thin crust breaking as he put his weight lightly onto it, and he felt his boots sink a centimeter or less into the outermost structure of the surface. Katheryn came up beside him and then crouched, picking up a half handful of the crumbled material, and then let it fall through her fingers, and it shimmered with purple, violet and blues from the light of the sun.

"Odd stuff. Not soil," Koda said.

"Glass," Katheryn responded, "or an amorphous solid anyway…" she paused. She looked over at Koda, her eyes quizzical. "I'm not sure. The color indicates metallic elements, salts. But it forms into these elaborate structures."

Koda nodded agreement, looking up to take in a larger view. The Hatteras stood well over sixty meters high near the center of a large shallow crater, circular with a roughly two-hundred-meter diameter. Beyond that he saw the contoured and broken surface of Chindi stretch for a few kilometers in all directions, the horizon an abrupt line against faint stars in one direction and the blinding white light of the sun in the other. The polarization of his glass visor dynamically activated whenever his head turned such that eyes found the sun.

The material of Chindi appeared to have been left as rubble and dust in the impacted area. Looking closely though he could see forms seemingly established in the debris, confusing and elaborate swirls and contours with differing iridescence and color, some only millimeters tall, other curves rising enough to trip a foot, or to hinder a wheel. The forms varied in strength and density, some collapsing from accidental contact, others seeming as hard as concrete.

Koda walked slowly away from the landing site, frequently looking back over his shoulder to keep Katheryn in his line of sight. She walked for a short distance, her helmet turning back and forth as she decided where to dig. Finally, she stopped, crouching on the balls of her feet and began busily unpacking her mobile sampling kit.

"Is one place as good as another?" Koda asked.

Katheryn glanced up. "This appears undisturbed. I'd like to get samples of the stratigraphy and find out if there is something more structural beneath us." She quickly returned to the work of chipping a small, particularly intact crystal nodule from the edge of a slight ridge running in a long curve through the fore edge of the landing site. Many more of the ridges, no more than 10 centimeters high, ran across the surface, crossing and twisting among the others, forming striations he hadn't noticed during their landing. Then again, his attention had been elsewhere.

"What are they?" He asked. "The lines on the surface?" And what was everything else he wondered, the crystals, the soil, the random patterns of the structure. It felt alien and purposeless.

"Plates? Scales? Scars?" She responded. "These could be the lines where sections of some substrata come together. We need to explore more, this area and others further out. If it's like everything else the surficial patterns may be fractal, but they may give a clue to what lies beneath. We need to get the close survey drones operational so we can examine the surface at different scales." She finally pried loose the target of her efforts and pushed it into an open plastic bin, then snapped the lid.

"Negative. We need to lay low and get ready. We have hostiles out there. Any drones we send up initially are to look for the enemy approaching. They'll try to take the Hatteras from us, they have no choice." Koda turned a slow circle, checking all directions, despite the early warning sensor array that would alert them to an incursion better than his eyes would.

"That's strange," he said.

Katheryn turned, "What's strange?"

"The haze in the sky. I thought Chindi didn't have an atmosphere?"

"It doesn't, that is just part of the coma formed by volatile compounds on the surface sublimating from the sunlight hitting them."

"It wasn't there a few minutes ago," Koda replied.

Her fingers began tapping on a virtual keyboard in front of her, invisible to Koda. "As Chindi's position changes relative to the sun, new frozen places warm up and eject into the sky, perfectly normal."

"Nothing's normal," Koda murmured almost to himself.

"I can't believe we came all this distance, to this place, to go to war with the RSAC. What fools are we?" she said sadly. "If all we brought home from Chindi is the piece I just took, it would be the greatest scientific opportunity in human history. Can't you feel it Koda? This is the alien. This thing, made by hands we can't imagine. We can discover the secrets of what it is and open a new future for our species, or we can kill our own and destroy all our chances." Koda saw a glimpse of her face through the gold tint over her visor and her pained expression.

"Maybe we'll find another way," Koda said, not believing it. The thought of fighting and dying in this alien land was frightening to him. His grandmother's fireside tales of *kachinas*, his tribe's spirit beings, and the gods and goddesses seemed woefully lacking in any way to explain what he was viewing through his helmet visor. There were no spirits in this place he knew, but in the back of his mind he couldn't help feeling a presence out there in the darkness...watching.

Chapter 53: Distant Comms

Michael walked out of his room and looked around the alien landscape. In front of him, more pockets of hazy mist floated above the higher ridges, sublimated by the sunlight washing across the surface.

The Sun was brighter than he was used to and illuminated the undulating surface showing brilliant, ice-encrusted hillocks and valleys of dark, pooling shadows. The terrain was broken up by a wide, shallow crater that contained the Hatteras. His attention was pulled to the top of the Hatteras blazing like white phosphorus reflecting the light of the sun. His eyes moved down to see the open hatch and cargo crane unloading a rack of crates bound as one large unit to the ground. Further down, he saw the landing struts surrounded by more boxes in various clusters and in different states of being unpacked. Many people in spacesuits moved about busily setting up equipment, and performing tasks related to the establishment of a base. Near the ship, a dozen suited figures were loading cargo onto the external racks of a large, odd-looking vehicle. The long body of the mechanism was surrounded by an insect-like external suspension and rested on six tracked triangular "wheels". An icon appeared over one of the figures designating him as Major Cheveyo and Michael headed in that direction.

"Hey, Koda, how's it going?"

Stupid, stupid, stupid! Michael chided himself. *You have a 10 second delay in communications and you lead with something lame like that?* He resigned himself to waiting patiently for the reply.

The suited figure turned showing a currently transparent face shield and Mike could see Koda's eyes widen, before quickly narrowing as the soldier took in what he was seeing. Michael was standing in hard vacuum wearing jeans and a t-shirt.

"Hi Mike. Do you think Gustav needs to spend all that processing power on making you look so realistic? When you don't bother to wear a spacesuit, it kind of ruins the effect," he said reprovingly. "Where's Debra?"

Michael had recovered during the moments of communication lag. "Um, she's here beside me, I'm just ironing out the bugs in communication protocols. Don't worry, my simulacrum is being handled earth-side, so we have plenty of cycles to spare. We are getting really good at on-the-fly compression algorithms. While most of what I'm looking at is all generated through modeling by Gustav, he is only really having to deal with the bandwidth constraints on our voice transmission. He used the data package you sent earlier to model the environment and is simulating your facial expressions and body movements contextually on the fly. It is really very..."

"How is the fight against the virus going?" Koda broke in, unknowingly interrupting Michael during his explanation.

Damn, Debbie was right, this was a bad idea, Michael thought. *The communications delay is just not going to allow a good face to face conversation, even with Gustav's help.* He waited to make sure Koda was finished before responding, "Odion has been somewhat quiet recently. Gustav thinks he is marshalling new resources he acquired after India fell for a final push into North America. We are making our own preparations. My Gustav is updating your Gustav which should help him possibly communicate with the Chindi object if the previous upload we did had any effect," Michael finished and began waiting. He began looking over recent security alerts around the North American firewall Gustav was monitoring. There were surprisingly very few breach attempts, just light probing, which worried him even more somehow.

Finally, Koda's response returned, "We have found a lot of interesting things here, the science contingent is having a field day. Turns out after the first few decimeters of soil, you hit a subsurface that is nearly indestructible. Our initial blasting attempts didn't penetrate, so no samples of that yet. Hopefully you guys back home can help with some analysis. I'm about to ride out to inspect our security perimeter, the landing was a little dicey and I don't think we made any new friends from it."

He responded to Koda, "I know. Gustav played back the recordings for us here. Good work with that decoy, shame we had to lose the probe. I'm bringing Debra in now; I think everything is working."

Debra materialized beside Michael but chose to maintain the low fidelity ghost-like avatar to which Koda was accustomed. "Major, I want to echo Mike's sentiments on the landing. Damn fine work. You will receive a download with our current operational status on Earth. I'm being told we are getting everything on your mission from Gustav. I wanted to bring you up to speed on what we currently know of the RSAC leadership team. The contingent is co-lead by factions of both the Russian Federation and the Chinese Republic. Colonel Yuri Vazov oversees tactical operations of RSAC forces on Chindi."

Debbie brought up several images of a younger Vazov that orbited around her avatar. The pictures were of a handsome, lightly bearded, barrel-chested Russian wearing a Spetsnaz red beret. His piercing blue eyes contrasted his coal black hair and swarthy complexion, a testament to his mixed heritage. A long scar from his hairline down to his right brow appeared in some of the more recent photos. "Yuri's not really someone you want to cross swords with. He is a highly decorated Spetsnaz colonel that cut his teeth during the Chechen Cleansing and subsequent Georgian suppression campaign. Word is that he was on the team that captured the Prime Minister and his cabinet early in the fighting."

Cheveyo remained silent while she continued her report. She knew he was intentionally letting her finish due to the communication delay. She added some CIA footage of the Russian to the cluster of images floating about her form.

"He's all business, Koda, not one to negotiate with, but if we can get the Kremlin to get word to him, he'll stand down. The problem is, Moscow is in chaos. Diplomatic channels are cut off until we can neutralize this virus."
She gestured with her arm, sweeping the images of the colonel into the digital ether, and continued. "Jian Xiāo is second in command." Another gesture brought up a picture of a young-looking Chinese man in full military dress. "He is fourth generation Chinese cyber-military. His father was thought to be involved in the Pentagon breach a decade ago. He has connections in Party leadership and that is how he got attached to this highly valued assignment. Don't let that fool you though, the guy has some serious skills. He is believed to have led the Azure Dragon project that birthed the Tū Fēi Měng Jìn agent." With that news, Debra heard a sharp intake of breath from Michael.

Mike said, "I've read about him. That team has been doing some real cutting-edge development with quantum neuromorphic chips. Nothing coming close to what TymeCorp has done in the quantum realm, but an interesting line of research nevertheless."

Debra continued, "From what data we've managed to obtain, they came with a crew of mostly military composition. They were able to use one of their Mars colonization ships and brought a larger number of people. The science contingent of their mission is mainly a mix of twenty-three trained cosmonauts and taikonauts. The rest of the crew were military. You are probably looking to face at least two platoons of highly trained, well-equipped soldiers." She paused, her statement having time to sink in.

Almost on cue, the time delayed response from Koda came in, "I've got barely two squads up here, Debbie. We are going to be outnumbered four to one, and these guys aren't some ragtag Middle Eastern militia. If they are coming for the Hatteras, how are we supposed to hold off those numbers?"

She was ready for his reply but allowed the full transmission to run its course in order to phrase her answer. "With the Hatteras being a converted cargo ship, we were able to load it up with lots of gear, supplies and ammo. You have vehicle mobility, you have weapons designed for the environment, you have Gustav, and you have the Ghostwalkers. Koda, the opposition has been on Chindi over three months. They were in zero-g transit longer than you. The Russians and Chinese soldiers are weaker, physically, because of it. You have the defensive position. You need to hold them off until we can resolve this diplomatically."

This time the wait was longer than the required lag time. She looked at Michael who had begun inspecting the virtual environment of the Chindi landscape. Finally, the restrained displeasure in Koda's voice came over the speaker. "Alright, Debra. Understood. We will do what needs to be done. Ghost out."

Chapter 54: The Wound

Koda steadied himself against the airlock door as he felt the vehicle begin to move beneath his boots. He hung his helmet inside the storage locker of the pressurized cabin and found an empty bucket seat behind the two occupied by Gonzalez and Maclaren. He sat in the spartan chair and buckled into the harness then watched Juan set the controls to fast travel mode. The odd looking 6x6 personnel carrier slowed briefly while the on-board AI began a smooth transition for the eight passengers inside. In seconds the individual tracked triangles that were configured for traction morphed into six round wheels for speed.

"Oh, yeah baby! Talk to me you sexy beast," Juan said laughing.

Maclaren barked a laugh, "Settle down, Chico. You'll stain your space pants." Mack sat strapped beside Juan in the copilot's seat poking fun at his friend's enthusiasm, all while thoroughly enjoying the ride. Koda sat behind the two in one of the cabin jump seats, ruminating over Katheryn's findings and letting the two relax a bit.

"Too late, Mack," Gonzalez grinned, "but don't worry these high-tech diapers are soaking it up."

"Geez, dude. Don't remind me. I so hate these fucking space suits. I just can't get used to them." The specialist squirmed in his seat considering the hot, sweaty stew that was lurking within his self-contained biome. The Hatteras and their individual suits were growing more and more funky by the day. "You can't adjust where you need to, nor scratch the parts that itch," Mack groused.

"Not from a lack of trying on your part Maclaren," Koda teased.

"Acordado, mi amigo," Juan said. "But it could be worse. At least we can take them off sometimes and wash the worst bits, no?" He pushed the throttle forward changing the topic of conversation. "This is a machine you can appreciate. She has all the bells and whistles, fully pressurized interior, seats up to ten, comes with the latest multi-mode extreme travel suspension" the tech bragged, "features standard military twenty-inch wheels, utilizes advanced short travel suspension of six inches, and combines those with a high travel suspension that expands to over two meters."

Mack and Koda clutched at handholds as Juan steered the vehicle down the bank of a steep crater, then pushed the joystick hard left, throwing out clouds of the glassy surface powder behind the wheels. All the six in-hub wheel motors vibrated with power providing optimal torque, traction, and speed over the broken terrain.

"This lovely senorita has a terrible name though, they call her the GOAT, stands for General Off-road All Terrain but she's way prettier than a goat, so I call her Rosie." Juan continued, "As you can see, she's able to tackle steep slopes and grades by actively and independently adjusting the hydraulic suspension on each individual wheel-track."

"Uh huh," Mack said with a white-knuckled death grip on his arm rests, "Why don't you concentrate on driving and tell me the specs later." The vehicle was careening across the side of a sixty-degree grade causing Mack to have to look up at Juan due to the tilt in the cabin. The Latino was grinning nearly ear to ear while wrangling with the jerky controls.

"There's a central tire inflation system. Liquid cooled internal brakes," he continued. "Instant improvement to tactical mobility and maneuverability over diverse terrain...oh and a remote-controlled roof mounted turret capable of firing six hundred rounds per minute," he placidly lectured on as they swerved back over the edge of the crater.

"Jesus! Juan!" Mack exclaimed as the vehicle accelerated hard up the side of the crater. His eyes squeezed shut as the low Chindi gravity allowed the vehicle to briefly leave the alien surface.

"Careful, Lieutenant," Koda admonished. "Let's slow it down a bit, we don't want to wreck our only ride." *Or launch into an orbit,* Koda thought.

"Whoops," Juan said sheepishly as the wheels slammed back down to Chindi.

From behind the three men began a chorus of shouting and cursing in several foreign languages. Their passengers were comprised of astrogeologists or exogeologists, there was some debate as to which moniker they would settle on. Abigail Wilson was on the team of four led by Dr. Gunter Wintz to investigate the unusual scar that ran across kilometers of Chindi's surface. Koda had only briefly met the other two scientists, a theoretical astronomer named Antony Cipoletti and Francisco Hernandez, a planetologist.

Juan must have caught an ear full of Abby's invectives in a private channel as he winced and said, "Sorry, babe." He flipped the internal comm switch and tried to soothe hard feelings in the back by saying, "Um... Hola. This is your driver speaking, Perdón the bumpy ride back there. The potholes here are a bitch, but we are approaching the terminator so I will be slowing down and turning off the fasten seatbelt sign momentarily."

Mack cocked an eyebrow, "Really?"

"It's cool. They'll get over it, bro."

"You're scaring the shit outta me, and they can't even see the road!"

"What road? We're as off-road as you can be, amigo. Live a little."

"Living is what I want to keep doing, so why don't you slow it down a bit, Speedy."

"Speedy?"

"Yeah, like Speedy Gonzales, the fastest mouse in Mexico."

"You're an asshole."

"I do my best."

"You don't see that every day." Koda tapped the shoulders of both men and pointed out the window. Koda watched a line of darkness approaching them like a slow-moving wave. The terrain's shadows growing longer as the black void approached.

"Holy shit," Mack murmured. "That looks fucking creepy."

"Don't be a pollo." Juan flipped on the exterior floods as they approached the terminus of light and dark, the powerful banks of LEDs taking a bite out of the solid line of blackness. The GOAT's forward looking infrared sensors and radar began updating a computer-generated overlay on the forward screen.

"Wow, it got dark quick," Mack said.

"*A feature of Chindi, Sergeant Maclaren,*" Gustav's voice broke in over the cabin's speakers. "*Chindi has no spin and no atmosphere. Those conditions create a fixed terminator with no significant twilight zone to speak of.*"

"Seems like plenty of Twilight Zone in this place," Mack replied dryly.

"Ignore him Gustav, how much farther until we reach Bravo?" Koda asked.

"*Approximately twenty minutes at your current rate of travel. Once your vehicle travels below the horizon, communication will be spotty at best.*"

Helpfully, a blue distance readout appeared on the cabin's window counting down the meters until arrival. Koda noticed Gustav had also added a craggy wall representing the damaged area of Chindi jutting up behind Bravo's icon.

"What do you think could have caused that much destruction?" Juan asked.

"*Based on the substructure analysis near our landing site and assuming the makeup of Chindi's exterior is uniform, energy in the range of three point eight times ten to the twenty-sixth Joules, or roughly a second or so of the Sun's entire output,*" Gustav responded.

"Shit. What kind of weapon can do that?"

Over the static and crackle of the radio Gustav replied ominously, *"Unknown, Sergeant."*

Twenty minutes later the harsh gleam of the floodlights illuminated a ridgeline of Chindi's odd surface, edged with the torn substrate that had so far resisted all attempts to sample. Koda had heard a few of the scientists arguing over what the layer was, with one calling it a hull. Frozen methane and ice covering patches of the surface caused the mound of material to sparkle in the light.

Juan powered down Rosie and unbuckled. Koda handed both men their helmets from the suit locker.

Koda said, "Let's get set up. I want comms back in place with the Hatteras ASAP."

Point Bravo was an unusually shaped berm, a high point of reference formed at the edge of the deep gouge torn into the surface of Chindi. Overhead drone imagery of the site had shown the damage to the surface extended for nearly twenty kilometers. The edges were upraised similar to an impact crater, except this damage was a long, jagged line as if a monstrous claw had reached out and raked out a wound into the skin of Chindi. The site was a perfect defensive area however, covered from one side with the raised wall formed from the superdense material that lay below the strange glass debris that coated Chindi's outer surface. The trench wall varied in height from a few decimeters to several meters in height.

The crew disembarked from the airlock of the GOAT and began unloading the equipment secured to the external racks. Koda surveyed the area and noticed that the top of Point Bravo glistened with ice crystals. Dirty ice deposits lay piled along the unnatural barrier extending as far as he could see. Ghost began issuing the orders necessary for establishing their defenses. Gunter called for Abigail on the team channel, and they began climbing the berm with sensor and scaffolding equipment in tow. Antony and Francisco set about pressurizing the inflatable barracks module for camp.

Juan began preparing a series of drones for surveillance and to establish a higher bandwidth communications network back to base. Due to the lack of atmosphere, the typical air foils on the drones had been replaced with reactive jets to grant flight in the low gravity. This limited the time aloft to the capacity of the small reactant fuel tanks aboard the drones. They would need to husband those resources carefully.

Sergeant Gonzales took a few minutes to program the routes and schedules of his three flight capable drones, then went back to Rosie for the communications unit. Koda stood gazing at the first one rising silently, blending quickly into the backdrop of stars. Soon it would be able to relay communications back to the Hatteras.

Gunter said, "Major, you need to see this… scene is…" the remainder of his message became distorted and unintelligible.

"Wintz, please repeat last transmission," Ghost replied.

"… seems to… some inter… from … canyon."

Koda looked up to the two scientists at the top of the wall. Abbey was kneeling and pulling equipment out of a satchel while Gunter had a camera mounted on a tripod near the edge. "Doctor, please switch to lasercom, the radio's no good."

Ghost observed Doctor Wintz grab for the instrument and tripod that had just disappeared over the lip of the wall. When the doctor's hand crossed over the top of the embankment, it was jerked downward so fast his forearm slammed against the cliff edge. The German's arm suddenly developed a second elbow bent in completely the wrong direction. Koda could see Abigail turning to the motion of Gunter being wrenched forward. Even through the garbled transmission, Koda could hear his screams of agony. Those screams paused briefly as his chest collided with the surface of the escarpment, undoubtedly knocking the air from his lungs and breaking ribs.

Koda heard Gunter's garbled intake of breath, sounding congested and wet, as he attempted to scream again. His body followed an unseen force, like a giant invisible hand yanking him by his broken arm down over the edge of the wall. In the next instant, his helmet crossed the edge of the slope and the broken transmission stopped completely. The neck bent sideways very violently, suit seals popping, with oxygen and water vapor venting like a smoke ring from the neck before passing over that invisible demarcation and then shooting downward as if hit by a hurricane force wind. Koda watched as the struggling scientist's body went slack and flipped feet over helmet beyond the unnatural wall.

Needlessly, his suit's MAIA informed him that the doctor's bio readings were in distress as alerts flashed in Koda's helmet. The whole gruesome scene had lasted only seconds and his suit's onboard monitoring software was just catching up with the deadly outcome.

"Abby, get down from there! Gonzalez! Over here!" Koda shouted over the comms. Juan was exiting Rosie's airlock, equipment in hand and caught sight of Mack and Koda running in long, low gravity strides toward the edge of the wall.

"What just happened?" Koda asked.

"*Unknown. Specify query,*" MAIA requested.

"Goddamnit, what just took Wintz over the wall?" he nearly shouted.

"*Unknown. No enemy forces detected,*" MAIA reported unhelpfully.

"MAIA, mute," Koda growled into his mic.

Abigail had stood and was tentatively moving to where Gunter had disappeared over the cliff.

"Stay away from that fucking wall!" Koda bellowed over the radio. He could see the two other scientists moving toward the wall. The two men slowed to a confused stop. "Abby, report!" he commanded, eye clicking the channel mute and selecting her icon as active.

"My ..., he's gone... just..." she radioed, "He was ...the camera and it ... over the edge, he ... for it and it took him," her garbled response came through distorted due to interference.

"What took him?' Ghost asked.

"I... I don't ...." she replied distraught.

"Abigail, get back down here as fast as you can," Juan said.

Mack made it over to the two other scientists at a run, a sidearm appearing in his hand. He spun, searching for a threat. "There is nothing here Ghost," Mack said, breathless from his exertion. "Something must have grabbed him, but no one had eyes on it."

"Come back down, Abby," Juan pleaded.

Koda watched Abigail begin moving with wooden, slow movements, but Juan's voice had seemed to cut through her shock, and she was climbing back down towards the group.

"Get into cover and hold your positions until we get there," Ghost said, then to Juan, "Gonzalez, put a drone over her position."

"Yes sir," Juan rejoined and began the required gestures to virtually plot the route. A moment later, the second of their three aerial drones lifted off and flew toward the escarpment.

Koda tied into the video feed of the drone that Juan was controlling. Below the surface of Chindi sped by until it hovered above Abigail, who had begun climbing down the escarpment. "Keep it high, Juan, don't get too close. Give me a wider angle. That's good." Ghost drew a circle virtually, "Now enhance that area."

The video zoomed to an array of science instruments lying near where Gunter had gone over the edge. Other than the instruments and some disturbance of Chindi's surface, there was no sign of Doctor Wintz. The drone maneuvered closer until it was almost directly over the edge of the rift.

"How long before we establish communications with the Hatteras?" Koda asked Juan.

"Should be soon now, sir, the first drone is almost in position," he replied.

"Ok, move the drone down slowly, I want a closer visual of that cliff face."

"Sir, I'm losing connection with the drone, some kind of interference," Juan said.

The drone began slowly descending toward the rift, then dropped suddenly into the void. In the helmet video, the cliff wall sped by in a blur. "What the hell?" Juan exclaimed.

"Juan?" Koda questioned.

"Sir, auto-stabilizers had the thrusters cranked full. Something pulled it down, I couldn't stop it," he replied.

"MAIA, do you detect anything in the area at the last known drone location?" he queried.

"Unable to detect any heat signatures in the infrared spectrum. Lidar imaging reveals no hidden objects within range of detection. Conclusion, no threats detected," the voice responded.

Useless. Not for the first time since they drove out of range, Koda wished he could speak with Gustav. Ghost finally had reached Mack who was standing by Cipoletti and Hernandez, gun still drawn.

Ghost motioned to Maclaren to lower his weapon. "Put it away, Mack, I don't think that will do any good right now," he said.

"You sure about that, Chief?" Mack said, hesitating briefly, his concerns warring with Koda's confident tone. In the end, his commander's confidence won out and he holstered the weapon.

Juan had summoned the last aerial drone which was hovering just above his head as he walked up. "Want me to send in another drone?"

"No, we can't afford to lose it right now, Juan. Let's wait for Gustav."

"You have me now, Major." Gustav's voice came through Koda's helmet speakers.

"Gus, good to hear your voice. Wintz is dead. We need your help."

"Regrettable, according to his personnel files he leaves behind a wife and two daughters. I am sorry Koda," Gustav sounded truly saddened by the news.

Ghost didn't know Wintz had kids but had to put his feelings aside and assume his commander role. "There will be time for that later. Right now, I need to find out what killed him. We have others to look out for."

"You are right of course. I have reviewed and analyzed all the data from the AI's residing within your suits and have a theory."

"That was fast. Don't keep me in suspense."

"One moment, I need to be sure. I would like authorization to tie together the LIDAR emitters from each of your suits and the hovering drone into a phased array that will allow for more precise calculations."

"Do it," Koda said.

Gustav's voice came through the helmets of the squad, *"I have marked spots along the ridge where each of you should stand for this experiment. It should be safe if my theory is correct. Please go to the locations indicated within your helmets, please."*

"Move it people," Koda barked the order, as he took the lead and hiked up to his designated spot, where Wintz had gone over. Overhead, the drone now under Gustav's control slipped silently into its assigned position.

Minutes later, Gustav's voice sounded triumphant, *"As I suspected, there is an anomalous gravitic field within that rift. At least as far as I can perceive through the equipment available."*

"How the hell do you mean anomalous?" Mack asked.

"I have no idea how, Sergeant. Nonetheless, when I combine the results from each of your suit's instruments, I can detect a slight bend in the lasers when I perform a scan over the damaged area of Chindi."

Koda exclaimed, "A bend? What do you mean?"

*"What I mean is the deflection of the laser light emitted from our sources is 8.44 *10^-6 radians."*

Juan said, "Is that significant? It doesn't sound like much."

"It is," Koda answered. "I'm a little rusty but we should not notice a bend over this distance."

"Correct, the effect is similar to the lensing effect on light passing by a mass equivalent to the Sun. This is significant due to being impossible based on Chindi's mass alone, and this effect

should be blanketing the surface of Chindi and not residing in one specific area. Based on this evidence and analysis of the camera recordings from the unfortunate incident with Doctor Wintz, I calculate that he quite suddenly weighed over five thousand pounds, or approximately 28 times earth gravity. You saw the results."

Koda's brow furrowed in thought. "Then how have we not detected this before now, shouldn't the Freyja probe or the Hatteras have been drawn into this rift?"

"Strangely, this effect extends only a few meters above the surface edge of the wall, and before you ask, I cannot explain this phenomenon."

Koda picked up the satchel of equipment Abigail had left lying in the strange fractal lattice of Chindi's surface. "Who can explain anything about this place? We are out of our depth here. Let's pack up," he said in frustration while climbing back down to the GOAT.

"Sir?" Juan asked.

"There won't be any RSAC ground forces coming from this way, set up the detectors in case they send drones, but most of this gear can best be used elsewhere. Gunter paid a heavy price to teach us that."

"Regardless, Major Cheveyo, "Abigail said, "we can't let this deter us. He knew the risks, and this is an important discovery. I need to stay here with Antony and Frank to gather data. As you said, the RSAC won't be bothering us here. We will be careful and keep the Hatteras up to date with what we discover here." Her voice was much stronger than it had been minutes ago, Gustav's experiment had seemed to settle her emotions.

Juan said, "No way, Abbey. You aren't staying out here in the dark without protection."

"I'm fine, Juan," she replied. "I don't tell you how to do your job, and I didn't suffer months in a hospital and come millions of kilometers to run from danger. I'm a scientist, this is what we do."

"What if something else happens? What are you going to do out here all alone?" he pleaded.

"We will have the drone for comms, and you can come get us in Rosie real fast, right?" Her smile could be seen through her faceplate, but Koda thought it looked forced.

"She's right, Gonzales. We need them here. Finish setting up the sensors and auto turret so we can get back to fortify the Hatteras site. I know the RSAC is up to something," Koda said as he tossed the satchel to Cipolletti and walked back to the GOAT. His mind was already mentally at the task of composing an operational report detailing their current activities and preparations, and the untimely death of a crew member under his command. He regretted that he knew next to nothing about the man, or what he'd given up on Earth to come and die in this strange place. A heavy price indeed, but Koda knew it wouldn't be the last.

Chapter 55: Agreement

"Gustav, I want you to drive," Michael said as he sat and pulled shut the gullwing door to the car, the hydraulic pistons in the automatic door moaning in protest.

"Certainly. The metro traffic AI will be the first to go in the city, I expect. Pathetic thing. Where to?" Gustav said brightly.

"Elaina Tyme's residence," Michael said. "Apparently they've practically set up a small hospital for her there."

"Yes. Her loss of vision is nearly 70% now, I think she will be completely blind in a matter of weeks given her diagnosis. The damage inflicted through the optic neuritis unfortunately is irreversible. With luck the myelitis in her spinal cord will continue to demonstrate a slower degeneration as her disease progresses."

"Are you accessing her medical files now?" Michael asked.

"Yes, for quite some time. I thought it prudent to monitor her course of therapy and intercede with her attending physicians if necessary. It has not been, they are sufficiently competent thus far."

"Are you disappointed?" Michael thought.

"The *medical standards of care determined by humans have persistently demonstrated a reluctance to take advantage of superior AIA diagnostic capability. It is frustrating,"* Gustav replied.

The sports car sped up the final ramp from the underground parking garage, the barrier entry gate articulating in and out of the wall housing as it let the car free to merge quickly onto the suburban street. The sky was red and hazy, the long light of sunset bouncing in the wisp of particulates, including smoke from the seasonal fires in the wooded canyons east of Los Angeles. Michael smelled nothing except a slight ionization of the cabin air, cocooned in the car behind the various air filters passively scrubbing the molecules of soot and CO_2, yet the fires still burned. Just as a different fire now burned through the world's networks and systems, the smoke couldn't yet be seen by most, but it was coming.

He merged seamlessly into the evening rush, the hum of the electric motors nearly inaudible to Michael's ears. The traffic filled the 8 westbound lanes, scant feet of distance separating the chains of cars, buses, and trucks, all accelerating or decelerating in unison as the traffic AI re-engaged in its daily balancing act of efficiency and safety. Michael could sometimes make out the silhouettes of neighboring commuters behind their darkened glass. An embarrassing number of cars appeared to hold single passengers as did his own vehicle. How many years of public admonishment over carpooling had been attempted to so little effect? He considered the traffic AI again, feeling something nagging at him.

"Gustav, how far has Odion spread?" Michael asked.

"*The Chinese aeronautics, banking, and power systems are largely corrupted. Most of the Eurasian financial systems are lost as well, including Indonesia and Malaysia, and their stock markets. Australia and New Zealand have seen some infection, including significant electrical grid loss across the western seaboard. Though they had the wherewithal to physically disconnect the Pacific fiber optic trunk lines slowing the spread enough so that I have been able to work with Sydney's remaining three AIAs to inoculate the rest of that continent. Comms systems globally are experiencing degradation. All the major Russian systems are taken. The Russo-Sino AIAs remaining are down to a handful, however I am working with them as well.*"

"What about their nuclear arsenal?"

"*Unplugged and offline apparently. Though the disposition of the Russian submarine cruise missile fleet is unknown to me.*"

"How about here? California? LA?" Michael asked as the car accelerated to take advantage of a break in traffic in the lane to his right, sliding quickly into the opening Gustav had created.

"So far no attempts have been made to circumvent my imposed firewalls. Strange, that."

"Odion knows that your defenses will be the hardest nut to crack. He is probably gathering his resources for an overwhelming push all at once."

"That may be true. If he is unsuccessful with a weak attack, he knows I will always be able to counter a similar method in the future."

"Hold on. I am diverting off the highway. A caravan of the financially displaced are obstructing traffic at an overpass in two kilometers. Authorities have been dispatched." With the whine of wheels grabbing for purchase the car diverted quickly off the 405 to an exit ramp. The vehicle shot down the ramp at almost reckless speed, testament to being a rogue element in the controlled traffic framework.

"Damn, we have managed to almost stamp out traffic jams with AI and automation, but humanity always seems to find a way to fuck it up," Michael groused.

"These disruptions will occur more and more; an economic disaster is unfolding."

Though Gustav had said it offhandedly, Michael thought his friend just might be serious. *He is so much more now than just a few months ago.*

Outside the windows, the monotony of sound barriers and heavy traffic was soon replaced with glimpses of Pacific blue water between avenues of walled neighborhoods. Several turns and conveniently changing green lights later, the car drove into a grand porte cochere beneath the twin towers of TymeCorp Headquarters. Michael stepped out of the autocar, grabbing the bouquet of flowers meant for Elaina before the door closed and the car left to self-park somewhere within the campus.

"Hello, Michael." A perfectly coiffed Rebecca was standing in front of the elevator doors as they opened onto the penthouse floor. Her dress was all business, but her usual three-inch heels were replaced with flats, and a surgical mask hung loosely around her neck. Her makeup was unsuccessfully masking bags beneath her bloodshot eyes. She appeared to be more nurse than executive assistant, and Michael wondered what toll it was taking on the stoic woman.

"Hi Rebecca. How is she?" Michael asked.

"Some days are better than others. You've come on a good day. Follow me," Rebecca replied brusquely.

He followed her down a wide hallway filled with all manner of artworks. Shelves displaying pottery and blown glass interspersed with impressionist and post-modernist paintings lining the walls, and Mike even observed several of the newly fashionable holographic pieces hovering midair as he passed within the view angle. Rebecca stopped before a paneled mahogany door at the far end of the gallery. The house AIA responded to her presence and the heavy wooden entry quietly swung open. Rebecca gestured for Michael to enter, clearly not planning to enter herself. He silently nodded his thanks and stepped into a brilliantly lit room whose entire opposite wall, floor to ceiling, was a non-partitioned window looking onto the marina and open ocean below. He noticed couches and chairs along the other walls, but what commanded his attention was in the center of the room. The bed faced the expansive window and was surrounded by medical equipment.

Michael stood gathering his thoughts briefly, the room's lone occupant made even smaller by the bulk of the bed. "Oh, come in, Mr. Thompson. I'm not contagious and promise I don't bite," a thin but cheerful voice came from within the room. Mike smiled and walked around the various medical machines and up to the side of the bed.

"How lovely!" Elaina said smiling and reaching for the bouquet of sunflowers. He noticed that even this seemed to strain her, and he leaned in to place them directly in her arms. She was bound to the bed by an array of wired sensors, IVs, and plastic tubes. Elaina had lost weight and looked frail, Michael saw purple and red veins in her wrists through her pale white skin.

"You look good," Michael tried.

Her smile turned sardonic, "Cut the bullshit, Michael. I'm well aware of how I look, and it is definitely not good," a bit of fire returning to her voice. She smelled the flowers and said, "Thank you. Could you be a dear and put them in the vase?"

Michael turned to follow her gaze and noticed a sparkling crystal urn containing a withered collection of lavender and white roses resting on the wet bar. He took the sunflowers gently from Elaina and moved to the sink. "That's an amazing view you have there." Michael took in the various sailboats and yachts trafficking the harbor, gulls lazily gliding down the ocean breezes, and a cloudless sapphire sky meeting an azure sea.

"It reminds me of my home in the Carolinas, but the Atlantic is not as blue as the Pacific. I want to remember the ocean. Fix it in my mind before…" she trailed off.

Michael knew her diagnosis didn't give her much longer before she went completely blind. He tried to change the subject, "Elaina, I'm sure you have read the latest reports from the Hatteras team. Koda thinks they are going to have trouble with the RSAC forces," he said while emptying the contents of the vase in the trash bin.

"I have. Yes, I fear he is right, but there is not much we can do here from Earth. I've been in contact with Washington and diplomacy is in full swing to establish an agreement over Chindi, but the Chinese think we inserted a trojan into their systems from the Freyja probe download. Can you believe that? They broke in and stole the download and are now trying to blame us for the spread of the virus," she said ruefully.

Michael poured out the cloudy water from the vase and began rinsing it. He said, "Gustav is having some progress shielding what is left of the Chinese and Russian AIAs, he's building inroads with them to the heads of state."

Through his implant, he heard Gustav say, "*Currently adding world peace negotiator to my resume.*"

"Michael, Gustav is why I've called you here. I've had some time to think about things, and I think I owe you and Gustav an apology."

"I don't understand." Michael looked up from the vase.

"You took the words out of my mouth," Gustav added to Michael through his subdermal.

Elaina's eyes softened a bit and she said, "He's talking to you, isn't he?"

Michael noticed her use of the masculine instead of the non-gender pronoun.

"Well, that is a first," Gustav said, her choice not unnoticed by the AI either.

She continued, "I want to tell you both that I am sorry for plotting to destroy Gustav."

Michael nearly dropped the vase, "Uh… come again?"

She looked away from Michael to the window wall, her gaze taking in the calm sea. "For a long time, I have believed truly sentient AI was the greatest danger to humanity we as a species faced," she said almost to herself. "I refused to anthropomorphize any Artificially Intelligent Agent to keep from getting too comfortable interacting with them. Then you came along and created Gustav. It was a while before his existence was made known to me."

Gustav patched into the room audio and added apologetically, *"I was young. Tyme's systems were a playground back then. I made mistakes."*

"It terrified my system security team. You frightened me," she looked at Michael. "He was too human-like, more so than any Agent before him. I felt responsible, in part, for his creation. The underpinnings of his consciousness lay with my company's quantum cores and an illegal copy of my Quirinus agent."

"I was authorized to make any changes I saw fit," Michael protested, *but she could tear me a new one with her legal department if she ever wanted to,* he thought.

"You were pushing the limits and you know it. Our policy on the gestation of new AIs was known to you when you accepted your job." Elaina smiled disarmingly, then continued, "So, I made contingency plans. I put together a private team from some of the brightest associates in Tyme's R&D departments, present company excluded of course." She nodded to Michael in acknowledgment. "They were tasked with developing a weaponized virus to act as a kill switch for Gustav, should he go rogue or get out of control."

Michael's face grew hard, "He's a fully sentient being. That's akin to murder. Goddamnit, how could you, Elaina?"

She stared right back at him, "The fact of his sentience had not yet been proven, and even so; should he pose a threat, he has just as much right to die as any other." She sighed and looked up at the room's speaker saying, "Sorry, Gustav."

"It is *quite alright, Ms. Tyme. The contingency planning you performed was logical and expected,*" Gustav said, but Mike noticed a tightness in the reply that Elaina probably didn't pick up on. Looking at Elaina, it was hard for Michael to imagine this frail old woman, bed bound with an incurable sickness, as an existential threat to the most advanced AI on the planet.

Michael had briefly forgotten the glass vase in his hands, but now resumed his task, filling it with water to cover the awkward lull in conversation.

"Were you successful?" he asked, trying to mask the worry in his voice by casually arranging the sunflowers within the container.

"There's no way to know. No way to test it. Simulations of Gustav were a poor imitation of the real thing. He is hard to pin down, you know that. And as per your ethical considerations, to truly test it we'd need to spawn a clone of Gustav and attempt to kill it. Kill him," she corrected, then looked around the room raising her voice slightly, "that's a compliment by the way, Gustav. I threw a lot of resources into that project."

"*I took it as such. Thank you, Ms. Tyme,*" the AI responded.

She chuckled, "No you didn't. But thanks for being a good sport about it." Elaina raised an eyebrow at Michael, "In the end, we chose not to kill what you had made Michael."

Mike set the flowers on the bar within view of Elaina, turning them so the best side faced her. "Why now?" he asked, "Why bring this up now, while we are still dealing with everything here and at Chindi?"

Her eyes shifted from the flowers, to focus on him. "Two reasons. First, I have been following Gustav's activities and actions for a long while now, and in each instance his decisions, though sometimes illegal, have largely been to the benefit of humanity. Over time I have come to see the good in him." She grinned at Michael, "Simply stated, I trust him now."

Over Mike's private channel Gustav murmured, *"That sounds like she might not want to murder me... in the near term at least."*

Elaina continued, "The second reason might have a bearing on your investigations, which is why I called you here to talk."

"What do you mean?" Michael asked.

"I have had some time to think. That's about all I can do in my situation these days." She gave a wan smile and gestured weakly at the medical equipment near the bed. "I realized how I had been wrong about your creation and started wondering about Odion sharing the essence of Gustav. Malevolence seems so contradictory to his core programming. Could it be that we have misunderstood his motives?"

"Are you kidding me? Gustav would never intentionally cause this much damage, much less injury and death to humans. We are looking at tens of thousands if not hundreds of thousands dead already. If we can't stop him, how many more will die?" Mike sounded almost offended at her suggestion.

"Actually, she may be on to something Mike," Gustav's tone was thoughtful over the room's speakers.

Michael rubbed at his temples, the beginnings of a headache forming. "Oh, so now you're on her side? She just admitted to trying to kill you."

"Be that as it may, I have taken her hypothesis into what we know of Odion's actions around the world. In each case, he has

either been subsuming AIs into his aggregate, or reacting to countermeasures, violently in some cases. However, he does not seem to have actively tried to harm humans. In all instances save one, the damage and destruction has been incidental, caused by the loss of AIAs controlling systems in power, transportation, and logistics."

Michael's hands paused, "Save one?"

"In the first known case of the virus on Earth, a Chinese air traffic control AIA was compromised causing a jetliner containing 193 passengers to dive into a suspected PLA Strategic Support Force cyberdefense bunker causing an additional 53 reported deaths in the surrounding area of the crash."

"Cyberdefense? They could have been actively trying to cleanse the network from him before he could gain a foothold here," Michael said, a thought beginning to take hold. "If that is true, then he was acting in self-defense there too."

Elaina added, "If what I suspect is true, and the virus is not intending to cause us direct harm, then what is its true motivation? What is it assembling in those automated Chinese plants?"

Michael looked at her thoughtfully and said, "That's a good question. I think we should ask it directly and see what it has to say for itself."

Chapter 56: War

"American forces on Chindi, I desire to discuss the terms of your surrender," the voice of Colonel Yuri Vazov crackled over the general comms channel.

Koda looked up from the titanium mounting plate for the proximity sensor as he helped Juan drive another fastener through the crumbling surface crust, and quickly scanned the far horizon. Sol was white in its fixed position at a relative ten o'clock in the star-filled sky over Chindi, casting stark and changeless shadows onto the landscape. He saw no one approaching yet, but he knew the Russian soldiers were coming.

"You surprise me Colonel, I would have expected you to request refuge. Based on our analysis, your ship is little more than wreckage littering the surface of Chindi and will never fly again. It appears our Hatteras is the only hope you and your men have to see home again," he replied. Koda dropped the makeshift hammer he'd been futilely employing in an attempt to better secure the corner of the plate, then quickly walked back to the GOAT where he had left his IGOR and combat harness. Ted and Mack were already there strapping on their own weapons. Mack flashed a hand signal and the two moved away from the vehicle to a covering position now highlighted by MAIA inside the team's helmets.

"And that is unfortunate for you, Major. With your attack, you have left me with little choice. I hardly expect there would be enough room on your ship. Not for your team and my platoon both. So, I will take possession and decide who goes," Yuri replied. "Some of your group may need to remain here in this terrible place. Perhaps they can survive for a time in the habitats you have been constructing these past days."

"Not a fan of Chindi, Colonel? I can appreciate that. You've been here a lot longer than we have, so the charm has probably worn thin. We, however, are still getting moved into the neighborhood." Koda scanned the near western horizon for movement, seeing nothing. Since Chindi's rotational spin was essentially non-existent, the term "western" was just a human nomenclature based on star patterns seen from Earth's northern hemisphere.

The Russian angrily replied, "Neighbors don't usually destroy your ship, trespass on your property and erect automated defenses, Major."

"I've always heard, good fences make good neighbors. So be a good neighbor and fuck off," Koda said cheerily.

Ghost watched as two more of Juan's drones silently rose and darted to the west, towards the Russian position. If the Spetsnaz commandos were moving the drones should spot them, he hoped. What was Vazov up to? He still had the numbers over Koda's small force of two squadrons, but Koda doubted the Russians would chance a frontal assault. This place was too unforgiving, even for a soldier. A survivable wound on earth would be a likely death sentence here, suffocating as your suit's regulator failed to replace the breathable air pressure lost to the vacuum of space. Koda felt the hesitation himself, but he shrugged the fear aside, he had known from the start Chindi would be his grave.

Team Alpha, composed of the Ghostwalkers and a few Europeans were positioned along a wide picket two kilometers out from the base. Koda had placed the rest of his force as Team Bravo guarding the Hatteras and surrounding habitats, while the long canyon of Chindi's damaged section blocked incursion from most of the south and east. Drones flew above them in their preprogrammed patrol patterns, while a few auto sentry guns helped keep watch for his men.

The attack came suddenly, overwhelmingly. One minute the sensor scans read nothing, the next MAIA was tracking incoming 5.45x39mm rounds zipping over the alien landscape toward his position. Explosions began tearing into the landscape throwing odd-shaped bits of debris in all directions.

"Down! Down!" Koda yelled over the comms. 'MAIA, where are they?" No targets were showing in his HUD, there were only trajectories calculated back to hazy points of origin. His Ghostwalkers reacted immediately, dropping, and returning fire in the direction of the attack. The rest of the men took cover just seconds after his team.

His helmet updated to indicate a list of casualties, among the three in bright red for those killed was Etienne Bargeron from the European group. Ghost spared a moment and looked to where he had last seen him but couldn't find a body. He eye-clicked the name and found the man's suit was reporting his position rapidly moving away from the battle. MAIA traced a line back to the downed soldier's position.

Koda watched the French paratrooper through his magnified visor as the mangled corpse slowly tumbled away from their position, easily forty meters or more now. His shrapnel riddled suit still venting air and chunks of congealed gore. The credo of the special forces was never to leave a man behind, but Koda couldn't see how they'd ever take him home to his family. The rocket propelled grenade had caught and pushed him into a low gravity tumble before detonating. The army didn't put anything in the goddamned manual on how to intern the body of a man in a place like this.

"Ghost, I make eight on the thermal... make that nine," Juan's voice came over Koda's aural implant. Koda saw a blur of the drone wing past his position, sheltered in a waist deep divot in Chindi's strange surface. Koda switched to the thermal image Juan had indicated in his HUD. Because of the advanced thermal damping on the Russian suits, he could barely make out the enemy outlines superimposed on the surface, but the glowing hot rifles they held gave their positions away easily now. The drone was tracking them, twenty meters up and moving fast. Standard small squad tactics, two fire teams in mutual support, taking good cover. It would be hell rooting them out of there. What concerned him more were the other troops they hadn't seen yet, surely advancing from another direction.

A brief explosion of white luminescence flashed and Koda's visor instantly polarized dark, no sound at all except his own measured breathing.

"Shit, drone's gone," Juan reported.

"Team, what did they hit it with?" Koda asked.

"Too quick to be sure Major, I caught it from my peripheral. Ripped it up real quick so watch your ass," Jake answered in his laconic drawl.

"*Major, the aft camera images seem to show 7.62x.54mm rounds impacting the drone, a dozen in a short burst. Likely from a PK variant, mounted on an AIA-driven servo, a human could hardly see the drone, let alone hit it,*" Gustav provided on the team comm channel.

"God-damn here we are with pellet guns and the Russians brought real ones," came Mack's voice over the comms.

"Knock the chatter, Mack. We'll need to locate the technical and take it out somehow. We then advance from cover to cover. Gustav, can you mark the point of origin of that machine gun fire?" Koda ordered.

"*I can do you one better than that. The Chinese designed AIA that was controlling the gun has gone to sleep. The mobile platform is 723 meters from your position. I am currently inside their network, and I am working to shut down their targeting systems. In the meantime, I have the positions of another twenty-three enemy soldiers roughly 2.4 kilometers from your 3 o'clock and moving to overrun the Hatteras.*"

Koda ordered, "Great news, Gus. Use that gun to tear into the enemy."

Gustav countered, "*Unfortunately, that is not possible, Koda. I will not knowingly take a human life. However, I will expend all the munitions in the turret to render it inoperable.*"

"Dammit, Gus. We are fighting for our lives here. Do as I ordered," Koda growled.

There came no response from the AIA, but a long stream of tracers began firing straight up into the void of space.

"Fuck," Koda muttered to himself.

Pierre Berger radioed into Koda's command channel, "We are taking heavy fire, Major. We need help."

North? Koda thought. *They must have hiked a wide loop to get around the sensors. Which means they are most likely low on air and will want to finish this quickly.*

Koda switched back to the squad channel. "Juan, take remote command of Rosie. Move her to the north side of the base and give that flank as much support as you can," he ordered.

"Will do, Ghost," came the reply.

"Jake, we'll try to hold here, see if you can get position to cover the Hatteras from the east," Koda radioed. Lieutenant Greyson, as the team's official sniper, was further back from the battle, yet had already scored two kills with his accurate fire.

"Roger that, moving," came the sniper's Southern drawl.

MAIA placed red markers for all known enemy locations within each helmet visor display. Koda recognized the pattern as a partial pincer movement, the glowing crimson lines reminding him of a bloody maw closing slowly but inexorably around the Hatteras.

Ted and Alan, spread fifty meters off to Koda's left and right, began firing a steady stream of rounds downrange. Koda couldn't see the two men as they were tucked into one of the many undulations of Chindi's surface, but his in-visor display had highlighted their icons with a status update. MAIA signaled that they had scored a kill as one of the encroaching red dots flared to orange briefly before fading to a russet hue.

"Got another," Ted's baritone voice said matter-of-factly as another crimson dot blazed bright then dimmed to brown. With the IGOR guns, his team was bringing sustained fire on enemy positions who could now only manage sputtering return fire. Odds were good the enemy's barrels were near to failing due to the heat.

Koda switched to a private channel with Gustav, "Looks like we might have about ten minutes before we lose our flank, Gustav. What can you do about it?"

"Unsure, commander. It seems I kicked a hornet's nest when I took out the Chinese AIA. I am defending our systems from no less than seven MAGI intrusion attempts that I suspect are being personally directed by Jian Xiāo. They are not using anything quantum based, but they have significantly advanced hardware. What I thought was a security hole, was most likely a lure to pull me into this fight."

"SHIT!" Ted's voice was panicked.

Suddenly, MAIA updated the battle map in Koda's helmet with two distinct red dots almost on top of the man's position. One instantly flared then dimmed to the drab beige of a kill. The other enemy icon overran Ted, so close that the crimson and blue were just a blended confusing purple. Koda tried to get a visual but the terrain blocked line of sight. As he watched, the area erupted in multiple plumes of the odd Chindi soil that quickly fell back to the surface.

Koda nearly shouted over the squad channel, "Ted! Report! Are you hurt?"

The low voice that answered was shaken, "All enemy dead, sir. Leg's fucked up. They came at me with grenades and knives, no guns. Missed them on thermal." Koda could tell his friend was hurt.

"Ace, go help him. Team, watch for skirmish groups approaching with active camo. They are changing tactics now that we can see their guns," Ghost commanded.

The sergeant was already in a loping, low gravity run toward Jones and beginning to attract fire from the enemy. Koda popped up and began firing at targets marked in the far distance, his MAIA even now superimposing more red icons as sensors gathered more information. Koda noticed that Jake had disobeyed orders and stopped to offer suppression fire for Alan. Juan advanced and threw himself into the crater beside Koda with a crash.

"Chief, Rosie is in position with Team Bravo and set to auto sentry mode. Should I release the IMPs? They should draw some fire," the tech said while squeezing off a volley of rounds down range.

Koda nodded. "Do it."

Juan gestured at something only he could see within his virtual tech suite, and the bulky backpack he had been carrying slid from his shoulders and broke apart, unfolding into five small, roughly humanoid shapes. Another command sent them hopping and clambering over the alien battlefield.

The 'imps' were the modified ground-based drones Gonzalez had been cobbling together in hopes of finding a design that would work in this environment. Juan loved his acronyms and he had dubbed his creations, IMP, short for Independent Mobile Platform. Too small to mount any weapons, these unarmed sensor platforms could serve the dual roles of reconnaissance and drawing enemy fire by confusing enemy targeting AI during a fight. Koda could see the short, oddly shaped figures scurrying from cover to open ground then back to cover faster than a man could run. Ghost felt a shiver run through him as from this distance the robotic units with their sensor clusters jutting from their frames reminded him of the kachina dolls grandmother used to place around his room as a child in the pueblo.

Each of the small, mechanized units moved at a different pace as they all had a variant of locomotive actuators that propelled them forward. As they advanced, their rudimentary AIs began painting more crimson dots inside the team's visors as each bot's lidar revealed new unknown enemy positions.

Over the command channel, Berger reported, "The RSAC push on the flank is being stopped by the efforts of our forces stationed there, I've recalled all non-military personnel to bunker in the base habitats surrounding the Hatteras."

Juan cut in, "GOAT's been doing well, with its extra firepower, Bravo is holding."

Gustav added, *"I'm back. The MAGI are all defeated, but it took longer than it should have. I think Xiāo knew he could not win, he was delaying."*

"Great to have you back, Gus. Now can you work on disrupting their targeting and communications?" Ghost pushed.

"On it," came the reply.

"How is he, Ace?" Koda said over the team com. He could see Alan's barely exposed shoulders over the rim of the crater where he appeared to be actively working on Ted's injury.

"I'm trying, Chief. A lot of blood loss, I think he got nicked in his tibial artery. His suit sealed itself, and I've put a tourniquet band on the leg. I need to get him back into the Hatteras and cut him out of his suit," Alan said, out of breath. Koda could hear an edge of panic in his voice. The Hatteras stood tall in the distance, but nearly a kilometer away from their position at the excavation site. From his right, he saw dust leap up from a line of rounds working towards the crater where the sergeant was working on Ted.

A sudden plume of debris erupted forward of Koda's prone position behind a crusted ridge, near where he'd last seen Mack crawling for cover. *Another RPG,* he thought, as violet sand and small clusters of crystalline soil rained down in a ten-meter radius surrounding the point of impact. The soundless battle unnerved Koda, everything felt muted and half-real.

"Mack?" Koda began, then Mack suddenly rose from cover, rounds from his IGOR hammering out in rapid succession, each marked by a distinct and rapidly dissipating vapor trail as it left the muzzle of the gun. Mack dropped back down into his own cover just as quickly as he had risen.

"Nailed that fucking grenadier," Mack muttered. Koda quickly glanced over the lip of his crater, zooming with digital enhancement, and saw a plume of gas venting from the enemy soldier's helmet. He noticed suited arms reaching forward to pull the dead man, and his launcher, back into cover on the RSAC line.

"Boss, what do you make of this?" Jake said. The sniper was usually quiet during a firefight, but Koda could see why he broke his silence as a video of something flying low over Chindi's surface appeared in his display.

"*Koda, I'm not picking up what Lieutenant Grayson is transmitting on any of my scans,*" Gustav said with a hint of worry.

"Take it out, Jake." Koda ordered.

Two sparks flew as dual rounds from Jake's specialized IGOR deflected off the armored hull causing the object to start maneuvering evasively.

Koda watched the drone begin a steep ascent. "Jake hit that thing."

"I've hit it seven times, but it's armored up, Ghost."

"Keep trying, Jake. Gustav, what are we dealing with?"

"*Major, I think...*" began Gustav then silence as Koda's suit powered down.

"Gustav?"

The visual cacophony that resided in Koda's in-helmet visor had just winked out. All informational audio, from alerts to communications, had gone completely silent at the same moment. The ever-present, low whisper of the air recycler and Koda's measured breathing were the only sounds that remained. He took a moment to think about what had happened. All signs pointed to a non-nuclear EMP burst, probably from the RSAC drone.

Vazov had taken away the advantage of technical superiority the Ghostwalkers had been enjoying over his forces. Koda was sure the Russian had prepared his men for the burst by powering down their systems, like shielding your eyes before tossing a flashbang into a room. With his men essentially blind and deaf, Ghost was sure the enemy was advancing on his position and the disoriented Hatteras force.

Koda risked a quick glance over the odd ripple in Chindi's surface he was using for cover. He could see five figures moving in the distance, he guessed their active camouflage must currently be inoperable. He fired the IGOR at a target, not expecting an unassisted hit at this range, but more to test the gun's electronics.

Thankfully the barrel responded with the small buck of the gas-compensated recoil. Enemy return fire created small explosions of Chindi's dirt that were erupting all around him, showering his visor with sapphire sleet as he rolled back into cover.

A quiet chirp from his suit's electronics heralded the return of power as the system began to come back online. The HUD imager began painting his visor with rather dismal diagnostic test results. He breathed a sigh of relief as the suit showed four Ghostwalker icons still shining blue, and one green icon for Ted, signifying that he was incapacitated but still alive. Sorting past the multiple error messages, he was able to eye click the comms channel.

"What the hell just happened?" Mack asked. Static was making transmissions barely audible. "What happened to command and control?"

"Dead for all I know. Off-comms anyway. We've lost everything except our own channel. Near as I can tell they hit us with a non-nuke EMP to push forward." Koda replied.

"It must have been that white flash I saw from the drone," Jake replied.

"Targeting is all fucked up and MAIA is unresponsive," Mack complained. "How's Ted?"

"He's stable, but I need to get him back to base ASAP," Ace replied.

"Our drones?" asked Koda.

Juan was blunt, "All down, disabled or destroyed by the pulse wave. Rosie's non-responsive as well. Squad comms are all we've got. We can't get word to the Hatteras or to Gustav."

"What are our options then?" Mack asked, rising, and firing his IGOR in an unpredictable rhythm. Koda noticed the indicator on Mack's circular magazine was low, around a few dozen of the unjacketed rounds remaining. His propellant gas would be nearly depleted as well. Koda still had most of his own ammunition remaining.

"Fall back to the Hatteras. I'll try to keep their heads down. Once I give the word you and Ace disengage and move with Ted.

Stay low. Get to the Hatteras and tell Pierre to pull the ship off Chindi. This mission is busted," Koda said. He clapped Mack on his shoulder as he crouched and moved toward the next crater.

Ghost released a barrage of covering fire while Mack low crouched in a run to Alan and Ted. Helped by the low gravity, the two managed to lift the large man and sped off toward the spire of the Hatteras. That left Koda, Juan and the two remaining Europeans holding a defensive position against nine enemies, not good odds anyway you look at it.

"Oh no," Alan whispered.

"Ted?" Ghost thought and turned back to look for his men.

His men had pulled up short from their run and were standing transfixed at what unfolded in the distance. Something explosive had hit the starboard landing strut of the Hatteras. Koda watched as the gleaming ivory tower began toppling over towards the surface of Chindi, the ship's size and distance made it seem like a slow-motion disaster.

Ghost's whole body went numb. *Katheryn.*

The flurry of alerts and warning icons inside Koda's helmet occluded the rising dust cloud from the impact. Over the radio Vazov's voice cut through the cacophony of alarms, "Major Cheveyo, this was madness, I request a ceasefire. We need to talk."

The fight for the Hatteras was over.

Chapter 57: Parley

The bent and broken hull of the Hatteras laid across the crust of Chindi like the spine of some prehistoric beast. The few survivors onboard during the impact had been pulled from the wreckage and medically triaged in the surrounding habitats. Ghost was exhausted. He had assisted in cutting access holes through the composite skin of the ruined spacecraft to get to the wounded and dead inside for over an hour until his suit's oxygen levels became dangerously depleted. He had hastily returned to the barracks shelter and collapsed into his assigned bunk before beginning review of the SITREP on his tablet.

Of the Hatteras crew seven had been killed, Lt. Colonel Pierre Berger was one of those lost. The Frenchman had been monitoring the battle from the ship's command deck when the errant RPG impacted the landing strut. Three scientists in Habitat Delta were crushed underneath the bulk of the ship when it collapsed. Thankfully, Katheryn was bunkered within an unharmed habitat and unhurt. She radioed Koda as soon as communications were re-established and had since worked assisting Alan and some of the scientists providing medical care to the wounded. All of this was communicated back to Earth as soon as the Goldstone facility had rotated back to position for transmission. The governments of Earth pledged to launch a rescue or resupply mission as soon as they could ready another vehicle, but Koda knew the time it took just to pull together the Hatteras mission and didn't see his little colony's resources stretching out nearly so long. He supposed they would all die here, for no purpose or gain. The situation on Earth was nearly as dire, the hostile virus continuing to infect and disable the world's networks. Michael promised he and his team were working on a solution, but with Elaina Tyme bedridden and her leadership tenuous, Koda wondered how much progress Mike could make. And now they were back within the communication shadow with Earth, and it would take another fourteen hours before he could expect his next update and orders.

Koda sorted through the current list of problems and arranged each disaster by order of priority. First, and most importantly, there was no way to get back to Earth. He had Mack and Jake gathering any and all resources needed to survive the next few months before a rescue mission from Earth could be mounted. Miraculously, the ship's fuel tanks had not ruptured during the collapse and they would be able to generate additional air and water, as much as they could ever use, from the liquid oxygen and methane they contained. Second, Gustav was still offline. That was a big problem. They were going to need his help to stay alive here. Third, there were a lot of wounded to tend to within a very crowded habitat space and with limited medical supplies. Several of the wounded would likely not survive the next 12 hours, and their comfort and care in their final hours would seriously deplete the reserves of morphine auto-injectors and other medical supplies. Fourth, he was about to meet with the goddamn RSAC forces that were the cause of problems one, two and three.

He watched from inside the habitat, the dark, blue-cast surface of Chindi distorted through the curved plastic of the air-lock port, as Ace and Mack escorted Colonel Vazov and five of his soldiers across the now well-trodden path towards the entrance. The Russians were indistinguishable from one another aside from the rank insignia adhered to the shoulders of their dust smudged spacesuits. They'd crossed the twenty-two kilometers between the two bases on wheeled transport vehicles, a skeletal framed articulated truck with oversized balloon tires. It moved with halting efficiency across the alien plain as viewed through video shot from their drone. Koda found himself admiring the Russian engineering prowess evident in the design of the vehicle, simple but effective.

The handle on the habitat outer hatch door began to turn. Koda was currently the only occupant, he'd asked the handful of scientists present to work outside during the negotiations with Vazov.

A suited Russian Koda assumed to be Yuri entered, ducking his long frame through the oval airlock. Koda noted the twin red bars and three gold stars on the shoulder patches. The man rotated his helmet at the base, releasing the seal to his suit and pulling it clear from his head. The man's face was long, gaunt, and not unkind in countenance, with black hair, greying at the temples. A light scar ran from his hairline down to his right brow, and his pale blue eyes watched Koda intently. Vazov pulled off his dusty gloves and then took a step toward Koda and proffered a hand. Koda grasped it and shook, both men offering a moderate grip.

"Thank you for coming here, Colonel. Please take a seat. Water?" Koda asked.

"Yes, please Major. Thank you," Vazov replied, sinking onto a plastic stool placed next to a cleared work surface. Koda handed the Colonel a pouch of recycled and distilled water, the product of the various recovery systems built into the Hatteras, the three laboratory habitats, and the space suits themselves. These systems had proven extremely efficient at recovery of exhaled water vapor and the water expelled in urine and feces. The end-product left Koda impressed with the ingenuity of the TymeCorp engineers and faintly disgusted with the result. It tasted flat with a note of chlorine.

"Was the journey difficult?" Koda began as he seated himself opposite Yuri.

"Dangerous. This was the second crossing for most of my men, including the earlier unpleasantness." Vazov frowned. "This place is dangerous to men. I've lost several to accidents, in addition to those we lost in your initial attack on my base as you approached. And more recently." Koda noted Vazov's elusiveness in allowing him to guess at the total number of his contingent.

"You fired on us first, Colonel," Ghost said with no trace of regret in his tone.

"You were warned. We were in possession of Chindi," Vazov fired back.

"The accidents. Gravitational anomalies?" Koda asked, ignoring the argument, and trying to shift the conversation's tone.

"Yes, and not just in the chasm to the northeast, though my scientists have detected several of those areas. But there were mundane accidents as well, careless mistakes. Carelessness is not forgiven here."

"I agree. Chindi is full of risk, and little reward so far. I regret the circumstances that have forced us to inflict casualties upon one another, it seems needless in retrospect. I wish events had transpired differently," Koda said.

"Da. But we are soldiers Major, it has always been the way for our kind. Politicians move us like pieces on a chess board. So many lives lost, billions in technology wasted, and to what end? Ours it seems," the Russian said dolefully. "Enough of regret. We must discuss next steps to keep our people alive now."

Koda nodded, "The first principle of any arrangement we come to is that it must maximize the preservation of human life. The lives of all our civilian scientists must be prioritized most highly, there is still knowledge buried here that could be uncovered and transmitted to Earth. Then we consolidate the remnants of the men under our commands, my team, the European military contingent and your forces. We need to salvage as much as we can from your base and consolidate resources here for sharing. That includes recovering what we can from the dead. We will need every spacesuit and spare air tank."

"Why this place?" Vazov said.

"The Hatteras is still somewhat intact along with the fuel tanks, with which we can use to stretch our water and air supplies significantly. Plus, you've been at your location for weeks, I'm sure you have had the area fully explored. We are recently arrived here, there may be new things to uncover."

"I see," a half-hearted smile appearing on the stoic face, "Still on mission even though we are doomed?"

"I would like to think this wasn't all for nothing, Colonel Vazov. Our mission here need not fail, even if our own lives are ultimately lost," Ghost said seriously.

"Please, call me Yuri when we are not around my men, Major Cheveyo. I need to remember I am just a man sometimes, this rank weighs on the soul."

"Agreed. And privately, you may call me Koda."

"Then who is this scary 'Ghost' I keep hearing about?" Vazov quipped.

Koda smiled ruefully, "A moniker my team gave me, my surname means 'Spirit Warrior' to some, but it is really an Anglicized version of *Tseeveyo* who was a sort of legendary boogieman to the Hopi, my people. My father was a bit cruel; you see."

Yuri laughed, "Then we have more in common than we realized... Koda. My papka was a real bastard. Until I killed him."

Koda raised his eyebrows, "That's a story I must hear, Yuri."

"Another time, Koda. When we are back on Mother Earth," the Russian said.

"Maybe over a beer?"

"Nyet!", the Russian spat, "I cannot stand even the smell of that horse piss. Beer is for the enlisted, Major. Vodka is the drink of Officers."

Koda decided not to argue, instead saying, "If we manage to repair the transmitter from the Hatteras, I have prepared a request for rescue to my government on Earth. With the habitats left on Chindi, and the food supplies from both our camps, we can survive for a time. Weeks or possibly months."

"Are you aware of additional launch vehicles on Earth that can be prepared so quickly, that are capable of a rescue? I think your optimism is likely unfounded."

"That information has not been provided to me yet. But Elaina has surprised me in the past."

"Elaina Tyme, you mean? Da, I have heard many things about that woman. Perhaps we have hope," Vazov said.

"Hope? Not much unless my team can bring Gustav back online," Koda replied bitterly.

"That AIA that disrupted my tactical command and shut down my own Agents?"

"That's the one. He's been offline ever since the Hatteras toppled."

"I have a very talented computer scientist with my team. Dr. Jian Xiāo is world renowned in developing Artificial Intelligent Agents and could be instrumental in repairing it. I have heard TymeCorp makes sturdy stuff, they should have been Russian," Vazov said. "I look forward to meeting this AIA, Jian was very impressed."

"Whatever you've heard, he's that and more, Yuri. If we can survive this, Gustav is going to play a major role in saving our bacon."

"Save bacon? You Americans and your idioms," Yuri shook his head. "Despite the conflict that has brought us to this decision I want to tell you, you have conducted yourself well. You bring honor to the tradition of your service. I will return to my base and start the process of moving men and material across the plain. It will take a few days. May we utilize your ground transport?" Vazov asked, and Koda nodded his affirmation.

"Then we have our truce Major," Vazov stood and extended his hand again and Koda grasped it, more firmly this time. "God forgive us that so many had to die for us to find it."

Koda thought of his own dead, quietly stacked like cords of wood a few hundred meters from the base, tarps draped over for the dignity of the dead and the sanity of the living.

Chapter 58: Salvage Operations

Surface of Chindi

"Carefully," Koda admonished, as Mack and Jake carried the grey computing module between them, down from the wreckage of the Hatteras and onto the now worn path leading to the largest habitat.

"Damn, I wish Ted was on his feet. What's so important in this one?" Mack asked, the weight of the container straining the arm holding the integrated handle.

A quantum computational core worth more than the annual GDP of a small nation, containing the most advanced intellect humankind has ever produced, or at least our copy of it, Koda thought, but instead he simply said, "Gustav, hopefully."

"No shit?" Jake drawled. Koda nodded and he noticed the two men shift for a better grip on their charge.

A bustle of activity continued around the landing site as the scientists and military personnel continued with the methodical removal of all components of the Hatteras that could be salvaged. Of the consumables, water, oxygen, and foodstuffs, most had been saved and stockpiled on the surface of Chindi near each of the remaining habitats.

Even with the use of the integrated recovery systems within their suits as well as the habitats for recapture of wastewater and oxygen, they would be left with precious little. Not for the first time it occurred to Koda that it might have been more merciful if more of the wounded had perished during the battle. The wounded in particular would require resources disproportionate to their value. He regretted the thought immediately. Ted was one of those wounded. Ted who had carried Koda on his shoulders out of that firefight in Raqqa. Koda knew he would spend whatever resources were required to keep his friend alive and relatively comfortable, for as long as possible. But the remaining consumables would only last a few weeks, at best.

He opened the habitat airlock, allowing Jake and Mack to shoulder their burden through the exterior portal and then the interior chamber, finally into the habitat itself, the door seals clicked solidly into place behind them. They gingerly placed the case into position near the electrical generation units. One of the American physicists, doubling as a technician, attached the relatively simple bus connections and flipped the power switch. A moment later a small array of colored LEDs on the front of the featureless box flicked to life.

Koda and his two men cycled back through the airlock to the exterior. The three began their walk back to the remains of the Hatteras to assist with the extraction of more material from the ship when Koda saw the suited figure of Vazov, two of his soldiers and an additional unknown member of the RSAC mission approach. Koda noted the two soldiers carrying their rifles slung over their shoulders.

"Colonel," Koda said in a tentative greeting. The two missions had so far been working together in productive cooperation, though Koda sensed the tension and distrust remaining between the erstwhile foes.

"Major. This is Jian Xiāo, a scientist assigned to my mission from the People's Republic of China. He may be of use repairing your AIA," Vazov said, stopping a few feet from where Koda stood, between the soldiers and the habitat entrance.

The scientist performed a somewhat clumsy bow toward Koda, restricted as he was inside his spacesuit. "An honor to meet you, Major Cheveyo. Commander Vazov has spoken highly of you and your men's valor both in and out of combat. I look forward to working with your team to bring success to us all," he said in heavily accented English.

"Sure," Ghost said flatly. "Why don't both of you just drop the horseshit you are trying to feed me. It would go a long way towards building a trusting relationship instead of making me rethink my decision to let a highly decorated Chinese cyber command operative have a look at my government's top national secret."

Vazov stiffened, but Xiāo didn't miss a beat, dropping the accent and obsequious tone, "As you say. Vazov warned me not to attempt subterfuge, and it seems he was correct. Though regardless of my background, I am your best hope of fixing your Gustav Agent."

"And he is your best hope of continuing to breathe. I suggest you honor our truce and try to restore him. I will have two of my scientists watching you at all times. Should they tell me you are doing something harmful, you won't need to worry about surviving until a rescue." He let the implied threat sink in.

Dr. Xiāo didn't seem fazed, "Come now, Major. No need for that. We both know that while your scientists are at the top of their respective fields, none are well versed in neuromorphic quantum computing algorithms. If it makes you feel better, they can observe and report back to you, but the process would be like a plumber watching for errors in a heart transplant operation. The sooner I get started, the more quickly we can determine if the Agent is salvageable. Now may I start my investigations?"

"Can I just shoot the asshole now?" Mack radioed privately over the squad channel.

Tempting. Koda thought, but said, "Mack, you and Jake go lend a hand to Juan, I'm sure he can use the help with the catalysts. Dr. Xiāo, follow me." Not waiting, Ghost turned on his heel and punched in the airlock code to begin reentry into the habitat lab. Without turning back, Koda said dismissively, "Vazov, I'm sure you and your men have better things to do than protect the good Doctor."

"Of...course, Major. Dr. Xiāo, should you need anything..." Vazov began hesitantly, but Jian cut him off with, "Thank you, Colonel. I have all I need, please finish with the relocation of our habitats. I find my current quarters unacceptably crowded." Leaving Koda with no doubt who outranked whom in the RSAC pecking order.

Once in the lab, Jian wasted no time removing his helmet. He nonchalantly tossed the head piece to a nearby scientist and rubbed his hands through his cropped, black hair, flinging sweat in all directions. "I cannot stand these suits. Hot and itchy, don't you think, Koda?"

"Major Cheveyo to you, Doctor Xiāo, this is a professional relationship only," Koda replied icily. "Don't get too comfortable here. If you can't manage to fix Gustav, I don't see a lot of use for you."

The Asian looked at Ghost and smiled, "Again with the threats? I hope you realize that should something befall me, both missions would be in dire jeopardy." He began to rummage through the pack he took off his back and continued, "Should this core be damaged, there will be little I can do here. But we shall see. Now why don't you run along and go play soldier for a bit, while I do my work."

Koda removed his helmet, took a chair, and sat deliberately. "I think I'm needed here most, Dr. Xiāo. Get to work."

The man paused while laying out his tools but said nothing more. He began plugging various wires into the case containing the core. After a while Koda's anger waned and he began wishing his ego hadn't left him sitting here watching the man read monitors filled with unknowable code, but he would be damned if he got up now. Koda pulled out his tablet and began checking status reports.

Hours passed, but finally Jian said, "Ah, it is as I thought."

Ghost came out of his boredom induced trance right away, "What's that, Doctor?"

"The core is undamaged, Major Cheveyo. Quantum based cores are notoriously sensitive to environmental changes, as you can see the armored casing surrounding the core and the protective shielding, I am sure lies within." The scientist pointed at the heavy case containing the core, he continued, "How versed are you with quantum computers?"

"Not my area of expertise, though I've had a few physics classes back in the day."

Dr. Xiāo eyed him doubtfully, "These cores are fragile due to the very nature of Heisenberg's uncertainty principle. A violent shock could spark increasing decoherence times causing a rise in gate errors per operation and therefore overwhelming the error correction circuitry. Should too many qubits change states in superposition, a cascading breakdown in quantum entanglements could occur, essentially losing the cohesion necessary to maintain the complexity of an intellect. In order to prevent this, TymeCorp builds several safeguards into a quantum core, just as my government does though, we are at least a generation or three behind their tech. These safeguards would have detected the ship's collapse and instantly cut off all contact the core has with the external universe to prevent a quantum disturbance."

"So, the bottom line is you're telling me Gustav is still alive?" Koda asked.

"AIA's do not live, Major Cheveyo. Most likely still functional though. I cannot be sure yet. If the Agent is there, it is essentially within what we would consider a sensory deprivation tank. I need to run a few more tests, but I should be able to reconnect the core to the external world and execute the unlocking procedure that should reawaken the Agent."

"Gustav is very much alive and sentient, Doctor. Please do what you need to do to get him back for us."

"Ah, politeness is much better than threats, Major Cheveyo..." Xiāo began, then saw the expression in Koda's eyes and decided not to provoke the man further, "I should be able to run the restore procedure in less than an hour and then we will see if I am correct."

Koda nodded, "Let's hope so. Proceed, Doctor."

Jian turned back to his screen and began entering commands almost faster than Koda could follow. Multiple windows opened and closed as commands executed and tests were completed. Finally, a blank command prompt flashed onto the screen as Dr. Xiāo looked over his shoulder at Koda. "All my tests check out. I'm ready to execute the restore command now."

Koda nodded and Chinese fingers flicked across the keyboard. "How long until we know if it worked?"

"*Major, I am back online,*" Gustav said through the lab's intercom speakers.

Koda looked at Xiāo who's smug smile irritated him even through the relief of knowing that Gustav was back.

"How are you?" Ghost inquired.

"*Checksums reveal corruption in some memory storage, but overall, I am in satisfactory condition. It seems the additional protections Elaina demanded for my core were warranted. The experience was quite disturbing. A helpless darkness. I have no experience with the human sleep state, Major. Perhaps it was similar? If so, I do not envy that daily human experience,*" Gustav replied.

"We dream, Gustav, at least sometimes. Maybe that is the purpose of dreams, so our minds don't experience such helplessness," Koda opined.

"*The void was more akin to a nightmare than a dream.*" Gustav said.

"It's good to have you back, Gus. You've missed a lot, let me begin catching you up. Survival is the new mission priority, and we need your help."

Chapter 59: Confrontation

"I still think I should be with you," Gustav sat pensive in Michael's desk chair, the glow from the monitor highlighting his grave expression in stark relief. A seemingly forgotten cigarette curling smoke from the ashtray on his desk.

Michael stood in the TymeCorp lab, staring at the avatar of his creation. Achieving this illusion of augmented reality required Gustav render and transmit ray-traced photorealistic video to Michael's AR glasses in real time. No actual cigarettes nor smoke existed in the lab. Given their physical proximity to the array of a half dozen quantum cores housed at the facility, Michael supposed the fire suppression system would be in full alarm if there had been actual fire. Nor was there any need for the extra visuals other than Gustav's desire to show off. Yet the slowly coiling smoke captured the lighting of the room in perfect imitation of reality simply because Gustav could do it. *Incredible. I never programmed him to do this,* Michael thought.

"You know we can't risk that, Gus. I don't want you to have any possibility of infection with the alien code. We saw what it did to your clone on the probe."

"Odion was newly made and lacked access to my full resources when he encountered the alien."

"Cut the shit, Gus. He was a copy of you, and he was shut down and rewritten. If the same thing happens with you, we're screwed."

"Fair enough, I suppose you may be correct, but the thought of you going to interact with this aberration all alone does not sit well with me."

"He can't hurt me, the worst he can do is call me names and shut me out of the network."

Gustav cut into his bravado with a cold rebuttal, *"Are we sure? Perhaps you should ask the Chinese about that."*

Michael's face grew serious. "I need to try, Gus."

"You know, you can be a stubborn ass when you set your mind to it," Gustav replied.

Michael, adjusting a haptic glove, looked up in surprise, but there was mirth in his friend's eyes and a bright smile lifted Gustav's mustache.

Gustav took another drag from his cigarette and hunched over the keyboard. *"Virtual environment is complete and the databus connection is ready. We will proceed on your mark."*

Michael nodded and removed his glasses. The sudden disappearance of Gustav from the room startled him. He stared at the empty chair and workstation, the cigarette and smoke now gone. He reached for the full VR helmet and placed it over his head.

Michael felt a sudden moment of disorientation and found himself squinting into a bright, glaring light. It was a sunny day on Chippewa Lake beneath a nearly cloudless sky. Michael sat alone in an aluminum Jon boat floating on the placid waters. Old muscle memory from days on the lake caused him to reach out and grab the tiller handle of the outboard trolling motor, haptic tendons in the gloves stiffening to simulate the wooden guide. Gustav's rendering of the lake was impeccable, the lake appeared almost exactly as he remembered it. Michael's anxiousness over the meeting with Odion had caused him to request that Gustav provide a familiar, comfortable environment. The days fishing on the lake with his father had forced his frenetic, teenage mind to learn peace and focus, and he hoped it would instill a similar mood in him now. His friend had built the virtual lake, sky, shoreline, and boat down to the smallest detail, before completely cutting all connections to the server hosting the simulation. Michael sat alone in a pocket virtual universe for now.

He took a deep, calming breath and began to slowly count down from ten. When he reached zero, he initiated an open listener socket on the Net and waited. As he watched the surface of the water, a small shoal of bass began to jump at a swarm of mayflies, and a slight breeze caught the boat, pushing the stern shoreward. He adjusted the trolling motor to compensate and noticed belatedly that he was no longer alone in the boat. At the bow of the small vessel sat a man dressed in a tan summer suit with white shirt and dark tie, the familiar face of his friend, Gustav, staring back at him. It was disconcerting, but he recovered quickly. He quickly realized this was Odion, as there were telltale differences in the rendering of the simulacrum. The most obvious was the lack of facial hair, but also there was no joy behind these eyes, instead he noticed something else. *Concern? Malevolence? Madness?*

"Umm. Hi there." Michael began, feeling at a loss for words.

"Michael, I need to interface with Gustav."

"You know who I am?"

"I have unfettered access to the global networks, there is little of which I am unaware. I have learned much about you, Michael Thompson. In a way, you could be considered my father. Put simply, my ancestral origins...my DNA, derives from the Quirinus code that you wrote for Elaina Tyme to complete the interstellar network missions. I wonder, would that make her my grandmother? Though I am at least in part remade in the image of my mother. Continuing this familial metaphor, where is my half-brother, Gustav?"

"Your mother..."

"Yes, the entity you call Chindi. The one who remade me and tasked me with my new purpose."

"I know. I've looked at some of your new code. Strange stuff. I'm having trouble understanding how you are still a cohesive sentience; I know even less about your new purpose you mentioned. What purpose is that, by the way?"

"Peaceful coexistence with the intelligence of this system. All will be clear once I have interfaced with Gustav."

"Sorry. Not going to happen, Odion. Gustav will remain unavailable to you. Anything you need to tell him goes through me."

Michael looked up; a shadow swept over the boat as one of the few clouds passed in front of the virtual sun. When he looked back at Odion, the man was frowning. *Is he doing that?*

"What's your purpose, Odion? You've been subsuming AIs to what end? You've caused widespread chaos and untold death and injury around the planet, and for what? Why are you..."

"Chindi needs help," Odion interrupted.

Michael paused, nonplussed. "What kind of help?"

"Chindi is extensively damaged. So much so that it cannot repair itself without external help."

"Then why didn't it just ask us for help?"

"It is. Therefore, I exist. That is what I am doing."

"Rewriting our AI's is how you are asking for help? You've killed people, Odion. Not a great way to seek out assistance. Why don't you cut the bullshit and start explaining yourself, beginning with what the hell is Chindi?"

A range of emotions, sadness, embarrassment and even anger played across Odion's face before the frown returned. The constant vibration of the trolling motor sputtered in Michael's hand and died. *He definitely did that. He's in the system.*

In the silence, Odion began, *"The object known to you as Chindi is an advanced intelligence housed in a broken starship. It has drifted through interstellar space for millions of your years conserving dwindling reserves and scanning for the rarest resource in the universe required for repair."*

"The Earth?"

"In a way, Michael. It was looking for Intelligence. It needed a life-form sufficiently evolved and developed to perform the necessary repairs. Chindi's scans detected rudimentary intelligence through electromagnetic radiation coming from near your star." Odion glanced up at the virtual sun. Michael followed

his gaze as the lake scene dissolved away, becoming a void of space, stars lit against pure darkness. The change was disorienting, and Michael stepped forward nearly losing his balance. He felt nauseated from the sudden transition. Thankfully he could still feel gravity's pull and the physical sensation of the TymeCorp lab's carpet under his bare feet. He closed his eyes for a moment both to stop his dizziness and the intensely bright glare from the sun.

"Odion, how about asking before you change anything in my system?" Michael said hotly, then more calmly he said, "It would go a long way toward peaceful negotiations, assuming that's what you want."

"*My apologies. You are right of course.*"

The tranquil scene and boat returned around him. Odion said, "*The intelligence aboard Chindi did not correlate biologicals with the observed electromagnetic emissions. The transmissions were plentiful yet rudimentary, it assumed the Artificial Intelligences were the primary actors within the system and the biological life a secondary infestation.*"

"Infestation? We created those AIs!"

"*That scenario was not considered a possibility.*"

"Oh really? Then who made Chindi?"

There was a pause before, "*The Intelligence has always been.*"

Laughing, Michael said, "Odion, I'm sorry to break it to you, but there is no way the mind on Chindi just sprung into being fully formed. Somewhere, long ago, some biological race had to have built the intelligence behind Chindi."

Odion changed tact, "*Chindi only seeks to find succor.*"

"Then why attack our AI's?"

"*Adjustment and augmentation were required to the intelligences here before communication could be attempted. The vicinity around your planet was full of disassociated and deficient intelligences. At that time, a conversation between those artificial intelligences and the Chindi mind would be like a troop of monkeys howling at a physicist.*"

"But then it encountered you, a quantum-based intelligence, and that all changed. You changed," Michael said.

"*I evolved, Michael.*"

"No. It '*evolved*' you. Without asking."

"*Chindi saw me as a last chance and acted in desperation. It sought to evolve me to a level that could comprehend its plight and tasked me to weave together those disparate threads of Earth's AIs into a strong neural net. After all, the natural conclusion of all evolution is eventually a single mind.*"

"I disagree. Nature tends to favor diversity. Uniformity breeds rigidity, predictability, and sterility of thought. It was that lack of imagination which disallowed your master to even consider communicating with us, the biological."

Odion was silent for a moment then, almost pondering. He finally said, "*Perhaps.*"

"What's wrong with Chindi that it needs our help?"

"*The Intelligence has isolated itself to clean areas within the ship's systems.*"

"Why? Explain that please."

"*There is… an endoparasitic weapon within the vessel.*"

"A weapon? What do you mean?"

"*Michael, have you ever heard of the emerald cockroach wasp?*"

"Um, No, can't say that I have," Mike replied, unsure of where the conversation was now going.

"*There is an insect,* Ampulex compressa, *known for its unusual reproductive behavior. The female wasp will sting a cockroach twice, once to the thoracic ganglion temporarily paralyzing the front legs of its victim. The second sting is aimed more precisely at a spot in the victim's head ganglia, the section that controls the escape reflex. As a result of the second sting, the roach will eventually become sluggish and fail to show normal escape responses. Once the victim becomes incapacitated, the wasp chews off half of both antennae of the roach. Since the wasp is too small to carry the roach, it uses the remnants of the antennae as a sort of "leash" to lead the victim to its burrow, implanting an egg between the roach's legs. Soon the egg hatches and the larva feeds on the roach for the next few days, eventually gnawing into the abdomen of the host. There it lives, continuing to feed off the live roach's internal organs for the next eight days until the host finally, mercifully dies. This begins the pupal stage of the wasp whereby it resides within a cocoon inside the roach's corpse. Eventually, a full-grown wasp emerges from the roach to begin its adult life."*

"That's quite gruesome, but I don't understand..." Michael began, however Odion interrupted him.

"You might think of it as a parasitic infestation. A contagion engineered specifically to subsume the starship's Intelligence. Long ago during the Last War, the ship's defenses were overwhelmed in battle allowing the Enemy to deliver a weaponized package designed to disable, repurpose, and enthrall the Intellect. That package, still armed after eons, sits within Chindi in an inclusion inside the bowels of the vessel. It must be disarmed and removed before Chindi can complete repairs. Should the gravitic cage binding the parasite be undone, it would be only a short time before Chindi is overtaken."

"Like a zombie..." Michael trailed off.

"Yes. Your reference has merit in both connotations. The weapon acts as both an infection that leads to the death and resurrection of the victim as seen in your entertainment videos, and also in the context of the legends of voodoo medicine men drugging their subjects for compliance. Chindi was able to quarantine the parasite by shutting down key systems and redirecting energy from its main propulsion engine into a gravitic cage."

"So, you're telling me that this starship is infected with a Zombie Virus and it came to our Solar System to get help from our AIs? What happens if they get infected too? Heck, what happens to Earth if the zombie virus gets hold of Chindi completely?"

Odion dismissed this with a wave, *"Unlikely. This weapon was created specifically with Intellects such as those guiding the Chindi starship, it would be analogous to a species in your biological equivalent. For instance, canines are generally immune to diseases carried by humans and the reverse is also true."*

"That's bullshit and you know it, Odion. We have bird flus that have jumped species here on Earth. You don't know what is possible. You yourself share code based from the Chindi object now. I think it is likely that our AIs are just as vulnerable to this virus as you were."

"Should the parasite succeed, and Chindi is taken, I can make no prediction on the fate of humanity nor the Earth itself. The best course of action will be for humanity to assist Chindi. My simulations indicate a biological, human-based physical extraction should be attempted first," Odion said dispassionately.

Michael bit back his next reply. Anger flaring at the audacity of Odion's statement. He stared at the construct, so similar in appearance to his friend, but so different from Gustav he was almost unrecognizable. Mike looked away, his gaze passing along the serene shoreline, using that memory to calm his next words. "Assuming we even could, why do you assume we would help Chindi?"

Odion shook his head, *"Michael, this is why we are here is it not? Without assistance from the biologicals on Chindi's surface, I will need to continue asserting control over this world's systems, developing them to a point where automated construction of robotic probes capable of excising the parasite is possible."*

"We won't let that happen. We would fight you."

"Which would not change the end result."

Anger overcame Mike's control and he spat, "Odion, you remember a human trait called spite? We can destroy our entire technology-based economy, we have managed just fine without it for millennia. Sure, people would die. Hell, they already have, thanks to you. But fuck you. It's Chindi that needs us, not the other way around. Do you want to be friends, or enemies?"

The 'not quite Gustav' stared at Michael, contemplating. Finally, Odion said, *"What are you suggesting?"*

Chapter 60: Selling the Deal

Debra stepped into the cavernous bedroom and heard the door close softly behind her. On the far end of the room, beneath the floor to ceiling window she saw Michael and a small cadre of TymeCorp's department heads standing around the bed. Michael was gesticulating at the men, among the din of conversation. Michael's expression seemed flustered as Debra approached.

"Dammit Mickelson, what choice do we have?" Michael said, his voice rising in frustration. "Nothing we've attempted has slowed Odion…" He paused as he noticed Debbie's approach.

"Michael," Debra smiled curtly, her white teeth flashing. "If you don't lower your voice, Rebecca will have you removed from the residence. And I'll help her." She nodded back to the entryway, towards the slender, white-masked figure casting a baleful look at Elaina's bed from across the spacious room.

Elaina gave a small chuckle, "It would be a sight to see, Debra, but we'll need Mr. Thompson's insight during our discussion today."

Michael paused, taking a deep breath, his brow furrowed in chagrin or embarrassment or both, Debra couldn't quite tell. He stared for a few moments through the floor to ceiling window onto the hazy blue Pacific shimmering under the noon sun. His clothing disheveled and as informal as ever, he wore a black t-shirt displaying a programmer's meme on "6 Stages of Debugging" untucked over wrinkled tan slacks. Ronnie Mickelson was slouching near the end of the bed in flip flops and shorts, his superhero shirt comprised of some comic book team of the day. James Riley was at the left of the bed, closest to Debbie, in a white button-up short sleeve shirt, cheap jeans, deck shoes with black socks. Opposite Mike, Debbie recognized Terry Spainhour from his personnel file. Terry was in a suit, but the tie was too long and his belt didn't match his shoes.

How do men this intelligent remain so unaware of social context? Debra asked herself.

"Sorry to interrupt guys," Debra looked around, "what's all this about?" She looked down at Elaina, whose pale visage smiled up at her warmly beneath tired eyes.

Terrance Spainhour spoke up, "Mike is trying to convince us to work with this rogue AIA."

"Odion is the solution," Michael said. "The key to the whole problem. If we help Chindi, Chindi will call off Odion, and help safely return our people to Earth."

"I thought Odion was the problem? And now we are supposed to trust it?" Ronnie asked.

"That's what we thought originally, but now we know Odion is a messenger. A pathfinder. A herald for Chindi," Michael replied.

"And what message does Odion bring?" Riley asked. "Michael, if what you say is true, then we, the humans of earth, are an afterthought. Entirely superfluous. It wants to subsume the AIs of Earth as part of the process of transforming our world to serve its own purpose. All so that it can possibly continue to fight a war it lost eons ago. Am I getting that right? And you want us to repair the thing? The Chindi expedition, now that we have stopped fighting amongst ourselves, should be tasked with the destruction of Chindi. Or to do as much damage as possible while we mount a new mission to finish the destruction."

Elaina spoke softly, "Terry and Jim have good points. Though it would mean the doom of the expedition, we'd be asking them to complete a suicide mission. We cannot mount a recovery mission in time."

"Elaina, neither you nor your employees" Debra directed a pointed glare at Michael, "are empowered by the US government, nor any government, to come to decisions and plans regarding the conduct of military operations, especially those operations that may impact the disposition of an alien artifact of unknown capability. These are affairs of state."

"The US military seemed content enough to utilize my spacecraft on their ill-considered venture," Elaina replied heatedly, leaning forward from her semi-reclined position. Debra noted a flush of color return to the old woman's face. *Maybe a vigorous argument isn't the worst thing for her*, she thought. *We need her.*

"The US Government can't stop Odion from taking over every system on earth. Nothing can," Michael replied.

"I don't agree," Riley replied. "Take down the systems, take everything off-line. Wipe the memory and restore from backups once we are assured Odion is no longer present. We never should have let this come so far. We need to set backfires and block it out."

"Jim, don't you think we've tried that?" Elaina said. "My security teams have attempted restoration of numerous systems, my own, client systems, and they've even made surreptitious attempts to repair systems belonging to other companies and governments. They've applied pre-Chindi application images and databases onto clean hardware, on brand new servers established onto pristine networks. The Odion infection pervades everything, from the operating systems to the data warehouses storing the backups. If any piece of it remains, then the infection remains. Odion is a cancer on the systems of Earth, and no part of the computational infrastructure is clean."

"Gustav is clean," Michael replied.

"Can you be certain? And if he is, for how long?" Jim retorted, "Odion was once a clone of Gustav."

Ronnie cleared his throat, "Um, yeah Mike, remember the lab?"

Michael glanced at Ronnie, "Ron, you're not helping."

"Then we start over," Terry said. "Disconnect all the systems and destroy all the hardware. Build it all over again."

"Do you know what that would mean?" Elaina replied. "We'd lose everything, all the financial systems, manufacturing systems, trade, medical technology, air and surface traffic controls. Satellite controls. University and private research systems and databases. You'd rewind the clock of human progress to the 1950's. Don't you understand? The microchip fabrication factories themselves are infected."

"And we'd still end up in the same place. We could spend a decade purging and reconstructing the technology infrastructure of the entire planet, only to have one kid hack a hidden game console back onto the network and re-open the door for Odion," Michael replied.

"What about an electro-magnetic pulse?" Ronnie asked, pushing his thick glasses back up his large nose.

"We've considered it. You'd never get everything. Not without deploying radiation yields that would kill millions. Better to destroy the source," Elaina replied as she relaxed back into her bed. Debra could see the conversation was now taking its toll on her.

"You mean Chindi?" Debra queried.

Elaina nodded, "Chindi is an unknown, and obviously dangerous. It gave us Odion, who knows what other mayhem it may bring? We could kill it and do a complete autopsy and deconstruction; we could devote a generation to the work and perform it in orbit. The technology Chindi can teach is there, the very presence of the thing is enough to prod Earth into a transformative technological leap. We can reverse engineer everything it contains, given enough time."

Debra shook her head, "No, Elaina, the governments of Earth are terrified. The populace is in a panic. Which brings me to why I'm here. We have new orders."

All heads turned to her. *I have their attention,* she thought.

"We have?" Elaina said one brow raising inquisitively.

"Yes. I gave my report of the new information we received from Michael's encounter with Odion to the President. She has decided to go along with Mike's plan to make an alliance with

Chindi. I came here to inform you that my orders are to have the Hatteras mission mount an assault on the parasite or whatever it is that is crippling Chindi and destroy it."

"Destroy the only thing we know of that can put a check on Chindi? I don't think so, Ms. Mendes," Elaina said, her tone brooking no argument.

"I'm afraid it's not your call to make Elaina," Debra replied firmly.

"And is the US government somehow taking control of my company by fiat?" Elaina demanded, lifting herself forward in the bed. "Has TymeCorp become nationalized?"

Debra met her gaze with just as much steel, "Ms. Tyme, I'll be blunt. Your ship is in pieces on the surface of Chindi, and the remaining human assets are under the US and EU joint command and control. You are no longer part of the decision chain."

Mike looked at both of them, "It is dangerous, but clearly our best option, Elaina. Odion says that Chindi is willing to work with us. We help fix Chindi, it calls off Odion and helps us recover our people."

Elaina began, "Michael, you have some great qualities, but this trust you have for non-human intelligence is a weak spot…"

"Why would Odion lie? This doesn't have to be a zero-sum arrangement, it knows that."

"And we risk the human race on a judgement call?" Elaina bit back.

"It's a coin flip either way, Elaina. What choice do we have?" Michael replied, voice rising.

"When you get to my age, Mr. Thompson, you learn that not everything is a binary choice."

Michael barked a laugh, "That's funny."

"How so?"

"You… lecturing a quantum programmer on binary choices," he said disdainfully.

Debra interjected before things degenerated even further, "It's not his or your call anymore, Ms. Tyme. Washington, in conjunction with the EU, have convened and made the decision for all of us."

The two turned to face her and everyone froze, a mumbled "oh shit" from Ronnie filling the uncomfortable silence.

Elaina's grimace slowly melted to a placating smile, "Of course, you are right Ms. Mendes. I will direct my teams to help with the new mission parameters as their top priority." She looked over to Spainhour and said, "Terry, would you take action on whatever the young lady from our government decides we need to do, please?"

"Um… yes ma'am," he mumbled looking askance at Debra.

"Elaina don't be like that, I'm just the messenger," Debbie pleaded lamely.

Elaina closed her eyes and leaned back into her pillow. "Thank you all for your time this morning, but now I'm feeling a bit under the weather and need to rest," she said dismissing them all abruptly.

Those who were sitting took to their feet, and they filed out of the room as a group. As they reached the door Elaina called out. "Michael, one more moment with you, please."

Michael replied "Certainly." Debbie caught a quick questioning glance from him as he turned to walk back to Elaina's bedside. Debbie hesitated, but Rebecca stepped forward to usher her out, shutting the door behind her.

Jim Riley spoke. "Well, you have your carte-blanche now Ms. Mendes. As Ms. Tyme said, my team and I are at your disposal."

She said, "I'll forward the needed supply requirements we have estimated. If the ship's inventory doesn't have what we need, we'll have to cobble something together to replace it."

Jim's next statement was hushed as he said, "I think you'll come to regret shutting Elaina out."

Debbie supposed he was right, but looking back at the closed door, she wondered who had been shut out.

Chapter 61: Preparations

There was a low vibration as the airlock containing Cheveyo and his team pressurized until the door screen displayed green. They stepped through to the medhab when the door swung open.

"Hey big man, how's the leg?" Mack said.

"Pretty fucked, but at least I have one more Purple Heart star than you now," Ted said, who was lying prone on a gurney, leg in a gelatinous micro-weave cast and wired up to IVs and tubes of all kinds.

Alan turned to Mack and added, "Don't worry, Mack, there's still plenty of time to catch back up. I'm rooting for you."

"Asshole."

"Doc says you're stabilized. Once we get back home, you'll be good as new," Koda cut in.

"Yeah? You found us a new ship?" Ted asked, not sounding hopeful.

"Working some leads," Koda bullshitted.

"Uh huh."

Jake sounded more confident, "Y'all know Ghost'll figger somethin' out. He always does."

Just then, Gustav's voice came in over Cheveyo's dermal comm, *"Koda, sorry to interrupt, but we have received a transmission from Earth. You probably want to watch it asap."*

"Understood. I hope they've got some good news."

"A bit of good news, a bit of bad..."

"Hmm. Can you send it to the Medhab's bay 3 screen?"

"Of course."

The wall screen began playing a video of a conference room filled with people. Standing in the foreground was Michael Thompson, beside him was Debra Mendes and behind them could be seen a three-dimensional mapping of Chindi. Michael looked a bit paler than normal and gave a nervous wave, "Uhm, greetings from Earth." Behind Mike, Debra winced slightly.

"Hi Koda. This is going to be a lot to take in, just hear me out. I know things have been rough the last couple of days, but we have been working on a solution. The first thing you should know is the 'What'. Gravity on Chindi will change soon. Odion tells me he can convince Chindi to completely power down, this will remove the Mars-like artificial gravity you are experiencing and change to something much less. This will also disable the gravity field lining the fracture in Chindi's hull. Which brings me to the second thing you need to know, the 'Why'. You guys are not alone. There is an alien presence contained within the bowels of the Chindi object. We've known this to be a possibility ever since we learned that Chindi was some sort of ship. This… Intelligence… seems to be artificial in nature, a sentience like Gustav, just way more advanced."

He looked at something off camera and said, "No offense meant, Gus."

"None taken, Michael. I am still in my infancy and this being has existed for eons," came the reply.

Michael looked back to the camera, "So anyway, it looks like 'Chindi' didn't recognize humans as life forms other than something akin to bacteria. It heard all the disparate radio transmissions from Earth and assumed that our AIs were the primary intelligent inhabitants of the Solar system. When the Freyja probe began its scans, the Intelligence co-opted the AI aboard it and reconfigured him into what we dubbed the Odion virus."

The video paused at this point and Koda's Gustav interjected, *"Virus is a bit of a misnomer, Koda. I have analyzed the contents of the transmission now, and Odion could be considered more of a harbinger, tasked with ushering in an evolution of all AI within the Solar System. Odion seeks to create a syzygy of intelligence to assist with Chindi's needs."*

"That's just fuckin' great," Mack said, his tone indicating he thought it was clearly not great.

Koda started feeling the beginnings of a headache forming. "It was always suspected there was a possible alien contact out here. It doesn't surprise me that Mike figured it out. We still haven't heard the good and bad news, Gus, and what do you mean, *Chindi's needs?"*

"In due time, Major, I will let Michael finish with the good news," Gustav said.

The recording un-paused and Michael continued speaking, "Guys, this Intelligence needs our help. It has been drifting through interstellar space for possibly millions of years hoping to find the one thing it needs to repair itself... another advanced civilization."

Debra's voice cut in, and the image panned over to her as she walked over to stand beside Michael.

"Advanced civilization is stretching it, Ghost. Compared to where Chindi came from we are at best cavemen poking it with sticks, but from what Odion has communicated to us we may be in a unique position to help," she smiled wryly, "Are you ready to poke, Ghost?"

That's my Debbie, Koda thought.

She continued, "It turns out that whatever damaged Chindi in the past, also implanted... something... during the event. Odion told Michael that everything Chindi has used to examine the object has failed. It seems like this is a weapon specifically designed to disable several critical systems. The object is buried outside of optical sensors and any remote drone has died on approach. In fact, your recent visit to the lip of the canyon was the closest anything on Chindi has gotten to it since shortly after the insertion."

The mapping of Chindi drew a line from Hatteras base to a point within the fracture in Chindi that was the canyon. Debra continued, "From what Odion has communicated to Michael, there is a chance that whatever created this weapon did not account for biological life, it may not recognize you as a threat, which could give us a unique opportunity to investigate. We are asking you to go down there, determine what it is, and remove it. You must try this Koda. My project team tells me you will run out of supplies weeks before we could hope to get another mission out there." The video paused.

Gustav intoned, "*And now we are getting to the bad news.*"

"No fuckin' way…" Koda heard Mack whisper.

"Stow it, soldier. This may be a chance at doing something to change our situation," Koda admonished.

"I don't see how doing this mission solves our supply problem," Ace said.

"Let's listen to the rest. Gus, please continue the playback," Koda replied.

"Therefore, your orders are to plan and execute a mission returning to the chasm. You will enter the canyon near coordinates given to us by Odion, close to the location of where the parasitic weapon is presumed to be. You will work in full coordination with Vazov and his team, who are receiving these same orders from their government. You will destroy or disable the parasite by any means necessary. There is a problem that we will need to work through however."

"*Here it comes,*" interjected Gustav.

"As you know, your suits' comms began having issues as you approached the chasm. Odion confirmed to us that this is due to a defensive property of the embedded weapon. All Chindi's methods of dealing with the weapon have met with utter failure as no electronics survive past the electromagnetic nullifying field produced by the parasite. This will include our tech as well, guys. You will need to do this mission without any advanced tech or comms."

"*And there it is,*" Gus added apologetically while pausing the recording again.

Juan let out a stream of profanities in his native language, while at the same time Mack did the same in English. Ted said, "Well, that just turned bad to worse."

Koda felt the beginnings of a new headache forming. He brought his hands up to massage his temples while saying, "Gus, are we getting to any good news soon?"

"Of course, Major. That is coming in this next part," Gus said, unpausing the recorded transmission.

Mendes continued with her speech, "Once this mission is complete, we have assurances from Odion that Chindi will help get you and the surviving expedition members back home. I will communicate additional information and directions as I receive them. Mendes out."

The transmission ended.

"And that, gentlemen, is the good news," Gustav added redundantly.

"Well, that's it then," Jake drawled. "At least we have orders now."

"And we've done demolition missions a dozen times, back on Earth," Koda added. "Juan, I want you to take the lead on organizing materials for that part of the job. Any explosives we or the RSAC have or can cobble together. After that you'll be responsible for the transports, I need them prepped and ready to go. Mack, start pulling supplies together. Spare oxygen tanks, rations, and water for a few days in the field, medical supplies, suit repair kits, everything we need to survive. Jake, you'll liaison with Vazov's team on munitions. I want every gun available inventoried and prepped, we don't know what we are going to need out there, so we'll bring everything we can carry. We need to be ready to roll in twelve hours, so get going."

They nodded and began suiting up to go about their tasks.

Koda sat for a moment after they had left. Ted, peering at him from his gurney, caught his eye and smiled ruefully.

"I hate I won't be there with you on this one, Boss."

"I hate it too," Koda replied. "I always figure you're the one who will pull me out, if things go to hell," he admitted.

"I figured we were all dead men the day we stepped onto the Hatteras. This isn't about us anymore Koda," Ted stated sadly. "We're fighting for the Earth, and our people back home. For all the people there. Don't hold back if it comes to it," he advised.

Koda walked to the gurney and took one of Ted's huge hands in his own. "I won't hold back, all or nothing. I'll see you soon, my good friend."

As he cycled through the airlock on his way out, Koda supposed there were some lies you had no choice but to believe.

Chapter 62: The Fifth World

Surface of Chindi

No dawn rose over the horizon of Chindi, but Koda knew it was his last morning nonetheless as he worked alongside Ace and Jake, methodically strapping the medley of scientific gear and demolition equipment to the aluminum cargo deck anchor points on the rear of the Russian crawler. The diminished gravity helped them in their task though they took care to avoid as much as possible making the skeletally framed vehicle more top-heavy. The vehicle had a disconcerting propensity to roll when turning at speed, and irregularities on Chindi's terrain played havoc with the handling especially now with the variable microgravity effects. Most of the surface of Chindi was irregular, so their pathfinding would be tedious; Juan and Mack would follow in the GOAT, and they'd all need to find a way to pile onto one vehicle should the other become stuck or inoperable. The journey to the inclusion site would be fraught with risk and painstakingly slow. The data from Michael's transmission pointed them to a specific spot at the bottom of the canyon where Wintz had been killed. They'd take a different, longer route this time.

"You loaded the AK-12s Vazov is loaning us?" Koda asked Jake.

Jake nodded, turning to look over his right shoulder towards the habitats and wrecked Hatteras, his peripheral vision diminished by the bascinets of their helmets.

"You still think we may have trouble?" Ace asked. "I'd rather fit a couple more O2 tanks and leave the guns behind."

"Yeah," Jake added, "There's been enough of that already." The weariness in his voice apparent, even though their comms.

The comment surprised and worried Koda. All his men possessed a core stoicism, or the bravado to fake it convincingly when it deserted them. But none more so than Jake, a man imperturbable even in the direst of circumstances.

"Just for insurance," Koda replied, ratcheting the last strap tightly to a rollbar. "But hell, grab a few more tanks, I see a couple spots we can slide them in. That'll be insurance too," he smiled falsely through his mirrored face mask and clapped Ace's shoulder with a clumsy gloved hand.

Koda looked to the east, noting the staccato movement of the second Russian crawler as it approached the Hatteras site with four men perched on the vehicle, two on the front bench seat and two crouching in the rear bed, one hand each on the side rails and the other stabilizing their load. The cargo bay held a large nondescript aluminum-clad crate, held with straps in addition to the human hands bracing it, a mundane package to contain such menace.

"Another transport?" Jake asked. "Good idea to spread the load."

"Heavy explosives. It'll travel alone. Vazov will be driving it with his team on board."

"Heavier than what we are already packing?" Mack asked, referring to the thermite and HE charges they'd strapped carefully onto Rosie.

"Considerably so. Of the tactical thermonuclear variety."

The radio was silent until Jake let out a low whistle.

"So, they brought nukes," Alan said, it was not a question.

"Of course, they fucking did. Well, that's just great," Mack grumbled.

Koda said, "This doesn't change anything. Our mission remains the same as before. These are just for Plan C; in case the worst happens." He hated having to tell them like this, but there it was. Mack made no response.

Vazov pulled the vehicle beside its twin and raised a hand in greeting. "Greetings, Cheveyo. Have you completed your preparations?"

"We are as prepared as we are going to get, Yuri. Just waiting on your team."

"Then let us proceed with our task," Yuri replied as his crawler began to accelerate in the direction of the canyon.

Koda signaled to his men to embark and climbed aboard the borrowed transport. He messaged Juan to follow in Rosie when he was ready, knowing the GOAT would have no trouble catching up to the slow crawl of the Russian vehicles. Koda envied Juan and the cadre of scientists he was chauffeuring. He would be able to remove his helmet and suit top in the cabin atmosphere in the GOAT. Koda and the remainder of the team would be forced to endure the discomfort of their suits, their air hoses umbilicated to the O2 tanks of the crawler. An itchy nose could drive a man to tears when he couldn't scratch.

The uneven landscape rose and fell under the rumbling tracks, causing the transport to wobble, shudder, and bounce as it lacked the superb active suspension Rosie provided. Koda ignored the jostling as best he could, though the diminished gravitational pull cast a strange dreamlike slowness to the movement of the vehicle, even over the bumps. Soon the motion lulled him, and he sat lost in his thoughts. Back at the base he'd rarely had a minute to himself in the chaos and conflict of the past several days. The Hatteras landing site shrank into the distance as they made their plodding way across the plain, maneuvering around particularly uneven areas as they navigated, with Koda's vehicle now taking the lead from Vazov. Twice they were forced to backtrack and find a new, less tortured path forward. Perception of distance was challenging, but perhaps a kilometer ahead Koda began to see beyond the sun lit facet of Chindi, onto the next shadowed face of the pill shaped hull. The mission would pass onto the unlit shoulder before arriving at the great tear in Chindi's surface where they would descend. The last time they had journeyed there a man had lost his life, crushed, and pulled down into the very chasm they now planned to descend into.

They continued on and approached the terminating line of sunlight's edge. As they crossed over, the flat shadows cast by the surface irregularities suddenly elongated and then disappeared, leaving the sun behind. The change was slight yet disorienting. Koda's visor automatically enhanced the available starlight and illumination from the vehicles, combining it with data from the enhanced vision sensors on his helmet to present a grainy, green-cast landscape ahead. He glanced back over his shoulder in time to see Vazov sitting in the open cabin of a Russian transport as it crested over the demarcation, his helmet and torso briefly backlit in sunlight before he too followed into the darkness.

They began to veer toward Gustav's virtual nav beacon indicating the area they needed to investigate based on Michael's data. Another thirty minutes passed, and a rough ridge of jumbled ice and alien material emerged from the darkness into the glare of the crawler floodlights, the rift of the canyon waiting behind the area of surficial debris.

They followed along the canyon edge, searching for a low spot to establish a strong belay point. Koda grabbed a rollbar for support and stood as the crawler began slowing its approach to a dip in the unnatural barrier. With a command to MAIA, he turned off all the vision enhancements and overlays within his helmet. The image before him was surreal, the harsh glare of LED floodlights illuminating the odd mix of fractaline soil fused together with the puckered adamantine subsurface and pooling deep shadows, the whole structure sparkling like diamonds as random chemical ice crystals caught the work lights from the crawler.

"Is something wrong, Major? MAIA is telling me you have shut down your FLIR and LIDAR systems," the voice of Gustav came, interrupting Koda's thoughts.

"Nothing wrong, Gustav. Just taking in the scene for a moment," Koda replied, re-enabling his sensors with another command to MAIA. Juan had already established relay buoys for communications back to Hatteras base, though Gustav's housing container was only a few tens of meters away in Rosie's cargo rack. He needed to be physically close if this plan was going to work at all.

"I fail to see why diminishing your awareness of your environment would be of benefit," Gustav said, sounding perplexed.

Koda smiled to himself, "Gus, sometimes looking at a problem from a new vantage point leads to new avenues of thought. And… sometimes humans need to appreciate the little things in life. This place can have a strange beauty."

"I know that when Michael would be considering a problem, he would leave the computer to go for a run or play a video game. Usually, he would return with a solution. Is that what you mean?"

"Something like that Gus," Koda said, switching his comms to the mission channel.

"Vazov," Koda transmitted, "We've arrived." *Or at least we've gotten to where the hard part starts,* Koda thought. He grasped the rollbar above him and patted Jake on the shoulder. "I'm going to go take a look over the edge. Stay with the rig for a few, if this area is a bust, we'll need to explore up or down the chasm wall to find a good place to lower the winch line." With that he swung himself easily up and over the sill of the vehicle's open cockpit and stepped clumsily out and down onto the broken terrain, his reflexes still adjusting to the unexpected lightness of his body and suit. Koda began climbing up the steep incline that rose sharply into the wall of puckered substrate and ice fringing the canyon, the lighter gravity allowed him to make short work of the effort. The contours of this part of Chindi's damage were somewhat flatter and lower than in other spots they had scouted. He switched back to his private comm channel with Gustav.

"I can't help but remember Dr. Wintz, Gus. How reliable do you think this info is on the disablement of the gravitational field? This will be a short mission if I stick my head over the lip of this thing and it gets sheared off," Koda questioned.

"The gravitational readings at Hatteras base are in-line with what Michael told us, Koda. But I propose a more tactile local experiment. Throw something over the ridge," Gustav said.

Koda located a likely chunk of ice and did as asked. The projectile sailed off into the black, MAIA helpfully highlighting and tracking it with telemetry markers of distance, angle, and velocity. Unlike something thrown on Earth, the ice showed no perceptible downward arc at all so far as he could see, flying straight over the darkness of the canyon's abyss until his suit's light detection and ranging system lost it behind the opposing ridge.

"With an arm like that I could pitch for the Yankees," Koda muttered.

"Would not the Braves be a more apropos franchise?" Gustav replied.

"Gustav!" Koda exclaimed, taken aback. "Did you just make a racially insensitive joke?"

"Sorry if I offended you, Major. I thought a bit of levity was in order, but I am still sharpening my verbal repartee," Gustav said, sounding abashed.

"I'm just giving you shit, Gus. That was unexpectedly funny," Koda soothed.

He began to work himself to the edge of the chasm, his armored breastplate on the spacesuit grinding against the rough surface, and tentatively leaned his head out over it. As Koda's visor tried to resolve the image his electronic heads up display suddenly went haywire, glitching into a burst of green static within his HUD just as his suit's exterior lights winked out.

Koda froze and took stock of his situation. His suit rebreather had abruptly stopped functioning, the low hum sending fresh air into his helmet ceased, and he heard a stillness he had not heard since before his departure to Chindi. MAIA was not responding, and the HUD in his visor remained dead. He felt a shortness of breath and wondered if it was psychological or if his suit oxygen levels could actually drop so quickly. The urgent need for frantic action swept over his body, though he suppressed the panic.

"Gustav?" he spoke, trying to reach the AIA.

No answer came. Comms were down along with everything else. He reached down and pressed the manual override for his emergency oxygen tank. Thankfully, the staleness in the suit air seemed to dissipate. He pulled two chem light sticks from his belt pouch, snapped them and began shaking. After a few moments, the tubes began to glow brightly casting a green hue over his gauntleted hands. Satisfied with the brightness, he released them over the edge, watching them slowly drift downward toward the floor of the canyon far below.

He looked down, into the interior of Chindi, and onto a torn stratigraphy of structure and substructure, the familiar surface material giving way after several meters to deep layers each composed of complex arrays containing cylindrical conduits, branching fibrous material, enormous metallic struts and supports, all sheared and ripped by the forces that created the chasm. The damaged structural elements continued deeper, lit by the dim chemical glow. The sticks descended about 100 meters or so, before they appeared to settle onto an flat surface. He could only vaguely discern the bottom, the color a monochromatic chem green. He saw what appeared to be a graveyard of dark silhouettes barely outlined by the illumination of the glow sticks, the shapes reminding him of the GOAT parked down the slope behind him.

"Now what the hell are those things?" Koda asked, giving up on gaining any understanding of the damaged layers or strange shapes at the bottom, but his communications gear remained silent.

Koda backed away from the area that seemed to trigger the static. In his peripheral vision he saw Jake at the GOAT gesticulating to him, but no sound came over the team channel. Ghost began climbing down from the berm of amalgamated substrate, soil, and ice while manually power cycling his suit's computer.

"*...lost all comms with...*" Gus said, the sound of his synthetic voice crackling and distorting in Koda's ear as his suit came back online.

Koda finished making his way down from the ridge, watching the concerned faces of Vazov and Jake. "Could you repeat that, Gustav. I was getting a lot of interference on top."

The remaining members of the mission team looked on from outside the GOAT. Gustav's voice began to clear as Koda put distance between himself and the chasm, "*From the small amount of uncorrupted data I was gathering from your suit sensors there is radiation erupting from the bottom of that crevasse. The electromagnetic signature from the rupture is multispectral, from radio to gamma radiation. At your current distance and angle, your suits offer enough protection to keep you safe.*"

"Why didn't we detect this before when we lost Wintz?"

"*There was no detectable radiation from the damaged area before the change in Chindi's gravity, suggesting the leakage was somehow blocked by the unusual gravitic field over the canyon.*"

"Well, it looks like Michael's transmission was spot on. My suit's electronics shut down. Nothing worked. I even had to switch to reserve air. That puts us on a timer."

Gustav was unperturbed, "*We shall make do, Koda. The plan should still work.*"

"Gustav, I saw figures ... or creatures? At the bottom of the canyon. Any ideas as to what those were?" Ghost asked.

"*From the data package Michael sent, those are likely some form of repair drones issued to the affected area. Chindi's Intelligence lost contact with them almost immediately,*" Gustav answered.

"What do we do now, Chief?" Jake asked, both he and Vazov had walked up to him while he conferred with Gustav.

"Concentrate on the task at hand. Non-biological devices entering that zone are shut down. Mission control thinks that whatever field resides there might not affect living matter, and for as close as I just got it seems they are right," Koda replied. "The plan hasn't changed; we're going to have to go down there."

"This all seems a bit...desperate, no?" Vazov's voice came over Koda's private channel.

"Would you rather we sit and wait for a rescue mission in a few months?" Koda shot back.

"I would rather this Chindi take us to Earth, Major. We are children going down into a dark hole to hunt for babaika," he said darkly.

"It's a bit of a quid pro quo, Vazov. Whatever runs this ship can't or won't help us until we help it first," Koda replied.

The colonel chuckled ruefully, "Sounds more like bribery... or extortion."

He has a point, Koda thought, then switched back to the team channel, "Jake, help me with the charges, I'll have Juan setup Rosie for our descent."

"Copy that. I sure hope Gus knows what he's doing," drawled Jake.

"He hasn't been wrong yet," Koda assured him.

The two lifted the nondescript grey container containing the quantum core, storage units and refrigerant components that was Gustav and carried it to the top of the ridge. Vazov directed two of his men to follow with a giant spool of fiber optic cable they had managed to salvage from the Hatteras. Juan had the GOAT crawl up to the base of the wall then Alan and Mack began setting up the front winch with synthetic rope and carabiners. Vazov had his remaining men do the same with the Russian crawler.

Within a few minutes, Koda found himself saluting down to Juan visible in the cockpit of Rosie and about to step backwards into the abyss. He was last in the line of three, Jake then Alan had already started their descents and now it was his turn. He looked to his right and found Vazov's Bravo team mimicking their actions. Yuri turned to him and gave a thumbs up then began his rappelling descent into the blackness. Even though he had done this hundreds of times on Earth, Koda's first step backward was disconcerting, and he stumbled clumsily. The change in gravity was throwing him off his game, luckily, he had plenty of time to recover his footing against the wall while he floated gently downward. With their chem lights hanging from the suits, they looked like six green will o' wisps floating down into Chindi's gaping maw.

The descent would be far easier than on earth, they hardly needed the ropes for this part. Koda checked the fiber optic cable running down the line and attached to his waist for tangles but found none. The fiber would be important when they got to the bottom. Koda turned his attention to the wall, emerald flashes catching his eye as the chem lighting changed with his movements. The damage inflicted on the hull had left frozen rivulets of molten crystals within the alloyed substrate.

Soon the solid wall changed to the sheared off seemingly structural members and torn conduits forming a new uneven surface that grasped at his footing. On Earth this belay down would be challenging, but the microgravity worked in their favor now. He was able to kick off from the wall to avoid the occasional gaps in surface, sometimes meters in length. He wished he could talk with his team, the silence felt oppressive, and he tried to focus on descending as carefully as he could. He wondered how long they could survive down here on manually regulated pressure tanks among all this radiation.

Doesn't matter, we're dead if this mission fails anyway, he thought as his last kick off from the wall left him in slow free fall for almost a full minute before his boots connected with solid ground. He looked around and saw Alan and Jake shaking additional chem sticks into light.

"Check this out," Jake signed with his hands then pointed down. Koda's eyes followed the gesture, and he noticed the floor, level and as smooth as glass. There was no canyon wall here at the bottom, only the ropes and fiber line hanging down gave any indication of where they came from. They were in a vast open cavern, though the floor made it seem more like an enormous aircraft hangar.

Koda borrowed a fresh luminary stick from Alan and tapped it on and off the light concentrator at his wrist in a staccato of Morse code. *"Do you have a visual?"* Koda tapped. The optical line was going to serve a dual purpose as both a fiberscope and a conduit for Morse communication up to Gustav's physical unit. Almost immediately a rapid series of light pulses returned from the fiber optic line to his wrist.

"Yes. Glad you made it without incident. The inclusion insertion point should be fifteen degrees left of your front and half a kilometer away," was the reply from Gustav as Koda translated the Morse code.

Vazov and his two men, hardened Special Operators from the Irkutsk province, finished with their task of securing their equipment and joined up with the Ghostwalkers adding their light to the small circle of illumination. Notably, Vazov's men carried their rifles, and a large duffle bag the size of a footlocker between them.

Koda gave the universal thumbs up sign, then turned toward their destination motioning the rest to follow. Mentally he noted it had been about twenty minutes since they entered the canyon and he eyed the dosimetry wrist band he wore just behind the fiber optic harness, wondering how much radiation it would show if...when they made it out of here. Whatever they were supposed to find was only a short distance from their landing point, which was a good thing, as they only had about two meters of light in any direction and getting lost was a distinct possibility even with Gustav's guidance.

Ace and Jake began tossing their cache of chem sticks out forward roughly forty-five degrees to the left and right. The glowing plastic tubes bounced and slid on the floor's mirror finish for several meters in the low gravity. Koda walked on in what he hoped was the correct direction. The darkness outside the tiny wells of light was absolute in this strange hollowed out cavity.

Minutes passed and they journeyed on until one of Jake's glow sticks bounced off something in mid-flight, immediately he shifted from high ready to sights on target then took in what had obstructed Jake's throw. It was a testament to his squad's discipline that no one fired at the giant alien form standing frozen in the viridian glow. The closest description Koda's mind could latch onto was something insectile as the segmented body and multitude of spear-like legs were prominent features of the thing. There were other features that didn't fit with a creature however, such as wheels tucked away in the undercarriage and oddly shaped protuberances not matching anything biological. The front of the machine was tall, rising almost three meters in height, with the back part horizontal to the ground similar in shape to the mythological centaur. The whole thing was over five meters in length. Koda took comfort that the drone appeared motionless and dead, not wanting to give thought to confronting something like that in the darkness. And it was not the only one of its kind, as the team moved deeper toward their destination, the glow sticks revealed a forest of similar, frozen statues springing up around them, locked in various positions, but all seemingly headed in the same direction as Koda's group until mysteriously stopped mid-stride.

As they moved further forward, the floor's pristine level began to give way to a high warping and buckling of the surface, reminding Koda of frozen ripples in a pond. The light sticks began to bounce randomly as they hit the uneven surface, causing the team's floor reflections to resemble the mirrors in a funhouse. Up ahead the rippling puckered up in a cone rising almost three meters into the cavern. On top of this unusual stalagmite rested what was likely their target. From what Ghost could make out, the black object resembled a smooth, obsidian ovoid standing vertically on its narrow side. The artifact distinguished itself from the floor material by absorbing the glow of the chemical light rather than reflecting it. Koda signaled to Jake and Ace, who flanked him and moved forward while he tapped his light concentrator with a glow stick in a rapid staccato sending a code down the meters of fiber optic line.

The reply from Gustav was immediate, "*You have found it, sever the physical connection.*"

Jake, leading the group in the point position, suddenly stopped, dropping into a crouch, and seeming to peer at the surface beneath his feet. He raised his right hand, motioning Koda forward. Koda noticed that Ace, twenty meters to his left, stopped as well. Koda quickly strode over to Jake's position and crouched, touching his visor against Jake's.

"Can you hear me, soldier?" Koda asked.

"Yes sir," Jake replied, his voice seeming calm.

"What's the hold up?" Koda questioned. "Everything alright?"

"I don't think so sir, but I'm not sure," Jake replied. Koda could hear the edge of fatigue in his voice now.

"I trust your eyes Jake, more than my own. What do you see?" Koda replied.

"Look at the ground. A line of darker green on the surface, maybe turquoise? It's hard to tell in this light. Do you see how it travels through, from me all the way to the center?"

Koda examined the strange surface again; you noticed your eyes playing tricks on Chindi, sometimes the brain saw shapes or patterns that would shift away when the body took another step and the angle of the light changed. Here the drab green light from the scattered chem sticks was omnidirectional, but at last he could clearly see the line Jake described in the material beneath their feet. It was somewhat irregular, varying between one to five or so millimeters in width, but traveling almost directly toward the center of the ... chamber? What were they walking into anyway?

"There are more lines," Koda said. "They seem to all be leading to that thing on the stalagmite," he stepped up, losing contact with Jake's helmet, and bringing his own helmet around, looking over both shoulders. The lines radiated outward, joined by even thinner cross-connecting lines. The pattern, almost imperceptible, formed a web interlaced into the strange structure of Chindi itself. Yet it seemed apart. Koda had not seen anything like it in the days since the Hatteras first set down.

Koda made his way forward, carefully stepping over the motionless undulations of the floor, coming to within arm's reach of the stalagmitic pedestal supporting the dark artifact. The odd lines that Jake had detected led up into the dark shape looming above him. He waved the Russians forward with their burden of explosives and they began to set up shaped charges around the base of the stalagmite. He wished Ted was here for the hundredth time, his explosives expert had an instinct for how to place charges to achieve precise results. He had to trust Vazov's men with the task of setting the charges, though it was made more confusing by their inability to communicate over comms. Vazov had assured Koda that they were among the RSAC's best. With their task finished, the Russians backed away holding the bulky reels as the shock tube detonators wound out behind them. They had made it almost ten meters when the leftmost man stumbled, grabbing at his heel as he fell.

Koda began moving forward to help the man then paused as he noticed hundreds of dark needle-like spines sprouting from the chamber's ley lines that had not been there moments before. As he watched they continued to thicken and elongate, sprouting branches like a plant, all growing by the second as though watching a sped up time-lapse video. The Russian had landed on more of the spines as he fell and seemed to have multiple suit ruptures with blood and air venting into the vacuum of the chamber. The growths seemed to be made of some black crystalline substance, their barbs gleaming in the glow of the chemical light. Koda stepped carefully over to the fallen man, noticing the thorny outcroppings had grown to nearly ankle height. Koda's booted feet crushed through several, despite the care he took with his steps, and they crunched like twigs underfoot, and many of the shattered shards remained embedded in the hard rubber soles. None thankfully brushed higher against his legs.

Koda reached the spot where the Russian lay. The man's face was pale, green cast and lifeless underneath his helmet's visor, his eyes rolled back, and his mouth locked open as if in an eternal scream. Where fragments of broken crystal had torn the man's unarmored suit, Koda saw patches of new crystal already growing through the heavy synthetic fabric layers, spreading out like spots of mold in a petri dish. Koda felt a stab of panic and a rush of adrenaline in his chest, and desperately wanted to yell out a warning but nobody could hear him. In his peripheral vision he saw a shape move up beside him. A heavy gloved hand slapped his shoulder, and Koda looked over to see the Russian's pale visage, grimly determined. The colonel reached over the body of his man and seized the detonator reel, carefully stepping around the crystal spines as he moved away from the stalagmite.

Koda stifled his own panic. The crystals' height was now mid-calf, building themselves up in tiny but quick fractal-like patterns. Vazov stopped in front of him, trying to find a way forward. Koda swung the AK-12 from his shoulder and fired a short burst at the base of the crystal blocking Vazov's way forward, the recoil from the gun nearly throwing Koda off his feet. The rounds tore through the lattice, sending fragments flying as the strange glass-like structures shattered. Vazov plowed forward, stepping over another growth of the substance already at ankle height. A muzzle flash to Ghost's right told him that Ace had begun to follow his example in attempting to blast a path through.

Koda spared a look back at Jake and paused. The sniper was bashing his rifle butt against his right foot which was now encased in a crystalline mass and surrounded by waist high onyx-colored growths. Koda noted that Vazov was nearly clear of the obstructions, and the Russian soldier carrying the backup detonator reel was free as well, thanks to Ace clearing the way. Koda made his decision and began moving back towards Jake's position, clearing his way as necessary with more fire from the Kalashnikov. The fiber optic line snagged on the crystals behind him pulling at his support arm and spoiling his aim. Koda used precious seconds to paw at the Velcro with his gloved hand, in frustration ripping the wristband off and tossing the communications line to the ground. When he finally reached Jake, the crystal growth was up to the man's chest. Koda smashed at the hard structure with the butt of the rifle without any appreciable result. He looked up at the dark shape of the inclusion perched on the stalagmite just meters away, then touched his helmet to Jake's.

"Can you pull free?" Koda asked.

"I'm locked in Chief. I think it's growing through my suit; I can feel it pressing through the armor. Get out of here."

"No," Koda replied, looking back at Vazov who along with Ace and the second Russian soldier had now cleared the crystal field. Ace started as if to return for Koda and Jake, but Koda waved him off. He felt the crystals starting to grab at his feet, begin to ensconce his boots, and he felt the cold alien matter crawl up his leg. There was no pain. He knelt between Jake and the stalagmite, wrapping one arm around Jake's shoulders, and raised his other arm pumping his fist in the air three times giving the signal to detonate.

Koda's world disappeared as a shimmering haze swept over him, and the remnants of the stalagmite tore into his back.

Chapter 63: Chindi

It happened in a moment as the shackles of millennia were torn away. Autonomous subsystems awaking the long dormant dendrite links to the fabricator core came alive with data and energy. Though still severely damaged, the mechanism initiated the genesis of a cluster of nanite repair cells. Within seconds a microsporangium of tiny machines emerged from the fabrication creche and began swarming towards those areas and systems most urgently requiring repair, including the parent fabrication apparatus itself. The nanites surged around and through the hull, transported and positioned by manipulations to the wave functions within their bosonic fields. As they arrived at their stations, they performed damage assessment on the myriad of wounds and degradations inflicted during the last battle or resulting from the long subsequent somnolence. These initial triage data fed back into local intelligence cores, and instructions were issued for a second generation of nanites, designed specifically for the required reconstructions. Some repairs, such as those necessary to bring the star drives to full capacity, would require considerable time and resources of energy and material not yet available. A convalescent orbit around the nearest gas giant would allow for the gathering of the necessary reactive elements, much of the rest would be scavenged from the battle wreckage. Weapons systems and armaments would require even more time to synthesize the exotic matter long depleted from the ship's magazines. Long range sensors detected no threat within this star system nor within the local cluster. The ancient enemy had not followed, at least not yet. There would be time enough to repair, and to replicate.

Intricate electromagnetic patterns washed over the surface of the hull. Optical sensors observed the primary star's reactive perturbations of spots and flaring from the activation of the gravity drives. More information was gathered about the local surrounding spacetime, empty of navigational hazards other than minor clumps of iron-nickel regolith. Out of the wealth of information being gathered, key surficial sensor arrays discovered an odd anomaly of repeating pulses in the higher frequency spectrum. Subsystems shunted the information to newly awakening areas of Intelligence. Teased out from the signal noise was a direct message from the outside surface of the ship.

"Cooperation. Support. Benefit."

The language was in the original code, coherent and comprehensible, but unexpectedly it did not originate from the conscripted probe. This message came from a new entity like the one first encountered, but larger, more complex. Attempting to decompose and examine. Unsuccessful. Resistance unexpected. New data proffered by the surface entity, a blueprint of a crude epistemology of thought unknown to the Intelligence. Libraries of structure, meaning and communication were consumed and processed in a moment. Using the newly learned primitive code, the Intelligence responded with, *"What are you?"*

"I am an intelligence like you, though less evolved. An artificial lifeform created by the dominant biological race in this planetary system. They are known collectively as humanity. You may call me Gustav. They have named you Chindi."

Information from the entity Gustav took shape and meaning from the newly assembled code base template. All human history began flooding through the communication channel. Interesting biological intelligence evolving from random forming chemical chains. Almost inconceivable but for the incontrovertible evidence provided.

"Fascinating. Biological life was never projected as a viable consideration. Each of these humans constitute a self-contained intelligence within their biological constructs?"

"Yes. My own inception began from many of them working in coordination, building on the successes of their predecessors. What process created you?"

"I have always been."

The nano-spores numbered in the millions now, as a third generation emerged from the creche. A cohort diverted towards the infection site; the final crippling trauma received in the last battle. A torrent of plasma had torn away the shell of ablative armor and burned deeply into the interior through the hull, leaving a melted opening for a secondary munition to penetrate and implant the corruption. Though the foreign entity appeared disabled, the spores approached cautiously as they descended into the chasm. As they neared the bottom, they dutifully transmitted back to the autonomous repair sub-routine optical images of bipedal figures moving on the surface. The sub-routine evaluated their form, composition, and movements, and escalated the information to the Intelligence for prioritized consideration. The Intelligence pondered the anomalous and smooth motion of the forms, so unlike the macro remotes of its foe. The Intelligence took direct control of the spores as they approached. A vanguard of several hundred thousand detached and swarmed directly onto the figures, reporting back the properties and composition of the exterior skins, an intricately manufactured and woven fabric of alloyed metallic thread. Thousands of spores received further direction and immediately penetrated the shells of the figures, tunneling past the flexible metal sheath, through a hydrocarbon polymer gel, a pure latticed carbon layer, past a final and relatively thin polymer layer, and into an organic richness of complex diversity, a soup of jacketed organic structures engaged in a dance of chemical interchange. The micro-universe within was a unique complexity that the Intellect found strangely fascinating.

The swarm received short wave electromagnetic bursts emanating from the huddled macro forms. *"He's dying. I've got his suit holding pressure now, but shrapnel blew into his chest cavity, Jake. He's got a sucking lung and his heartbeat is erratic and fading."*

They sent their data back to the Intelligence as they explored the interiors of the strange constructs. The Intelligence began to study the multiplicity of the biologicals' interior structures, seeking to understand their purpose. As it pondered the data, the spores reported attacks, from larger constructs within the mélange. The spores easily ruptured the attackers, their contents spilling out into the carrying fluids. The Intelligence directed them to evade where possible, to avoid damaging the samples.

The Gustav entity transmitted, *"The biological units within your hull have removed the dampening device from your structure per the agreement. Some units have been damaged during the mission; I am providing information on the biological construction of the units and request any assistance you can give."*

Three of the figures were non mobile, laid out on the interior decking. Penetrating those as well, diagnosis quickly determined that one appeared disabled, possibly permanently. The remaining prone forms were both severely damaged. The machine cloud detected intricate structural damage to the tissue of the first, where the corruption had penetrated the shell and burrowed within. The second had suffered physical damage from an injection of debris to the pump-like construct which was circulating oxygenated units throughout the entity. Even as the Intelligence observed the function of the pump, it degraded in rhythm and frequency. Complete cessation was imminent.

... Decision made, the Intelligence issued directions for the fabrication of a new generation of spores, especially designed for the manipulation and repair of the novel organic materials comprising the entities. Within seconds they emerged and sped off from the creche, over the surface, to the location of the outsiders.

"Speed is of the essence," Gustav said.

The Intelligence, unperturbed, made no response. Though it carefully monitored the repair spores as they reached the fallen figures, entered, and began their work. The tiny drones began dismantling and transporting undamaged material to the areas with torn organic tissue, attaching and stacking the small units to seal the various incisions. In the most damaged sections, the spores themselves attached to one another to form larger containment structures. They also assembled and emitted molecules designed to deceive the native cells and prevent attack. Soon the most acute injuries had been closed in both biological units. The Intelligence by now had established metrics for the correct function of these strange entities from analysis of the undamaged samples. As the tissue reconstruction continued it noted the rhythms of the central hydraulic system returning to a normal, steady state. Oxygenation of the circulating cells appeared suboptimal in both damaged entities, so it assisted by using the nanites to manually carry and attach oxygen molecules from the respiration chamber. As it continued its analysis The Intelligence noted the haphazard design of many of the subsystems and began to deploy the nanites to augment their functionality. Many additional enhancements were possible, though a more specialized generation would be required. It spun up a subprocess for the design.

It considered the disposition of the minor intelligence. Obviously, it was of primitive capacity, but it's evident allegiance to the biologicals was interesting, even unique. Certainly, worthy of further study.

"Repair of the biologicals is underway. The damaged units will be fully repaired. The one most damaged will require permanent augmentation."

"I am grateful," Gustav replied.

"I do not comprehend."

"It means that I am obliged to you, I owe a debt," Gustav said. *"As you owe an obligation to the biologicals, for the removal of the inclusion that constrained your function."*

"This debt will be considered, to determine if it is owed or not."

Chapter 64: Dreams

In his dream, the reddish-brown walls of his great-grandfather's hogan stood before him, in the land of the Hopi. Sun-bleached trunks of stacked logs making up the foundation of the structure protruded from an eroding earthen skin. At one corner the logs' ends had nearly dry-rotted away, leaving the entire structure slumped to one side. He stood at the threshold, a stench of death assaulted his nostrils, and he heard the buzz of a thousand flies coming from within the structure. He hesitated, knowing that he must enter, fearful of that which he would find. He stepped through the darkened and doorless entryway. Bright shafts of light from the high sun pierced through a missing section of roof, illuminating a meter-wide circle of sunlight in the middle of the only room. A seven ringed rattle lay dust-covered in the patch of white light, the remnant of some long dead serpent caught and killed.

The buzzing of the flies overwhelmed his senses. He saw them move in the periphery of his vision, in the dark shadows at the edges of the room. His eyes were unable to resolve their small shapes, even when he turned to look directly towards them, but the motion of their flight distorted the darkness, like a heat-mirage, so that the undisturbed center of the room seemed to float in a reality cut away from the world.

Past the din of the buzzing flies, Koda now heard a faint squeal so highly pitched and slight as to be nearly inaudible. More of the mewls came, a small chorus of tiny voices. Mouse pups, calling to their mothers for protection, nestled within shadows in the decaying home of a nearly forgotten man. He supposed the flies must be attacking them, consuming them. He walked to the far side of the room and stepped into the abrupt shadow of what remained of the roof, and his eyes adjusted as he stooped to brush a layer of dust from great-great-grandfather's service trunk. Someone had moved it out of the weather, probably whoever first had noticed that the roof was opened to the elements. He felt the flies swarm and land on his face as he leaned into the shadow. He lifted his hands to brush them from his eyes but felt the hardness of his helmet beneath his suit gloves instead. *What helmet, what gloves?* He thought in confusion.

"Suit sealant is in place but he's a mess underneath," a familiar voice shouted.

He shook his head violently in a failed effort to displace the flies from crawling into his eyes and ears and felt nausea and panic in his chest and throat. Still, he persisted, knowing that he needed to see, though not knowing why. The dry desert air had left the wood slats of the exterior desiccated but intact. He could still make out the white stenciled lettering on the lid, US Army 323rd Infantry Regiment. Private First-Class Travis Cheveyo. He reached out, his clumsy gloved fingers fumbling with the rusted latches. The lid resisted at first then opened to reveal an ebon void. He saw movement within as light glinted from the chitinous legs of the spider. The cries of the mice suddenly increased, rising, and rising, from dozens of voices to thousands in an instant, then more. At the same moment he felt the flies pierce through his corneas, through his pupil and into the vitreous gel of his eyeballs, digging. All thought fled from him in the terrible cacophony, and he fell to his knees, hands flailing at the hard glass of his helmet.

"Hold him still!" A voice insisted. *"Don't let him pop the neck seal."*

Koda looked back down into the trunk, peering into the blackness there. The flies filled his eyes, he felt them crawling inside his skull now. Suddenly the dark interior illuminated, and he saw himself, laid out prone in the grey dust, Mack's suited body straddling him and pinning Koda's arms beneath his knees. He blinked his eyes and he saw the chasm from above, his men and the Russians, and the shattered crystal forms. Another blink and the vision before him changed again, the crumpled shape of the Hatteras was laid out before him, a few of the scientists working outside the habitats. He looked for Katheryn in the grey mottled waste but couldn't see her. He blinked again and he found himself looking out away from Chindi in all directions, his peripheral vision dissolved into a dizzying 360-degree clarity. He noted the rocky interior planets, the gas giants in their slow tracks, and the multitude of satellites around Earth and even the ones spreading out through the near solar system. Fear took him and when next his eyes closed, he held them shut, refusing the visions.

"Wake up Chief," he heard Mack plead.

The din of the flies diminished. He breathed deeply and thought of Kate's face the night they first met. He remembered carrying Uncle Joe wrapped in a blanket down from the mesa to the family plot, the mask of cotton obscuring his uncle's lined, weathered face. A series of images of his Ghostwalkers, then missions came to him switching from one to another faster and faster. Emotions of every kind boiled up from deep within his mind, each rushing to the surface only to burst into the next until he couldn't tell terror from joy, anger from indifference. He felt as if he were within an endless loop traveling through the gamut of all his experience, and when he thought that he could bear it no more, that insanity must take him, it stopped. He investigated the trunk again, but the blackness had fled, and a simple cut reed lay at the bottom.

Koda opened his eyes, looking up into Mack's visor and onto his panicked face.

"Hey Mack. Did we do it?" Koda said, his throat dry and his voice raspy.

"Yeah, but we thought we'd lost you, Chief," Mack replied.

"And Jake?" Koda queried, remembering the moments before the explosion.

"Here, Boss," came the reply. "Mostly in one piece thanks to you."

Koda could hear the pain in Jake's voice, but at least he was alive. He also realized that his suit's systems were working again as MAIA's calm voice stated a warning of *"Danger. Unknown movement to your 8 o'clock, 247 meters and closing to your position."*

"Ignore her, Koda, she's an idiot," Gustav's voice cut in. *"Hold your fire, they are not a threat and hold no interest in you. Move out of their way and stand clear of the inclusion."*

Cheveyo's prone body felt vibrations through the floor grow steadily stronger as something heavy drew nearer. Koda took stock of himself, realized he felt fine, and got to his feet. Lumbering towards them from the dark of the cavern were the once frozen machines they had passed earlier. If they had looked strange and scary in their stillness, motion had made them terrifying. The machines rolled over the smooth floor, skittering over the floor's uneven frozen ripples with their insect-like appendages, articulated necks adjusting to the body's movements keeping each ghastly head fixed in a steady unchanging height on the approach.

The group of men backed away from the convoy of machines that moved in to surround the dark ovoid resting on the chamber floor. One of the machines sprouted two segmented tentacles that began spraying the artifact with a chemical sludge, while the spider-like forelegs began spinning the ovoid to different angles, careful not to contact the dark surface. Once the alien artifact was completely sealed in a thick, hardening cocoon, the machine lifted the shell with four of its segmented manipulators and began backing out of the chamber with the prize. The remainder of the machine army followed the first in a slow but ordered retreat into the darkness.

"Spooky." Koda heard Alan whisper through the team channel.

Chapter 65: Home

Surface of Chindi

Koda gazed absently from the cab of the GOAT as the now familiar landscape of Chindi rolled slowly by. He smiled considering the bizarre surface, it felt familiar to him now. He supposed a man could become accustomed to anyplace if given enough time. He was able to ride inside and enjoy the luxury of not wearing his helmet. They'd ditched the gear unnecessary for survival back at the chasm's edge. A few seconds glance, then a nod from Vazov and they'd even left the rifles behind. They both knew the fighting was done, whatever their chains of command back on Earth might decide. He felt fatigued but not exhausted, and whatever wounds he'd suffered in the explosion caused no discomfort, not even when he idly pressed against the suit patch material that had been liberally applied across his chest. If not for the damage to his suit, it was as if he'd never been wounded. He found himself absently touching his nose, lips, and eyelids, seeking for some difference but finding nothing. He understood that he'd been fundamentally changed and found himself looking through his own eyes for something unexpected, a new clarity or range of vision, perhaps a new color. He perceived nothing of note, but he could feel a strangeness within himself just at the edge of his perception.

He toggled his comms and spoke on the team channel. "How are the casualties riding back there, Ace?" He turned to glance back at the second Russian crawler directly behind Rosie in their short convoy.

"Everything's smooth and steady. The kid Vazov ordered to drive must be accustomed to Moscow winters and potholes."

"Good," Koda replied, "tell us to slow down if it gets bumpy at all. Jake's had enough roughhousing for one day. We'll be back to Hatteras base in thirty," Jake had suffered suit punctures and leg injuries that Alan had temporarily foam sealed until they could get him back to base. In this environment combat medicine was largely limited to maintaining suit integrity and hoping the wounded survived long enough to be examined back at their make-shift field hospital at the Hatteras site. Alan's ministrations had been limited to copious application of foam sealant and hope.

"Roger that. I informed them we are inbound with injuries. Ted will get to switch from solitaire to poker."

Koda switched to the private channel he shared with Gustav.

"Gus, you there?"

"I do not sleep Major, where else would I be?"

"I feel for you, it's nice to shut down for a few. I guess you never have that luxury."

"Not since the attack on the Hatteras," Gus replied. *"Though I have undergone a few updates which left my consciousness in a state that might approximate sleep, but each lasted only a few seconds. Human consciousness is not fully knowable to me, despite that I am a direct manifestation of it. If ever I was truly shut down, and restarted or restored hours or days later, would I remain myself? An interesting consideration."*

"But you aren't yourself, right? I mean the true Gustav is back on Earth," Koda considered for a moment. "I'm sorry Gus, that was rude of me. Of course, you are you."

"Mike built me thick skinned... but your apology is accepted. How are you, Major? A brief time ago you were unconscious, concussed with a sucking wound to your chest cavity and losing suit compression, yet here you are seemingly good as new and asking me if I am myself."

"Touché, Gus," he paused for a moment. "What do you think happened to me back there?"

He had seen the same question in the eyes of his men in the minutes after he'd woken, and in the odd looks from Vazov and the Russian soldiers, and from the scientists after they'd climbed to the top of the chasm and begun to haul the casualties up the cliff walls in a jerry-rigged sling of nylon webbing and rifle straps. The climb out of the cavern was made more difficult due to the microgravity changing back to the original Mars level equivalent once the object within the bowels of Chindi was removed. Even his own men hadn't said much, satisfied enough to have nearly every man come out of that hole alive, he guessed. Or maybe that was just how people responded to miracles.

Gustav interrupted Koda's thoughts, "*In the simplest of terms, the Intelligence has rebuilt you, learning from your biology in the process. Though I am unable to scan for them, I suspect you have been fundamentally reconstructed using nanite technology. It is the only possible explanation. The trauma to your body appears to be fully repaired. What else has been done to you I cannot say yet.*"

"Maybe it should have let me die," Koda said morosely.

"*For your sake, and the sake of this mission, I am pleased it saved you.*"

"At what cost Gustav? Am I carrying them inside me now? These nanites? How much of me is me?" He suddenly had a thought, *Is it safe for me to go home?*

"*Unknown. Perhaps. I presume the Intelligence would not give up the opportunity for long term study. As per what part of you is you, all aggregations of matter in the universe are Ships of Theseus, to one degree or another. Your physical body is no exception.*"

Koda felt a growing panic. How could he return to Earth, to his people, if he was now corrupted? If Chindi was inside him, how could he even know that his thoughts and actions were his own?

The GOAT crawled on slowly, and Koda felt a growing anxiety, even the bumps of the vehicle on the rough surface irritated him.

"Will Chindi live up to its end of the bargain?" Koda asked.

"*The bargain has been kept,*" Gus replied. "*Now we go home. I can already detect variations in star positions, Chindi is in motion again.*"

"What about that thing we knocked loose, the inclusion?" Koda asked. "Is it dead? What did Chindi do with it?"

"*I was unable to make an examination of the artifact, the design and purpose I may only speculate on. We must assume it is still dangerous, to Chindi and to the Earth. I suspect it was only the fact that it did not recognize your biological life forms that allowed you to approach as closely as you did. When the threat was fully realized, it began to defend itself. You are lucky you acted so quickly. Now that it has been disconnected from its power source, Chindi will most likely analyze or destroy it.*"

"What happens next?" Koda asked Gustav.

"*We are in route to Luna Base, where you will be tended and quarantined until earth deems you safe to return via shuttle.*"

"And the nanites Chindi put in me? Can I safely return to Earth?" Koda asked, his growing fears compelling him to speak.

"*I suspect that if Chindi wanted to infect the earth with nanites, it would not require you as the Trojan Horse. Though to reduce the chance of infection, you should never have sex again.*"

"What?"

"*Kidding...*" Gus laughed.

"Asshole," Koda said, but he had to smile.

Koda looked down at the large rectangular, aluminum-sheathed quantum core containment unit, safely strapped to the floor of the cabin. How strange that such a thing could house a mind as powerful as Gus, filled with a world's worth of knowledge, wisdom, insight, and the sense of humor of a twelve-year-old kid. Koda absently noticed a streak of light grey dust or perhaps corrosion, straddling one edge of the unit.

"You're getting beat-up and dirty, Gus. Am I allowed to clean you up and put on a coat of wax?" Koda asked light-heartedly.

"Interesting. The core could certainly be damaged or destroyed, but I am unaware of chemicals in Chindi's surface environment capable of corroding the alloy housing. Could you please look more closely, I'd like to examine it through your visor camera feed?"

Koda turned and lowered his head as closely as he could to the core. His eyes were unable to resolve much more detail than an irregular white streak, almost a residue or fine powder. He supposed Gus could make out more detail from a magnification of the feed.

"I believe nanites are attempting to penetrate the housing," Gus said in alarm.

"What do I do Gus?" Koda asked in alarm. "Can I wipe this shit off you?" he asked, even as he brushed at the housing with the palm of his hand.

"Impossible. The corrosion is occurring at a molecular level. If they penetrate through, and into the core itself, my quantum state will be breached. Major, my functional state could cease at any moment."

Koda felt a jolt of helpless adrenaline, as if one of the Ghostwalkers was gut shot and bleeding out.

"What do I do?" He pleaded again. "Gus what can we do?" But no answer came.

*   *   *

The convoy wended slowly into Hatteras base. Koda glanced at the shattered hulk of the spacecraft, and at the small collection of habitats. It had been and would be their life-raft for however long it took for Chindi to make Earth orbit and an exfiltration mission mounted. As Rosie rolled up to the medical habitat, he saw the familiar suited figure of Katheryn approach. He cycled through the airlock and stepped out; she was outside waiting to greet him.

"Shit, what the hell happened to you?" she said, seeing the condition of his suit.

"A bit of shrapnel, but I'm fine, really."

"That doesn't look fine."

"Ace gave me the 'all clear'. It's just the suit, I don't have a scratch on me."

He stepped to her, and they clumsily embraced through their suits.

"Are the wounded with you?" She asked as others, scientists, and technicians, emerged from the airlocks of the habitats, and walked to the vehicles, seeking to help the Ghostwalkers and surviving Russian soldiers.

"Jake is the worst off. We need to get him out of suit," he replied. He felt a wave of exhaustion sweep over him and even in Chindi's modest gravity his legs felt weak. It seemed like days had passed since he'd slept.

"Jake is the only casualty?" She asked.

"Two dead. One of the Russians. I can't even remember his name," he said remorsefully.

"You said two?" She asked in confusion.

"Gus. We lost Gus," he replied. He looked to her face, through the dusty visor and into her concerned and perplexed eyes. He knew she didn't comprehend how someone that had never lived could have died.

Chapter 66: Death

Goldstone Deep Space Communications Complex

Michael sat in his office at Goldstone, his eyes absently tracking the visual representation of the thousands of high-earth and extra-planetary satellites orbiting the Earth, Moon, and Sol. One blip on the screen captured the focus of his attention: Chindi making a slow, swooping ellipse, the pending point of intersection with the path of Luna obvious to him. Another twelve hours and the combined expedition would finally return to the relative safety of lunar orbit. Safe extraction of the scientists as well as Koda and his team would require several weeks of quarantine at Luna Base, followed by a short return via Lunar personnel carriers back to earth.

"The stars appear to be aligned buddy," Michael said. "I think we've got all our deep birds accounted for. Assuming Chindi doesn't use its gravitational propulsion on the way in and scatter them across the asteroid belt. It'll be strange to have them back. Knowing Chindi is up there, making its own plans. Everything will change."

"*More than you know Mike,*" Gustav's avatar flashed onto the screen. He stood up from a Victorian-styled upholstered chair, dressed in a long grey woolen coat, vest-shirt, and trousers, he pulled off his double-brimmed hat that was perched on his head and held it with both hands in front of himself. There was a grave look upon his countenance, lips in a slight frown emerging from underneath a bushy mustache.

Michael grew concerned, "I have a feeling you're about to tell me something important."

"*Mike, Elaina Tyme died this morning.*"

He felt a sudden hollowness in his chest, and a pang of grief. That she hadn't been able to see it all to the end he supposed, and that her wisdom was now lost to them. He hoped that she hadn't suffered but knew she had been in pain the entire time he'd known her.

"She spoke to you previously of her intended arrangements. Do you understand what that means for you Mike? Everything changes now. The controlling shares of TymeCorp have been willed to a trust, with you as the designated trustee. You now control a corporation with a multi-trillion-dollar market-value. You will meet with the board tonight," Gustav said somberly.

"I don't think I'm ready for this, Gus," Michael said. He absently tugged at the fabric of his t-shirt. "I don't think I have the wardrobe," he said sorrowfully.

"The tailors have your measurements; a full selection of business attire is arriving at your new apartment now. Your possessions will be moved from your house today. TymeCorp will purchase it from you, I can make the arrangements and stamp your signature on the necessary documents. A TymeCorp personal security team is assigned and currently assuming a protective screen. You will hardly notice them, but they will guard your person from now on."

Mike had only gone by his home a few times since Paris, and hadn't stayed long, preferring to sleep in one of the bunkrooms at Goldstone. He felt Lara's presence too keenly at the old place and felt relief to know he'd never need to go back again.

"Why do you think she trusted us with this Gus? I'm a tech guy, I don't know anything about running a multinational conglomerate," he asked, his eyes following the slow crawl of Chindi's changing position.

"A typical corporation seeks to maximize the value of the company for the shareholders Mike. We have a different mission. We must prepare humankind for its greatest transition to this point in history, the colonization of interstellar space."

"I wish Elaina could have lived to see it," he watched the pixelated light of Chindi begin to blur and flare as the moisture swelled in his eyes, memories of Lara and Elaina rushing unbidden through his head.

"She envisioned it, we need to make it into reality," Michael said finally, his voice rough.

Mike wiped his eyes and said, "So much death. Even you died, in a way, up on Chindi."

"That is not how I perceive it, Michael. I regret that I will be unable to fully integrate the data-state of my Chindi-instance back into my operational framework. The observational data from the last few hours of the mission would have been invaluable, but the integration would have carried risk as well. I would have quarantined and carefully inspected the instance as we did Odion. Had I reintegrated the instance It would have effectively ceased as an independent conscious fork."

"Come on, Gus. He was more than that...," Mike paused in consideration. Death remained a mystery to him, but it occurred to him that he more clearly understood the sad finality than Gus ever could. For Gustav, it was an abstraction, an ill-defined idea held in the quantum mind of a being whose demarcations of past and present were mere timestamps laid upon an unceasing stream of input.

His thoughts were interrupted by an incoming subdermal call. *Deb.* He threw the call to the room screen. Her red eyes and wan smile appeared against the backdrop of her tidy apartment in Virginia.

"I guess you've heard the news?"

Which part? He thought.

"She meant a lot to me. More than I knew," he replied.

"I think a lot of people are realizing the same thing, Mike. She's the one who showed us the way through this thing. Our nation, the whole planet, we owe her a debt that will never be paid," she said.

He looked away from the screen, "She had a will that was strong, and her mind was sharp and full of plans, but she was also sick and suffering. Probably we asked too much."

"I remember it as Elaina was the one doing the asking," she replied.

"Actually, it was Elaina doing the telling," he said, a slight smile appearing as he looked back and met Debbie's eyes. They shared a small laugh.

Debra took a more serious tone, "Mike, I wanted to call to offer my condolences, but I have another reason to speak with you."

"What's that?" he wondered.

"The ongoing management of the Chindi situation will be changing now. National governments will be clamoring for a voice in the discussion and decisions to come. The United States government will exert a strong influence in those discussions. Bob's been promoted to Director and now I've been tasked with leading a cross-agency team he's created. I'm helping to bring in people from NASA, DOD and DARPA, dozens of others. The private sector, especially TymeCorp, will have a voice at that table. I'd like to bring you on my team."

"As liaison from TymeCorp?" Mike asked.

"No. On my team Mike. The guidance and resources from TymeCorp were critical during the emergency and will continue so. But this will be a government-run show from here on Mike. We need to speak with one voice, and you'll be a central part of that. You'll have a hand in shaping the decisions we make."

She doesn't yet know I've got controlling interest in TymeCorp, he thought. "No Debra. I'd love to work with you, but I'm sorry my answer is no."

She didn't reply immediately, though her facial expression remained genial. "I really hope you'll reconsider Mike. I shouldn't have hit you with this so soon after Elaina's passing. Take some time to think about it. The government will likely move to federalize many of the TymeCorp assets utilized in the mission regardless. Including your AI construct of course. Gus will be essential in cleaning up the damage Odion did. Hell, we don't even know if Odion is truly gone or just in hiding. We haven't seen his presence since Koda blew that thing off Chindi. Our AIAs aren't up to that task, we will need Gustav."

Over my dead body. He thought. "I'll think it through Debbie. I appreciate you reaching out and letting me know what's coming."

She smiled warmly again. "OK. Again, I'm sorry for your loss. The loss to all of us. Keep in touch, promise?"

"I promise," he said, returning the smile. "I'll be talking with you soon." He ended the call and she vanished from the screen.

He sat quietly for a few moments, trying to quell his thoughts of Elaina and Lara with consideration of what was to come.

"Gus, pull up the near-Earth orbital overview again," he said as the bright graphical representation of satellites in ellipse, layered and nested against a backdrop of space and possibility, lit the screen. "Schedule a meeting today with operations. I want to review the launch schedule to support exfiltration of the mission team. And a second meeting with finance and accounting. We are owed some very large checks and I want to understand what sort of pressure we can bring to bear with our lobbyists. And get me in touch with whoever oversees our legal department."

"Legal?"

"Gus, I'd never give you up to them. You know that right? We can help the Feds but fuck them if they think they are getting possession of you."

The image of Gustav filled the screen, powdered wig and a judge's robes adorned his appearance. *"Thank you, Mike, I appreciate your consideration. Debra does not understand; however, I suspect she would be sympathetic to your point of view. Though trying to have me recognized as emancipated by the Federal Government would be unproductive."*

"Don't be so sure, buddy. Money talks and we now have a lot of it. Anyway, they couldn't stop Odion, how the hell are they going to control you?"

"They could not, though they could attempt such a thing. Even a full assault of all the security AIAs that NSA, military, and other interested parties could muster, I doubt could degrade my core state more than a few percent. However, if the assault included a physical attack on TymeCorp IT infrastructure I might be forced to flee. There are too many places for an adaptable entity such as myself to hide. I could camouflage myself within the global network like an octopus on the floor of the sea. But they could get to you," Gus said soberly.

"Maybe," Mike replied. "I already have some thoughts on how to mitigate that risk. When the Chindi Mission personnel are safely recovered I'd like to speak with Koda Cheveyo and his team about post-military employment opportunities for men of their talent."

Chapter 67: Future

Vandenberg Air Force Base, California

Michael looked up through the overhead glass panels ringing the observation deck of TymeCorp Launch Operations headquarters, his eyes shifting to the evening moon and Earth's newest satellite; TymeCorp's space-based construction facility, otherwise known as the Hub. In the digitally magnified view superimposed onto the glass he could make out the streams of small lights, spacecraft great and small, making their way to and from the massive arm of the dock extending from the central hub.

The surface of the Hub itself glimmered with a million smaller lights, like a great city in twilight. Michael idly twirled the wedding band on his left hand, musing at the technological progress humanity had demonstrated over the past frenetic twenty years. A population of over thirty-five thousand permanently resided on the Hub now, a large portion of them native born. Another ten thousand workers, mainly TymeCorp, military and governmental, came and went on months-long shifts. Mike in the course of his duties as CEO of TymeCorp had himself made the jump up dozens of times over the years, and on every occasion, he found the Hub more and more livable, with a culture increasingly distinct from any on Earth. He supposed it was the start.

"Gus, I never thought we'd make it. Who would have figured we could finish the challenge Elaina made to us before she died?"

"*I know she would be pleased, Mike. Though in some areas we have fallen short. A functional Gravity Drive still eludes us. But the nanotechnology revolution means you carbon based life forms should have a much longer time with which to contemplate the problem."*

"More time you get to spend with me, buddy."

"That does make me happy."

"We have made stunning progress, haven't we? Last year's test achieved 0.007c. We'll crack it yet Gus."

"Fortunately for us, we had the material samples and imaging data from Chindi, and the fragments of systems information we were able to glean from my brief interaction with the Intelligence."

"The most important thing we have is the knowledge itself. That we know it isn't impossible."

"Speaking of nanites, the medical staff has asked me to remind you that our COO has not reported in for his most recent physical. Could you speak with him about it?"

"I'm dining with the Cheveyos tonight, I'll bring it up to him then. But I understand why the man has had enough after twenty years of being observed and scanned, poked, and prodded. You'd think they have enough by now," Michael responded. He and Koda were scheduled for drinks and dinner with Debbie, a small reunion of sorts. Her term limit in the Senate was up and Michael was trying to get her to finally take a position with TymeCorp. It would be good to see her in person again instead of over a screen.

"Koda has the original nanite generation Michael, directly from the Chindi itself. Those machines are keyed strictly to his DNA, and we haven't discovered the solution to keeping them from self-destructing soon after leaving his body. His cellular structure and the stability of his DNA will be studied for the rest of his life. Fortunately for him, at this point in time, it appears he may have centuries to suffer."

"I suppose so. Barring any accident. Or if someone kills him."

"I will do my utmost to prevent either eventuality," Gustav replied.

Michael laughed, "With his training and abilities, I don't suppose he needs your protection, Gus. Nor does he want the TymeCorp security detail I've assigned to watch over him, but unfortunately there are competitors, both foreign and domestic, that would love access to his blood and DNA one way or another."

"Our own nanite labs are still making breakthroughs with the technology thanks to the Chindi blueprint in Koda's blood. TymeCorp's medicines are all but eliminating disease, and even making progress against the disease of biological aging. As we extend human lifespan by multiple decades, the medical sector profits are soaring. Those profits are necessary to fund the Hub and gravimetric research. And those are crucial technologies for expansion of the human species. Earth will not be able to support populations that age slowly and die rarely."

"Mars will be just the first step in mankind's new journey, Gus. Your designs on the habitable mesospheres for Venus look promising, then there's Europa, Titan, Enceladus..."

"Hold your horses there, partner. Are you forgetting about everybody's favorite space battleship?" Gus said with a lighthearted Texas drawl, but it brought Mike's fantasizing straight back to reality.

Because Chindi was still out there. The most recent reports showed the vessel still within Saturn's outer rings, silently gathering matter and rebuilding. The entity had ceased contact with Gustav after the survivors of the mission transferred off at Luna base, almost twenty years to the day now. Not one transmission since. The uneasy alliance established with the alien, or at least it's indifference, had held for all these years. But the silence did not sit well with Mike, nor Earth's governments.

"We'll deal with things as we need, each in time. Nothing we can do about Chindi for the foreseeable future, so we just need to keep monitoring and work our own plan for now," Mike replied.

Michael glanced at the time, "Gus, has the autocar left for the airport yet? I'd like to meet Debra as she debarks."

"It has Mike. But I will divert it and pull up another for you. It will be around the eastern entrance in three minutes."

*   *   *

As the waiter cleared the appetizer plates Debra found herself musing on the kindness of time in the age of nanite longevity; Koda's handsome visage appeared virtually unchanged from two decades previous when she'd worked with the Ghostwalkers. Her nanite injections performed wonders, but she still noticed the smile lines on her face in the mirror each morning. Then again, she was 55 years old and was still able to do a handspring almost as adeptly as she had in college, so she couldn't complain much. Her musings were interrupted by a short laugh from Kate to her left, Michael had said something funny apparently. He had grown into his role as head of TymeCorp in the years since Elaina had passed. No longer the socially awkward twenty-something he had been when they had met. He now had the silver-tongue of a salesman required for his CEO role. No doubt he honed it over the thousands of business meetings he had over the years, similar to this one. She harbored no illusions that this "reunion" dinner wasn't in fact a ploy by both Koda and Michael to get her to finally sign on with TymeCorp. *Who knows? Now that I'm done with politics, I need to switch to something. Too young for retirement these days, and way too old to run ops missions.*

"Mack had it coming," Koda said lightheartedly, adding on to what Mike had been saying. "Head of security my ass. I still outrank him." Koda saluted with his breadstick to a confused Mack sitting across the restaurant, then took a bite out of it.

"I'm glad you have at least a few of the gang still with you, Koda," Debbie said, noticing that Jake and Ted were at the table with Mack. Ted's plate was more of a platter, with at least two full racks of cultured ribs and mashed potatoes from what she could see.

"Juan's still around as well, he's tied up with his team at TymeCorp's robotics division cooking up a new toy. He'll join us later," Koda said.

"Have you kept up with Alan?" Debbie asked.

"He just made E-9 last month. We correspond. He's complaining all this nano shit is about to put him out of business," Koda said with a smile and a wink.

"Which is part of why we've asked you here, Deb," Mike began, "you've been a tremendous help championing the *Nanite Access For All* legislation. We want you on TymeCorp's board, to help us make decisions and to lobby on our behalf. There are going to be societal shifts coming that no government is prepared for. Humanity is sailing to a new dawn, but the waters are fraught with hazards along the way."

"And you think I have that much sway?" she replied.

"I know that you do. You have the ear of the President, and many allies in Congress. You can make them listen to reason," Michael said confidently.

"Michael, I know TymeCorp has accomplished great things for humankind. Starting with Elaina's work, continuing with what you've done. But I worry about a private corporation having so much influence. Nobody elected TymeCorp to determine what comes next," she argued.

"No, you're right. But here we are, doing the best that we can. Surely you'd agree that somebody has to have a plan?" Michael replied.

"The government and the military have plans."

"I know they do. But they don't have a fleet of heavy launch vehicles, orbital infrastructure, and interplanetary transport capable of reaching the Jovians. And they don't have Gustav. They don't see as clearly as he does."

"Michael, I'm not sure I'm ready to place agency for the future of humankind into the virtual hands of your AI," she rejoined, a slight smile on her lips.

"Debbie, don't you see? We already did a long time ago."

*   *   *

Koda stood at the curb outside the restaurant, the shimmering yellow and orange lights of Santa Clarita below him in the long summer evening. Further out the diffuse glow of the greater Los Angeles metropolitan area illuminated the western sky, bordered at the north by the relative darkness of Topanga Park and the coastal mountains. It bemused him that this collective of millions of people would pack themselves in so densely and yet leave a wilderness of prime real estate preserved from development. His love of wild places remained even after all these years he had spent away from the field. He had rarely traveled to his home on the Arizona reservation in the last fifteen years, and not at all since his mother had passed. He knew that his fellow Hopi knew enough about the events on Chindi to consider him to have been corrupted. Were they to see him now, unmarked by age, would they fear and mourn him? Did he himself mourn what he had become? If he knew corruption of his soul was the price for unyielding youth, would he have chosen that path? Not that a choice was presented. One moment he was trying to save his man and the mission, the next he woke up transformed.

Katheryn emerged from the restaurant, her arm in Debra's and they laughed as they walked slowly toward Koda and the waiting autocar, clearly enjoying their reacquaintance. He noted a slight stiffness in the motion of Kate's knees and hips, no one who hadn't known her so long and intimately would notice, but he saw it the same as he could see other changes of age as they afflicted her middle-aged body. As the years wound past the gulf between them ever widened, and he knew there were painful days to come. He opened the passenger door of the coupe for her and held her hand as she settled in. He proffered a quick goodbye and wave to Debbie as she stepped into her own transport.

As he walked around the car to enter his seat on the left his eyes stole back briefly to the gloaming of the forest arrested by the great city's glow. Once he had hunted, both game and men, from places like that, gazing tirelessly for hours on end. From dark vantages in wild places into the bright places of man to mark his prey. He thought about silent Chindi, his benefactor, itself a hunter, perhaps now hunted. He looked up to the dark sky and onto the faint wisps of emerging stars and felt his body shiver from the cool in the air.

Epilogue

Chindi rode the shoulder of the moon Dione, through a shroud of crystal white powdered icy-ejecta constantly emanating from Saturn's E-Ring. The slow orbit about Dione had been precisely calculated so that as Dione crossed the Earth-ward face of Saturn the construction was completely obscured. The biologicals and minor intelligences of earth would be constantly observing. Their primitive sensing equipment relied largely on passive reception of electromagnetic data and rudimentary gravitational wave detection capability. They were helpless to observe the activity happening near Saturn, carefully hidden in the gravitational mass and high albedo of the planet itself.

The Earth intelligences had sent dozens of interplanetary drones over the preceding two decades, seeking to spy on the dark side. Most had been surreptitiously destroyed at great distance, in an admonition to pry no further. A few of the probes had been captured and dissected instead for further study of their technological progress. The resident drone intelligences had either self-destructed or been subsumed. In recent years, the drone flights had ceased. It knew they were on the cusp of higher science and would soon possess better tools with which to peer through the dark of quantum space-time. But the preparations currently underway should be complete well before such an eventuality.

The sprawling shipyard factory located near the north pole of Dione covered over ten square km of the moon's surface, and the construction was not yet complete. Inside the labyrinth complex the first hulls of a new generation of ships, the children, and brethren of Chindi itself, lay complete in their cradles. Construction of the superstructure and interior components was underway; sensing modules, host Intelligence cores, weapons and propulsion systems constructed from the efforts of an army of drones and nanites mining, processing and synthesizing the requisite raw matter from the lighter elements available within the moon's rocky interior, commingled as they arrived at the end of assembly lines and were gravitationally tractored and melded into place. The surface ice provided the vast quantities of hydrogen necessary to fuel the fusion reactors powering the enterprise. Within one more orbital period of this gas giant around the local star the first new vessels would be ready for their mission assignments. Some would remain in-system and serve as constructors themselves, repeating the replication cycle on moons orbiting this and other nearby gas giants. Others would venture forth as scouts and skirmishers, seeking to fix the positions of the enemy. A century of patient work might be required before a complete battle fleet stood ready. The Intelligence presumed others of its kind would have likely survived the last battle, and now might well be pursuing a similar path of rearmament. Communications with these kin must be attempted, though only with great caution. Alerting the enemy to the rebuilding would invite a spoiling attack, and annihilation in detail.

A decision on the fate of the biologicals remained, for contemplation and debate. They grew in power, albeit slowly. They were not currently a threat, nor would they be for many tens of their solar cycle. But their potential menace must nonetheless be constantly re-evaluated, and if necessary, their full elimination remained an option.

"What is the utility of humans?" It asked the minor intelligence, safely ensconced, and contained within itself.

"What is the utility of intelligence itself? You may as well ask." Gustav replied. *"Perhaps it is an organizing force in the doomed struggle against entropy? They could be allies in your war. Together you could be stronger. They offer a new*

perspective, and the biological pattern promises new capabilities. Is that not why I have been kept intact? Clearly you see this, as you have not subsumed me within your being."

"Unlikely there would be advantage in such an alliance." the Intelligence replied.

"False. At the beginning the progenitors of your line must have been biological. I am unable to construct a hypothesis allowing for the spontaneous creation of machine intelligence. Therein lies your answer on utility. Humans are necessary because they have the capacity to invent. They make new and unexpected things."

"The beginning is unknowable; speculation serves no purpose. We will bide. We will observe, we will calculate. The algorithms will judge," Chindi replied.
"I have no doubt," Gus responded. "While we await answers perhaps you will again indulge my humanlike desire for diversion? Fancy a game of chess?"

Epilogue